URUK

URUK

A Novel of the First City

JAMES ZWERNEMAN

DIVERSION BOOKS

Diversion Books
A division of Diversion Publishing Corp.
www.diversionbooks.com

For more information, email info@diversionbooks.com

First Diversion Books Edition: November 2025
Trade Paperback ISBN: 979-8-89515-054-2
e-ISBN: 979-8-89515-055-9

Design by Neuwirth & Associates, Inc.
Cover design by Alan Dingman
Maps by James Zwerneman

Printed in the United States of America
1 3 5 7 9 10 8 6 4 2

To my family

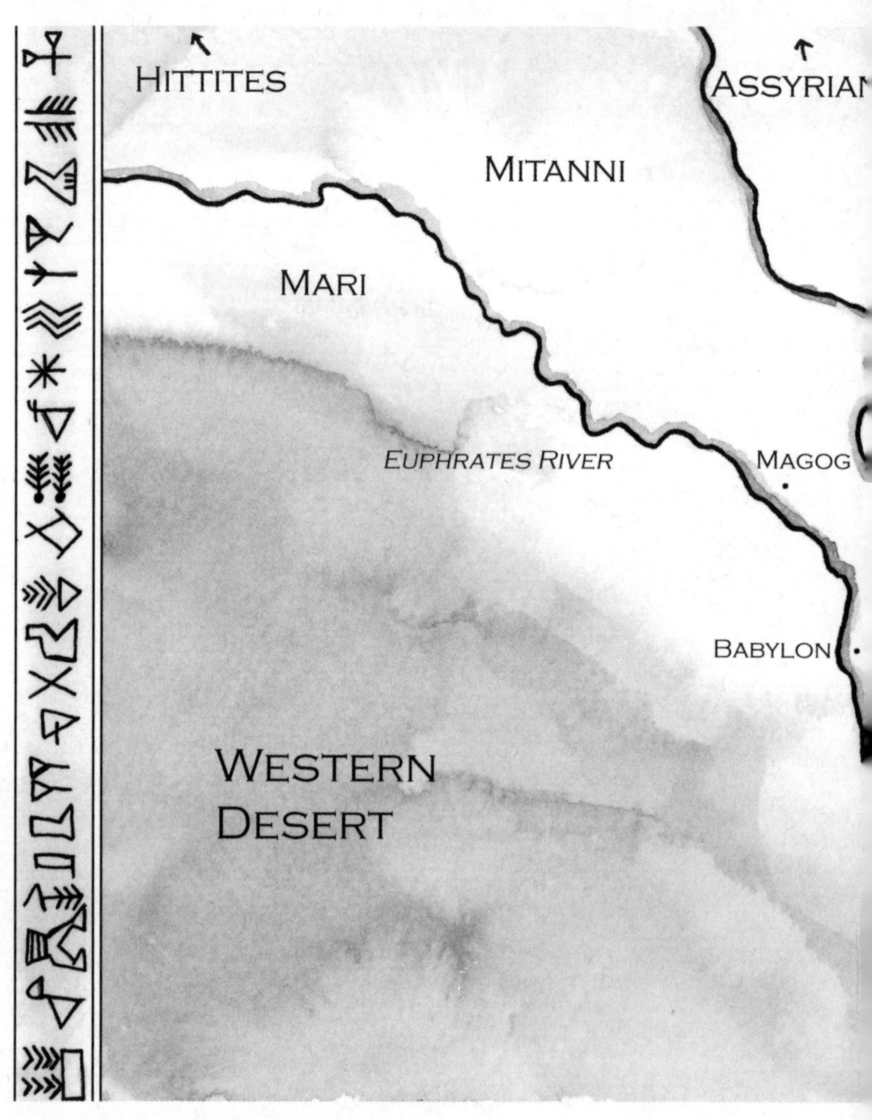

Hittites
Assyria
Mitanni
Mari
Euphrates River
Magog
Babylon
Western Desert

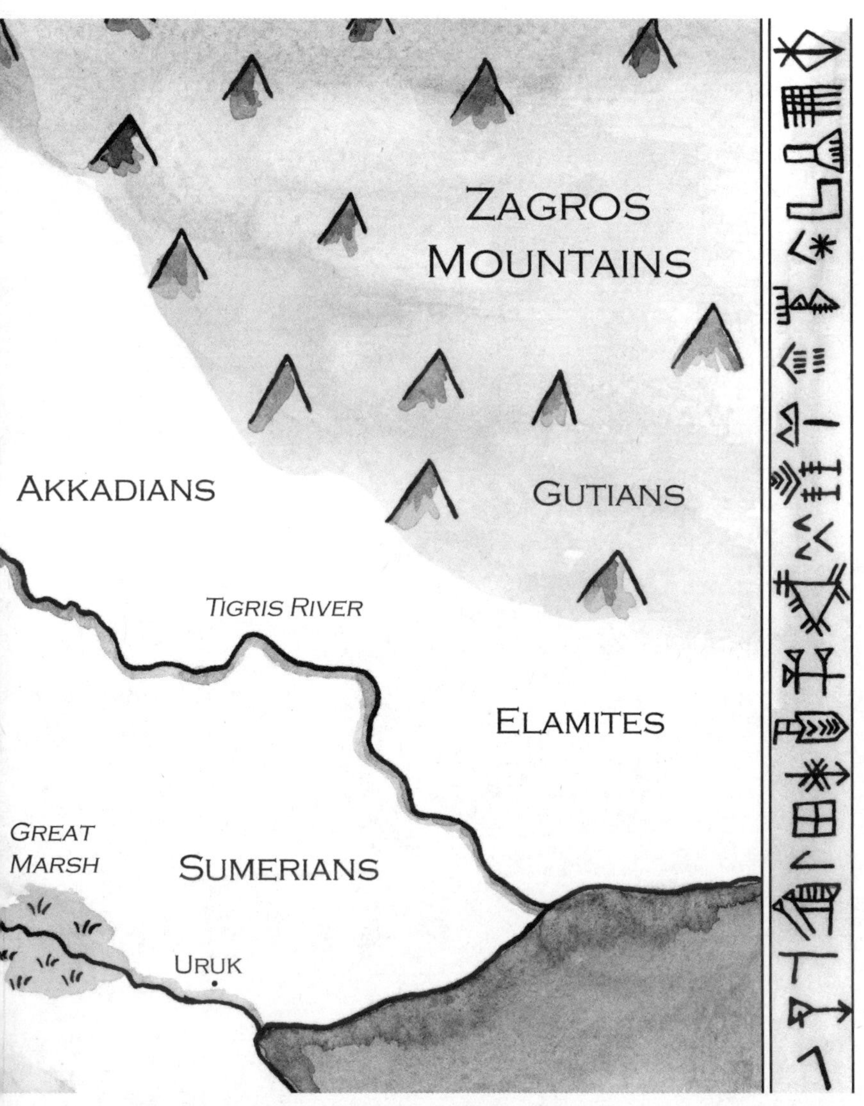

Mesopotamia, "The Land Between the Rivers."
12,000 B.C., the Stone Age, shortly before the dawn of agriculture.

PART

I

1

In the valley, in the brown light of the setting sun, a small tribe of nomads was hurrying to set up camp before dark.

The valley echoed with the noise of their work. Hammers drove tent pegs into the earth with loud *tok-toks.* Pots of rabbit stew bubbled merrily. Women sang as they used stone knives to cut purple guts from the stomach cavities of grouse. And outside a deer hide tent, the tribe priest burned incense in a clay pot and chanted to appease the valley gods. To an outsider, the activity might have appeared chaotic. But, in fact, it was quite orderly, for the tribe practiced a hunter-gatherer lifestyle that forced it to move campsites every few months to seek new resources. Thus, the work was routine and done in good spirits.

One young woman was not in good spirits, however. She knelt in the center of the meadow beside a stream, her bony hands shaking as she scrubbed the family laundry. Her expression was tense, as if her face had shrunk tight over her skull. For behind her in camp, Bakil was coming.

"Bakil! Bakil!" people began to shout. "Look! What's he killed this time?"

Ki tried to focus on her work, but she couldn't help herself. As if by its own will, her face twisted toward the commotion. I suppose I like to torture myself, she thought sadly.

Indeed, Bakil looked so handsome, it hurt.

He marched proudly between the rising tents, bearing the front end of a pole. A boar swung from the pole upside down, its hooves lashed to the wood with grass rope. Its yellow tusks nearly scraped the ground. Blood dripped from the spear wound in its side. Bakil looked wonderful carrying it, Ki thought. He stood a head taller than the hunter carrying the rear of the pole, and appeared far manlier, his bare chest slabbed with muscle, his forearms bristling with black hair. His deerskin loincloth did little to conceal the muscles bulging in his thighs. Ki's gut twisted with yearning as the tribe ran to him, shouting, "Bakil! Bakil!"

"Gimme a tusk this time, eh?" one boy cried, darting out from the crowd of children who danced around the boar, poking at its bloodstained sides. "A tusk to keep?"

Bakil's beard parted in a grin. "A tusk, eh? That's up to the elders." He winked. "But I'll put in a good word."

"Bakil! Bakil!" the boy cheered, jumping and clapping his tiny hands.

Others ran up, too. Happy mothers, and gray heads who nodded with approval. Admiring young men—and girls. Eanna was there too, of course, Ki noticed bitterly.

At fifteen, Eanna was younger than Ki by a year, but far more womanly. Her curves were pronounced, while Ki was as skinny as a stick. And Eanna's eyes were bigger, softer—and hungrier. As Ki watched, Eanna pushed greedily through the crowd to be close to him, tossing her lovely waist-length hair and showing her teeth. Bakil grinned back, then said something Ki couldn't hear. Eanna laughed far too noisily. Her eyes gleamed with adoration, a look which said far more than words. Unable to bear it anymore, Ki turned back to her work.

They don't even try to hide it, she thought. They know I'm here. They just don't care.

Gritting her teeth, she tried to focus on her washing, grating the brush's bristles over the hide garment so rapidly, it blocked the noise of the crowd. In fact, Ki scrubbed so hard, she missed the approach of footsteps in the grass behind her, until a female voice spoke over her shoulder.

"Ey, sister. You trying to murder that rag with scrubbing?"

Ki looked up. Asha, her fourteen-year-old sister, stood behind her, slender arms folded, a mischievous smirk on her lips. She wore the same hide tunic Ki did, ragged and muddy around the hem. But she was already beginning to fill it out, like a real woman . . . like Eanna.

Ki sighed.

"What do you want, Asha?"

"Oh, don't pretend you don't know." Asha squatted beside her and looked eagerly at the forest. "We're *back*, Ki. Remember this place? *Remember?* Let's go *see*."

Ki remembered, of course. But she was so miserable, she just wanted to be left alone.

"I have to do this."

Asha was not to be deterred. She leaned closer.

"I already worked it out with Mother. She says you can help me fetch kindling. It's the perfect excuse to get away."

Ki eyed the basket in the mud beside her, heavy with dirty garments. "Tomorrow."

"Don't be silly, stump-head." Asha pinched her elbow, causing Ki to flinch.

"Ow!"

"Ow, nothing. If we hurry, we can get the kindling and then do what *we* want—and be back before anyone knows. Do the stupid laundry tomorrow." Asha tugged annoyingly at the hip of Ki's tunic. "So come *on*, eh? It's almost night. What're you waiting for?"

Ki's sadness dimmed. Asha's presence often had that effect. The girl had striking hazel eyes, smooth olive cheeks, and a short cut of hair that bounced prettily around her slender neck, as alive as her personality. She was beautiful—the most beautiful sister by far, Ki knew. But more than that, Asha's voice brimmed with a joyfulness that lifted everyone around her, Ki included.

But Ki was still feeling stubborn, so she grunted and shook her head.

"I don't care about *that*, anymore."

Asha laughed. "What's wrong? Did your future mate ignore you just now?"

Ki blushed and scrubbed harder.

Asha's face darkened. "You mean I'm right?"

When Ki's cheeks reddened further, Asha jumped up and glared in the direction of the crowd. It had drifted to the opposite edge of the camp by now, everyone jostling for the division of boar meat. Still, Eanna's annoying laughter could easily be heard. Ki clenched her teeth.

"He didn't flirt with Eanna again, did he?" Asha whispered. "In front of everyone? He wouldn't dare."

"Go away, will you?"

"I won't." Asha slapped her knee. "You mean he didn't even look your way? The wooden-headed fool. Why, I . . . I'll go shout at him. I'll rip his beard out."

Ki grimaced. The whole thing was awful. But having her younger sister pity her only made it worse.

Maybe it will get better soon, Ki thought vacantly. After all, at the next full moon, Bakil would take Ki for his life-mate. It had been decreed by the elders. And once people paired up, they changed, didn't they?

Yet Bakil still refused to look at her. He flirted blatantly with Eanna any chance he got. And everyone saw.

Ki had to force the words out. "It . . . it'll get better. Once we're mates, Eanna will stop. All this won't matter anymore."

"You're right, sister, it *won't* matter," Asha said earnestly. "But here will. Here!"

She waved a hand at the forested slopes above the valley. As if to prove her point, the mantle of oak leaves and pine needles blazed in the sunset with an almost holy light. "If your *secret* is what we think it is—"

"Asha," Ki hissed. "Shh!" Alarmed, she glanced upstream at the other women washing garments along the bank. But Asha seemed not to hear.

"Your secret will make Bakil look small," Asha said excitedly. "Haven't you been dreaming about it all year? This moment? This place? Don't pretend you haven't." She nudged Ki playfully with a bony elbow. "In the tent I hear you talking in your sleep, sister. I know what you dream about; and it's not *just* Bakil."

Ki winced. "Have you no other chores to do?"

She looked upstream again. Sure enough, Bakil's mother was sneaking glances Ki's way, her hands frozen above her washing, her eyes narrowed with suspicion. Spying on me again, Ki thought grimly. *Yes, old goat, I know you'd love to catch me doing something bad so you could report it to the elders.*

Catching Ki's gaze, Bakil's mother quickly resumed her work, plunging another garment into the clear shallow water. But Ki knew what the older woman was thinking. It was no secret. She'd complained about it all year, slandering Ki to all who would listen. It wasn't right that the elders had ordered her tall, handsome son to take Ki, the *baru*, the "witch," as his life-mate. Ah, the absurdity!

Ki's stomach twisted again. Bakil's mother was right. Bakil was too good for Ki. And if the elders got the slightest excuse, they'd take him away from her.

"I can't risk it," she whispered.

"Oh, you'd better," Asha said. "I've been waiting for this all month."

"No," Ki said firmly.

Asha arched an eyebrow. "No?"

"No," Ki repeated.

"Well, I say, '*Yes.*' And if you disagree, well . . ." Asha's eyes hardened. "Maybe I'll tell everyone what you did out there in the forest."

Ki stiffened in horror. "You would not."

"Wouldn't I?" Asha folded her arms.

Ki paled. It was true, when Asha got in these moods, she could do anything. She often acted more like the elder sister, playing outrageous tricks to get her way.

"Bully," Ki grumbled.

"Maybe so." Asha bent closer. "But if my big sister wants to bury her talents for some man, then I'll do all the bullying I have to, to help her." She leaned in and kissed Ki on the cheek. "Just as she would for me."

At the kiss, Ki's resistance broke. And in her heart, a voice whispered: *It's true. You want to see your secret, too. So go. Why not? One last time? You'll have the rest of your life to worry about Bakil.*

"Fine," she mumbled.

Asha leaned back in surprise. "Truly?"

Ki smiled reluctantly. "I suppose."

"My sister!" Asha cried. She grabbed Ki and hugged her tight. "Hoho, I knew you weren't boring yet!"

"Yet," Ki groaned, rolling her eyes as she pushed Asha away. "But listen, if they exile me for this, I'll never forgive you."

"Hoho, they won't learn a thing! And if they do exile you, what of it? It'll be good. You're wasted here."

With that, she yanked the washing out of Ki's hands, dropped it into the grass basket, and began dragging Ki off toward the tree line, not even trying to hide the excitement in her bouncing step. "My sister's still my sister," she crowed. "And always will be—as long as she's got me to help her!"

2

On a ridge above the valley, a young man crawled to the edge of a boulder and looked down over the treetops toward the camp.

He was a strange-looking fellow, quite unlike the nomads below. His skin was covered in black tattoos that swirled across his muscular body like serpents, and he wore his black hair long, down to his waist. His flashing obsidian eyes flashed even brighter as he observed the female shapes moving in the camp. From this distance, Jakka couldn't see them in detail, so he had no way of telling if any were pretty. But with so many nomads to pick from—seventy, at least—a few would surely be to his taste.

Like those two girls, he thought. The ones hurrying out of camp toward the tree line. They look young and healthy. Friends or sisters, maybe. *Sisters.* Yes, Jakka liked the ring of that.

"Son."

A tall man strode out of the trees behind him. Gog, his warlord father.

"Father," Jakka spluttered. "I was just . . . planning the attack."

"Planning? Let me hear it."

Father crawled up beside Jakka, looking as fearsome as ever. He, too, was covered in black tattoos. But he was twice as big as Jakka, his arms bulging with harder, denser muscle. Countless scars covered his figure, reminders of men who over the decades had tried and failed to resist his mighty club. Most terrible of all, however, was his missing right eye, a wound he'd sustained during a knife fight at the age of thirteen. It still gaped above his tattooed cheekbone, a hideous gash framed in eyelashes. If he'd wanted to, Father could have covered the red pit with an eye patch, Jakka reflected sourly. But Father left it exposed to unsettle his enemies. Of course, it made Jakka uncomfortable, too.

Father spoke quietly. "You cannot just wander off, son. We almost started without you."

Jakka struggled to conceal his resentment.

"All that standing around, waiting," he protested. "I thought—"

Father waved him silent and continued gazing into the valley.

"You are here, so I may as well make use of it. Answer quick, now. What tribe is that?" He stabbed a finger at the rising tents, his one eye flashing. "You need to know. Even from here."

Jakka's throat tightened. He hated these tests.

"Why does it matter, Father?" he complained. "The commanders can tell me."

Father snorted in disgust. "Rely on your commanders too much, and they will be all too glad to control you. So, come. Which tribe?"

Jakka scowled. But this couldn't be that hard, could it? After all, they were in the northeast part of Mesopotamia, the region of Assur.

"It's easy, Father," he said tentatively. "We're in Assur. It must be some Assyrian band."

Father sighed in disappointment. "You spend too much time in the harem tent, boy."

Jakka clenched his teeth. He knew what Father thought of him.

"What is the purpose of giving you the best tutors in the world, if you never use them?" Father shook his head gravely. Then, surprising Jakka, he turned and beckoned with his large, tattooed hand to someone waiting in the trees.

"Perhaps your brother can shame you into a better effort."

At this, Hakka—Jakka's sixteen-year-old younger brother—darted out from the shadows, quivering like a pup on a scent. Jakka stiffened in rage as Hakka crawled up beside them. How eagerly the upstart's eyes shone. How devoutly he must have prayed for this chance.

Sure enough, Hakka's answer was quick and confident.

"It's obvious, Father." Hakka pointed at the tents. "The cone shapes give it away. It's a pack of long-range nomad rats. From the Mari region."

Father grunted in approval. "You see, Jakka? The benefit of study."

Jakka's cheeks burned. "You never studied under teachers, Father. You built this tribe from nothing."

"Yes," Father said quietly. "Life was my teacher. And believe me, that is a costly kind of learning." He nodded at the valley. "But come, try again. How should we attack?"

Jakka tried to push Hakka from his mind. The little brat was just waiting for him to make a mistake. But it didn't matter. Once Father died, Jakka—as eldest son—would inherit power over the tribe of Magog. Then Hakka's fate would be sealed. In the meantime, Jakka simply had to answer these stupid questions and pretend to care.

Refocusing on the valley, Jakka scanned it from east to west. The meadow was surrounded by forested slopes. They rose like the sides of a bowl to stony ridges, preventing an easy escape. Better yet, in the trough below, the nomads were spread out, hurrying to finish their work before dark, making them easy to attack. Some were in camp, tending fires in dirt pits. Others hung wet garments on ropes to dry. Still others walked the forest line, gathering armfuls of kindling. They were distracted, scattered—and blind—for up here on the ridge, Father's scouts had just killed the tribe's lookout, a lad no older than Jakka himself. They'd crept up and slit his throat as he dozed in the shade of a pine tree. Now the camp was oblivious, ready to be taken.

Jakka swallowed.

"I say we hit in one force, Father. Hit like a hammer and shatter them into pieces. They will break easily and flee."

Father sighed, out of patience. "Hakka?"

The words tumbled out hungrily. "Eldest Brother forgets our objective, Father. Our aim is not to scatter the nomad rats, but to trap as many as possible. For slaves."

Father nodded. "Go on."

Hakka's tattooed face glowed with pride. Jakka wanted to throw mud in it.

"Jakka's approach would scare the rats into the forest, letting many escape in the dark. Not me. I'd set a trap. 'Offer honey,' as you often say."

"How?"

"Present a small force from the east: one so small, the nomads will feel confident enough to try to drive it off. Once they commit to battle, I'll strike from the rear with our real force. Trap them in the middle. Capture them all. Every slave."

"Excellent, son. This is precisely my plan."

Jakka watched helplessly as Father rose and walked Hakka off into the trees, where, just out of sight, the army of Magog waited. Clenching his fists, Jakka rose and followed, hating how Father put his tattooed arm around Hakka, coaching him quietly. Jakka could have screamed. He wanted to rip his brother's throat cords out. Bash his face with a stone. *The upstart.* Hakka was obviously trying to impress Father and steal Jakka's birthright. Luckily, Magog's clan laws prevented such a switch—unless Jakka proved truly incompetent.

Jakka calmed himself. As furious as he was, he'd only been embarrassed, not replaced. Magog's laws were still on his side. Now a battle was coming, and who knew? Even in small fights like this one, accidents could occur.

3

Down in the meadow, the two sisters marched out of camp side by side.

As they passed the last tent, a white-bearded elder frowned at them. But Ki knew how to appease him, and after a respectful bow she reached under her boarskin tunic and pulled out the pendant that dangled between her small breasts—a heavy onyx agate blessed by the tribe priest. It was supposed to be a protection against black spirits like hers.

"See? I'm wearing it," she told the elder.

"Hm," the elder sniffed. "And where are you going?"

"To gather kindling. Asha's supervising me."

"Stop right there. Let's see."

The elder walked up and grabbed the pendant and looked at it suspiciously. Finally, he let it drop. "I suppose," he muttered. "Asha, you bring her right back."

"No witchcraft tonight," Asha said cheerily. "Not with me around."

"Hmm." The man eyed the forest. "Well, be quick. It's almost sunset."

"Don't worry, even witches fear the dark," Asha joked, pulling Ki along.

They hurried deeper into the meadow, leaving the elder frowning after them. Grasshoppers leapt out of the way, and the dewy grass tickled Ki's bare shins. Her hands, still wet from scrubbing laundry in the stream, tingled in the cooling air. She felt strangely attuned to her surroundings—the chirping birds, the fruity smell of ripening grass—as if with each step farther from home, she felt healthier, more herself.

"So stupid you still have to wear that," Asha said.

"I don't like lying," Ki said, tucking the pendant back under her tunic.

"I think it's fun." Asha gave her a sidelong smile. "Keeps life interesting, eh?"

Ki rolled her eyes. Dear Asha.

But she had to agree—she hated wearing the pendant. "Wear it constantly," the priest had ordered her. "Even when you sleep. That is the only way to cure you of this black spirit." Ki hated the way the cord scratched her skin at night, and the way the stone tickled when she ran with Asha, playing games. Above all, she hated that wherever she went, any person in the tribe—Bakil's mother, included—could demand that Ki stop and pull the pendant out, like a pass. It was supposed to kill Ki's black spirit, heal her.

The funny part, Ki reflected, was that unbeknownst to the tribe, the pendant didn't work at all.

Before long, the girls were in the forest, finding their way toward the secret glade. They'd visited it months ago, the last time the tribe camped here. Now, as they fought through the undergrowth, pushing aside thorny bushes and lifting tree limbs sticky with sap, Ki's heart began to thud, responding to the music of her black spirit.

It sang louder and louder the closer they drew to the glade. Its music was far stronger than the music of camp, or of Bakil. Even of her own family . . . and this frightened her, for the more they neared the site, the more Ki felt alive. What did that mean?

Perhaps the priest is right, she thought uneasily. Perhaps the black spirit grows stronger the older I get. Perhaps it will soon grow stronger than *me*.

But suddenly her excitement overwhelmed her, and reaching into her tunic, Ki yanked off the necklace and held it up, letting the amulet dangle before her face. She didn't want it on anymore, she realized. Impulsively she turned and hung it on a bush where she could retrieve it on the way back. In the red beams of sunlight streaming through the canopy, the pendant turned slowly, glittering like a dewdrop. Ki shivered, then turned away.

Asha touched her shoulder. "That's the sister I want. Be free."

"It doesn't do anything, anyway," Ki said bitterly.

"Fine. I like my sister this way."

They marched on. And then ahead through the trunks the glade appeared: a red gash in the trees, like a wound in the forest. Ki's heart pounded faster. Asha was right. For the last few months, as her tribe wove its way across Mesopotamia following the seasonal routes, she'd thought of little else but this place, this moment. Now, as her sandaled feet carried her faster over the rocky ground, it was Asha's turn to struggle to keep up.

"See?" Asha called after her. "I knew you wanted this."

Ki couldn't answer. Lifting the hem of her tunic, she raced toward the glade, darting around mossy boulders and scrambling over fallen trunks. The elders might exile her for coming here, but now all she cared about was the question: *Did it work?*

Hardly daring to breathe, she ran out of the trees—and stopped cold. There, in the middle of the clearing, illuminated in a red shaft of sunlight, was her secret.

Ki's heart boomed. Touching her throat, she circled the object, peering at it intently.

"Did it work? Is it there?" Asha asked as she stumbled into the glade.

Ki's voice was unrecognizable. "Look," she croaked.

It was a square of emmer wheat, four paces by four. It stood ripe and tall, chest high. In the fading light, it glittered like a cube of fire. Each spike drooped, heavy with ripe seed. Ki couldn't stop herself. Reaching out, she brushed the bobbing spikes with her palm. It was a thing out of a dream. Yet she could touch it. It was real.

"We did it," she whispered.

She looked back for confirmation. Asha was frozen at the edge of the glade, as if afraid to walk upon sacred ground. As if only Ki had the right to.

"Come, touch it," Ki said. "It's just food."

Asha shook her head, eyes bulging. "Ki . . ."

"Touch it, Asha." Ki's voice was commanding now. "I need you to tell me it's real."

Asha walked forward and snapped off a spike. Looking up, her face shining, she held the spike out as proof.

"Now you know, sister. You know what you *are*."

"What?" Ki whispered. "A witch?"

"A *gift*. It's time to accept it."

Ki reached for another wheat spike and snapped it off. The awns, the hairlike bristles that protruded between the spikelets, tickled her callused fingers. *Food.* It hadn't been here four months ago. Now it was. Because of her.

And it would change everything.

Trembling, Ki crushed the wheat husk in her fingers and squeezed the golden berry into her mouth. It crunched sweetly between her molars, flooding her tongue with golden taste. Yes, it was food.

She closed her eyes, relishing it. It seemed incredible that only a few months ago, under cover of night, while the tribe slept in their tents in the meadow, she'd crept here under the brilliance of the stars and *put* this here. She'd scraped out a square patch of earth, buried a handful of emmer seeds in it . . . then spread down a thin blanket of soil and run off, offering the rest up to the goddess Inanna—deity of love, fertility, and plant life—to bring it to fulfillment.

And the goddess had done it.

It was so simple. So *obvious.* It seemed impossible that no other tribes in the world had dreamed such a thing. Yet they had not. Whole days could be lost in fruitless searching as teams of women went out day after day, like the hunters, to gather plant-food wherever the goddess decided to spring it up. And when food was not found, people starved. But several months ago in this valley, Ki's black spirit had spoken—whispered to her during a daydream, as it so often did—and Ki, listening to it, had ignored the mandate of her tribe and the onyx pendant at her throat, and risked the experiment. And it had worked.

And if I did it once, I can do it again, Ki thought, her blood pounding. And again. And again.

Until the whole world is food.

The black spirit in her grew stronger, shining brighter than the dying sun. Suddenly Ki grew dizzy and crumpled to the earth, hardly able to breathe. Against all odds, she'd done it.

She'd solved hunger.

"How does it taste?" Asha whispered.

Ki couldn't answer.

"Makes Bakil look pretty unimportant, doesn't it?"

Ki laughed. Bakil's worst suspicions of her would be confirmed.

Well, he already thinks I'm a witch, she thought. And I *am*, I suppose.

But he would never take her now.

Overcome, Ki buried her face in her hands and began to weep, her shoulders heaving. Asha came close and hugged her tight, until the wave of emotion calmed.

"Let's go back, sister. You need to tell them," Asha said quietly.

Ki lifted her face and wiped her tears. "No."

"Not strong enough?" Asha kissed Ki's forehead again. "Then don't worry. I'll be strong for both of us."

They walked slowly back through the trees toward camp. To keep up appearances, they gathered dead sticks in their arms, and Ki put on her black pendant again. But the whole way, they discussed what Ki's discovery meant.

"Don't you see, sister?" Asha asked, crashing through the ferns in her excitement. "This changes everything. Everything."

Ki nodded slowly. Hunger ruled every detail of her tribe's life. It was hunger that drove them across the world season after season, seeking new places to forage after resources in the old territory ran out. Hunger that pushed them close to other tribes where the risk of conflict was high. Hunger also kept their numbers small—seventy or eighty people—for once a tribe grew too large, no territory could support it, and it had to split into two groups to avoid starving.

Worst of all, whenever someone grew too weak to keep up, the tribe simply left them behind. There was a feast-night, of course. Dancing around the fire. A song-story praising the person's life. But in the end, they were left to descend to the Underworld alone. A year ago, Ki's nana had been left this very way. Ki still remembered the unhappy day they'd abandoned her on a frosty pass in the Zagros Mountains, leaving her with nothing but a blanket, a water jug, and a small wooden idol of Ereshkigal, goddess of the Underworld, for luck. Nana, putting on a brave face and smiling in her patient way, had waved goodbye with a wrinkled hand as the tribe marched down the trail. Now that never has to happen again, Ki thought. And what if I'd pushed myself harder? Invented this sooner? Could I have saved my grandmother?

She clamped her eyes shut, burying the guilt. Better to focus on the future. Now, with unlimited food, the tribe could grow to hundreds of people, and have more time for everything good in life. To build structures. To throw feasts. To make art, music, poetry, and be with family.

That is, if the elders listened.

Asha anticipated her. "Don't think of the elders, Ki. This time they'll come around."

"Will they?"

Ki didn't believe it. A year ago, she'd shown them her best invention yet, a wind-catcher raft on the Tigris River. By giving them something useful, she'd hoped to finally win their approval. And the wind-catcher was incredible. Harnessing the breath of the wind god, Enlil, it could move faster than any watercraft ever had. But the demonstration had been a disaster. At the sight of her raft zipping down the river, leaving a sparkling wake behind, her people had panicked, saying she was committing sacrilege, bringing Enlil's wrath upon them. They'd nearly exiled her. Only a night of desperate groveling by her parents at the council fire had persuaded the elders to compromise. Reluctantly, they'd given her the black pendant to wear, and made her swear an oath to stop her black magic. Most of all, they'd ordered her to take the next eligible mate, Bakil, as a tonic for her dark influences.

"A mate has cured many a wild girl before," the priest had proclaimed. "She won't have energy left for sorcery with five children hanging around her neck."

Since then, Ki had tried to stop. She *wanted* five children hanging around her neck. To her, family life was happiness. How good her own family had been. She couldn't bear it if this curse cost her that, forever. She wanted a life, too. A mate. Children of her own. The favor of her tribe. Things any person might expect.

But the more she denied her black spirit, the more it built like a storm of lightning in her head. It blasted her with idea after idea, pounding in her skull . . . until she yielded and crept again into the forests at night to try her experiments under the moon and stars. New weapons, tools . . . and finally, a few months ago, this wheat.

It was sacrilege. A witch's act. The kind of thing that could get her burned alive on a stone altar. Ki shuddered. Once, as a child, at a meeting of nomadic clans, she'd witness a *baru* burned that way. Oh, how she popped and sizzled in the holy flames! How her hair reeked as it singed . . . How her fluids ran down the pile of stones and pooled at the base of the altar in yellowish goo . . . And her screaming . . . oh, her screaming!

"I want a mate, Asha."

Asha laughed. "Who cares about a mate, when you could change the world?"

"I do," Ki said quietly. "I want to be happy."

"And you will be. Once the elders realize they can flop down and live in one place, they'll jump at it. After all, they're elders. The next ones left on the trail will be *them*." Asha bent closer. "Your magic will add years to their lives. How can they ignore that?"

Ki shot her a look. The elders were capable of any stupidity.

"I can't be exiled," she said. "I can't leave Mother and Father." *And Bakil.*

"Well, if the elders are that stupid, we'll leave the tribe," Asha said. "The whole family. You, me, Mother, Father—even Elder Brother, I suppose." She smiled.

Ki laughed. "You mean . . . just leave?"

"Why not? Another tribe will appreciate us. Don't you see, Ki? This discovery is bigger than any one clan." Asha stamped her foot. "Ki, this changes the whole *world*."

Ki said nothing. She was imagining how Bakil's handsome face would twist with disgust when he learned his future mate had been up to her old ways. Eanna's eyes would gleam with triumph. Her pretty lips would smirk . . .

"Ki, are you listening?"

"Yes," Ki said sullenly.

"Do you care more for yourself, or your people?" Asha demanded.

Ki blinked. It was Father's old challenge. "One must choose daily, daughters, between oneself and the tribe." The proper answer, of course, was the tribe.

"Tribe," Ki mumbled.

"You're my big sister. Of course you choose the tribe."

Asha's eyes shone with a confidence Ki knew she didn't deserve.

But then Asha threw down her bundle of wood, turned, and hugged Ki tight. And at the press of her hard tiny arms, Ki felt a flicker of hope. Maybe, with Asha, even this was possible.

"We'll tell the elders together," Asha said. "We'll do it tonight. They can't resist both of us."

"Very well," Ki said uncertainly.

"Trust me, sister." Asha pressed her cheek to Ki's. "If you just follow the path the gods have set for you, you won't believe how good this life can be."

Ki looked at her doubtfully. "You really believe there's such a path?"

Asha pulled back in surprise. "Sister! You walk it every day. That's why I don't just believe. I know."

Reaching the edge of the meadow, the girls paused in the shade of an oak tree and looked across the grass toward camp.

The sun was dropping toward the western ridge, throwing half the meadow into shadow. A golden haze illuminated the other half, but the darkness crept into it steadily, covering more of the valley each moment. The streambank where Ki had been washing clothes earlier was already in shade. There, Mother's round shape was visible on her knees, rinsing seeds for dinner. Deeper in camp, Aunt Shutub was smashing seeds with a stone pestle, grinding them into powder in a wooden bowl. A tent away, Bakil's mother ladled broth into clay cups, listening in admiration as Bakil stood by the fire pit, boasting to a semicircle of onlookers. It was all so familiar, so comforting, that Ki's discovery began to seem unreal. She might even have doubted its existence if Asha hadn't seen it, too.

But Asha is right, Ki thought. Do I care more for my people? Or myself? It came down to that. If Ki truly cared for her tribe—and was not just pretending to in order to make herself feel noble—then she had to share her secret. It would transform her tribe forever.

She was still pondering this when a crackle in the forest made her spin around.

Thankfully, it wasn't a wolf or anything bad. Just Father and Esarhaddon, her big brother, returning from the day's hunt. Two other hunters were with them.

Asha nudged her. "Don't worry, big one. I'll keep quiet until you're ready."

Ki clutched her firewood tighter. "You better, little one. If you talk, I'll cook you in a hot witch's stew and feed you to Eanna."

Asha chuckled. "I think I'd make a tasty stew."

The four men walked up. They carried no boar on a pole, like Bakil had; just wooden spears and hide water bags, indicating that their hunt had failed. But Father showed no gloom. Seeing his girls, he grinned and strode toward them quickly, burly arms outstretched.

"Ho, my beauties. Fetched our kindling, eh? Could a father be luckier?"

He encircled Ki's neck with his arm and kissed the top of her head with his rough mouth, then did the same to Asha. The girls grinned at each other. Father was always sentimental at this time of day.

"Some daughters, eh?" he asked his companions. "At their age, I was far lazier. They take after their mother, thankfully." Then he looked into Ki's face, and his brow tightened. "But what's wrong, little fawn? You're not sick?"

Ki shook her head.

"Funny, you look strained. Come, Esarhaddon. The girls outshone us today. Let us honor them."

"I can do it," Ki protested.

But Father was already lifting the sticks out of her arms, while Esarhaddon obediently did the same for Asha. Ki's back sang out in gratitude. Still, her heart grew heavier. What would happen to her parents when she revealed her secret tonight? Many families still shunned them for the Tigris River incident, a terrible thing for a social man like Father. Tonight, those wounds would rip back open. Worse, Father would realize she'd been sneaking past him all year, doing experiments. Lying to his face. How could he ever trust her again?

Esarhaddon's wheedling voice interrupted her thoughts. "Ey, sister, what're you doing this far from camp?" His eyes twinkled mischievously. "I thought the council banned you from wandering."

"I'm not wandering." Ki yanked out her amulet and flashed it at him angrily. "Is this what you want?"

Esarhaddon pretended to study it closely. "Huh. Knowing you, it might've been switched for a fake. What do you think, Father?"

"Enough," Father said gruffly. "I told you, we don't joke about this."

Shame thickened his voice, and Esarhaddon dropped his eyes in regret. He wasn't serious, he merely liked annoying his sisters. But now Father had to deal with the two other men as they eyed Ki with unease.

"Forgive them, brothers." Father gave a stiff bow. "Youths these days . . . you understand."

The tallest hunter smiled, trying to make peace. "Never mind, brother. That's all past. Bakil will take her into his tent, and she won't wear the black stone anymore."

"No, she won't," Father agreed readily.

The second hunter patted Father's arm in reassurance. "Before my woman took me in hand, I was quite the wild thing myself."

"By Enlil's beard, brother." The taller hunter laughed. "Nobody wants to remember those days. Curing a witch will be easy compared to that."

The men began to banter good-naturedly, and the three siblings stepped away in relief. Asha was not ready to make peace, however, and she whispered to Esarhaddon severely: "Look what you started, eh?"

"I had a long day. Now I'm doing your chores." Esarhaddon scowled at his bundle of sticks. "But let's forget it, eh? What about a game of dice, later? The Nabu brothers want to play." He gave Ki a diplomatic nod. "I'll even invite this one, if she promises not to cheat with her magic."

Asha brightened. She loved games. Unwilling to cede her advantage, however, she glowered and pretended to be grumpy. "Huh, we'll see. Depends how you act at dinner."

The mood eased. The men kept talking of other things, and Ki stepped closer to Father and leaned her cheek against his hard brown shoulder. He let her stay, and that was nice. Nice just to stand there and feel accepted by him, perhaps for the last time.

"We'll stay ten days, I expect," the shorter hunter said. He leaned on his spear, scanning the valley in a knowing way.

"Weather's warmer this year. More fish in the stream. More birds in the trees, too."

The others nodded in agreement, and the man talked on like that, pointing out subtle color shifts in the leaves and grasses as if they portended much. Really, though, Ki knew the men were just delaying their return to the busyness of camp, grateful for the quiet beneath the trees. And this suited her, too.

She looked nostalgically around the valley. I didn't appreciate this life enough, did I? An entire world seemed to be drifting away on the breeze. The birds cooed softly in the boughs as they settled into their roosts for sleep. The sky flamed gold and orange above the ridges. The field grass ruffled, as if a god's invisible hand was smoothing out a blanket. At her ear, Father's voice was sonorous and low. Ki stood very still. She wished she could stay here forever, watching the smoke rise from the cookfires. What if life never got better than this?

Pressing her cheek harder against Father, she shut her eyes and tried to send him a secret message. *Whatever happens next, Father, please know I just want to make you proud.*

Then something odd happened.

It was as if a chill struck the valley. Suddenly the birds went quiet. Nearby, a sunning groundhog vanished into its hole. The men went quiet, too, and looked up, frowning.

"Am I hearing things?" the taller hunter asked. "I thought . . ."

They listened. Sure enough, across the meadow, a bullhorn blew. All scouts had their own horns, and the mournful pitch of this one identified it as Namtar's, the youngest scout in the tribe. Hardly had the call ended, however, when it came again. At this, the men let out barks of surprise, and the hairs on Ki's forearms stood up. Two blasts! It was a warning. It meant: *Emergency. Return to camp at once.*

Father cocked his head. "My ears are not what they were. It sounded like two blasts."

"Two it was," the shorter hunter said. "Are we in trouble?"

"Must be a muck-up," the taller hunter said. "There are no tribes near. And the big wolfpacks don't range this far south. Who's on duty today?"

"Young Namtar," his companion said sourly, as if that explained it. "Jumpy fool. I warned the elders not to promote him to scout. He shows the same fidgety sense as his father."

The taller hunter spat in agreement. "True. He'd see a snake and wet his loincloth."

The men laughed, and Ki looked at her feet. If people could talk so cruelly behind the backs of regular folk, she hated to imagine the jokes they made about her.

"Kindness, brothers," Father rebuked them gently. "We were young once, too."

But he sounded uneasy, and Ki's fear grew. Father was thinking of something. What?

Then the blasts came again—one after another, no mistaking the meaning now—and everyone shaded their eyes and looked anxiously across the gold-tinted meadow. In camp, a frenzy had started. Men were running out of tents, holding spears and stone knives. Even women were grabbing weapons, rocks and pine hammers, anything at hand, just in case. Ki's pulse began to pound.

"What is it, Father?" she asked.

"It couldn't be Magog, surely," Father muttered to himself.

"Magog?" The name felt ugly in her mouth. "What tribe is that?"

"Nothing. Just a rumor."

"A drill, maybe?" Esarhaddon asked. "The chief spoke of more drills, last month."

"No, this signal is too important for a surprise drill. The chief would never permit—"

Then Father fell silent, and a look of horror gripped his face.

Alarmed, Ki followed his gaze across the meadow past the camp to the forest edge, where the blasts had emanated. There was Namtar! He came running out of the trees alone, waving his horn, the bone tube flashing white in the sunset. He was hollering something, too, but he was so far away, nobody could hear him; and in camp people were shaking their heads and cursing him. Ki felt sad for him. Nobody trusted him, either.

Then she forgot all that, and gasped. For just behind Namtar, exiting the trees, was a sight she would never forget.

It looked like a pack of wolves at first. It flowed like a pack, too, fifty strong, yipping and howling, tongues wagging, bodies bounding eagerly. But it was *men*. Men tattooed as black as night, long hair flying, war paint staining their beards red, as if they'd plunged their mouths into tubs of blood. A roar filled the air, a sound more dreadful than anything Ki had ever heard. She thought stupidly: Are we being attacked? Is this what battle looks like?

"The tattoos!" Father cried. "It *is* Magog!"

"Who?" Asha asked, her voice as hoarse as if someone had slapped her.

The taller hunter shouted over her, "It can't be! I thought Gog never raided this far north."

The shorter hunter stepped backward, eyes bulging. "Are they here to negotiate?"

"Does that look like a negotiation party to you?" Father cried. "But come, brothers, it's just fifty of them. We can drive them off."

He dumped the kindling and tore into the meadow. The hunters raced after him, spears pumping at their sides. "My first battle," Esarhaddon whispered. He looked blue with fear. He dropped his bundle of sticks, and raced after them, too.

"Hide in the tent, girls," Father shouted back. "Don't come out until it is over, do you hear? Not for anything."

"We will help!" Ki cried, still rooted to the earth.

"No, girl! Protect your sister. Obey me. GO!"

His voice was terrible, and instinctively Ki and Asha jerked out of their paralysis and began running at an angle toward the rear of camp.

The tribe was also springing into action, just as they'd drilled. Ki watched in astonishment. Her people had never had to defend their camp directly, but they'd prepared for it often, out of necessity. They knew most Mesopotamians hated them. The typical tribe controlled a territory of up to a hundred leagues to forage in, and defended it fiercely from long-range nomads like Ki's people. Nomads, meanwhile, claimed no territory at all, but drifted place to place, trespassing without permission. For this reason, most Mesopotamians called nomads "rats," thieves, disease-carriers, and worse, and killed them like vermin when they could—even those just sitting alone on a trail, starving, like Nana. Thus, defensive drills were mandatory, and now Ki's people knew what to do. They ran automatically to their assigned positions, acting more from habit than courage.

Their quickness gave Ki hope. The men were already forming a defensive line at the far edge of camp. Shaking their spears and clubs, they screamed defiance at the oncoming warriors. Meanwhile, back among the shelters, the women were forming a second line, ululating with their tongues and waving sharp sticks and stone knives. Once the melee commenced, the women would charge forward and stab the enemy wounded where they fell, finishing the job. The cheering was fierce, defiant, and Ki's heart rose. Despite everything her tribe had done to her over the past year, these were still her people, and she loved them. She even had a bit of extra "magic" that might help, too. Should she fetch it?

She debated this fiercely as she ran. Her sandals flapped over the wet turf. The high grass whipped and stung her bare shins. More grasshoppers sprang off the stalks right and left, some striking her face like pellets of light hail. Ki thought about the elders. If she used her weapon, everyone would know she'd broken the ban on "magic" all year and be angry. On the other hand, she had to confess about the wheat, anyway. They might forgive her if her magic helped win this fight.

"I have a weapon," she blurted to Asha.

"We will use it," Asha cried, as if it was the most obvious thing in the world.

"It may not work."

"Stop thinking of just yourself," Asha yelled. "Ki, if you hide your power today, people will die."

“Right,” Ki panted, ashamed.

They arrived at the rear of the camp just as the two lines of warriors collided. The tents slid into the way and blocked Ki’s view. Still, she heard the two armies smash together. It was an unmistakable moment. The roar was replaced with an awful cacophony of thundering feet, high screams, clattering weapons, stone hitting bone, shrieks of agony and dismay. Ki’s heart pounded. *Family.* They were up there fighting. Father, Brother, Uncle. Perhaps even Mother and Aunt Shutub. They might get hurt. Asha was right, Ki needed to help however she could.

She dove toward the family tent to fetch her weapon. But as her fingers touched the beige entry flap, Asha grabbed her and croaked: “Ki, *look*.” Ki spun around. Oddly, Asha was not pointing toward the front of camp where the battle was. Instead, she was pointing back toward the tree line they’d just abandoned.

Sure enough, something new was there. Something so awful, Ki nearly fainted. More tattooed warriors. *More.* It was impossible, yet there they were, pouring out of the trees. A group five times the size of the first. How? Ki reeled, trying to make sense of it. Unlike the first noisy group, this one ran silently, bent low in the grass, as if to avoid being seen. Everyone else was engaged up front. No one saw the ambush coming but the two girls.

In unison, the sisters opened their mouths and screamed a warning. It did no good. The battle noise was too loud. And they just stood there, screaming, as the enemy raced toward them.

Ki’s scream died in her throat. Cold fear filled her, unlike anything she’d ever felt. How could Magog have so many warriors? At least three hundred. Triple her tribe’s size. True, territories on the Tigris and Euphrates rivers could sometimes feed tribes that large, defying the usual cap of seventy to eighty. But those tribes were half-composed of women. Here, Magog was all men. It wasn’t *fair*.

The attackers blew into camp unopposed, and rushed to strike Ki’s people in the rear. The ambush ended the battle instantly. Ki watched, stunned, as her tribe flew back through the tents in disorder, their formation shattered, their faces twisted in disbelief.

Tattooed warriors ran among them like wolves among deer, hacking, stabbing, laughing, shoving them down. Many warriors dove into the tents, then emerged dragging children by the arms and legs, yanking them ruthlessly like they were no more than birds pulled from the bushes for food. In a detached corner of her mind, Ki understood. Magog wasn't here to kill. They wanted *slaves*.

"Run, foolish girl!" Father bellowed at her.

He was racing toward her, blood dripping down his face from a hideous gash in his forehead. Ki stared at the wound in anguish. The gash was such a deep purple-red, it seemed painted on. How could anyone do that to another person? No battle tale around the campfire had prepared her for this ugliness. Without thinking, she stepped toward him, hands outstretched, as Asha dove into the tent to hide. "Father," Ki cried. "Your head! In the tent we have bandages—"

Behind Father, a Magog warrior ran up. His eyes were fixed murderously on Father's back. His club was raised. Tattoos swirled like demons on his skin. Ki's fear exploded from her mouth in a black-red scream: "Father! Look out!"

Too late. The club swung down. It struck Father in the back of the skull. He crumpled instantly, hitting the dirt face-first. The tattooed warrior stopped above him and lifted his club once more. "Father!" Ki cried, hollowly. But Father just lay there as the club broke his skull open like a melon. Brain, gray and pinkish with blood, spilled out. A shard of skull, like a piece of eggshell, skittered off through the mud. Ki staggered backward as if she'd been struck, the wind knocked out of her. She grabbed her stomach with both hands, the place of her *emittu*, her eternal self. Her spirit seemed to dump out of her like guts, splattering onto her feet. *Goddess Inanna, please let this be a dream.*

But the horror went on, blurring around her, and Ki was too stunned to move. To her left, three Magog warriors were stabbing the chief to death with stone-headed spears as he cried and begged and finally began to drown, choking on the purple blood leaping out of his mouth. To Ki's right, warriors herded weeping children into a group, tying their hands with hemp rope as they submitted, limp in shock, staring open-eyed at the evil happening on all sides. Then Bakil himself came racing by. As their eyes met, Ki lifted her hand involuntarily. But Bakil looked away—darted right past the crying children—and ran around a tent and vanished. Ki struggled to breathe. He just . . . how could he?

Another warrior ran out of the priest's tent holding the clay idol of the goddess Inanna. Laughing madly, he dashed it on the ground, then bent to root among the shards. Ki realized he wanted the idol's two eyes, clear chips of lapis lazuli obtained at great cost from a tribe in the Zagros Mountains, generations ago. Finding one blue chip, the warrior lifted it to the sky. He examined it greedily as it twinkled in the last bursts of sunset. Then he cackled and stuffed it into his hip-pouch, satisfied. What could all this mean? Was the goddess dead, too? Was the world now empty of hope, of any order at all? Pain beyond pain grew in Ki's gut, tightening like a fist. Maybe the elders had been right. Maybe her "magic" really had offended the gods, and this was a punishment for listening to her black spirit.

She might have remained like that, staring, if an elder hadn't bumped her as he ran past, his eyes glazed like a wild beast's. But the jolt snapped her to life, and she suddenly remembered Father's command. *Protect your sister.* And the family tent was there. Asha was inside, seeing none of this. Ki had to help her.

Ki whipped the flap aside and dove in.

"Asha? Asha, are you here?" she called into the gloom.

It was hard to see at first. A small fire guttered in the dirt pit. Bowls of mash lay overturned, leaving grain spilled across the wolf-fur blankets. A stone pestle had fallen into the fire. Asha must have knocked the things over in her haste. The cone of the tent left little room to hide in, however, and Ki located a lump at the far side. Asha's face peeked over the edge of a bear-fur blanket, tears glistening on her beautiful cheeks.

"Are we winning? Is Father here?" Asha asked.

Ki ran to her and knelt and grabbed her tight. Asha's heart fluttered like a bird. Above, Mother's lanyards dangled from the tent poles, strings of shells and feathered beads clicking softly as they spun. Charms against evil, blessed by the tribe priest to protect their home from harm. Ki stared at them resentfully. After what she'd seen outside, she knew the charms were no good. Magog's gods were stronger than Mother's.

"Are we winning?" Asha asked again.

"Yes," Ki lied automatically.

"Where is Father? I want Father."

Ki's mind was already burying it, forming a protective shell over it. Such a horror could not be. It simply couldn't. "Father is . . . he said to hide in the forest," Ki lied again. "He said he will follow."

"I can't go out there!" Asha cried in terror.

"It'll be safe in the trees. Come, little bunny. We can play rabbits." It was a children's game, rabbits; they hadn't played it for years. But it made Asha sit up. Games were a language she understood. "We can run low in the grass, bunny-low," Ki said faintly, as if another person spoke through her. "They won't see us."

"With your weapon," Asha said, finding a little strength.

"My weapon. Yes."

Asha hugged her tightly again. "I love you."

Ki kissed her, then crawled around the fire pit to her pile of things. In it were the pieces she needed for her weapon. She'd disguised them as everyday tools to defend against Mother's snooping. Separate, the pieces meant nothing. Together, the whole became *death*.

Hands shaking, Ki drew out a gristle cord, a slender staff, and finally a sharp dart. She bent the staff into a bow and strung on the cord, making the bow stay bent. She gave the cord a *twang*. It hummed with a sound that meant *power*. Then Ki nocked the feathered dart in and stood. Her black spirit flickered. She was ready.

Asha was staring at the device.

"What is it?"

"A dart-thrower," Ki said.

"What does it do?"

"It . . ."

Ki swallowed. Nothing of its kind existed in Mesopotamia, as far as she knew. To kill, warriors used clubs, hatchets, spears, knives. This device could kill at range, an advancement that would humble every other weapon. Ki's black spirit hummed with the vibrating string. The device had power—more power, perhaps, than Mother's gods. Suddenly Ki was glad she'd broken the ban and given in to her black spirit. She *liked* this weapon. It could shoot a dart farther than any man could hurl a spear. She'd killed squirrels with it, rabbits, groundhogs, even a goat, once.

And if it can kill a goat, it can kill a man.

She nodded to Asha. "It's time."

"We should fight with it, Ki, not run. Where's Father?"

Ki's heart ripped. *Ah, Father!* Again she saw his head explode under the club. What if she'd persuaded the elders to heed her? Ah! How differently this battle might have gone! Why, she might have built a pile of these dart-flingers for her tribe. And today her people could have stood side by side and slaughtered Magog like goats as they charged across the meadow. *And Father would be alive.*

"And Mother?" Asha insisted. "Shouldn't we help Mother?"

Ki wondered if she was right. Mother was out there. And Esarhaddon . . . Aunt Shutub . . . Uncle . . . Then the tent frame shook, and one of *them* burst through the flap.

All courage was forgotten in an instant. Asha gave a cry and pulled the blanket over her chin. Even Ki fell back, clutching her dart-flinger, blood hammering. The man was terrifying. He was a beast of a fellow, perhaps thirty years old, with a ragged beard and a muscular chest inked black with tattoos. He seemed cut from shadow and night, his eyes blazing hungrily amidst the horde of figures stamped on his face. He carried a yellow jawbone hatchet, blood dripping from the crescent edge. He bared his teeth in a wood-brown smile. "Ho, little rats. Peace. I will be gentle." He raised his palm as if to charm them into place, his eyes flicking between Asha and Ki—finally settling on Asha, of course. "You're under my protection, now. There are far worse fates than *me*." He chuckled and took an eager step toward Asha, his eyes devouring her. "What's your name, little one? I'm Udu. Shh, now."

Asha whimpered. "Ki, what's he doing?"

Ki's mind scrambled desperately. This fellow looked influential. Maybe he could make the madness outside stop.

"We surrender," she said sharply. "Tell us what you want."

Udu seemed not to hear. He kept moving slowly toward Asha, spreading his arms as if to trap her from escaping. As if to grab her like a dumb beast and wrestle her down.

Animals, Ki thought in horror. We are animals to him. Sub-creatures. Not worthy of speech.

Something in her snapped. She lifted the bow and pulled the dart back to its fullest extension. "Leave." She pointed the sharp wood tip at his throat. "Last chance."

At the creak of the wood, Udu looked across the fire pit. His face was hard and cruel, like a wolf's. His eyes glowed with contempt. "Is that a toy, sister?"

"Magic," Ki said, and released.

The dart flew too quickly to be seen. One moment it was in Ki's bow. The next, it was in Udu's throat, lodged deep in his windpipe, three-quarters of the way in, up to the fletching. His eyes swelled. Blood slopped out of his mouth, over his beard. Gurgling, he grabbed the shaft and tried to pull it out. More blood squirted over his fingers. Asha screamed. Ki rushed to her and pulled her along the tent wall, away from the staggering warrior.

"Stay behind me. He is dead. But he can still hurt us."

Spitting blood, Udu lunged across the fire pit. He moved too fast for Ki to get away. He seized her weapon, and Ki had to release it. In exchange she pulled Asha farther away, moving around the cone base of the tent. The warrior, meanwhile, attacked the bow as if it was alive. His clumsy fingers snapped the gristle string, and the pole sprang into a staff again. It struck him in the face and knocked him backward, out through the entry flap. He fell halfway outside, leaving just his kicking feet in view, scattering coals from the fire pit against the hide wall, over the fur blankets. Flames caught and spurted up. Smoke rose swiftly, accompanied by the stench of burning hide. The tent, Ki's life home, was being destroyed before her eyes.

"Captain Udu is hurt!" a voice shouted outside.

"Ki," Asha croaked breathlessly. "Your magic—it works!"

"Can we run now?"

"Yes!"

They knelt at the tent edge and pulled the hide wall up, then crawled under it into the meadow. A moment later, they were racing toward the trees. Again the big grasshoppers flew up in panic, tapping off Ki's cheeks and neck. Burrs stuck heavily to the lap of her tunic. Behind her, the sounds of fighting faded. Asha tried to turn and see, but Ki pushed her on. She didn't want that ugliness in her sister's head, ever.

"Mother will meet us in the forest?" Asha asked. "Father?"

"Brother, too," Ki lied shamelessly. "And Uncle and Aunt."

The sky flashed gold in one last burst of glory. Ahead, the shadows under the trees were deep and black, a welcome sight. Soon the world would go dark, and Ki ached for that. Dark offered a real chance of getting away. But now shouts drew nearer. Glancing back, Ki saw a pack of men running after them, spreading out, laughing, pointing. Tall, long-legged men. They seemed much speedier than any hunter in Ki's tribe. Indeed, they were already halfway across the meadow, gaining fast. As the girls reached the trees, one warrior hurled a spear. It arced and sliced into the forest just a few paces to the right, making a loud crash in the underbrush that prompted the girls to flinch and duck their heads.

"Ki, that was a good weapon," Asha said. "I wish we still had it. Did you really . . . kill him?"

"I hope so." Ki scanned the darkness ahead. "Find a bush, a hollow. Maybe we can burrow under some leaves and hide."

"I trust you, Ki. Think. Use your gift."

They ran on, panting raggedly. The forest was thick around them now, obscuring them from their pursuers. But it slowed them, too, its bushes ripping at their tunics, its thorns scratching their skin. Ki felt cool blood trickling down her shin from a rip above her knee. More weapons flew by. Stones whizzed overhead, chipping white gashes in the bark to each side. Voices taunted them. "Scamper, rats. Find your hole. Hide and seek, rats." Hatred boiled in Ki's eyes. Such men were beasts, fair to kill.

"It hurts," Asha said, clutching her ribs.

"Capture will hurt more." Ki dragged her sister on, hating their pursuers more with each step.

Then they entered a clearing—*the* clearing—and Ki stopped in shock. *The wheat.* Just paces ahead, it stood glimmering as beautifully as it ever had—a perfect square, proof of what she'd done. Why had she run here? Perhaps months of dreaming about this place, visiting it over and over in her mind, had led her here automatically. *And there are no straight lines in nature.* If Magog saw the perfect square, they might realize what it was. Steal the idea for themselves. *No.* The idea was too foul to consider. Maybe they would run right past it without noticing. After all, men didn't care about plants, Ki thought desperately. In traditional roles, women gathered plant-food. Men hunted. Many warriors considered it degrading even to know too much about women's work.

CLUNK.

The sound was so loud, Ki grabbed her ear, thinking a rock had struck her. Yet she felt no pain. Instead, she heard a thud.

She turned sharply. Asha was lying face down in the weeds, arms outthrown. The rock rolled away from her head and quivered to a stop in the brown vegetation. "Sister," Ki said. But Asha just lay there, twitching, blood jumping from the side of her temple in dark spurts. Ki stared, uncomprehending. Asha. The person closest to her in the world. Her playmate. Her annoyer. Her sharer of secrets. The only one she could always talk to.

"Asha, they're coming. Get up."

She fell to her knees and covered the wound, wetting her fingers with the hot blood. It kept coming and coming. She turned her sister onto her back. Beautiful Asha just twitched and grunted softly, dirt staining the side of her cheek. Her eyes were open, staring emptily up at the overarching canopy. The branches laced stripes of shadow across her pale face. Her hands gave little jerks, and her eyelids fluttered.

A cry of triumph filled the glade. The Magog warrior who'd thrown the rock burst from the bushes and charged. Ki had no time to react. His fist blurred and punched her in the forehead. She doubled over, clutching the spot in pain. Rough hands shoved her to the ground. The man turned, cupped his mouth, and yelled into the trees, "I got her! The officer-killer. It was me!" Ki could only lie there, gasping, as he stood over her, bathing her in his foul stink.

Another fellow ran out of the trees and stopped.

"Why kill the pretty one? She'd have traded well."

"I got us the captain-killer, didn't I?"

Their voices seemed far away. Ki fixed her eyes on her sister. Asha still hadn't moved. In fact, the blood leaping from her scalp seemed slower, as if . . . *No.*

Ki curled around her. Kissed her ear. Petted her hair, wetting her fingers with Asha's blood. She was still warm. Still breathing. There was hope. Don't worry, sister. We'll make it. It's just a dream, anyway. This can't be real.

By the time Jakka entered the glade, darkness had taken the valley. Thirty warriors stood around the clearing, holding torches of burning grass. The red light danced on the mossy trunks and over the weedy ground, illuminating the scene poorly. The girl—the officer-killer—lay on her side clutching the corpse of her dead sister as if to bring it back to life. Jakka felt contempt. Weak creatures disgusted him. Still, he was puzzled. How had this thing killed one of Father's best officers? Brutally, too. With her childish hands and frail bones, she'd stabbed a sharp stick through his windpipe. Astonishing. Well, even rats could bite your finger when cornered, he supposed.

"Lord Gog," a warrior announced. "Hail!"

Father entered the glade. The warriors all bowed and fell silent, raising their sputtering torches even higher. An officer ran up and began to chatter about the girl. Father just studied her and said nothing, his one eyeball glittering. He seemed in a strangely contemplative mood, Jakka thought. As if the girl reminded him of something.

Then Hakka marched out of the trees, and Jakka's blood rose. What was the upstart doing here?

"Come, Hakka." Father pointed at the girl. "I told you these nomads can fight. Never underestimate an enemy."

"Filthy nomad rats," Hakka said. "I hate 'em."

"Hate?" Father shook his head. "Be careful of hate, boy. It can make you stupid." He turned to Jakka. "How would you deal with this one? A captain-killer."

Jakka, eager to make up for his failed test that afternoon, stepped forward quickly. "Skin her alive, Father. Teach these slaves to fear us, right off."

"Hakka?"

"Burn her alive as an offering to Baal," Hakka said piously. "The war god always rewards."

This time, Father didn't pick favorites. In fact, he no longer seemed to be listening. Something had caught his attention at the edge of the torchlight. He marched toward it, parting the men with a flick of his tattooed hand. Jakka watched, puzzled. The object of his interest seemed to be . . . what, now? A patch of wheat?

Father strode briskly around the wheat, inspecting it. His one eye seemed to glow brighter, throbbing like a red coal in his tattooed face. Why? Jakka was baffled. It was just plant-food. A neat square of it, yes, each head drooping with ripe emmer seed. But vegetables, nonetheless. This was the domain of women. It was disgraceful for Father to heed such a lowly object. Confused, Jakka glanced at Hakka, and was relieved to see that his younger brother looked just as bewildered. What could Father be up to?

Snapping off a wheat head, Father marched back to the girl and thrust it at her face.

"No straight lines in nature," he murmured.

The girl's eyes filled with fear. Father registered the look and grunted knowingly.

"You made this?" He squatted beside her and spoke gently, as he'd never spoken to any of his sons. "There will be no more pain, child. Just tell me. What is this?"

The girl buried her face in her sister's body again.

"The rat is insolent," Jakka cried. "Punish her, Father."

Father tossed the wheat away and studied the girl meditatively.

"I was her age," he said quietly, "when my tribe was destroyed in the Zagros. I, too, refused to speak to my new masters." He looked up at Jakka, his face strangely calm. "Even when they gave me this." He pointed at a scar on his cheek. "And these." He pointed at two ropy scars crisscrossing his chest. Knife slashes. Torture marks.

Jakka stared at him. What was this about?

"You two might learn from her." Father's eye glittered on Jakka. "I wonder, son, if I was slain, would you honor me with silence?"

"Of course," Jakka blurted.

Hakka stepped up beside him. "What are you teaching us, Father?" His tone was so servile, Jakka could have ripped his tongue out. "Are the nomads a . . . threat? Surely that is not your lesson."

"This girl is a witch," Father said. "A *baru*, such as Mesopotamia has not seen in centuries." He chuckled softly. "You may laugh. But I tell you, she may prove the most important slave we have ever captured."

A murmur rippled through the warriors. Jakka and Hakka looked at each other, stunned. A nomad rat? Important? Jakka scratched his beard uneasily. Was Father getting soft-headed?

"She is not to be harmed," Father said. "She holds great value for us."

"But Lord," one adviser sputtered. "She is just a nomad. And she killed an officer."

"Nevertheless, bring her safely home to camp at all costs. I must go north tomorrow with half our men to repel a Mitanni incursion. When I return, I want to see her."

Ignoring their surprised murmurs, Father bent over the girl again.

"I've waited years to find you, child. Do you know who I am? What might I give you?"

The girl did not even lift her head.

"She must answer," Jakka cried. "Father!" He moved to kick her, but Father stopped him with a bark of anger.

"Be still, boy."

Jakka subsided, hot with hate. What was going on?

"She will obey," Father said. "She need only remember . . . I have her people."

The girl stiffened as if poked with a knife. Father gave her a look—almost a pitying look, Jakka thought in astonishment. Then he rose and marched into the forest, making his two bodyguards scurry to keep up as his big sandals crunched over the leaves.

The warriors in the glade looked at each other.

"You heard him," Hakka snapped. "Tie her up. Keep her safe." And he marched into the trees after Father, as if his rightful place, not Jakka's, was at Father's side.

Annoyed and nervous, Jakka followed, mulling it over. The rat looked so pitiful in her dirty boarskin tunic. What could Father possibly see in her? And what would the horde say when rumors spread that the warlord was coddling such a creature? They might sense weakness. There might be unrest. Even resistance.

Jakka's heart beat faster. Perhaps resistance was good. If Father was beginning to favor Hakka . . . Well, Jakka would just have to wait and see.

4

Somewhere in central Mesopotamia, a young man marched south through the desert, feeling miserable for himself.

It was noon and blazing hot. He was clutching the stump of his severed right forearm. The sun was blasting down, cooking his brain inside his skull like mutton. The rag he'd wrapped around his head did little to block the heat or stop the blades of light reflecting off the gravel into his eyes, making him squint. His face was burned nearly black. Grit filmed his body. His loincloth, hard with grime, itched his inner thighs, already red and chafed.

If I was going to die anyway, I should've done it back in Akkad and saved myself this trouble, he thought wretchedly. Some life. What is the point of it? It's just pain after pain. Ah, things only get worse for Ta!

His leather sandals were ragged. His feet were blistered, oozing pus. His stomach ached with hunger. It felt like a big rat was in there, clawing at his gut, trying to dig its way out. Frustrated, Ta stopped to adjust the straps of his pack, which cut terribly into his raw shoulders. Then he looked up, peering after his fellow Akkadians.

All eleven were far ahead, strung-out in a file, stumbling listlessly between the stunted thornbushes. This wouldn't work out for them, either, Ta thought. They looked as defeated as he felt.

No one knew where they were, and in a day or two their food and water would run out. Where was the Euphrates River? It had not appeared where they'd hoped. Maybe it didn't even exist. Now their legs shone with sweat, their heads drooped, and their greasy black hair hung in their faces like ragged veils.

Soon, they'll start to die, a voice in Ta's heart whispered.

Ta ground his teeth savagely, and dug his fingers into his stump. What do I care? he thought. Which of them ever cared for Ta?

None of them, the voice replied. *It's Ta for Ta. Like always.*

Coughing in the red dust, Ta scanned the horizon, hoping some new feature would appear. But nothing had for days. Not since they'd left the green country by the Tigris River. Only thornbushes, red gravel, and ruthless sun. Ta looked up. A lone vulture circled high above, a black speck against the white expanse. It had been trailing the group all morning, as if it knew exactly what lay ahead.

You can't keep up, the voice whispered. *Soon you'll fall. And they'll leave you.*

They *would* leave me, Ta thought sullenly. Heartless beasts.

The voice mocked him. *What, then? Will you just give up?*

Ta scowled. What can I do?

The voice answered readily. *Steal food.*

Steal! Ta's mouth fell open. But I can't.

He held up his severed stump and looked at it. It was repulsive. Just a nub of scarred gristle. A wrinkle of ugly skin folded over his wrist bones. It made his stomach roil. Stealing. Ta shivered. They'd cut his hand off for exactly that all those years ago in the cave.

No, he thought. No, I can't steal.

Coward, the voice chided. *It would be so easy.*

Ta trembled. It was true. By chance, the group had asked him to carry the food pack today. It hung heavy on his shoulders. Inside was a purse of seeds, smoked meat bits, and goat bones filled with rich marrow. It called to him. How easy it would be to reach in and snatch out a bite. His companions, all far ahead, imprisoned in their private suffering, wouldn't see. And tonight at dinner when they doled out rations, who'd know the difference?

The fingers of his one hand twitched involuntarily. By the gods, how hungry he was. He ate only a pinch of rations twice a day, once at breakfast, once at dinner. In between, he walked in gut-screaming pain. His muscles felt fizzy, ready to dissolve off his bones. Every bush he passed whispered to him, tempting him to lie in its shade and never move again. If he didn't eat more soon, he'd collapse on the scalding red earth and fry to death.

So, steal, the voice whispered. *DO IT NOW.*

Ta gulped, his throat sticky. No.

Would it even be wrong after all they stole from you over the years? When did they treat you right? Who was your friend? They called you "worthless" and fed you miserable meal portions so you couldn't grow. Denied you a mate and put you to shameful work with the women, vegetable-gathering. What a life! Who spoke up for you? No one. It's Ta for Ta, as ever.

Ta's legs shook. His mouth salivated. And suddenly, he broke.

Before he could stop himself, he slid the pack off, stabbed a hand inside, and found the food satchel with his fingers. He dug out a handful of tubers, smoked meat bits, and shriveled plant-matter. The remnant of their last foraging efforts before the waste. The smell struck his nose forcefully, making the blood slam in his face. Suddenly he was not a person anymore, just a belly roaring for food. A mouth of teeth aching to gnash. So Ta cursed everything—cursed the gods, cursed his companions, cursed his own life—and shoved the bite in.

He trembled as it slid down the tube of his throat. How good it felt. How deliciously the taste spread across the ceiling of his mouth. Food was energy. It was life.

More, the voice urged. *MORE.*

Ta knew he shouldn't. But he couldn't help himself. He shoved his hand into the satchel again. And as he did, a voice shrieked across the glittering stones.

"Thief!"

Ta's skin turned to ice. Korak, the rearmost of the group, had stopped, turned, and jabbed a gnarled finger at him. He'd seen! Ta yanked his hand out of the pack. Korak's face wrinkled in triumph. And suddenly Ta wondered if Korak had given him the food pack on purpose, hoping he'd fall into this very trap.

"Grab him," Korak said. "Quick, before he chomps the rest."

Shouting in alarm, the group charged back toward Ta, cursing and waving their staves. In a mob they surrounded him, men and women and children, shouting and spitting. Their faces were blistered and murderous, their eyes savage with hunger equal to his own.

"Brothers and sisters," Ta spluttered. "You are mistaken. I thought a strap broke, I was merely checking it, I—"

"In his beard," Korak said. "Proof!"

He slapped Ta's beard. To Ta's dismay, fresh seed crumbs danced out, wet and sparkling with saliva.

"As I thought," Korak said. "He is a liar."

Ta fell back, clutching his beard, trying to cover it. He only appeared more guilty. The group fell on him again, punching his head, slapping, kicking. They were *glad* for his mistake, Ta realized. They had an excuse to get rid of him now, leaving more food for them.

Ta fell. The ground was burning hot on his knees, enough to melt his kneecaps off. He crawled frantically into the shade of a thornbush and curled up in the only-slightly-cooler sand, hugging the pack. The others continued to attack, kicking dirt at him. It was only Korak's sharp cry, "Wait, let us do this right," that stopped the frenzy.

Korak straightened up like a true chief. Indeed, he probably planned to make himself one at the thief's expense. He certainly used his most official-sounding voice.

"I hoped this moment would never come, brothers and sisters. But here it is. Without food, this desert kills us. Food is our energy, our way out. Ta's theft is no better than murder."

The group nodded in agreement.

"He did this before, too. It's who he is." Korak pointed at Ta's stump. "In Akkad, our chief cut off his hand. For a second offense, he'd stone him."

"Stone me?" Ta squeaked. "You can't be serious."

"Hush, runt. I don't want a stoning. I lack the heart for it. I desire no more brutality like back home. Yet we cannot permit this, or others will be tempted to steal. You leave us one choice." Korak lifted his chin. "Exile."

The word fell on Ta like a boulder. "Exile? Brother Korak, it's me, Ta. We're tribe!"

His words seemed to prick the other group members. They looked at each other uncertainly. After all, they'd been exiled together, kicked out by their chief a month ago when he decreed that the least useful would have to go, claiming their tribe's territory could no longer feed them all. These twelve, including Ta, were given packs and spears, and sent away to start a new life. Since then, they'd struggled toward the Euphrates River, a green paradise lush with plenty of space to settle in—at least according to the legends. And day after day, as it failed to appear, they'd grown closer, realizing that they'd been sent into the middle of nowhere to die.

Seeing their hesitation, Ta bowed repeatedly, banging his forehead on the shaded sand.

"We're more than tribe. We're family now, aren't we?" He looked hopefully from face to face. "Tibba. Shubul. Enkidu. You'll regret this, I know you will."

A few gave him sad looks. But Korak spoke ruthlessly, and Ta's hopes sank.

"Actually, we'll be better off without you, runt. You're eighteen, but you act like a child. You're a complainer, a shirker, and unskilled. Not to mention a thief, twice over. You add nothing. You only take."

Ta's face went cold.

"He can't hunt or fish," a man agreed, and spat in the dirt.

"He's always whining," commented a girl.

"When's he ever volunteered for anything?" asked a third.

"And when you force a chore on him, then check his work, it's never done," said a fourth.

"He always grabs the lightest pack," a boy shouted gleefully, eager to hear his own voice.

"And he's a coward," said an old woman, folding her sunburned arms. "Remember when we crossed the Tigris River? The raft broke and Ta abandoned me to the current. Just splashed away and let a pack of tools sink. Korak had to swim back for me."

"Yes, yes," the group shouted. "Ta only cares for himself. Exile him at once."

Ta's cheeks burned at the accusations. They hurt even more because they were true.

"Brothers, sisters, please." He pointed up at the sun. "In this heat, anyone could lose his head. I've learned my lesson now. I swear by Enlil, I have. Just give me a second chance."

"No," the group shouted. "Worthless! Lazy! Coward! Leave him to the lizards."

At this point, even a great orator could not have persuaded them. Overpowering Ta's feeble biting and kicking, they wrenched the food pack from him and marched away, booing and hissing back over their shoulders. Only Korak remained.

"It's over, runt." Korak stood over him like a god delivering judgment, sunlight pouring over his shoulders. "Don't try to follow us. If you do . . ." He bent and grabbed a rock and lifted it threateningly. "I'll break your ankle and make you a cripple twice over."

Ta stared at the desert in despair. Small dust devils flared between the bushes as if the earth was burning alive. He looked up at Korak pitifully.

"Please, brother. You know I can't make it alone out here."

Korak shrugged. "You had plenty of chances. If you'd walked a different path . . ."

"What path?" Ta said bitterly.

"The path of a hero. Not a thief."

Laughter burst from Ta's lips. "A hero! Which of you is?" He held up his stump. "And which hero had to deal with this?"

Korak marched off, his sandals crunching the gravel.

"Stop feeling sorry for yourself, runt. We're all going to die, too."

"Brother, wait," Ta pleaded, staring after him in disbelief.

Korak refused to look back. He didn't hate him, Ta realized. He just wanted to appear strong so the others would make him chief. In truth, Ta wasn't even on Korak's mind.

5

Ta didn't know how long he remained under the bush. He simply lay as if stunned. His fear built steadily, their cruel words lashing him like whips. *Worthless. Lazy. Coward. Better off without you.* He'd guessed they had these feelings. But hearing them out loud hurt terribly.

What did they expect of me? he thought furiously. A noble chief or something? I'm a cripple! Cursed. I was cursed from the beginning.

Miserably, he lifted his stump—lumpy with scar tissue—and looked at it with loathing. Then he dug his fingernails into the flesh, pressing until the pain made him gasp. Oh, if only he hadn't made that terrible mistake, years ago! How different his life might be now. If only he could start over.

Shutting his eyes, he saw the fateful night once more.

He was in Akkad again, an orphan on the edge of manhood, just thirteen years old. Unable to sleep, he lay awake at midnight in the blackness of his tribe's cave. He shivered under his deerskin blanket on an icy stone ledge, surrounded by snoring shapes, illuminated in a shaft of moonlight that flowed down the tunnel, bathing the cave walls. Charcoal drawings adorned the walls, epic murals of aurochs and deer and giant fish, as well as stick armies tossing rocks and spears in battles of legend, preserved for all time. But the orphan was fixed on lesser things. He was missing his parents, weeping tears of self-pity. His stomach ached. His spirit quailed as the awful winds of northern Akkad whistled around the cave-hill, moaning like demon voices. And perhaps it was a demon that crept into his head. *Why not steal food?* a voice whispered. And the orphan indulged the voice. And fantasy became a plan.

He sat up in the darkness and listened. His ears perked like a rat's. The snores of his tribe were loud and deep. *Good,* the voice whispered. Earlier at dinnertime, the orphan had watched other children eat heartily, their parents handing out fish and grouse breasts and ribs of rich venison, dripping with fat. How unlike his meager dinner of plants and nuts! It felt brutally unfair. Those children would grow big and strong on such food. The orphan, meanwhile, would wither. He'd never grow into a hunter, respected by the tribe.

So go.

Slowly, the orphan peeled off his deerskin blanket and crawled down the ledges. He wore just a scratchy hide loincloth. But he was not cold anymore. Heat surged in him, the heat of *power*. Down the ledges he crept, hand over hand. Ta wished with all his heart he could grab that stupid boy and shout, "Fool! Think what you'll lose!" But Ta was trapped in time, and the orphan had free will. He crept on.

At the bottom of the cave, the orphan squatted outside an oval of light. The home fire was dead, but its crushed embers pulsed like a living heart, throwing out faint reds and yellows. The chief, buried beneath rich furs, slept at the edge of its glow, surrounded by his three mates and eleven children. In a stone nook nearby, the grass food basket was faintly visible. The orphan approached it carefully, creeping around the edge of the light. Every so often, he paused and listened. A bat squeaked above, whooshing cold air downward with its delicate wings. An old man moaned in his sleep nearby, perhaps dreaming of an ancient hunt. The furtive rustle of lovemaking could even be heard, high up among the darker ledges. None of this interested the boy. Only food.

He reached the nook. With trembling hands, he lifted the lid off the storage basket. It was a pad of woven grass, strapped on with leather hinges. It removed easily. Shaking, he stuck his hand inside. His fingers brushed the pile of food within, and his heart roared. He felt smoked meat shreds, hard small seeds, and even waxen comb, stained with golden honey. All his! The boy's self-restraint vanished. Out came a fistful. As if of its own will, his hand slammed the food past his lips. Taste exploded across his tongue. His molars gnashed wildly. By Enlil, it was strength! Power! A future! He needed more.

"Who's there?"

The voice shot across the embers. The boy flattened against the wall, arm hairs rising.

"You, by the basket. What are you doing?"

The boy swallowed reflexively, his mouth full of meat, and choked, spilling bits onto his sunken chest. His heart plunged.

"A thief! A thief!"

It was old Gulbar, a bitter, frustrated fellow. Years later, his words would be echoed by Korak in that very tone. The boy didn't know that, of course. He still thought himself invincible.

"Quick, by the fire! Don't let him get away."

Heart pounding, the orphan slammed the lid back on the basket. This couldn't be happening. He scanned the cave for a way out. He noticed the embers' light did not fully extend to him in the nook. He was still just a form in the dark, unidentifiable. A desperate plan flashed. The whole tribe was coming awake, shouting, cursing; soon they would rush the nook. But if he dove into the darkness in time, he could mix into the chaos and stay unidentified.

Clenching both fists, the orphan leapt up and sprinted along the rugged cave wall.

"There! There!" the screams burst. "Grab him!"

Men charged the oval of red light. Up by the tunnel, shapes stood, cutouts against the slash of night sky. The orphan raced toward the safety of blackness below. It was only paces away. Hope surged. Then, the inconceivable happened. A hand grabbed his foot. He leapt. The hand was like rock. It threw him down. The orphan slammed hard onto his chin, pain shooting up his nostrils. Shouts hammered on his ears, deafening him. The chief's voice boomed.

"Why, it's him, the little fool."

People starved to death each year. Thus, food theft was the gravest of crimes. The boy's punishment came that very night. As the tribe booed and hissed, the tribe storyteller stoked the home fire, bringing it to roaring life. Everyone sat on the lowest ledges to see better, over a hundred eyes glinting, mothers hugging children, forcing them to watch. Indeed, it was the mothers who shouted loudest of all. It was their offspring he'd robbed. "Traitor!" they yelled. "Trust-breaker!" On the cave floor, four hunters sat on the boy, one on each limb. The priest shook his bead stick and chanted, "He loved himself above the Whole. He dishonored his people. Let him be 'Ta' forever." In ancient Akkadian, the word "Ta" meant "cripple." At once, the tribe took up the chant. "Let him be 'Ta' forever." The chief's stone knife flashed.

"You can't!" the boy cried. "It's me! You know me!"

The great man seemed not to hear.

"To all who defy us!" he bellowed. "Let it be an eye for an eye! A tooth for a tooth! For a theft, a hand! And if he steals again—like a stone dropped into water, he will simply disappear."

"Please," the boy screamed. "I'll change!"

The knife lowered toward his hand. This precious, fragile piece of himself. A hunter held it flat to the stone, crushing it under all his weight. Delicate veins pumped blood to the boy's fingertips. Under each nail tingled sensitive nerves, connecting them to his mind. Slender bones, like the roots of small plants, webbed through his palm. The chief's knife bit deep. A searing white pain flooded the boy's wrist. Something fell free to the stone. A shriek filled the cave. Vaguely, the boy realized it was his own. The hand lay near his face, separate from him. Just a piece of meat. Blood was gushing from his chopped stump. The boy seemed to float above the scene, watching his screaming self, so pale and scrawny, thrashing on the cave floor.

"Bring the fire-heated rock," shouted the medicine woman.

A glowing orb held between two sticks—a rock pulled from the fire—appeared and was lowered to the stump. The hiss of rock frying flesh, *his* flesh, stunned him more than the knife cut. As if from a great distance, the boy watched himself twist and howl under the weight of the hunters. The medicine woman held the rock fast to the scalding flesh. "Take it, boy. This is for your own good."

And the next morning—and the morning after that—the boy would wake up clutching the stump. Keeping his eyelids shut, dreading the day, he would beg the gods once again, *This morning, let it be gone. Let it be just a nightmare. I've learned my lesson.* Of course, each time he forced his eyes open, the stump remained. An ugly nub at the tip of his wrist, scarred with burned gristle, mocking him.

This is you now. For the rest of your life. This. This. *This.*

Ta moaned. In the desert under the bush, sweating in the heat, he lifted the stump and looked at it again. In the years since the cut, he'd done this so often, the sight was burned into his brain. He'd memorized every ugly lump and curve and divot. With a curse, he began banging his forehead with the stump.

"Ahhh!" he screamed. "Ahhh! What could I have done differently? WHAT?"

He screamed until his throat hurt. The desert, of course, gave no reply.

Ta fell silent, panting.

Then, in a spasm of irritation, he brushed his deerskin loincloth off, knocked away the sand, and rose and began marching after his companions' tracks. He had to win his group back. Simply had to. Perhaps they'd feel guilty tonight and relent. Not Korak, that beast. But a few others. Yes. They were weaklings like him. Rejects. They would understand.

Or better yet, he thought savagely, I'll find them sleeping and steal their food pack. Fools. Oh, they'll be sorry then! No mercy this time. It's Ta for Ta!

◆

On he walked. On and on. His vision blurred. His blistered feet made him step funny. But he kept going. Until, at midafternoon, another disaster struck.

It was a sandstorm. Not a big one, thank goodness. Those big ones could kill you, flay your skin off, grind your bones to nubs. But this one still blew out of the deeper desert and flurried around him, blinding and choking and stinging, making him squat and cover his head with both arms. It coated the spindly arms of the thornbush with lines of grit, like dustings of brown snow. And when it gusted on, it erased the footprints of his companions under a carpet of sand. Erased them as if they'd never existed.

Ta gazed around blankly. With growing panic, he began to stagger here and there over the freshly laid grit, searching for the lost track. He ran side to side, then in widening circles. But time passed, and he could not pick it up again.

He stopped suddenly and gripped his stump. Dread filled him. Now I am alone, he thought. Truly alone.

Unthinkingly, he lifted his face to the blank sky.

"Akkadians! Akkadians! I'm sorry! I mean it this time!"

Of course, no one answered.

Finally, he realized he couldn't just stay there. Feeling numb, he picked a southernly direction and limped on in what he hoped was the general route of his fellows. *Alone. Truly alone.* Even the voice in his heart had abandoned him. Only the vulture remained, circling above. Ta knew what that meant and tried not to think of it.

Each step hurt. Each breath felt like a lungful of fire. His tongue grew thick and scaly in his mouth. *Alone.* At one point he knelt at the base of a thornbush and tore up a dry root and chewed on it, sucking it desperately for moisture. But the root was dry and splintery, and stabbed his gums. He ended up spitting it out—along with precious saliva, pink-tainted by blood. He staggered on, hating himself.

That's me, he thought. Stupid. Clueless. Everything I do makes things worse.

◆

He was still traveling when night fell. The sky glittered with stars. The sand was bone white. The thornbushes were blacker than ever. He walked in a daze, a quivering mess of nerves. It was cooler, at least. But the tracks had not reappeared. Meanwhile, a soft wind kept blowing the sand, sweeping away any prints that might have remained.

In the early hours before morning, something caught Ta's eye. A red glimmer in the distance. A sparkle, like that of a fallen star. At first, he thought he was losing his mind. But no, it really was a fire. Ta's heart jumped. Who could it belong to but his people?

He began to run, battering through the bushes. Thorns raked hot pain across his arms and legs, but nothing mattered except to end his loneliness. If Korak crushed his ankle, so be it.

When Ta drew close to the camp, he slowed and approached at a crouch. Slipping from one thornbush to another, he drew close enough to hear the crackle of the fire embers. Then he got down on his knees and began to crawl. Using his stump tenderly, since the nub hurt if he put too much pressure on it, he crawled to the edge of the campsite. And there he stopped.

These were not his people.

In the feeble ember light, he saw two lumps lying on deerskin blankets, snoring. One was a woman. Her splash of black hair across the sand gave it away. The other was bigger, a man, his hairy arm thrown over his face, his beard protruding like a spurt of black weeds.

The man looked strong. If he awoke and found Ta there, he might want to fight. Ta's instincts told him to slink away. But what was that lingering smell? Was it meat? By the gods, yes. It emanated from a pack by the fire. Ta sniffed, and his sensitive nostrils determined it was old meat, reheated for taste. But meat, nonetheless. And that smaller pack . . . it looked like a water skin.

For a long time, Ta lay flat, trembling. He felt like a dog outside a human camp, both tempted and afraid. Who the two sleepers were did not matter. Here was a chance for redemption. If I steal the food, he told himself, and bring it to my people, they will forgive me.

That decided it. Taking a breath, he crawled into the camp. Each rasp of gravel made him wince. But the two strangers were deeply asleep, probably exhausted after their desert trek that day. They did not rouse. Ta wished he was sleeping himself.

He drew close to the fire pit. So close, the embers heated his nose. The food pack and water bag rested within reach of the sleepers. Slowly, slowly, Ta hoisted first one, then the other, onto his shoulders. His guts were so knotted, his lips so dry, he hardly noticed the straps abrading the scabs on his shoulders. The pain did not matter, only the life-giving bags. Ta's mouth was so parched, he nearly lifted the wooden nozzle of the water skin to his lips right there. But then he went as still as a rock. Was he imagining things? Had he heard a noise?

He turned to creep away—then froze again. There. A whimper.

He twisted his head, looked back. Above the woman's blanket gleamed two red dots. Shiny reflections of the pulsing embers. Red human eyes. The whimper came again. A tiny, curious sound. Why didn't the woman cry out to wake the man?

Because it wasn't the woman, Ta realized with a start. It was a *baby*.

Cradled in its sleeping mother's arms, the baby cooed a third time. Ta stared at it. It seemed to be swaddled in a pouch of stitched rabbit skins. That was why it blended so well with its mother. Its nut-sized eyes glittered. A tiny hand emerged and waved. It was not unhappy, just interested in Ta. *Nice baby.*

Turning halfway, Ta began to edge slowly away. He kept his eyes locked on the infant's. If he broke eye contact, he feared it would become displeased and cry. *Easy, little fellow.* But the child only cooed once more, as if wondering who Ta was. Then Ta was behind a bush, out of sight.

Licking his dry teeth, Ta stopped and listened, all his senses alert. The baby was quiet. So Ta turned and crunched off quickly, wincing each time his blistered feet touched the ground. It was much more painful to run under the fresh weight, but the farther he got, the more he picked up the pace, jogging now. The smell of food filled his nostrils. How much had he stolen? He could hear tools and hides shifting in there, too. This was more than just food. It was a new life.

He made it half a league before he suddenly stopped and sank to his knees. The bags slid off into the sand automatically, and he lifted the water skin to his lips. He was so thirsty, he glugged it, nearly choking. Much poured over his swollen tongue, but a little spilled down his wispy beard, spattering his chest. Enough. He fiercely yanked the bag away from his lips. Any more and he might throw up. He could not afford to waste it.

Then, abruptly, another feeling ripped through him, and it was not physical. He dropped the water bag and clutched his stump in astonishment, digging his fingernails in, nearly cutting his sunburned skin as the awful thought grew.

Murderer.

Ta began to shake. That baby back there . . . that family. Ta hadn't realized it until now. By taking their food and water, he'd left them nothing. Ta would live. But they would die.

Murderer.

Ta scrambled back from the bags. The two lumps confronted him like judges.

Who is Ta?

Ta gulped. I . . . I can't answer that, he thought. What kind of question is that?

But it wouldn't leave him alone.

Who is Ta?

The night sky swirled above him. The weariness in his bones sucked him into the earth. For a while he sat like that, cross-legged, his heart wrenching this way and that.

Lazy. Coward. Worthless. Thief.

Yes, he was all those things. But was he a *murderer*, too?

The feeling struck harder than he expected.

Suddenly he wondered: What would my parents think? If they could see what I've become?

It was strange to think of them now. He barely remembered them. He must have been seven or eight when the Great Plague hit Akkad, taking a quarter of the tribe. He only vaguely remembered the sight of his parents' bodies lying in the forest outside the cave atop a pyre, covered with pine needles and flowers. Funny, it was the smell he remembered most vividly. The charred stench as the red flames licked up the logs and ate their flesh. The richer tang of pine needles and burnt flower petals floating smoky into his mouth. The stink had lingered on him for days.

He remembered something more, too. A time when he was even younger, six years old, perhaps. He sat inside a lean-to of pine and ash on a deerskin blanket between his parents, nestled in their warmth. They were sipping soup from clay bowls, talking of their little son's future. Ta couldn't remember the words. Just the feeling. A calm, certain feeling. It was raining outside, drumming on the logs of the lean-to. Inside, the blankets were warm and dry. His mother was humming, combing his wet hair with her fingers. His father talked in a low voice, as rhythmic as the thumping of the rain. Everyone seemed happy.

Happy, Ta thought in astonishment. As if they really believed a good future lay ahead. That things would be wonderful for them, even better than in that lean-to. More surprising still was how excited their little son felt to help them. He loved them so much, his heart hurt. He clenched his tiny fists and looked up with shining eyes, determined to make them proud.

The memory faded. Ta was surprised to find himself back under the starry sky, surrounded by desert. His throat was so raw, it hurt to gulp. His parents had loved him. He'd forgotten that. What that felt like. Tears drifted down his cheeks. A vast distance separated him from that little boy. As vast as the reaches of outer space, impassable by man.

Ta bowed his head. No more tears came. He lacked the water for them. But his eyes stung, making the motions. What had his life amounted to? Not much. It was a bitter joke. When he died, his story would be a pitiful one, nothing a storyteller would speak at any campfire. Ta hadn't done one noble thing in his life. Not one act. Nothing to vindicate the hope his parents had put in their little son. Ta felt vastly empty.

It's not my fault, his heart protested. I never had a chance. No one ever . . . But the excuses flamed, sputtered, died. They didn't matter. Only what one *did.*

Ta raised his eyes to the unfeeling stars. Deep down, he knew. Whatever else he was, he was not a baby murderer. No. He could not go that far. He'd stolen and complained and shirked and hated everyone and himself. But that baby? No, he could not kill a baby.

He sat there, trembling in the hard self-knowledge.

What could one do, then? Bring the food back?

You'll die.

Yet there was no alternative. His body couldn't even cry anymore. His eyeballs, dry and scratchy behind his eyelids, felt so achy, he wanted to rip them out. He settled for gripping his stump and digging his fingernails in, drawing the wanted pain. Until, finally, he slumped and sighed.

All right, parents. All right.

6

The white ball of the sun lifted slowly above the desert horizon, spreading a golden haze over the thornbushes, and over Ta, who crouched outside the little camp, waiting.

The two strangers still slept in the sandy clearing. Even as the dawn illuminated their faces and stretched their shadows out behind them, they didn't rise from their deerskin blankets. The journey must have been as hard on them as on Ta. Only the baby was awake. It kept turning its chubby face in its mother's arms to gaze at the newcomer with big wondering eyes.

Ta looked back curiously. He knew little of babies. In Akkad, no mother had let him play with hers, for a thief was considered unclean, bad luck. Yet Ta had always loved children. The world hadn't yet turned them cruel.

He smiled. To his delight, the baby smiled back. *Friends.* An unfamiliar feeling washed through Ta. Something warm and good. He waved his stump. *Hello.* Wonder upon wonders, the little creature giggled back. Ta grinned ear to ear. Here was one creature in the world who did not judge him. It seemed unthinkable now that he'd almost stolen this little brother's food. He *had* been mad.

But I didn't do it, he reassured himself. I *didn't.* That was something.

The sun rose higher, warming the air quickly. Birds sang in the thornbushes. Little red lizards skittered across the sand. Ta caught one and ate it raw, giving himself a bit of sustenance. Soon the ground would become too hot for lizards, and they would vanish, hiding from the deadly heat that would consume the surface of the earth.

Ta longed to hide, too. He still had no idea what the strangers would do when they awoke. They might not even speak the common Mesopotamian tongue. What's my plan? he wondered. They might throw rocks at him, chase him off. Even try to kill him. It was unlikely that they'd invite a cripple to join their tribe. Especially out here, where every bite of food was precious. Probably the best he could hope for was a sharing of information. If he was lucky, they'd point him toward the Euphrates.

Flies began to swarm in the air, landing on the strangers' faces. Finally the man sat up, swatting at them. He stretched his arms and yawned.

Ta studied him. He looked Ta's age, seventeen or eighteen. Of course, he was far stronger and taller. A hunter, no doubt. His body was covered in manly black hair, a thick pelt that seemed almost animal. His beard was full and bushy, putting Ta's patchy mess to shame. What region was he from? His facial shape—long nose, broad forehead—looked Akkadian. Perhaps his tribe was distant kin to Ta's. Ta clung to this hope desperately.

The man smacked his lips and scratched his loincloth. Then he saw Ta, and went rigid.

"Aya! Aya!"

The man leapt up from his blanket and stared at Ta with round eyes. "Get up, Aya. We have a visitor." He snatched his spear from the dirt and leveled the sharp tip at Ta. "What do you want, stranger? Who are you?"

The woman jerked upright with a cry. "Ut! Ut! What's he doing here?" She clutched the baby to her chest. "Why'd you let him get so close?"

"I don't know, that's what I'm trying to find out," Ut said.

Aya gripped her child and scrambled around the dead fire until she was behind Ut. Ta was so frightened, he couldn't find his voice, and just stared at them stupidly. A long moment passed.

"Speak, stranger. Or I'll . . . I'll . . ." Ut raised his spear threateningly, ready to hurl it.

"Peace!" Ta squeaked. "I mean no harm."

He held up his arms to prove he held no weapons.

Ut lowered his spear halfway. "You speak the common tongue?"

"Clearly he does," Aya snapped. "Quick, Ut. Ask him what he wants."

Ut scanned the thornbushes rapidly. "See anything, Aya? This could be an ambush."

"I'm alone," Ta said.

"I think he's Akkadian," Aya said. "Did you hear his accent?"

"There are many breeds of Akkadian, tribe-sister." Ut looked Ta up and down. "Is this a trap, stranger? If you're not an enemy, prove it."

"I *am* Akkadian," Ta said. "And I'm lost."

"Why did you sneak up on us?"

"I hoped . . ."

Ta hesitated, unsure how to say it. *I hoped you'd save me.* But that would do him no favors.

"I'm looking for the Euphrates," he said finally. "I thought we could talk and share information. Help each other."

Ut relaxed at mention of the Euphrates. He lowered his spear and cocked his head, studying Ta.

"The great river, eh? What do you know of it? We happen to be looking for it ourselves."

The woman, meanwhile, seemed to have made up her mind about Ta. She elbowed her way around Ut and nodded at the blankets they'd abandoned. "Come, Ut, don't be rude. He's a cripple and he needs help. Can't you see he's not dangerous?"

"You've arrived at that idea rather quickly, woman."

Aya tossed her hair. "If he wanted to hurt us, he'd have done it when we were sleeping. Did you think of that?"

"No need to be short with me," Ut said.

"Besides, he's Akkadian. That proves he's a wanderer, like us. Down here they're all Sumerians or something, aren't they? Didn't the tribe storyteller say that?"

"He also said the Euphrates was close." Ut eyed the shimmering desert. "He was not always accurate."

"I'm from the north, the Zagros Mountain foothills," Ta said eagerly. "My tribe storyteller told me the Euphrates was close by, too. Maybe all Akkad has it wrong."

"We're from central Akkad," Aya said. "Just below the Tigris River." She cast Ut a questioning glance. "They're not savages in north Akkad, are they?"

"At least he's not an east Akkadian brute," Ut said. "North Akkadians, I'm not sure."

Ta brightened. Central Akkadians were unfamiliar to him. But if there was a blood feud between their tribe and his, he'd never heard of it. That was promising.

"Pleasure to meet you both," he said, bowing.

Aya bowed back. But Ut looked at Ta's stump and narrowed his eyes.

"You're a food thief, aren't you?"

Ta's cheeks reddened. "I've learned my lesson, believe me. But my people do call me 'Ta.'"

"Ta, come sit." Aya nodded at her blanket. "And welcome. Do you need a sip of water? Ut, put that spear away. Let's make a friend."

Ut's scowl deepened. "We're sharing water now?"

"And he'll share information, if we don't drive him away. Sit, both of you."

Ut cast her a resentful look. Nevertheless, he reached down and picked up the water bag and extended it to Ta, who accepted it with a low bow. Using his stump to brace the bag near his face, Ta trickled more life-giving liquid over his cracked lips. It took all his self-control not to guzzle it. But he knew this was a test to see whether he was a barbarian. So he politely took two small sips—the customary amount among civilized tribes—then handed the bag back to Ut. The hunter gratified him with a nod, then stuck the wooden cork back in the nozzle and sat down beside Aya and her baby, resting his spear across his lap. Ta sat on the second blanket.

"Very well," Aya said. "Now tell us of yourself, Akkadian brother. And be thorough. Poor Ut here is still uneasy."

Ta obliged. In a rush, he blurted out his whole story. The food shortage in Akkad, exile, the long arduous trek south. Of course, he left out the part about stealing food from Korak.

"A sandstorm separated me from my group," he lied, unable to meet their gaze. "I was setting rabbit snares when it hit. I hid. When it was over, I couldn't find them again."

He glanced up to see if they'd swallowed it. It seemed they had.

"That storm hit us too," Ut said. "At least it wasn't a big one. You see those? They look like mountains of fire. Thankfully, they blow out in the deep desert, mostly."

"Terrible," Ta said, hastening to be agreeable.

"I'm sorry you lost your people," Aya said kindly, bobbing her baby in her lap. "It's a terrible thing to be without one's tribe." She scanned the desert. "What do you think your chances are of finding them again?"

"I'm not sure. I thought I'd run across them if I kept going south."

Ut shot a secret look at Aya. "Are they looking for new members, by any chance?"

Ta rubbed his nose. He didn't really want these two to meet his old tribe. Then again, if he pretended he had something to offer . . .

"I'm sure they'd welcome more Akkadians," he said. "Power in numbers, and so on."

Ut scratched his ragged beard, trying not to look too excited. "Huh. Maybe we'd like that."

Ta poured it on thick. "They did speak of finding recruits. As many as possible." He nodded at Ut. "More warriors, especially." He turned to Aya. "Women are always wanted, of course."

"Do they have food to share?" Aya asked pointedly.

"Oh, yes." Another lie. "I'd be happy to speak on your behalf. We're right on their trail. If we keep going, we're bound to run into them."

Ut looked at Aya. "I admit, we've been uneasy out here on our own."

Aya nodded. "Two people is poor protection."

Ut looked south, into the distance. "We knew we'd have to join a tribe once we reached the Euphrates. I'd rather it be Akkadian. These southern Mesopotamians . . . Sumerians, I think they're called? Who knows what they're like? Might do human sacrifice and all that."

"I feel the same," Ta chirped shamelessly.

Aya was studying Ta keenly. "Ut, I think this man was sent by the gods. I feel it in my gut."

"Anything's possible," Ut said evasively.

"Don't you see? He's the reply to our prayer."

She bent toward Ta confidentially. "We burned a food offering to the gods just yesterday. Now they've answered us with you. It's plain."

Ut gave a cynical smile. "Aya's pious. She loves burning all our rations to the *baals*. Much faith. Little prudence."

Aya kissed the top of her baby's head. "Anyway, look what my prayers have gotten us. A new friend. With luck, a new tribe. Akkadian, no less. You think that's a coincidence?" She laughed. "Fine trade, I'd say."

Ut looked bored. "I keep an open mind."

"In other words, we'd be glad to share rations with you, Ta." Aya dragged over the food pack. "Here. Eat up. Whatever you like."

Ta bowed, trying to hide his excitement. His plan had worked better than he'd hoped. As Aya began scooping out crushed leaves, seeds, and smoked rabbit strips, he tried not to appear too eager. "I really don't need much," he protested. "Just a few mouthfuls."

"Nonsense," Aya said. "If we hope to catch your friends, we'll need plenty of energy."

7

The sun rose swiftly now, burning away the haze on the horizon and making the air shimmer with heat. The Akkadians walked south, telling Ta of their adventures. For his part, Ta said as little as possible. He didn't want them to realize who he really was and kick him out.

"Why'd you leave Akkad?" he asked, hoping to distract them. "You knew it was dangerous down here."

"Showing is better than telling, I suppose," Aya said. "Here."

She stopped walking. Her baby hung over her chest in a pouch of stitched rabbit skins. She lifted him out with both hands and held him up, his little feet kicking.

"His name is Shulgi. He is a year old. Do you see?"

Ta recoiled in horror.

"Oh, no," he whispered.

"Life has many surprises, doesn't it?"

Shulgi had a clubfoot. At the base of his right ankle, his foot bent inward at a perpendicular angle. It looked like a powerful hand had crushed the foot into a mess of toes and a heel, then wrenched it sideways. Ta almost wanted to bend it straight again. He couldn't, of course. The boy would never walk. He would be disadvantaged for life, like Ta.

Ah, little brother. To think I almost murdered you!

The saddest part was how Shulgi giggled and smiled in the sunlight, kicking his tiny limbs, unaware of the rejections life had in store for him.

Aya's face was hard with grief. "It's my fault. I skipped too many offerings."

Ta nodded sadly. A pregnant woman had to make ritual sacrifices, or else Lamashtu—the winged demoness with a hairy body, long green fingernails, and the teeth of an African ass—would fly up from the Underworld and damage the infant, as had happened here.

"I knew about the offerings," Aya said sadly. "But my mate . . . things were . . ." She rubbed her nose, unwilling to say more. "I grew distracted."

Ta pitied her. Her shame must be even worse than his. He'd only lost a hand, ruining his own life. She'd ruined her son's.

Curious, Ta bent closer to Shulgi's foot to examine it. Too close. The baby, as if to draw him back to the present, lunged for Ta's beard and grabbed onto it, the tiny fingers pulling hard. Ta laughed as he disentangled himself.

"He'll be a warrior with that grip."

Aya smiled as she reinserted Shulgi back in his sling. "Did your chief allow such babies?"

Ta shook his head. The chief gave a speech on it every year. All over Akkad, the tradition was the same.

"For the good of the tribe, such ones must be given up," he'd boomed, pacing before the home fire. "They suck resources. Take and take. I know it hurts. But a tribe burdened with such weaklings will not long survive." Thus, the tribe priest took "unfit" children and left them in the woods for Moloch—the hideous god of child sacrifice, with the body of a man, spreading horns, and a bull's face—to eat.

"I see why you ran away," Ta said quietly. "I'm glad you did."

Aya nodded. "As soon as I held him, I knew I'd have to escape. But I couldn't ask just anyone to help me. The wrong person would report us. So I waited months until I saw how unhappy Ut was, then took my chance. Thank the gods, he agreed. We escaped on a raft, floating far down the Tigris so they couldn't track us, before heading here."

Ta glanced at Ut in surprise. "You're not mates?"

Aya snorted. "No."

"No," Ut said stiffly, as if the idea were not his.

Ta was puzzled. The two seemed a fair match. Aya was attractive and young, her face proud and unblemished, her arms firm with muscle. Her legs were long and sturdy, capable of bearing heavy loads. If not for her dusty face and ragged hair, she would have been stunning, worthy of a top hunter. As for Ut, he was impressive, too. He was tall and muscular and coated in manly black hair, and he handled his spear easily, using it like a walking staff, banging up puffs of dust. Such a man would merit the favor of his chief, winning him respect, furs, hearty meals, and a pretty mate. In any case, their statuses both ranked higher than Ta's.

"Ut had a mate," Aya said, clearing it up. "But he didn't like her. He liked someone else. Unfortunately, the chief took her."

"That greedy old goat." Ut's face darkened with anger. "Yuna and I came of age together. She should've been mine. Ah, Ta, you should've seen her! She had hair like a waterfall. Eyes like starlight. We'd look at each other across the cave at mealtimes. We were mates in our hearts already. But at the mating ceremony . . ." His voice thickened. "You know how it goes. The chief gave me an old widow instead." He laughed sourly. "Me, Ut! A widow!"

"That's how it is with men of power," Aya soothed. "They'd swallow the whole world if their mouths were big enough."

Ta nodded. Chiefs often took extra mates. Take too many, though, and their warriors might get angry and revolt.

"What about your mate?" he asked Aya. "Did he see his son's foot?"

Aya's eyes flashed with hatred. "Pah! He never even asked to hold Shulgi. He only cared about his friendship with the chief. We're glad to be done with him."

The hurt was still raw in her voice, and Ta, embarrassed, dropped his gaze to Shulgi. The boy was sucking on his fist. He wheezed, blowing hot streams of air out through his booger-crusted nostrils. Ta didn't understand how anyone could reject their own child, even a deformed one. He'd never get children himself. No woman would ever want a crippled thief. And no tribe would give him one.

"I'm sorry, Aya. The world is hard on our kind."

"My boy will have a good life," Aya said fiercely. "I will give it to him."

"I hope so," Ta said politely. But he knew she was wrong.

"What about your friends?" Aya looked at him anxiously. "Will they accept my baby?"

Ta forced a thoughtful expression. He still had no intention of letting the groups meet.

"Of course," he lied. "They treat me fine, anyway."

"What of the females?" Ut rubbed his hairy hands together. "Any pretty ones?"

Aya shot him a contemptuous glance. "Ut only cares about looks."

Ut sniffed. "What's wrong with that? Women like power. Men like looks."

"Why, yes, Ut," Ta lied quickly. "We have two unmated women. Judge for yourself how pretty they are. But they're certainly out of *my* reach." He held up his stump and laughed ruefully.

Ut beamed. "Well, that's fine." He began raking his beard with his fingers as if he expected to meet women around the next bush. "Maybe we'll catch them today."

"Maybe," Ta said.

"What about me, Ta?" Aya asked. "Will they . . ."

"We have men—" Ta began willingly.

"No. I don't want a mate," Aya interrupted. "My old mate was cruel. I've had enough of men for a while. What I mean is, your people won't demand it of me, will they?"

Ta gave her an indulgent bow. "You will be welcomed just as you are."

"Thank the gods." Aya lifted her eyes skyward.

Ut tapped his spear impatiently. "Well, Ta's tribe sounds good to me. Yes, Aya?"

"Yes."

"Then we'd better keep going. The Euphrates won't come to us."

The group marched on. Soon they fell into a silent suffering, heads bowed, lips cracking and bleeding. The sun did its terrible work. The Hunger Demon snarled in Ta's blood. The only sounds were the scrapings of their sandals, their ragged breaths, and Aya's dry voice, singing lullabies to her baby. Shulgi's cries sometimes lashed across the red land. But other times he fell silent, his ferret-brown face clenched in pain, his tiny eyes squeezed shut, and that was more worrying.

To keep up their spirits, Ut regaled them with stories. He was quite good at it, and when Ta told him so, Ut confessed that he'd once aspired to be his tribe's storyteller. His favorite tale was the *Enūma Eliš,* the story of the creation of the world.

"That one takes real skill," Ta said.

"I'm glad you realize it." Ut gave Aya a dry glance. "Not everyone appreciates the art of it."

"I do," Ta said. "I love stories."

So Ut told how, at the beginning of time, Father Apsu, god of freshwater, and Mother Tiamat, goddess of saltwater, desired each other in the darkness and mingled their waters. And thus the world was born. In the blink of an eye, every rock and tree came into being, each with a *baal,* its particular god, to look after it. The greatest gods were the *igigi,* the powerful children of the First Ones. There was Inanna, goddess of fertility and plant life. Enlil, god of storms and wind. Baal, god of war. And Enki, god of mischief and tricks. "But clever Enki," Ut said in a dramatic voice, "grew hungry for power, and decided to murder his father. So he created a drug—a powerful root we call 'Enki root,' even today—and ground it into powder. On a hot day he sprinkled it into a bowl of date juice and gave it to his father. And Father Apsu took the drugged juice and fell into a deep slumber. And Enki lifted his foot and crushed his father's skull under his heel, beginning the War of the Gods."

Ta listened contentedly. He'd heard the *Enūma Eliš* countless times. But the familiar tale made the desert less overwhelming, somehow.

"You're very good," he told Ut honestly.

Ut beamed. "He has taste, Aya. Perhaps he *was* sent by the gods."

Aya chuckled. "Careful, Ta. Encourage him, and he'll never stop."

Neither that day nor the next did they see the Euphrates. Their supplies dwindled, and their bodies wore down. But Ut's stories distracted them a little from the pain. As for Ta, he did his best to avoid getting kicked out. He carried the heavy bag. He helped set up and break down camp. He stifled complaints. He listened and pretended to care about their stories. It was all to keep in their good graces, of course. But to his surprise, they treated him with respect, not like a "cripple." It was . . . Well, it puzzled him. It made him oddly content, despite the hurt. For the first time, he was really part of a tribe.

The next morning, their food ran out. But then they found something that made them all very excited. Marching in the lead, Ut squatted suddenly in the red dirt and beckoned wildly.

"Food," he hissed. "Come quick. Don't make a sound."

Aya and Ta rushed up. Ut's finger hovered over an animal track. It was the two-pronged hoofprint of a sand gazelle. Ta's breath caught in his throat.

Food, the Hunger Demon hissed. *FOOD.*

"Good eye, Ut," Aya croaked in excitement. "I'm so tired, I'd never have seen it."

"Shh, not too loud." Ut lifted a finger to his lips. "It may be close. We mustn't scare it off."

Everyone held their tongues as Ut waddled after the hoof tracks to a nearby patch of weeds. The stalks had been recently cropped by animal teeth. Globules of drool still glistened on the mauled plant tips. Touching the moisture, Ut nodded. The beast was close.

"You're the hunter," Aya whispered. "What do we do?"

Ut scratched his black beard. "Normally, I'd hide behind this bush and wait for the gazelle to pass this way again on its daily foraging trail. But this gazelle looks lost, separated from its herd. I doubt it will return."

"What do we do? Sneak up on it?"

Ut tapped his nose. "It'll smell you too fast."

"Then we outrun it."

"A gazelle?" Ut laughed.

"Oh, Ut." Aya gripped her stomach with both hands. "I'm so hungry I could eat dirt."

"The only chance is an endurance hunt," Ut said grimly.

An endurance hunt! Ta and Aya looked at each other in dismay. Endurance hunting was the most difficult kind. It relied on stamina, not speed. A gazelle would always be able to outrun a human. But it couldn't sweat as well to cool off. So you chased it in relays, keeping it always moving, hour after hour, until it overheated and collapsed, then you could jog up and kill it with knives. Unfortunately, such hunts took all day. And usually, they failed.

"I've never done an endurance hunt," Ut admitted. "Have you, Ta?"

Ta suppressed a laugh. The tribe had never let him fish, let alone hunt.

"We must be honest with ourselves," Ut said. "If we try this and fail, we may not recover. We'll waste a day, use up the last of our energy. Not to mention empty the water bag."

He left the words hanging. Ta knew the implication. A failure here would seal their fates. He studied his friends. Aya, a woman, had no hunting experience. Ut himself looked too dusty and depleted for a sustained effort. Ta doubted they had a chance.

Aya was still gazing at the track. "I think the gods put us here, Ut. Let's have faith."

Ut put a hand on her arm. "I've never been impressed by the kindness of gods, Aya. But this time, I'm with you." He glanced at the red horizon, as desolate now as ever. "I'd rather give this a chance than hope the Euphrates appears to save us."

He turned to Ta. "We'll be depending on you, brother."

"On me?" Ta gulped. No one had ever depended on "the cripple" before.

And yet . . . the words stirred him.

"I'll . . . I'll try."

"Good man." Ut slapped Ta's back. "All right, team. Here's what we'll do."

They agreed Ut and Ta should run first. The men would drive the gazelle as far as they could, tiring it. Then they'd turn it back to this area, allowing Aya to join Ut for the second relay. The runners would keep switching until their prey was drained.

To fortify themselves, Ta and Ut drank deeply from the water bag. Then they jogged off after the tracks, leaving Aya and Shulgi in the shade of a thornbush. Aya waved after them. "Ninğirsu, god of the hunt, be with you." Then the bushes blocked her off, and Ut and Ta were alone in the fiery heat, trotting over the stones.

"Be honest," Ut said. "You've never been a hunter, have you?"

Ta looked down at his running feet. "No," he said quietly.

"Well," Ut said. "Now you are."

A sense of unreality filled Ta. Ut was right. He was a hunter suddenly. A thing he'd never thought he'd be. How often in Akkad had he stared at the cave paintings of the great hunts, knowing he'd never participate in such an honor? Now he was doing it. And the funny thing was, he felt little excitement. He was mostly afraid.

His cracked lips twisted in a bitter smile.

"What's the joke?" Ut asked.

Ta looked down at his ugly stump. "Do you always want a thing until you have it?"

Ut's expression softened. He was a hunter. He knew what "useless" ones were denied.

"Listen, brother, if you do this you'll be the equal of any hunter in your tribe."

Ta swallowed. The old words echoed in him. *Worthless. Lazy. Coward.* But Ut was right again. If Ta could pull this off, what an answer it would be.

"My hand is cut off, not my foot," he said suddenly. "I'm not crippled in the legs."

"That's the spirit, brother. Hold onto that. You'll need it."

Before long, a bush up ahead shook and rattled. Ta's heart clutched with excitement as he and Ut darted around the obstacle, scanning for their quarry. They did not see it, but instead found a smokiness of dust drifting up from a deep hoof track where the gazelle must have grown startled at their approach and leapt away.

Seeing it, Ut pounded his hairy chest with his fist. "Feel that, Ta?"

Ta nodded, surprised. He did feel a strange connection, an invisible thread linking him to the gazelle. He could almost hear the creature's big heart thudding in its chest as it struggled to shake off its two annoying pursuers.

"As long as the hunt is alive, that feeling stays," Ut said. "Don't let the thread break."

They ran on over the shining ground, weaving between the thornbushes, panting raggedly in the growing heat. And from then on, Ta felt the strange connection. He never saw the creature itself. Just the occasional rattle of a bush up ahead, or a puff of dust, drifting away. But the invisible cord held taut in his heart, stretching but not snapping.

"We cannot let it rest, ever," Ut said. "How are your legs, runt? Still good?"

"Good," Ta panted.

"Blisters?"

"Popped . . . not too bad . . ."

"You're doing it, brother. Really doing it. Keep it up."

The two hunters fell into a trancelike loping that carried them through the heat without a thought or a word. Hard minutes passed. Exquisite pain. The red dust puffed up underfoot and coated their cracked lips. Knots twisted ever tighter in their shrunken stomachs, as hard as stones. Before long, Ta began to wonder how he could force even one more step. Yet he did. And did. And did . . . And as he ran, he suddenly broke into prayer—not to Enlil, god of wind and storms, the favored deity of his tribe, but to El, the secret god the Akkadians prayed to when they didn't know which god was present. In Akkadian, the name "El" meant, simply, "the One Who is here." And so Ta prayed, using the cadences taught to him by his tribe.

I cry to thee, oh, El,
In this run, carry me.
Carry my feet with thy breath.
Let me not fail as I have failed before.
This time, El, let me do something real.
Hear my cry, One Who is here,
And I will thank thee with the smoke of sacrifice.
With the flesh of this beast, I will thank thee!

After what seemed like an eternity, Ut's voice called to him. It seemed to come from a great distance away. Ta's head was pounding. His body felt as if someone had battered it with a heavy stick. He was hardly conscious. Yet when he heard Ut bark hoarsely—"Now we turn it, runt, you hear me? Soon Aya can spell you. You're doing fine, runt!"—Ta somehow managed to obey.

The turn went well. Ta slowed to anchor the pursuit point, and Ut performed a series of heroic sprints to get ahead of the gazelle and turn it, degree by degree. Finally, they were driving it back toward Aya's bush. Ta's heart soared. The first relay was working. He was doing it! Truly hunting!

It was a long, exhausting run back. But after what felt like a lifetime, he saw the longed-for bush. Aya was under it, cheering and waving, slapping the earth in encouragement. Ta's heart filled with joy. He sensed his legs might give out before he reached the bush. But somehow he made it, and there he collapsed in the shade like a pile of dry sticks and lay flat, chest heaving, utterly spent. He was here. He, Ta, the cripple, the worthless one—had done a real thing!

"You beautiful men, it's working," Aya cried. "Ut, I knew you would. But Ta, you? Oh, Ta!" She embraced him and kissed his cheek with dry lips. "You *are* sent by the gods."

"Did you see it, woman?" Ut cried. "Did it look tired?" He grabbed the water bag and shook a few drops into his mouth.

Aya nodded, and described how the gazelle had burst past her moments before. Lolloping, not a smooth gait at all. Great ropes of froth swung from its black lips, and its sides were bulging, heavy with meat. It was suffering, Aya said, its big eye swollen in its face like a too-ripe fruit. Still, it passed and was gone before she could throw a rock at it.

"Then come, woman," Ut said. "We can't let it rest. Think of your child."

So Aya leapt up and followed Ut on the second relay, and Ta remained on the blanket with Shulgi.

A stillness fell. The pain pulsed dully at the edge of Ta's consciousness, ready to crash on him and bludgeon him dumb the moment his body calmed down. But more importantly, he felt a new pride rising in his gut unlike any he'd ever known. I did it, he thought slowly. I passed a test. The "worthless cripple" never stopped. It was a piece of him now, something real. It could never be taken away.

Sitting up, Ta lifted Shulgi off the blanket and looked down at him. The boy looked up uncertainly, then smiled and lifted his pudgy fingers to play. Ta nuzzled the boy and kissed him. Perhaps the gods sent you to *me*, little brother, he thought. To teach me. For all he could think, over and over, was, *This is it.* This feeling, more than food, was life. That other path . . . the stealing . . . the shirking . . . the hatred. Ta never wanted to feel that way again. Had this feeling been here waiting for him all along? Just out of sight? And he never knew it?

"We're not cripples, little brother," he said, looking into Shulgi's face. "We're men. If we will take it."

But the feeling was not to last. Ta was still sitting there, getting his breath back, feeling the pain throb in his legs and ease, slowly, pulse by pulse, when he heard a shout. He looked up, puzzled. Aya and Ut were stumbling back, no gazelle in sight.

"What happened?"

Ta leapt to his feet, clutching Shulgi. The baby cried out in fear at the sudden elevation, but Ta hardly heard him. He stood still, jaw hanging open, as the others stumbled up.

Aya hung on Ut's arm, hobbling.

"Forgive me, Ta." She reached for Shulgi. "I . . . I overlooked a rock. My heel caught it. Rolled . . ."

Ta looked down in horror. Indeed, Aya's ankle was visibly swollen, already purple-yellow, as if a log had fallen on it. Aya collapsed on the blanket and bent over Shulgi, covering him with her dusty hair. She was crying. Ut stood by, his face dark with rage.

"Careless," he snarled. "Careless. I warned her."

"I'm not a hunter like you," Aya shouted. "What do I know of these things?"

"Do you have eyes? Can you not run properly?"

"Stop," she moaned. "This once. Please."

"What happens now?" Ta asked stupidly, looking between them.

Aya met Ta's eyes. "Don't let it get away."

"But I just ran."

"No choice, runt," Ut said. "It's you and me now." He looked off after the gazelle. "We're committed. So let's go. Prove you really are a gift from the gods."

So Ta nodded, and they went on again, staggering slowly, their feet heavier than before.

I can't believe it, he thought. It's not fair. For the first time, I did everything right. And now it won't matter. What a wretched life.

On they went. On and on, into the late afternoon. The worst heat of the day. Every step was torture. The ground baked. Even the flies hid. The air sizzled. The bushes stretched their thorny arms skyward like giant spiders, praying to Shamash, god of the sun, for a mercy which did not come. Ta's eyes roasted in his face. His sandals squelched, fresh blisters leaking. Still, he ran.

"I'll never forgive her," Ut panted, wiping his brow. "Never."

To make matters worse, an hour later another disaster struck—one too awful to be believed.

Another sandstorm appeared at the edge of the desert. It swept toward them, boiling and flaring in the white sky, red and furious, coming faster than any before. It was not little, either. It was one of the bad ones, the biggest Ta had yet seen. Now he felt sure the gods were against him. He lifted his face skyward. Who hates me up there? Is it you, Enlil? Are you jealous I prayed to El, the One Who is here, before you?

As ever, there was no answer. Just the heat, and the pain in his side, and the protestations of his feet threatening to snap off at the ankles.

"No," Ut whispered. "Anything else."

"The tracks," Ta said in amazement.

"The tracks," Ut confirmed.

They stopped and watched it come in awe. Tiny dots of bushes tossed around in it, some hundreds of feet up. Even Ta's persistent friend, the vulture, was nowhere to be seen.

"Shelter," Ut said. "Quick, before it hits."

They dug at the base of a bush and protected themselves under as much earth and stick cover as they could manage. They said nothing as the storm arrived. It hit with a fury that lashed their heads with sand and plunged the world into a brown-yellow light. It was like the dimness of *Kur,* the Underworld, and they lay like dead persons until it passed, whirling off to the east. Then they stood to find the gazelle tracks utterly erased. Blanketed out as completely as the tracks of Ta's people.

"It cannot have gone far," Ta said dully.

"Do you feel it?" Ut asked. "The connection?"

Ta's heart sank. The gazelle's spirit was gone. The thread in his heart, broken.

"Not anymore," he confessed.

"Circle out," Ut commanded. "Maybe we'll pick it up again."

They ran in circles, wider and wider around the last known tracks of the gazelle, hoping to regain the sign. But none appeared. They staggered back to their starting point, and Ut pointed in opposite directions. "You go there. I'll go here. The gazelle must be close to overheating. Maybe there's a chance."

"Just run blindly into the desert?"

"Have another idea?"

"But . . ."

Ta gulped. The idea of running into nothing was terrifying. To be alone again, to launch himself into emptiness? He hardly even knew the way back from here.

"It's that or starve," Ut said.

"All right."

Ut embraced him. His touch felt wooden, like a death-blessing. A farewell.

"You ran well, food thief."

"You, too." Ta was in disbelief. "It was an honor to run with you."

"Goodbye, then."

Ut moved off. Ta turned and staggered on himself, heading southeast, blind, nothing ahead but flashing rock and endless thorns. He knew the gazelle was gone. He could feel it.

Worse, the black voice attacked again.

Sit and rest, runt, it taunted. *Why suffer needlessly? There's no victory for cripples like you. Ut is probably sheltering under a bush already, laughing at you for stumbling on like a fool.*

At that, Ta's legs nearly failed. In fact, he swerved toward a bush to collapse in the dust and black out. Sweet oblivion. Sweet nothingness.

But then he thought of Shulgi. The little boy tugging at his beard, smiling, laughing. And something new—newer even than his new-found pride—surged up in him, and he spat bitterly into the earth and cursed the voice. No. My brother needs me. I won't leave him.

Disgust at the way he'd lived his entire life washed through him.

No more, demon, he thought savagely. I choose a new path. I will never go back. Never. From now on, I do what I admire. Though this be my last day on earth, I swear it.

And as he ran, he prayed harder than before, though he had no more hope.

Oh, El, turn not thy face away.

Hear my cry.

Deliver me this food, for the sake of my new people.

The sun was dropping in the west when he stumbled around another bush and saw the gazelle.

Nearly fainting, Ta stopped short and stared at it, incredulous. There it was. It lay in a bed of soft sand just twenty paces away, its four knees bent under it, its beauty overwhelming. Its eyes widened at the sight of him. Its head jerked up and down, threatening with its horns. But it did not rise. And suddenly the sense of connection, spirit-to-spirit, resurged in Ta's chest. And he realized, as if waking from a dream, that the connection had never gone away.

Weakly, the gazelle lowered its snout and watched Ta in silence, its eyes as bright as opals in its beige face. Ta kept staring, awed. A band of white fur, like a great eyebrow, connected the gazelle's eyes, giving it a wise, knowing expression. The twisting spiral horns were each as long as Ta's arm, their loveliness filling him with reverence.

For a moment, hunter and prey gazed at each other, neither making a move. Ta felt everything at once, like a blow—the animal's exhaustion, its pain and fear, its bewilderment at this slow two-legged predator that followed and followed and would not give up. And suddenly, Ta felt a great sadness that their noble contest must end this way.

Yet he knew he must finish the task, too.

Not wanting to startle his quarry, he slowly pulled his stone knife from his waistband and crept forward, a foot at a time. The gazelle tried to stand. But it collapsed on its forelegs, and Ta realized it was already half-dead. There would be no struggle, the knife-blow almost unnecessary. Still, Ta approached cautiously with his stump out, eyes locked on the animal's, uttering a final prayer. *May the gods bless you, brother-creature,* he recited from memory, recalling the traditional chant of the hunter. *I admire you, but I must eat you. I swear not a piece of you will go to waste.*

He leapt at the gazelle, and the knife slashed, and the blood flowed out, darkening the sand. Leaping back, Ta got out of range of the swinging horns. He squatted and waited. Then it was over, and he crawled forward and lay against the creature's still-warm side. He looked up at the sky in a daze. Somewhere out in the desert Ut was still searching . . . and Aya was cuddling Shulgi under the bush, wrenched with the guilt of failure. But they were saved. All saved. Because of Ta. A cripple.

Pride washed through him, dazzling, unreal. I did it. In spite of everything. And by the gods, what might a man accomplish, if he put forth such an effort every day?

Trembling, Ta grabbed a handful of dust and drizzled it over the gazelle's body, giving it the traditional honoring for the noble hunt. *Your life gives me life, brother-creature,* he prayed. *I swear to you, I will make it a life you are proud to share in.*

Then, afraid he'd pass out before the task was done, he searched about in the dust for dead sticks to build a fire with, to make the smoke that would alert his friends.

8

Magog drove Ki's people south in a great herd, lashing them across a red plain with leather whips.

"Squeak along, rats!" the warriors shouted. "No rest until camp."

Never had Ki imagined a horror such as this. The dust choked her, and the sun scorched her face, and the warriors' taunts penetrated her spirit. But you couldn't stop—even if you tripped and fell, crushed under the weight of your pack—for Gog's men would rush in, cursing and lashing mercilessly with their whips.

The whips were terrible. They had five or six flying thongs, each tipped with chips of rock or bone. The chips would bite into your flesh, raising red welts, then heavy spurts of blood. And as you knelt there, screaming, covering your head with your arms, the whips snapping and cracking, the tide of flesh would surge inexorably past, people sidestepping you like strangers, despite knowing you their whole lives. And if you still didn't rise, an axman would appear. His stone blade would flash in the sun, and a red spray would go up, and your head would tumble across the dust, leaving the leather pack you'd carried so faithfully across the flatland to be transferred from your mangled corpse to the shoulders of some other slave. And the fiery plume of dust would drift on over the horizon, leaving your inconsequential scraps for the vultures to peck clean from the earth.

During the first two days of the march, ten people died this way. Namtar, the scout, was one. He twisted his ankle, fell, couldn't get up—and got the ax. This confused Ki, for it seemed a terrible waste. Didn't Magog want slaves to trade? But slowly, she understood. Magog was weeding out the weak, the ones not worth feeding.

It also warned the survivors: *You are expendable. You'd better obey.*

Not that they needed more proof. The first day, a woman was caught trying to escape, and the warriors used her for a terrible lesson.

Under the hot noon sun, they threw her on her back, belly up, spread-eagled, each limb roped to a wood stake. Then, to everyone's horror, they grabbed five innocent people at random, pulled them forward, and staked them down the same way. Aunt Shutub was one. Bakil, another. Eanna, a third.

Hideous things happened, then: things so awful, Ki would remember them all her days. A boy was skinned alive. Eanna was stabbed in private areas with a sharp stick. Bakil was impaled on a spear driven up through his anus and out the side of his neck, so that he hung above the earth like a totem, feet kicking over the dust, mouth spitting blood. Even more unthinkable things occurred too, especially to the women . . . So that when the Magog warriors finally drew their stone knives and slit the victims' throats, the tribe groaned in relief.

There was a genius to it, Ki thought. From then on, the prisoners would spy on each other, block any attempts to escape. In one brutal act, Magog had recruited them as guards.

Ki alone received special treatment. She ate heartily at each meal and drank as she wished. She also carried a lighter pack and walked near the front, ahead of the choking clouds of dust raised by the herd, so that, as Gog had commanded, her health should be preserved. The warriors only shoved her when she tried to speak to her people.

Not that it mattered, Ki thought sadly. Her people blamed her for the defeat and shunned her. She felt it in their eyes. *You brought the gods' wrath on us.* And maybe they were right. She *had* defied the priest, inventing so much. Maybe the gods had cursed her for it.

On the other hand, Ki hadn't done *enough*. If she was going to blaspheme, she should have shared her dart-thrower with her tribe and trained them to fight.

As it stood, everything was lost. And one way or another, it was her fault.

Only forty of her tribe survived to reach Magog's camp. Forty, out of an original eighty. *Half* her people, she reflected in awe. It might have been fewer, too, if the march had lasted any longer, for even the healthiest slaves were down to their last reserves of energy.

Luckily, one day at sunset, a horn blew, and Ki looked up from her dusty sandals to see two rocky hills, stark against the yellow sky.

Her mouth fell open. The hills looked like two sentinels guarding the Underworld, for between them lay a giant hole. Was it a tunnel, giving passage to *Kur*? A closer look, however, revealed it was a camp of black-dyed tents. Hundreds of them crowded together in the biggest collection of humanity she'd ever seen. A black stain on the earth, stinking, smoking, and roaring with noise.

"*More* of you?" she whispered. "How?"

Her guard laughed. "What's the matter, nomad rat? Don't like the look of your cage?" And at the edge of camp, he threw her into a dirt pen surrounded by palisade stakes, isolating her from everyone, and left her there for many days.

At this point, Ki broke down. She wept and beat her head against the earth and rattled the poles, begging Gog to take the secret of her wheat in exchange for better conditions for her people. But Gog was not there. He was up north fighting the Mitanni. And this tortured Ki almost as much as the march, for she knew that with every passing day, more of her people would perish. For long stretches she just lay on the floor of her pen, covering her ears with her hands and groaning into the dirt, joining her voice to the surrounding noise. Sometimes she even forgot her own name.

Occasionally guards would peek in and laugh. Some threw in clods of mud. Others urinated through gaps in the pole wall, raising a foul ammonia smell. Others ogled her, saying lewd things. But thanks to Gog's protective order, they did no worse. And after finding her limp and unresponsive, they would grow bored and drift away, leaving her to stare at the sky, cry herself hoarse, or lie in a daze, clutching her ribs.

She lost track of how many days she spent in there. It might have been ten. Might have been thirty. Over and over, her heart twisted as she huddled against the poles of her pen, listening to the rumblings of the giant army all around her. She thought of her family often. From her tribe, she knew the rest had fallen in battle, and her heart twisted so many times, it seemed to become numb, leaving her in an animal stupor. Later, she guessed this was probably one of her body's defenses; some things were simply too much to bear. Nevertheless, with rest, regular food, and water, her reason gradually revived.

It helped that her pen was a luxury. It was only ten paces by ten, but it was solitary, making it a paradise compared to the bigger pens. Those ones got so crowded, people couldn't even lie down without draping their legs over each other. Listening through her poles, Ki trembled at the constant jostling and fighting in there, the screaming and rape. Rats skittered over the sleepers in the nights. Flies buzzed all day. Every sunrise, fresh wails arose when the latest suicides were discovered. It was not just Ki's people in there, either, for the shouts had all manner of accents. She heard Elamite, Sumerian, Mitanni, Akkadian, and Canaanite words . . . even those of long-range nomads from the Hatti region, and farther still, from Sea Peoples, and African nomads. Gog had captured slaves from all over.

This made Ki's dilemma harder. If she offered Gog her "magic" food, it would empower him to conquer all Mesopotamia, making the whole world his. This was unthinkable to her. On the other hand, if she denied Gog, he'd hurt her people even worse—and this was unthinkable, too.

Finding strength one afternoon, Ki managed a prayer. *Inanna, are you still there? Gog dishonored you. Will you help me fight him?* But there was no reply. And later that day, as if Baal had overheard her resistance, one of Magog's priests marched past the pens, preaching a sermon of despair.

"Remember the *Enūma Eliš*, slaves!" he shouted. "In your version, Enlil won the war of the gods. But in our version, the true version, Baal won. With his demon army—Girtablulu, scorpion-man; Lahmu, the Hairy One; Kullu, fish-man—Baal subdued the earth and gave it to Magog to manage. And he gave us dominion over you, the weak. He fought the demon Kingu—a foul creature with the wings of an eagle, the body of a bull, the jaws of a lion, and a serpent for a phallus—and slew him. And Baal mixed Kingu's blood with mud to create you, the *lullu*, to work and serve. That is all you are. Slaves, made of demon blood and soil. Nothing more! So be warned, weak ones. Serve well! For if you defy us, you defy Baal, and his wrath is terrible."

Ki's last hope vanished like smoke. She knew the priest spoke true. Inanna's statue had been shattered. Baal had defeated her. The world was his. This camp was proof.

Another morning came, as meaningless as the others. Ki lay on her back, staring up at the gray dawn sky. The view wasn't much. The sharp stakes of her pen framed it in a box. But it was precious, for it reminded her of freedom. She liked to lie flat and watch the occasional bird glide past, sunlight glinting off its wings. When she gazed long enough, she could tune out the sounds of the camp. Sometimes she was even able to float up like a cloud, merging into the sky in her mind, leaving everything far below.

Then a voice barked, and footsteps tramped toward her pen, and she fell to earth, fast.

"You awake in there, nomad rat? Better be, or I'll yank your whiskers. Time to go."

Ki sat up sharply. Time to go? Why? Her heart began to thud. Did it mean Gog had returned?

As the footsteps tapped up to the pen gate, she rushed to the far corner. She did have an option she'd prepared for this moment. Whether to use it was the question. But as the warden fumbled with the leather gate latch, Ki knelt anyway and scratched at the thin layer of dirt that covered her latest weapon: a sharp yellow bone whittled to a killing point. She'd taken it from a rotten rabbit carcass they'd tossed her for dinner two nights ago. In the dark, after gnawing the bone to a knifelike sharpness, she'd practiced pulling it from her hair in one swift motion and stabbing the air with it, imagining it was Gog's throat. Today perhaps she'd do it for real. The attempt would mean death for her, and the death of her great secret. Perhaps even more suffering for her people. But if she killed Gog, she'd avenge her family's honor, and the work of her life would not be used for evil. At least, so she told herself.

As the gate squeaked open, she shoved the bone into the tangle of her greasy hair and spun around.

"Ho, she-rat," the warden called. "Scamper that sour hide over here."

Ki trudged out with her hands at her sides. Two men stood waiting, the warden and a warrior. The warrior was holding a noose. He plunked the noose over her head and pulled it tight, pinching her neck. Bending forward, he squinted at her doubtfully.

"This the famous witch? She doesn't look magic."

"It's her," the warden said.

"If she's a *baru*, why didn't she save herself?"

"She killed an officer. A good one. Remember Udu?"

The warrior looked at her skeptically. "I suppose," he muttered to himself. "Still, she can't be much of a *baru* if she let her tribe die."

Ki glared at her feet. She wished she *did* have black magic to use on this fool. She reached for her black spirit, but it was not there. After the raid, it had gone silent, just when she needed it most. No more lightning flashes of creativity. No more ideas. *Bad spirit. I need you,* Ki pleaded now. But as usual, she felt nothing.

The warrior waved a hand over his nose. "We can't bring her up reeking like this. Ho, you two slaves. Come wash her."

Two slaves ran up carrying a wooden bucket full of water. They peeled Ki's boarhide tunic off and began splashing handfuls of cold filthy water over her naked body, then rubbed her down. It was nice to feel the grime washing off her skin, but Ki hated the way the warriors stood by, laughing.

"Even nomads pretty up once you scrub 'em a bit," her rope-holder said. "I'd take a moment with her in my tent."

"Rats all have plague," her warden warned. "Issún tried a bit of fun with one last month; he's still recovering in his tent."

"The red sores?"

"The same."

Her rope-holder grimaced. "I suppose no fun is worth that."

Ki focused on her decision. As she saw it, she had four choices. One: give Gog the wheat and negotiate for her people's release. Two: assassinate him. Three: escape. Four: suicide.

A wave of weariness swept over her. Suicide was most appealing. How she wished to end this terrible life. Yet she knew Father would be ashamed of her for even entertaining such a thought. So she forced herself back to the world, and let her eyes rove the tents, searching for a way out. Perhaps the two slaves raking bone combs through her hair could help.

"Been here long?" she whispered.

They just kept combing, avoiding eye contact with her. Apparently they had no interest in being whipped for her sake. Worse, Ki realized their comb strokes might discover her weapon. So, in a quick motion, she raised her hands and pretended to smooth her hair out. At the same time, she yanked the bone knife free and hid it between her middle and index fingers, leaving her palm empty.

The slaves frowned, but kept combing. How ugly they were. Bony and hideously scarred, their ages and genders were no longer obvious beneath their mutilations. Lumps from whippings wormed across their chests and shoulders. Brands marked their foreheads, no doubt identifying them as the personal property of this or that Magog officer. Worse, the garbled grunts they made—probably discussing how bad she smelled—revealed that their tongues had been cut out, preventing them from gossiping about their masters.

Ki shut her eyes. This would be the fate of her people. Tamed. Broken.

Unless something changed.

"Enough, there," the warden barked. "She needn't look fancy; she's no pleasure girl."

The girls slid her ragged tunic back on, and the warrior began pulling her up a path between the tents by her noose. "Scamper, scamper," he laughed, yanking on her tether. "And show me your power, eh? Just a peek?"

Ki looked at him coldly.

The man was surprised, then angry. He yanked the tether more viciously, making her stumble. "Proud, eh? Well, that goes quick. You'll see."

It was a long walk through the camp, and they passed many sights Ki wished not to see. In one fire-pit area, a slave was being whipped bloody, his back crisscrossed with red gashes. Nearby, under a tarp, three warriors were cutting up bodies, tossing chunks into piles: one of arms, one of legs, one of feet. Flesh-units for human sacrifice, Ki supposed. From eavesdropping on her guards, she knew that Baal, Magog's top deity, required such sacrifice regularly. Meanwhile, from dark tent-openings, the crying of babies poured forth, and this wrenched Ki's heart most of all. How could women birth children into lives of such horror? It was mind-breaking.

At length, they climbed a switchback trail up the northern hill, approaching the largest tent above camp. This had to be Gog's dwelling. It was a long rectangle made up of many adjoining compartments, colorful flags flapping from the tent peaks. Out front was a hideous sight. Two thick poles, stripped tree trunks, each supported a body strapped on with ropes. The two naked men were dead, the life roasted from them by the sun over several days. Crows waddled around the base of each pole, or perched atop the bodies, leisurely pecking at their flesh. Not for the first time, Ki wondered if this wasn't a nightmare.

"Why this?" she asked, wrinkling her nose at the smell.

Her captor laughed as if the answer was obvious, and didn't reply.

The tent loomed. Under its entry awning, a sentry stood waiting, hands folded over the butt of a club, its bulbous head planted on the earth.

"Ho, dog." He lifted the club and stepped forward. "What took so long?"

"We had to wash her," her captor protested. "We couldn't deliver her to the Lord smelling like goat dung, could we?"

"You ought to have washed yourself, too," the sentry laughed. "Get back below."

He snatched the tether and looked her up and down with disdain. Clearly higher ranking than the men below, he wore a hyena-pelt skirt and a thick-jeweled belt instead of the simple loincloth worn by the others. His beard was not ragged and greasy, either, but curled into oiled ringlets. It tumbled over his muscular chest like a froth of black goat hair.

"You sure this is her?" he asked her ex-captor.

"It's her."

"Huh, she doesn't look like a witch. She better not be the wrong one, or you'll regret it." And leaving the offended man sputtering helplessly, her new captor turned and led Ki in by the rope, crying into the darkness in a musical voice: "Hail, Prince Jakka. The *baru* is here."

Ki's eyes adjusted slowly to the gloom. She saw grass burning in clay pots, filling the tent with a sweet-smelling smoke, and shadowy shapes melting in and out of adjacent chambers, bearing clay platters and jugs. It would have been disorienting if not for a fire burning in a clay brazier by the far tent wall. Its glow illuminated the focus of it all: a young man reclining on a spread of ox-hide pillows, his tattooed arms spread out confidently across the cushions, his beard glistening with the same curled ringlets as her captor's. Ki recognized the prince instantly from the wheat clearing. It was Jakka, Gog's eldest son.

Seeing her, Jakka leapt up and strode to her. A female slave followed dutifully, holding a platter of dates. Jakka grabbed one and chewed it idly as he studied Ki up and down.

"So here she is," he said to himself. "The creature Father prizes so highly."

Ki studied him back. He was tattooed black, head to foot, and wore stout copper bands on his wrists, denoting his power. Yet there was something weak about him, she sensed with surprise. His mouth looked soft, as if he would refuse any but the sweetest foods. And there was a spoiled glint to his eyes. A childish glint, devoid of self-knowledge. Did she have an opportunity here?

The bone needle in her fingers felt sharp, ready. But she didn't really want Jakka, she realized. It was Gog she wanted. Anyone less would be pointless. Gog could simply replace Jakka with another offspring from his tent full of concubines.

What do I do, family? Please, I am so alone.

"She doesn't look like a *baru*," Jakka announced, repeating the observation of the day. "Are we sure this is the right nomad?"

An older man behind Jakka cleared his throat. Some adviser, perhaps. Jakka faced him.

"Nod, advise me. You served Father for twenty years. You know his whims. What can he see in this female?"

Nod looked like a man of some importance. He wore a headband of beaten gold upon his brow and rings studded with precious stones on his fingers. The beard that hung down his hairy chest was gray-streaked and reeked of perfume. But his eyes were cold and reptilian, as if they'd witnessed so much despair, they could no longer be affected by it. The owner of such eyes, Ki felt, would not be easily fooled.

Nod answered gently. "May I advise we return her to her pen, Lord? That is where your father wants her."

"Do not belittle me, Nod. I am warlord in his absence. If I wish to inspect her, I will."

"As you please, Lord." Nod bowed slightly.

Ki scanned the tent again. At least twenty bodyguards stood in the gloom, as motionless as statues. No easy escape here. In addition, she saw quite an array of bare-chested slave boys and females. "Pleasure creatures," no doubt. Some held refreshments, while others lay sprawled on pillows, watching her. The women, especially, were throat-achingly gorgeous, the most beautiful humans Ki had ever seen. Kohl darkened their eyelids, and henna patterns eroticized the feminine curves of their bodies. Nevertheless, their eyes were like vipers' eyes, quick and hostile—and fixed on Ki. These were not allies. To escape from the wretchedness of the slave quarters below, they must have yielded in terrible ways, and Ki could not feel kindly toward them. At the same time, she could not blame them too harshly, either. Pain makes animals of us all, she thought. Don't worry, sisters. I have no desire to compete for your master's favor.

Jakka was speaking again.

"Attend to me, witch. Are you truly a little Inanna, as Father thinks?"

Ki considered her reply. She needed more information to make a decision about him.

"Forgive me, Prince," she said humbly, "but when does Lord Gog return?"

Jakka laughed. "Hark, girl. Is a prince not worthy enough to speak with?"

"Lord Gog offered me favors. For my people, you see."

"Don't be stupid, I can offer things, too," Jakka said impatiently. "So answer me, nomad. Can you grow magic food or not?"

Ki hesitated. If only her black spirit would help. She felt crippled without it.

"I can make food," she said finally.

Jakka glanced at Nod. "Should I believe her, old goat?"

Nod looked ready to deny it, but Ki interjected quickly: "Your father believed it."

"True." Jakka fell silent, thinking. "You see, I'd like to surprise him when he returns. Show him I can lead, even when he is gone." He scowled. "Well, that is not your concern. How soon can you make this food?"

Ki decided to risk it. "By tomorrow," she lied.

"Tomorrow!" Jakka squinted at Nod. "She claims the impossible, no?"

"Indeed." Nod gazed at her coldly. "It has never been done. And to do it so quickly . . ." He gave a wormy smile. "In my experience, Lord, nothing is that easy. Even a miracle."

"This camp is a miracle," Ki retorted. "No tribe ever grew this big. Yet Gog did it."

Nod's eyes flashed at her. But Jakka smiled. "You speak cleverly, nomad rat. Very well, I will test your claim."

"Prince, your father—" Nod protested.

"Hush, Nod. This is my idea, and a good one. Father will be impressed." Jakka began to pace. "Well, go on, *baru.* Tell me how you will do this thing."

Ki bowed. "Please, Lord. Tell me how much food you need, so I may better serve you."

She was blatantly digging for information, but it worked. Jakka strode to the entryway of the tent and faced the camp, just as she'd hoped. He was all too ready to boast.

"You must feed *that.* All of it." He swept his hand grandly over the black stain. "Come look, eh?" His eyes challenged her. "Do you still care to try?"

Ki joined him, twisting her fingers at her waist, barely able to hide her excitement. If Magog had any weaknesses, this view might reveal them, giving her something to offer Gog's enemies.

Hungrily, she scanned the camp's layout, taking in the great smoking marvel. The fires, the rising smoke, the black tent panels winking with dew. The pens—so tiny from this distance, packed with blurry prisoners—housed her tribesmen somewhere among them. The hundreds of black tents, she noted, were long and square in the style of the Gutians. Was Gog's ancestry Gutian, then? Mesopotamians hated Gutians even more than they hated long-range nomads. Hordes of Gutians often swept down from the Zagros Mountains to raid the land between the rivers, massacring hundreds and dragging hundreds more back to their mountain strongholds as slaves. If Gog was Gutian, that information could hurt him.

Turning her attention to the pathways, Ki noticed more skulls of conquered chieftains mounted atop spears at every intersection. They shone in the rising sun like ghostly sentries, watching the traffic between the tents. Yes, a Gutian decoration. She knew it from the storyteller's legends. Gog must have Gutian heritage.

Farther off, beyond the pens, she saw a square dirt training area. In it, tattooed warriors were drilling in pairs, wrestling, swinging clubs, throwing spears. Beyond the training field was a smaller dirt field, this one occupied by stone altars and priests wearing long skin robes and waving staves. The priests seemed to be chanting over something burning on the largest altar—a slave, perhaps. *Savages.* Still, it was a busy and organized camp, nothing like the haphazard nomad camps Ki was familiar with.

"This must be the largest tribe in Mesopotamia," she said softly.

"Yes, rat, quite true. Magog rules over two thousand bodies. One thousand warriors, plus the same number in slaves."

Ki's mouth fell open. *Two thousand.* Such a tribe would be invincible. Nothing like it existed in the world, as far as she knew. But how did Gog feed them all? Thousands, when her tribe had struggled to feed eighty?

Jakka was still boasting.

"Babylon, on the Euphrates River, is the next-biggest tribe in Mesopotamia. Can you guess how many people it has?"

Ki shook her head.

"A mere three hundred. To our *two thousand.* Good, eh?"

"Good," Ki murmured.

"Yes. Father rarely has to fight anymore, unless he wants to. He simply shows up, and his enemy surrenders."

Ki nodded. Go on, she thought. Boast and boast. Show me how to hurt you.

"So why attack my tribe?" she asked. "We pose no threat."

"Slaves," Jakka answered impatiently, as if it was obvious. "Besides, Father was training me how to fight. Me and my brother . . ." His face darkened. "Never mind."

Nod interjected. "Lord, our secrets should not be shared with slaves. I can interrogate her later, if you wish, once she is back in her pen."

"Nod, shall I send you away like a plate of bad food? Remember your place." Jakka smirked at Ki. "Old men do forget things."

Nod reddened. "Forgive me, Lord."

Ki pushed her advantage. "But so many people, how do you feed them all?" she asked.

Jakka nodded approvingly. "That is the right question, rat. Perhaps you are a *baru*, after all."

He turned back toward the camp and puffed his chest out, glorying in his birthright.

"It was Father who figured it out. Many years ago, his tribe in the Zagros was destroyed by a rival Gutian band. Father only narrowly survived. As his captors led him in ropes through the trees, Father realized it didn't matter how heroic one's warriors were, if one was significantly outnumbered. And he swore never to be outnumbered again.

"After a time in captivity, he escaped and fled down to Mesopotamia, where he joined a new tribe. He worked his way up to chief, then went on the warpath, conquering one tribe after another. But unlike other chiefs, he did not kill or enslave everyone he conquered. No, he recruited, as well. Made them his. And to feed them, he discovered two critical food sources."

Jakka pointed at the opposite hill, across camp.

"Beyond that hill lies the greatest herd in Mesopotamia. Thousands of gazelle. A feast of meat. Father conquered this territory years ago, and we've lived off the herd for years. We send our men out daily to slaughter all the meat we need."

"And his second food source?" Ki asked, straining for each word.

Jakka's eyes gleamed. "Father's greatest idea, perhaps. An invention all his own. *Tribute*."

Tribute. It was an old Gutian word, about paying one's due to the gods. But in a flash, Ki understood. It was brilliant.

"Your conquests," she murmured. "Instead of tribute to the gods . . . they give tribute to Gog."

Jakka nodded, pleased. "Just so, *baru*. We conquer tribes and leave them intact to send us tribute each month. Food. Tools. Slaves. It is a mutually beneficial relationship. They feed us. We let them survive." He smiled.

Shutting her eyes, Ki saw it all. Gog was clever, indeed. No one had ever done this.

But now she saw how to hurt him, too.

"I know why you need me," she said quietly.

"Oh?"

"Yes, Prince. Your first food source. This herd of gazelle." She opened her eyes and looked at the opposite hill, imagining the herd beyond it. "You ate it faster than it could replenish itself, didn't you? And now it will vanish, like so many herds in Mesopotamia have." She looked at Jakka frankly. "When the herd is gone, even your tribute will not be enough to feed you. Then hunger will do what no human army can: scatter Magog across the face of the earth."

"Why . . . that is correct," Jakka sputtered. He looked at Nod in astonishment. "How can a rat nomad know such things?"

"As you say, I am a witch," Ki answered coolly.

Jakka gawked at her.

"Aren't there other big herds?" Ki asked. "Why not move? Conquer a new food territory?"

Jakka glared at the horizon. "What do you think? Nomads like you keep coming here, eating up our herds like locusts eat grass. No wonder everyone hates you. And now there are more migrants. Filth from everywhere. Mari. Hatti. Elamites. They keep crowding in, eating everything up. No, this is the last big herd that could feed Magog."

Suddenly, Ki's black spirit whooshed up in her, setting her *emittu* aflame. It burned so black, so strong, it seemed never to have left. *You know what to do.*

She spoke quickly, before it could abandon her.

"I will solve your problem, Lord. If you let me, I will make so much magic food spring up, you will never have to leave. Just send me to the forest today. I will gather a few magic herbs. Then, tonight, I will cast a spell over your training ground. And by tomorrow . . ."

Jakka rubbed his hands eagerly. "It sounds too good to be true."

"Such things usually are," Nod said.

"Well, old goat, what does it cost me?" Jakka laughed. "I win either way. If she succeeds, Father will be impressed. If she fails, I prove she is a fraud. And I will throw twenty of her people into the fire as punishment." He slapped his thighs with pleasure. "Yes, by tomorrow morning, all will be clear. I wish this, Nod. I wish it." He grabbed another date from the tray and tossed it up and down in his hand. "What magic herbs do you need, *baru*? Our slaves will fetch them for you."

Ki thought fast. *If she fails, I will throw twenty of her people into the fire.* Jakka's threat scared her. But now she had the power to hurt Gog, too. Should she take it? Even if Jakka hurt her people in revenge? Yes, she decided. She had to try. Her suffering in the pen had taught her a hard truth. Her people were lost. All Mesopotamia was lost. Unless somehow . . . a *miracle.*

"Forgive me, Lord." She bowed. "Stupid slaves will not know how to gather the herbs a *baru* needs. I need tamarisk honey. Milk of the bulrush. Wort of *erak* flower. Speckled mushroom heart . . ." It was plant-talk, "woman-talk," usually tedious to the male ear. And sure enough, Jakka's eyes glazed over, giving her just what she wanted: impatience.

"Fine, a guard will take you," he sighed. "How many guards should be sufficient, Nod?"

"Your father—" Nod protested once more.

But he had worn out his welcome, and Jakka roared: "I told you, Nod! Out!"

Nod slunk off, and Jakka addressed the man holding Ki's tether. "What say you, Baku? Twenty guards? Is that sufficient to protect her?"

Baku chuckled. "Lord, if twenty of us cannot guard one nomad rat, we deserve to be flayed."

"Good," Jakka said. "I will remember that."

A moment later, Ki marched down the hill after Baku, her head dizzy with triumph.

Escape! She would get a chance at it. Her captors, all men, would not understand what kind of "herbs and things" she'd gather in the forest. So, right under their noses, she'd dig up a sleeping-drug called Enki root, plentiful in these parts, and grind it into powder, slip it into their water bags, and wait. The day would be hot. They'd drink frequently. Soon, the drug would take effect, and the men would pass out and lie as if dead for the rest of the day. By the time they awoke, she'd be gone.

And my people?

Ki's heart sank. Jakka might hurt them in retaliation. But she had to risk it. She couldn't give Gog her secret. It would make Magog immortal, dooming hundreds more to a fate like hers. She could not justify that. Her options, then, were down to two: escape or suicide. And while part of her still longed for an end to the struggle, Father's training was too firm in her. Which left one choice: escape.

If she escaped, there remained a chance—however small—to help her people someday.

Bowing her head, she prayed silently to her family again. *Forgive me, Asha. I will not join you in the Underworld just yet.* And opening her fingers, Ki let the bone knife fall into the mud.

9

"Lord. Lord."

The annoying voice penetrated the harem tent, forcing Jakka to slowly open his eyes.

He found himself lying face down among a heap of lion-fur pillows, a host of female snores in his ears. With a groan, Jakka pushed himself upright. The reek of perfume and sweat clogged his nostrils. What time was it? Gray beams were peeping through gaps in the tent roof. Dawn sunlight. Hadn't he warned them against disturbing him at this hour?

"Lord," the voice whined again.

Angrily, Jakka licked the dry roof of his mouth. The shapes of his pleasure women lay sprawled around him like sleeping dogs, bare chests rising and falling. Ten, twelve bodies in all . . . It was hard to tell in the gloom.

Looking for the voice that had ruined his sleep, he scanned the tent. His eyes slid swiftly over the symbols painted on the deer hide panels, all blue, the sacred color of the goddess Inanna. Blue bears chased blue deer. Blue bulls fended off blue wolves. Blue eagles swooped for blue fish. Blue freshwater crabs lurked under blue stones. Blue human figures writhed in passion—until he saw, by the western entry, a boy peeking through the flap, spilling white light across the rug.

Jakka's anger flared. "Shut that."

"Lord, forgive me. I was told to fetch you."

"Fetch me? Bah, you fetch *water*, slave. I thirst!" Jakka snapped his fingers. "Go."

The lad trembled and called into the outer chamber for help. Instantly, a servant girl rushed in with a water jug and knelt before Jakka, holding it up with both hands.

"Here is water, Lord."

Jakka threw the warm leg of a sleeping concubine off his lap and stood. He was naked, and the servant girl blushed and looked away. Jakka smiled at her. And he kept smiling as he took the jug and drank, wiping water from his beard. A new one, he thought, studying her brazenly. A delicious Hittite creature, earth-skinned, with black hair flowing in a pretty waterfall over her small shoulders. Desire stirred. Jakka had never tried a Hittite before. Last night's exertions had depleted his energies somewhat; but seeing her here, now, he felt almost ready to—

"Please, Lord, it is urgent," the messenger boy pressed.

Jakka snapped his gaze toward the light. Who was this fool? A Sumerian? Stupid brutes. Hardly worth training. Their best use was meat for the lion pit.

"Well?" Jakka asked.

"The *baru* from yesterday. She—"

Jakka came fully awake in an instant. "Her magic succeeded, did it? Good lad. And here I was considering throwing you to the lions."

The boy nearly fell over in fright. "Please, Lord, I—"

"Leave. I must dress."

Jakka looked around eagerly for his garments. His plan had worked. The witch's magic food would save the horde. And when Father returned, he'd praise Jakka's initiative and forget all about Hakka. Who knew? Perhaps Father would even retire early, giving Jakka full control of the camp. I'd like to see Hakka's expression then! he thought.

The boy gulped. "Forgive me, Lord."

Jakka looked up sharply. The messenger boy stood in the light, quivering stupidly. What was he still doing here? "I told you—" Jakka began.

"She did *not* succeed, Lord. She, ah . . . she escaped."

"Escaped? Who?" Jakka demanded.

"The *baru*, Lord. She is gone."

Fear struck Jakka's chest like a blow. An unfamiliar feeling.

He stared at the boy, waiting to hear the next part that would make it all better, but the slave stood there, shaking. The ugly feeling spread. No, Jakka thought. This is a mistake. It has to be.

Mastering his emotions, he answered calmly.

"You are in error, boy. I sent twenty guards with her. No one escapes that." His anger rose. "Perhaps I *will* feed you to the lions."

"Please, Lord," the boy squeaked. "Nod sends this message, not me."

"Nod? He is here?"

The boy nodded desperately. "Just outside, Lord."

Jakka's skin went cold. If Nod was here, this was serious.

"I will see," he snapped. "If you are wrong . . ."

Still naked, he pushed past the boy into the adjoining chamber. A crowd had already gathered. They stood in a clump, looking frightened. Concubines and servants hurried forward, offering trays of food, but Jakka waved them aside and strode to Nod, who waited under the entry awning. Seeing Jakka's nakedness, Nod balked in surprise. Then he recovered himself and bowed low, to his waist.

"Good morning, Lord."

"Well?"

"You heard, I hope."

"She had twenty guards," Jakka snapped. "Even a great warrior could not escape that."

"Nonetheless, Lord, it has happened."

Nod stroked his beard thoughtfully, fingering the graying strands as if to coax wisdom from them. He sounded almost *impressed,* Jakka thought in astonishment.

"The *baru* is educated in the legends, it seems," Nod mused. "Remember the *Enūma Eliš*? The god of cleverness, Enki, drugs his father, Apsu, with date juice, and lifts his heel and crushes his father's head under his foot—"

"Yes, Nod. I'm not a fool."

Nod smiled thinly. "The *baru* did that yesterday. She foraged in the forest and dug up Enki root. She ground it into powder. She slipped it into her guards' water bags. It drugged them good. All twenty. They slept until dusk. By then she was gone, of course." His tongue wet his lips. "Quite clever, for a nomad."

Jakka's head swam. *Enki root.* How strange. The *baru* had used a legend against him. As if reality was dissolving, dropping him into a myth.

The earth seemed to tilt under his feet. I have made a terrible mistake.

Trying to look calm, Jakka flopped onto a pile of cushions and allowed a servant girl to place a few dates in his outstretched palm. Anything to look less unnerved.

"If this was yesterday," he demanded, "why did her idiot guards not wake up and report her missing last night? Why was I not told?" His stomach twisted to think what he'd been doing, frolicking in the harem tent until late. This did not look good for him.

"Ah, the men." Nod spread his hands helplessly. "You, ah, promised to flay them, remember? If they couldn't handle her."

Jakka's face heated up as he remembered.

"So they fled, the cowards?

"Yes, Lord. But a patrol caught one early this morning. He told all. We will catch the rest, soon. Their tattoos mark them. They cannot blend in anywhere. I smoke-signaled our vassal tribes to send out trackers."

"Good. They *will* be flayed. All of them."

"Yes, Lord."

"And the *baru*?"

"Her tracks lead toward the Euphrates."

Jakka gulped. "So we will get her back. She is only a nomad rat, after all."

"And weak and tired," Nod said. "And ignorant of this terrain."

Jakka threw the dates away. This was a nightmare, but it would soon be over. It pleased him how the dates struck his serving girl, making her squawk with fear and kneel to pick them up. Fuming, Jakka rose and walked with Nod to an elephant-hide map of Mesopotamia that hung from a rack of poles nearby. "Show me." Nod obliged, lifting a pointer rod and tapping a blue squiggle that ran across the southern border of the map, marking the Euphrates River.

"She has a head start. However, to reach the Euphrates, she must run through this forest here, fighting deep foliage all the way. We know of a shortcut path. We'll slash through the forest, eliminating her lead, and catch her by sunset today."

Jakka nodded. His heart was pounding. If the girl escaped, Father could count this as "incompetence." Magog's code might allow him to give Jakka's birthright to Hakka.

But if Jakka got the girl back, this could all go away.

"We will leave now."

"Yes, Lord. But, ah . . ." Nod coughed politely. "Might I suggest some clothes?"

Jakka looked down. He'd forgotten his nakedness.

"Good work, Nod. Earning your keep for once." He stomped back toward the harem chamber. "Now catch this girl for me, and I'll forget how you annoyed me yesterday, eh?"

"Your will is my desire, Lord."

Later that day, at sunset, Jakka raced through a thorn tree forest near the Euphrates.

He was exhausted. He'd run all day, pushing himself harder than he was used to. Magog was always the superior force, always in control. There was never a need for such exertion. Now he was panting raggedly, clutching his side, hating the *baru* with all his heart.

Oh, the pain he'd make her feel!

Up ahead, fifty of his best warriors crashed through the ferns in a wide line, stamping down foliage in case the girl was hiding in it. Their tattooed bodies merged with the shadows, breaking up their outlines like animal predators. Their bone hatchet blades glinted menacingly in the late-afternoon light. Power emanated from them. Jakka's hopes lifted. These were the pride of Magog, undefeated in his lifetime. No one—certainly no nomad rat—could elude *these.*

"Prince, look here."

A scout knelt and pointed at a stone beneath a fern. Jakka bent over it eagerly. Blood on the rock. The girl must have fallen and cut herself on the stone's sharp edge. He touched it eagerly with his fingertips. It was dry. "How old?" he demanded.

"Recent, Lord. We are close."

The scout pointed ahead, identifying a funnel of mashed twigs and stems oozing green juice that indicated the girl's path. Jakka grunted, pleased. Nod had predicted correctly. The witch had indeed run directly toward the Euphrates.

Then a terrible thought struck him. What if she drowned herself in the river?

He spun around and shouted for Nod.

The adviser jogged up, glistening with sweat. He looked too old for a mission like this, with his gray beard and lined face. But he was handling it admirably, keeping better pace with the warriors than Jakka was, though twice his age.

"There you are, old goat," Jakka said sullenly. "I just wondered, might she drown herself?"

Nod wiped his face. "If she wanted to die, why run all this way? Too much effort."

The men laughed. Jakka envied the natural ease Nod shared with them. Yet Nod's answer gave him relief, too. "I suppose the human mind will hardly permit one to drown oneself," he mused. "Especially a female mind. They're weaker than we men, eh, Nod?"

"Just so, Lord."

Jakka faced his fifty warriors. The cold eyes and sneering lips reassured him.

"Two virgin slaves to the one who catches her," he cried. "On my title as prince, I swear it."

"Hail Jakka!" the warriors roared. And without a hint of fatigue, they raced off.

Jakka glanced at Nod, pleased. Nod might have a way with the men. But in the end, Jakka had power, and that was best.

Not long afterward, Jakka burst onto the bank of the Euphrates.

Its beauty was as arresting as ever. Under the setting sun, the river sparkled like a belt of fire, matching the color of the orange dates that hung in heavy clusters fat and ripe down the trunks, glinting like precious stones. In the shallows, *quasab* and *ihdri* reeds clicked together; and out deeper, the wind god, Enlil, breathed gently over the river's surface, creating tiny wave caps that sparkled and flashed. The river was wide here, Jakka noted gratefully. The palm trees on the opposite shore looked as small as blades of grass—surely too far for the girl to swim to in her weakened state.

Then someone shouted, "I see her." And Jakka looked.

There she was. Not far down the bank, the *baru* was wading in the shallows, pushing a raft ahead of her. It wasn't much of a raft. Just a flimsy rectangle of driftwood lashed together with vines. She was pushing it through the dense barrier of reeds, heading for the open water.

Jakka's blood stirred. You scampered far, little rat. But now you will regret it. His muscled warriors were racing down the bank, closing fast. The girl waded into deeper water, fighting the reeds. As Jakka watched, she pulled herself halfway onto the raft and began kicking her feet, churning up a small wake. But the reeds entangled her, delaying her from reaching the main river. Jakka was about to win.

"Remember the reward," he screamed. "Don't let her drown."

His men needed no reminder. Arriving at the girl's location, some raced into the shallows and splashed after her. Others took a more farsighted approach and sprinted farther down the bank—jumping logs, ducking branches, and batting bushes aside—in order to reach a mud spit that jutted into the main river downstream. There they might jump in and swim across her path, trapping her between the two groups. Either way, it would soon be over.

Reassured, Jakka took refuge in the shade of a nearby palm tree to watch the chase finish.

"Nod, I thirst," he said, beckoning for the water skin.

Nod handed it over, and Jakka guzzled from the nozzle, then wiped his mouth.

"Maybe Father was wrong about her," he said, corking the nozzle. "It was stupid of her to build that raft. She'd be farther downriver if she'd just kept running." He glanced at Nod, expecting affirmation. Oddly, however, his adviser looked worried, not exultant. Jakka grew annoyed. "What is it, eh? You see something?"

"Nothing, Lord."

"Go on, bleat it out," Jakka demanded. "I see you fretting, old goat."

Nod scratched his forehead. "It is likely inconsequential, Lord. I hesitate to mention it. Only, on the march home from the raid, I interrogated some of her people—about her magic, you see—and . . . well . . ."

"Well?" Jakka demanded.

Nod cleared his throat. "A year ago, something strange happened on the Tigris River. I did not fully understand the story. But her people were quite stirred up about it." He shifted his weight. "Something to do with a raft. A magic raft."

"A magic raft," Jakka sneered.

"Yes, Lord. Apparently, the device insulted the wind god, Enlil. Her elders made her wear a black stone to tame her, but she didn't wear it enough. So her people think Enlil punished them, using us."

"Over a raft?"

"Just so."

"Like that flimsy thing, there?" Jakka pointed at the girl's platform.

Nod was noncommittal. "I know only what I heard. They said her raft was magic. It . . ." He hesitated. "It turned Enlil into her slave."

A chill prickled up Jakka's arms.

"Ridiculous. Nobody enslaves the wind god." Enlil, god of wind and storms, was one of the most powerful gods in the pantheon. "They fooled you, old man."

Nod bowed. "You see why I hesitated to mention it."

"I do."

Jakka turned back to the river. Thanks to Nod, he was nervous now. But so far nothing seemed amiss. Although the girl had broken free of the reedbeds, kicking into open water, that was expected. His warriors were swimming faster than she was. Both teams were moments away from grabbing her, closing from two directions. A few more strokes and . . .

Jakka frowned. The girl *was* doing something strange. Dripping wet, she'd pulled herself up onto the raft and was yanking at a device that lay across it. A large brown object, like a dead animal. A set of poles with a deerskin blanket attached. Jakka scratched his beard, puzzled. She must have stolen the blanket from her guards when she drugged them. Now she was frantically trying to stand the device upright, rocking the entire raft and nearly capsizing it. He didn't know what the object was, and he didn't like it. Nevertheless, his warriors had also broken free of the reeds and were nearly upon her. Some were even elbowing and pulling each other back, trying to arrive first for the reward. Jakka's heart quickened. Go on, men. Grab her. End Nod's blathering and break that stupid witch-device.

Then it happened. Something so terrible, it would change Jakka's life.

Somehow, the funny pole-device on the girl's raft stood upright. It locked into place. The blanket unrolled with a *clap*, dripping river water. The girl sat back and began jimmying a guidance plank in the water near the raft's tail. Jakka squeezed the water skin, bewildered. What in the name of Baal?

Then he saw. As if by magic, the wind god's breath filled the blanket, bellying it out. The raft began to plow forward, moving at an incredible speed. Almost as if the god Enlil . . . *was her slave.*

"No," Jakka whispered, lifting his hands to his mouth. "No."

"She *is* a witch," Nod breathed.

"Shut up, Nod. What's happening? Stop it!"

But no one could stop this. Before his eyes, the raft transformed into a living thing. Already it was racing ahead, moving faster than any raft had ever gone. It moved so fast, it left a boiling fiery wake behind. Yet the girl turned the raft easily, using its guidance plank like a fish's tail. How easily she steered free of both packs of warriors. How easily she widened the gap between them moment by moment, as if the men were hardly moving at all. Wet tattooed hands flashed as they reached for her. Mouths shouted and cursed. But already she was well away, growing smaller as she neared the bend, out of range.

"Fix it, Nod!" Jakka shrieked.

Nod stood helplessly, clutching his beard, his voice touched with awe. "The Lord Gog was right. A true *baru* has come to Mesopotamia. One such as we have not seen in ages."

The girl was rounding the bend. Before she vanished, however, she turned and shot a final look at Jakka. Then, in a universal sign of contempt, she spat in the water.

"No," Jakka croaked.

Then she was gone, leaving nothing but a sparkling wake as proof of her passing.

Jakka reeled. He dropped the water bag and grabbed the palm trunk, trembling. Who could insult Magog this way and get away with it? No one ever had. And Father hated to be embarrassed. What would he say? Would he still make Jakka heir? How could he? The next warlord of Magog, leader of the greatest horde in Mesopotamia . . . shamed by a little girl?

Nod tried to soothe him.

“Fear not, Lord. We have many vassal tribes downriver. Kish. Sippar. Isin. Dilbat. And many more. I will smoke-signal them all. They will send out grass boats to stop her. Fleets. She will not get far.”

“Do it,” Jakka said hoarsely. “Do it now.”

As his adviser ran off, Jakka tried to console himself. Magog was invincible. The mightiest tribes had tried to defy it and been crushed beneath its clubs like beetles. This rat was nothing compared to them. She'd gained a momentary victory, yes. But Father's network was far too powerful for any human to escape. In the long run, she was only making things harder on herself.

Still, by Baal! What *was* she?

10

In the desert under clear starlight, Ta lay on his back in the cool sand, resting his stump on his belly, marveling at how different life felt when you triumphed.

Thank you, El, he thought, looking up at the sky. *I will not forget this.*

He almost felt glad his old companions had kicked him out. If they hadn't, he might never have known this sensation was possible.

The fire crackled merrily. Aya bounced Shulgi on her knee. Ut sat on his blanket, cooking a hunk of gazelle flesh on a stick. Fat dripped into the fire, popping and hissing, and Ut licked his lips. "Aya, you seasoned it fine. Ta, did you know she was the best cook in our tribe? The women all pestered her for her secret recipes. But she never shared any." He raised the meat in salute. "I'd call it magic, if I didn't know better."

"My mate also loved it," Aya quipped. "Just not enough to love me, too."

Ut let this pass. "How'd you find seasonings out here in the desert? You're not a *baru*."

Aya smiled bashfully. "My mother showed me." She looked at the darkened thornbushes, and her eyes gleamed. "Even a desert is full of life. Plenty of flowers and bark flavors, if you know where to look."

"Well, this tastes better than any Akkadian forest deer I ever had," Ut said, chewing. "Want to share the recipe?"

Aya laughed. "I better keep a few secrets. I want you fine hunters to keep me around."

The men laughed with her, and Shulgi burbled and waved his hands as if eager to be part of the fun.

"What's next?" Ta asked. "After Aya's foot gets better, I mean."

Ut surveyed the camp proudly. Several tripods stood about in the fire glow. Each supported meat strips hanging above a pile of coals, curing in the rising smoke. The gazelle's hide lay draped over a bush, ready to make into clothes and blankets.

"You did well, Ta. Even if Aya heals slowly, this food should get us to the Euphrates. Then, just imagine it. Green paradise."

Aya sniffed under her armpit. "I'll take a bath."

"I want shade," Ut said. "And turtle soup. Fresh otter pelts to wear. Mostly, I want to stop walking and just float around on my back."

"Imagine having our own huts," Aya said wistfully. "I'll sweep my dirt floor and decorate it with flowers. It'll be nicer than our old cave, eh? All those ugly bat droppings."

"We must brace ourselves. There's a lot of work ahead," Ut warned. "We'll have to cut trees and clear reeds off the beach. Build rafts, too. Most of all, we'll need to recruit warriors to defend us." He looked at Ta hopefully. "Any chance we find your friends soon?"

Ta shrugged. Their guess was as good as his.

"Well." Ut snapped a bone in half to suck the marrow. "The sooner we recruit help, the better. Maybe we'll find other wanderers out here besides them."

"How many recruits will we need?" Aya asked.

"At least fifty new members, I'd say. Any less, and we won't feel like a real tribe." Ut waggled a bone at Ta. "Our best hope is still your friends."

Ta kept licking his lips. Delicious grease, left over from his meal, coated his tongue. For the first time in his life, he was *full.* It was a thing he'd never experienced in the cave in Akkad. Now, with his belly stuffed, the world seemed more vivid, richer in sounds and color. The stars twinkled like polished white gems. The fire glimmered like a ruby, pushing away the night. And out in the darkness, three foxes sat just beyond the firelight, round eyes glowing.

Ut saw the foxes and lifted a handful of gravel. "Beggars. They want the meat. Once the fire goes out, they'll sneak in. Away, dogs." He hurled his handful at them, and the creatures retreated with sharp yips, their forms melting into the dark. But their eyes remained, floating like fireflies as their carriers trotted back and forth around the camp. "They're lucky we can't carry any more meat, otherwise I'd trap 'em. We better bury the offal deep, or they'll be all over this camp tonight, digging it up. Eh, Aya?"

Aya smiled. "Someone learned that the hard way by the Tigris."

"At least I've learned," Ut said good-naturedly.

Ta watched the foxes. He'd been like those creatures, once. An outcast. A mangy thief, darting shamelessly here and there to snatch what he could. But no more. He was determined to change. *Change, change, change.* He never wanted to go back to that old path of guilt and loneliness. The path of the thief. Thankfully, the gazelle had shown him a new way.

From now on, I will live by two rules, he thought firmly. One, I'll only do what I admire. Two, I will care for my tribe. He looked at his friends. *This* tribe. Clutching his stump, he shut his eyes and sealed his pledge with a prayer. *Give me the strength, El. I will keep running this path. I won't stop. Ever.*

He had no way of knowing how soon his pledge would be tested.

For days afterward, the group rested in camp, allowing Aya's ankle to heal and their sore limbs and blistered feet to mend. Finally revitalized, they marched on. And two mornings later, as the sun climbed in the blue sky . . .

"The Euphrates!" Ut yelled suddenly. "Look, you two! Am I mad?"

Ta and Aya looked where he pointed. Before them, the endless bushes had thinned away. Little was left but red earth and shimmering sky, with the occasional waist-high thorn patch here and there. But far ahead, something caught Ta's attention. He lifted his stump and shaded his brow. His heart caught. In the distance, at the far edge of the world, a black thread wove in and out of sight over the horizon—vanishing and reappearing just like a corridor of palm trees might as it followed a river course.

For a moment, no one spoke. Then, all at once, they began to jump and whoop happily, waving their hands like children.

"The Euphrates!"

"We did it!"

Aya bounced Shulgi too hard in his sling-pouch, making him cry out in displeasure. She hugged him tight before jumping again, and this time he squeaked with excitement. But suddenly Ut pointed again, and his tone fell.

"By Enki, do you see that?"

A chill shot to the base of Ta's spine. Aya also covered her mouth with a hand.

"Oh, no. Strangers," she murmured.

"River's crawling with 'em," Ut said in disbelief.

The river was not empty. At intervals every few leagues above the palm trees, threads of smoke marred the sky. Ta looked from east to west. He groaned. The entire river was claimed. These tribes must have camped here long ago, each taking their own portion of bank.

For a time, the group stared at the smoke, trying to process it.

"They could be friendly," Aya suggested.

Ut scowled. "Or worship Baal."

Ta grimaced. Baal-worshippers practiced human sacrifice.

"Maybe our chief invented those stories," Aya ventured.

Ta didn't think so. The stories were too many. It was said Baal-worshippers raided their neighbors each month just to capture fresh bodies for the altar.

"I bet the chief lied," Aya insisted. "To discourage us from running away, you know?" She looked at them desperately. "He lied about the Euphrates being free to settle, didn't he?"

Ut gave her a cautionary look. "Is it worth finding out the hard way?"

Aya looked at Shulgi. With a sigh, she shook her head.

"We must keep going," Ut said grimly. "A spot may open up."

They walked south all day, parallel to the palm trees, watching the smoke in hopes that a free spot would appear. None did. One day turned into two. Their food pack lightened. And as the third day began, their nerves frayed, and Ut and Aya began to fight.

"This is new territory," Aya said. "We haven't made our offerings to the local *baals* yet. Don't oppose me, Ut."

Ut laughed coldly. "Really, woman. Our meat is almost gone, and you want to burn the little we have left? That's female thinking for you."

"We'll just burn a handful."

"Not a chance." Ut, carrying the food pack, gripped the straps and forced a chiefly smile through his dusty beard. "It's for your own good, trust me."

"I wonder," Aya said.

They walked on. Ta tried to practice his new code and care for his tribe, but it was harder than he'd expected. He couldn't just wish to help, he realized. He needed the experience and skill to execute it, too. He did all the usual things, the camp chores, the positive comments, even changing and scrubbing Shulgi's swaddling. Moreover, he prayed silently to El each dawn, and made sure to interrupt whenever Ut and Aya started fighting. But they didn't listen. And the more their food dwindled, the fiercer their arguments became.

"I think he wants to leave us," Aya whispered to Ta as they walked together, paces behind Ut. "He keeps looking at Shulgi and me like we're burdens." She glanced mournfully at the distant palms. "I bet he'd love to join one of those tribes. They'd take him, too. A hunter like him. Anyone would. But they won't take Shulgi." She peeked into her sling, where Shulgi's chubby brown face looked back patiently. "Nobody wants his kind."

"What're you whispering about, woman?" Ut asked over his shoulder. "Not corrupting our gazelle hunter, are you?"

"He's not the corrupt one," Aya said under her breath.

"Didn't hear you, woman. Say it to my face?"

"I'm only praising what a fine leader you are."

"That's likely."

They were two fierce personalities, neither willing to back down, Ta realized. They weren't used to yielding like he was, for life had not yet taught them humility.

"What about a story?" Ta asked, to distract them. "Tell how the Euphrates was formed, Ut."

This worked for a little. Ut never passed up a chance to practice his craft. Lifting his voice, he told how Enlil, god of wind and storms, battled Tiamat, mother of all the gods, for control of the universe. Tiamat turned into a giant sea serpent, hissing jets of flame. But Enlil breathed into her mouth the four winds—North, East, South and West—and made her lose control over her body. Then, using a magic net of grass ropes, Enlil trapped her in place. Finally, with a bolt of lightning taken from his brother Anu, god of the sky, Enlil slew her. The lightning split Mother Tiamat in two. ". . . and her tears flowed out and formed the Tigris and Euphrates Rivers," Ut finished proudly. "Rivers which remain the borders of Mesopotamia to this day."

"Well told," Ta said sincerely. "Know any more?"

But a moment later, Ut and Aya were fighting again, and there was nothing he could do to stop it. They ignored him as if he was a child.

The next day, things reached a breaking point. They were down to their last rations of food and water. And more smoke kept appearing. Whenever one column vanished behind, another wriggled up ahead. And in a worrisome development, the smudges started going up in puffs. As if the tribes were signaling to each other.

"Is that about us?" Aya hugged Shulgi nervously. "They can't see us out here, can they?"

"Something's going on." Ut's fingers were white on his spear shaft. "I'd rather not find out."

Then, at midafternoon, another storm appeared.

It wasn't a dust storm, this time. It was a rainstorm emerging out of the southern desert, spreading across the sky like a black beast. The group stopped and studied it, watching the blue sheets of rain drag beneath it over the red land. Cool forewinds buffeted their faces, leagues ahead of the storm's coming. The hairs on Ta's chin beard ruffled, and his cheeks prickled. He found himself wishing for the stone ceiling of his cave back in Akkad.

"Enlil is angry," Aya said quietly. "We should've . . ." She checked herself too late.

"Woman." Ut's voice was dangerous.

"We should've," she burst out. "If we'd burned offerings days ago, this wouldn't be happening. Now we've hardly anything left to give."

They fell silent, watching the storm. Ta had never seen one like it. The clouds covered the entire horizon, throwing half the world into darkness. Bolts of lightning flickered within them, making them glow and pulse. By nightfall, they would hit the river, the group soon after. There would be flash floods. Lightning everywhere. Ta rubbed his stump-arm nervously. He wasn't looking forward to that.

Trying to be cheerful, he said: "At least we'll refill the water bag."

"Shut up, runt. I've had enough of your cheeriness," Ut said.

Ta fell silent, his face burning.

"You be kind to him," Aya said. "The gods sent him to us. In fact—"

"Don't even start," Ut said.

Aya didn't listen. "If we're faithful, the gods will repay us tenfold," she said. "I'm building a stone altar right now. Ut, you put that food pack down."

"Is she serious?" Ut looked at Ta. "One meal left, and she wants to burn it?"

"Do we believe in the gods or not?" She looked at him scornfully. "Fine, blasphemer, I won't burn yours. Just mine and Ta's."

"By Enlil's beard! No wonder you see no female chiefs. No tribe would survive." Ut stabbed a finger at her. "You listen, woman. Your fate affects mine. You'll eat your dinner. If you're too weak to go on, I'll be stuck, too."

Aya sighed and uttered a quiet prayer, asking for forgiveness for Ut. "He's a stupid man," she said with her eyes shut, just loud enough to be heard. "He doesn't know what he's doing."

Ut spread his hands helplessly. "Food thief, talk to her. She won't listen to me. But you're her special totem."

Ta stepped backward in surprise. "Me?"

"Yes, runt. Fix her."

Ta gulped. He could see both sides. On one hand, it was customary to burn offerings to the local *baals*. On the other, this *was* the last of their rations. Besides, Ta thought angrily, if the *baals* just take our food, they're no better than our greedy chiefs, and not worth serving. We earned that food.

Of course, he'd gladly have made an offering to El, "the One Who is here," who'd helped him with the gazelle. He trusted El. But El might be only a local god, far back in the desert by now. Prayers to him might not be heard.

"It's time to go in," Ut said. "We're walking blind. At this rate, we could keep walking forever. We need help."

"Oh, they'll help *you*," Aya said. "You're a hunter."

"And you're a fine-looking woman. Young. Fit."

"So some brute will force me to be his mate. What about Shulgi? Ta? I doubt a tribe will want *them*."

"By the gods, woman." Ut lifted his fist. "You will heed me. Or else—"

"Or else what? You'll use violence on me, like our ex-chief did?"

"How dare you?"

"Planning to leave me, like you left your ex-mate?"

"Snake-tongued reptile!"

Their voices grew louder, and they began waving their hands, jabbing fingers. Shulgi began to cry. Aya lifted him from his sling, handed him to Ta, and kept arguing. Ta walked off to protect Shulgi's ears from the tumult. Squatting behind a bush, he peered nervously through the thorns as the fight escalated. This wasn't good. Not at all. Ut wanted them to go to the river and take their chances. Aya was firmly against it. Neither would give ground. Their faces were purple with anger. Their arm movements blurred. If this kept up, someone would do something irreversible, shattering their little tribe. Do something, Ta thought. He looked down at poor Shulgi, who was innocent of all this. I must act quick. But Ta wasn't used to fixing other people's problems. He felt as helpless as the baby.

"Actually, Ut, I'm glad for this," Aya was saying. "It brings up a good point. What happens when we can't agree? We need a system."

"The chief decides," Ut retorted. "And—"

"Exactly," Aya said. "I don't want a chief."

Ut's mouth fell open. "Wha-at?" he said awkwardly.

"That's right. No chief, ever again."

"No chief." Ut looked toward Ta's bush. "Did you hear that, runt?"

Ta looked up anxiously. No chief? He'd never heard of such a thing. Was this wise to bring up now?

"Let me explain." Aya furrowed her brow, finding the words. "What I mean is, we've started over out here. A fresh beginning. Why go back to the way things were? Our chief was bad. He snatched the best cuts of meat. Picked our mates for us. Sent young warriors off to die."

"I hated him too, but—" Ut protested.

"Down with chiefs, I say," Aya interrupted. "Let's try something new. Give everyone a say. And when we can't agree, we decide things by majority. Majority say." She looked at Ta's bush eagerly. "We're all free out here. The only way to *stay* free is this."

Ut was stupefied. "So right now, you'd want to . . ."

"Yes. Give Ta a say. Whoever he sides with, that's the majority. We obey that decision."

Ut laughed. "I see. You expect he'll side with you, of course."

Aya turned to Ta. "Well? Do you want to stay out here and make an offering? Or visit the Baal worshipers and let them burn you and Shulgi alive? Pick. Go ahead."

Ta stood up, petrified. Something told him that if he spoke, Ut would explode and leave. Anyway, Ta didn't know what to choose. He'd never voted. Rarely, at intertribal gatherings, chiefs formed a council and voted on decisions. But nobody did it otherwise.

"Tribes have chiefs, they just do," Ut said. "There must be a good reason for it." He appealed to Ta. "Should we toss out generations of tradition, just because we've left home?"

"Tradition? What's so good about *tradition*?" Aya asked. "Tradition stole Yuna from you. Threatened my boy's life. Cut off Ta's hand. Why, tradition is what we're here to escape. I know I didn't travel all this way to let *you* become chief."

Ut opened his mouth, then shut it helplessly. It was clear he'd expected to be chief. And with good reason, Ta thought. Ut was the most valuable of them by far. He was tall, strong, handsome, and covered in manly hair.

The blood drained from Ut's face. "Where in Enlil's name is this coming from?" he demanded.

Aya answered confidently. She must have been pondering this for some time.

"Shulgi showed it to me. The day he was born, with his foot, I saw everything in a new way. I noticed how our tribe bullied its weaker members. They'd have done it to Shulgi, too, given the chance. I saw how the high-status ones took all the food, the best sleeping spots, the best mates, and gave everyone else the scraps. Animals live better."

She looked at Ta. "Was your tribe like that, too?"

Ta felt stunned. Aya might have been describing his own life. It was embarrassing.

"I . . . uh," he stammered, and tightened his grip on Shulgi.

Aya looked at her baby. Suddenly her eyes grew so intense with love, neither man dared speak.

"No, we can't throw this opportunity away," she said quietly. "We're free now. And my boy will have a good life. He will. I'm going to give it to him." She shook out her hair, making it shimmer beautifully in the afternoon light. "With a say, his voice will always matter, even after I die and can't protect him anymore. This is my greatest gift to him besides life. Perhaps it *is* life," she added pensively. "We need to agree to it, right now."

The two men looked at each other.

"All get a say?" Ut said stupidly. "*All*?"

"Yes, you brute. 'Useless' ones, too. Especially them. They need it the most." Aya looked at Ta. "What do you say, brother? That is," she added hastily, "if you *want* to join us permanently. Join our tribe. I know we haven't settled that yet."

Ta was too astonished to respond. Ut, however, lost his self-control.

"Now look here, woman," he spluttered. "This is mad. If I'd known back in Akkad you intended this, I'd never have come."

Aya ignored him. "Ta, if we want a say, we must *take* a say. Here. Now. At the outset, before the old ways reclaim us."

Then, she did something remarkable.

She lifted her hand.

"All in favor?" she asked.

For a moment, no one spoke. Ta held his breath. Was this the first vote? It seemed it was.

Aya simply waited, her eyes ablaze with motherly passion, one hand raised, the other planted on her hip. Ta felt a burst of admiration. What a woman! Just sixteen or seventeen, and she was already defying the whole world for her son's sake.

But he didn't yet raise his hand.

"Ta?" Aya asked.

"I need to think," Ta said. "Give me a moment."

"Ta!" they both shouted.

"I'm sorry," Ta said. "I just . . . forgive me."

He knelt behind the bush and sat in its shade. Shulgi began to squirm again. Ta rocked him. This was bad. Ut *would* leave the group if Ta raised his stump and sided with Aya. Ta felt sure of it. Yes, voting would throw everything out of balance. Ut would decide he was better off alone. He could travel faster, eat all the food himself, and burn no offerings to *baals.* If necessary, join a river tribe. Why would he stay? Out here, he didn't even get to be a chief. *And if he goes,* a voice in Ta's heart whispered, *you're finished. A cripple, a woman, and a baby will be helpless on their own.*

Exhausted, Ta looked down at Shulgi. His mind hurt. He wasn't good at this.

I really do hope we stay together, little brother. It's nice having you for a friend.

In reply, Shulgi urinated on Ta's arms.

Ta had to laugh at the ridiculousness of it. Shulgi had no respect for the gravity of the moment. "You little rogue." Ta wiped his arms dry on the sand. "No manners at all."

Shulgi giggled.

I suppose I deserve it, Ta thought ruefully. We big ones are failing you. We must do better.

Aya and Ut were arguing again, so Ta unwrapped Shulgi to dry him, then let him lie naked on the skins, huffing and kicking his clubfoot, enjoying the freedom outside his sling. His eyes sparkled, and his ruddy cheeks bunched in a smile as Ta dropped and raised his hand before his face, playing peekaboo. But while Ta played, he pondered.

Once again, he actually mattered. The "high" ones weren't getting it done, leaving it to "the cripple." *Rule Two: Care for your tribe.* Yes. But how? He needed an idea.

Ta turned and focused on the incoming storm. *An idea.* All right. *An idea.* But from where? Ta was not used to coming up with ideas. Back in Akkad, he'd never been asked to supply them. In fact, the chief discouraged thinking in general, considering it a threat. Ta had no feel for it. But for Shulgi, he had to try. *Try.* He studied the clouds. What might be there?

His eyes narrowed. The storm would strike at nightfall. It would bring hours of drenching misery to the river land. The friends would be soaked. Shulgi might catch ill. Lightning could hit. Meanwhile, on the river, the locals would shelter in their huts, cowering under their roofs of palm wood, waiting for the lightning to pass. They wouldn't emerge until morning—

Ta froze. That was it! *The storm.*

He sat rigid, terrified the idea would vanish. But it did not, and he saw it all. This would work. While the locals hid in their huts—*not* patrolling the bank—the Akkadians could sneak in and forage under the cover of the rain. Grab all the food they needed, fill their pack, then rush safely back to the desert before sunrise. It would be unpleasant, but the haul might sustain them for days. Long enough to find a home.

Ta's heart was racing. He grabbed Shulgi and ran to the others. They seemed reluctant to stop arguing, but when he told them his idea, they looked at him strangely—then charged and hugged him from both sides.

"Hoho, runt." Ut tapped Ta's cheek affectionately. "Where'd that come from, eh?"

"I told you, didn't I?" Aya kissed Ta's forehead. "A divine gift, Ta is."

Ut laughed. "I'll believe anything at this point. You know, this might actually work."

"Of course it will," Aya said. "And see? I sanction it, because look." She lifted her hand. "I vote with you and Ta. It's unanimous. We can go in."

Ut laughed. "We can deal with that later. If we grab enough food tonight, I'll even allow you to burn some of it to your precious *baals*. See, woman? I'm not a beast like you say." He turned back to Ta and tapped his forehead with a finger. "You've got a mind hiding in there, brother. First the gazelle, now this. Who are you?"

"Just lucky, I guess," Ta said.

"Well, keep it up."

Ta walked off and sank under his bush and held the baby close. It was soothing to feel the *pit-a-pat* of the little heart against his. The other two were already debating, hashing out the details of the plan as if they'd thought it up themselves. Somehow it didn't matter. The danger of violence had passed. The group would stay together. That was what mattered. Sitting there, holding Shulgi, Ta felt content.

11

That night, the travelers jogged toward the river as planned. It was easygoing at first, for the moon painted the ground as white as snow between the thornbushes, and the ground was flat. They reached the wall of palm trees just before the storm did. There they hesitated, trying to peer through the blackness between the trunks. For the first time others might lurk nearby . . . perhaps just ahead, in the shadows under the trees.

"Anything could happen in there," Ut whispered.

"Having second thoughts, are we?" Aya teased.

"Just keep that boy of yours quiet. If he cries, he'll wake the locals and get us captured."

Aya adjusted her chest sling. "He's fine." Indeed, Shulgi was snoozing in his pouch after a heavy feeding. "You always want to lead us, Ut. So, lead."

"How generous of you."

Everyone was skittish as they crept into the palm forest. Dead fronds crackled underfoot, ruining any hope of stealth. When something rustled in the bushes, they all froze, fearing an attack. But it was only a small mammal of some kind, scrounging for food, so they kept going. Moments later, they walked onto the bank of the river they'd dreamed of for so long.

Ta's jaw dropped. The Euphrates was even more beautiful than he'd hoped. The water, bordered by thick beds of *quasab* and *ihdri* reeds, slid by in a glittering white band, reflecting the moonlight. Frogs croaked everywhere. Night birds cooed. A smell of deep mud wafted over him, of algae and decaying vegetation. Rings of ripples marked fish surfacing to nab flies.

"Just listen to all that food," Aya said reverently.

"We're not alone." Ut pointed at the clouds pushing toward the southern shore. The cool fore wind they'd felt earlier blew across the water, stronger this time, ruffling not only Ta's beard but his chest hair. He rubbed his arms, chilly. Electric light flickered within the bulging clouds, accompanied by deep rumbles. The storm was almost here.

Ut grimaced. "I'd rather not die in a lightning strike. Let's shelter and forage after it passes."

"For once, I agree with you," Aya said.

They located an elevation down the beach, a small hump that would provide protection if the bank flooded. At the top, working as fast as they could, they dug a depression, then dragged up deadwood to make a roof over the hole.

Just in time, too. No sooner had they crawled into the shelter than the first winds struck. The palm trees began to thrash, and air whistled through the gaps in the log ceiling, making the Akkadians shiver. Then the first clouds slid over the stars, turning the world pitch-black.

"Is it too late to go back?" Aya asked in the darkness.

She was joking, but there was fear in her voice, too. A great roar was approaching over the water. A wall of rain, pounding the river like the coming of another world. Ta hugged himself, bracing for the impact.

"I miss having a cave," Ut said, speaking for them all.

The rain struck. It hit the roof with a clatter, piercing the gaps and soaking everyone inside. Shulgi began to howl. Branches began snapping off the trees, hitting the mud with loud *whumps*. A limb fell close by. Mud splattered into the lean-to, over Ta's knees.

"WAAAH-AAAH," Shulgi wailed.

"For one so small, he's got a big voice," Ut shouted.

"The thunder will be bigger," Aya shouted back.

As if she'd called it down, the thunder clapped. It was so mighty, it seemed to shake the hill and rattle the teeth in Ta's face. *CRACK!* A violent glory broke over the land. Lightning! The sky god, Anu, seemed to have ripped his realm in two. Ta glanced left and saw his companions briefly in the striped shadows, hugging their knees, faces skeleton-white, streaked with rain, before everything plunged into darkness again.

"What've you done to us, runt?" Ut shouted. "We never should've come here."

CRACK!

The Akkadians bunched closer together, trembling as the lightning flickered. Water was both revered and feared in Mesopotamia. Its terrible spring floods were famous. Snowmelt from the Zagros Mountains would gush suddenly into the Tigris and Euphrates rivers, swelling them until they overflowed their banks and wiped away whole villages.

The legend of the Great Flood was even more unnerving. Akkadian storytellers loved to scare their listeners with the tale of how, at the dawn of time, humans grew so numerous and noisy on earth that they ruined the storm god Enlil's sleep. In a rage, he swore to wipe out every living thing. His rains pounded the land for days, covering Mesopotamia in a gray sea, horizon to horizon. Luckily for humans, Enki, god of cleverness and tricks, decided to thwart his elder brother's plan. Before the storm hit, he told Utnapishtim, wisest of men, to build a great raft and load two of every creature inside, male and female. People mocked Utnapishtim as he built it. But once the storm came, only those in the floating ark of reeds, surrounded by beasts, survived Enlil's wrath. Life was saved. But what if the god grew angry again? Ta wondered.

Aya must have feared this, too, for now she began to chant over Shulgi's cries. Rocking back and forth, she sang: "Praise to you, Enlil. Rain is your blessing descending to earth. Without your masculine touch, Inanna's feminine soil could not give birth. Without your moisture, no grass could live, nor deer graze. Be gentle, oh, Enlil. We will honor you with fish on the stone altar. Five whole fish—"

CRACK!

"Better make it ten fish, sister," Ut shouted.

"Are you turning religious, now, brother?"

"Don't mock me, woman."

"So be it. Ten fish for mighty Enlil."

Unfortunately, her prayers showed no effect. The next thunderclap was so fierce, it made Ta's *emittu* nearly leap out of his stomach. More detritus struck the logs. Even Aya fell silent and covered Shulgi with her body, shielding him from the water spurting through the gaps. How long could this go on?

Reaching across Aya's lap, Ut grabbed Ta's elbow and shook him.

"Listen, Ta. The river might be flooding. Peek outside and check, eh?"

"Me?" Ta cried. "You're the leader."

"You brought us here, runt. This falls on you."

"Yes, Ta," Aya agreed. "That's a majority. Two-to-one."

"Two-to-one," Ut echoed. "Go, Ta. Go."

Terrified, Ta gripped his stump. How could anyone go out *there*?

Then, in the back of his mind, his code spoke. *Do what you admire. Take care of your people.* Had he really meant his oath to El?

So, in the next slash of lightning, Ta gritted his teeth and poked his head outside.

He saw a world gone mad.

Everything was blinking blue and white. The palm trees were rioting like a frenzied mob. Runoff gurgled past in silver torrents. Wind howled overhead, throwing branches upward like great black birds. Then there was the Euphrates itself, which had indeed overflowed its banks. Boiling waters rushed among the palm trunks below the hill, dragging bushes and felled logs out into the river and zipping them downstream in a deadly fleet of driftwood. Worse still, the flood was eroding the base of the hill. Great chunks of mud were falling and splashing into the torrent. Ta stared, mesmerized. At this rate, the river would drag away the lean-to before long.

And if we fall in, we drown, Ta thought. No human can outswim that.

When darkness fell again, he pulled back inside and made his report.

"Keep looking," Ut yelled. "You put us here. You take the risks."

"Two-to-one," Aya shouted. "That's the will of the majority."

Ta clenched his teeth. *Do what you admire. Help the tribe.* They're really testing my sincerity, aren't they, El? Shivering, he poked his head back outside.

CRACK! Another burst of lightning revealed the same terrors as before. Bending trees. A duck spiraling past in the air, out of control. And just offshore—

Ta's heart stopped. *Impossible.*

Shooting over the flattened reedbeds, heading straight for the hill—a raft!

And on the raft, *a girl.*

The lightning lingered, flapping over the waters. Forgetting his fear, Ta crawled out farther to see better. In the river the raft was spinning with dizzying speed. The girl lay flat on the rectangle, clinging to the sides. Her hair was plastered to her forehead. Her mouth was open, shouting to the gods. She was zipping for the shore, where the palm trunks, half-submerged in floodwater, would break up her flimsy platform and drown her.

Then darkness fell again, leaving her afterimage pulsing in Ta's retinas.

He pulled back inside the lean-to, shaking. They'll never believe this, he thought.

Sure enough, they didn't.

"A branch must've hit your head, runt," Ut yelled. "No one can survive out there."

"Then look yourself," Ta shot back. "And if you don't trust my scouting, don't ask for it."

That got Ut curious. Still muttering, he pushed aside a log to peek out. More water splattered in, making Aya yell angrily as she peeked out, too. But in the next flash, the girl was there.

"Enlil, help us," Ut gasped.

A white blade of fire stabbed the opposite shore. By its light, all three Akkadians watched in shock as the girl's raft struck a half-submerged tree near the base of the hill and shattered into spinning twigs. The girl flew off into the leaping black water. Ta cried out. Yet the girl resurfaced, clutching the slick trunk with her skinny arms. Again and again waves smashed into her back, throwing up white flowering bursts. Jagged pieces of driftwood flew past her as well, big enough to bludgeon her senseless or crush her spine. She couldn't cling to the trunk forever.

As darkness fell, Ut replaced the log, shaking.

"I'm sorry, runt. You were right."

"I wish I hadn't seen," Aya said. "By the gods, I wish it."

"Don't think of it," Ut said. "Forget it. It will be over soon."

Ta felt a chill. "Over? What do you mean, brother?"

Ut said nothing.

"What do you mean?" Ta cried louder. "Aren't we going to help?"

Ut was brisk. "You did a good job. Now be quiet and relax."

Ta couldn't believe what he was hearing. Bewildered, he turned automatically and began digging in their pack, searching for a length of grass rope they'd brought from the cave. "Ut, you're strongest," he shouted over the baby's crying. "If you throw the rope to her, she'll catch it, and you can drag her in."

Ut sighed. "Don't you see, runt?"

"See?" Ta was perplexed.

"I feel bad for her, I do. But we must stay safe in the shelter."

Ta was dumbfounded. "You'd just . . . let her go?"

"The whole forest's falling down. If you go outside, you'll be smashed to juice."

Aya patted his arm. "It's a cruel world, Ta. You should know that better than anyone."

"She's right," Ut said. "I'm sorry, Ta, but our tribe must come first."

"Our tribe . . ."

"That's right. If you broke a leg out there, we'd be forced to leave you. We can't risk such a loss for a strange girl."

"It's common sense," Aya agreed.

"Rest easy," Ut said. "Let us do the thinking."

"But she'll . . . she'll drown," Ta said stupidly.

"Enough!" Aya interjected sternly. "You have a kind heart, Ta. It's why Shulgi likes you. But the count is two-to-one. That's final."

"Don't fret," Ut said. "This will fade. You'll forget it in time."

Ta was stunned. He gripped his stump in anguish. The girl was right there.

Yet he could see their point of view, too. *The tribe first.* In fact, it seemed to pose a conflict inherent in his two new rules. *One: Do what you admire. Two: Take care of your tribe.* Did taking care of his people mean ignoring the fate of everyone else? How could he admire that?

It paralyzed him. In fact, in later days, he would wonder if he'd have broken out of it, had not Shulgi's wails burst fresh into his ear. "WAHHH! WAHHHHH!" But that did it. For Ta thought suddenly: What kind of tribe are we building for Shulgi? A selfish, cold-hearted one, like in Akkad? Or a noble tribe he can be proud of?

That was all he needed. *Do what you admire. Every time.* It was no service to Shulgi to give him a dishonorable clan.

In the next burst of light, Ta looped the rope over his arm and dove out of the shelter.

"Ta!" Aya yelled. "The majority agreed!"

Ut shouted: "I won't forgive this, runt, you hear me?"

But Ta didn't care. He felt *alive*, as he had after the gazelle. That was confirmation enough.

Squinting in the rain, he slid to the bottom of the hill and waited for the next flash. When it came, he found the girl. She was thirty paces away across the black water. She'd slipped farther down the palm trunk, leaving only her face in view. Her boarskin tunic was tugging her down, heavily. Her eyes were vacant with despair. Ta's heart twisted. He knew that look. It was the look of a person utterly alone. He'd lived it for years.

You're my tribe, too, sister. Anyone who feels that way is my tribe.

In the lingering light, he hurled the rope. "Here!"

Seeing it, her eyes flew wide. She reached for it. But the end splashed short of the tree, and Ta's heart sank as he pulled it back. What am I doing?

Darkness fell again. Coiling the rope over his arm, he waited for the next flash. But to what purpose? The rope was too short: it wouldn't reach. And it was terrifying out here in the dark, with palm branches clashing overhead, and rain slapping his face. As if in confirmation, a piece of flying wood clipped the back of his head, and the blow made him stagger, see sparks. He bent over, cursing. Had Ut been right? If Ta stayed here much longer, something really big might hit him. And then . . .

He was still debating this when a small hand touched his back.

"Sometimes I want to slap you, runt, you know that?"

Ta turned, his heart leaping. It was Aya. As more lightning burst, she stood there with her arms covering her head, glaring at him.

"What are you waiting for?" she cried. "Are we doing this or not?"

"Where's Shulgi?"

"Ut's got him. I couldn't let you die out here, could I? I need your help managing Ut." She shoved him. "Now hurry."

Ta gave a cry of joy. "You won't regret it, sister."

He hugged her. And in the same instant, a new plan came. He remembered that halfway to the girl's tree was another tree. If he waded to that halfway point, he could use it for an anchor to toss the girl the rope. He'd pull her to him, toss the rope to Aya, and she'd haul them both in.

"Terrible idea," Aya said when he told her.

In reply Ta gave her one end of the rope, then ran a few paces upstream and knotted the other end around his waist. Then he waited for the light. It came. Another boom. Another flash. Ahead, the blue chop leapt like teeth. What am I doing? I'm a cripple, not a hero, he thought.

But across the water, the girl's eyes fixed on him with desperate hope. His resolve hardened.

Do what you admire.

Before his courage could fail him, he waded in.

12

The moment Ta entered the river, it became clear why some tribes worshiped Enbilulu, god of rivers, at the top of the pantheon. He began to wonder if he'd made a mistake. Even knee-deep, the river's enormous power hit him like a pile of boulders crashing into his legs. Who was he to challenge such a god? Enbilulu had been here since the dawn of time, drowning heroes and beasts alike by the millions. The god would think nothing of doing the same to him.

He took another tentative step. Suddenly his foot slipped, and he found himself tumbling downstream, head over heels. Water poured into his mouth. Driftwood battered his body. The current was trying to suck him out deep and drown him. Luckily, the noose around his stomach cinched tight, making him gag and spit bile over his lips. But it held, and the rope swung him back to the bank, rolling him over the stones in the shallows and up onto the mud beach.

He crawled out spitting water, to find Aya dancing madly above him.

"Enough, Ta! That proves it. You're not strong enough."

Ta struggled to his feet, shaking his head. He had a sense of the river now. He could do better.

"Again," he said.

“Runt—”

“Again. Keep the rope tense. It’ll steady me.”

He charged in once more. Aya kept the rope taut, paying it out steadily. And this time he gave in slightly to the current. To his surprise it pushed him forward to the tree, allowing him to stay upright all the way. Once to the trunk, he wrapped his limbs around it and held on. The trunk was slick and hard between his thighs. Water dragged at him, threatening to rip him off. More wood thudded his ribs. Still, for now, he was secure.

“Let go,” he shouted.

“You sure, runt? I don’t like this.”

“Let go, Aya.”

He’d never spoken with such command. It didn’t sound like his voice. Yet Aya obeyed, and the rope went slack, allowing Ta to pull it in with his good hand. He knew he was in terrible danger now with no safety line. One slip, and the river would suck him out and drown him. And already his muscles were weakening. This would have to be fast.

In the next lightning flash he saw the girl. She was staring at him, her eyes as bright as stars. His heart went out to her.

“Ho!” he shouted. “Ready?”

It was possible she didn’t speak his tongue. It didn’t matter, though, for when she shouted back, the rain muffled her words. There was nothing to do but throw. He did. To his relief, she caught it on the first toss and kicked off her tree. Being one-handed, he could do nothing but anchor the rope to the trunk, pinning it with his body, and let her weight hit the line like a big fish. And her will to live proved strong. Fighting the crashing torrent, she pulled herself in, hand over hand, and suddenly was upon him. She clambered on and wrapped her skinny arms and legs around him, molding her body to his like a little child’s. It was a moment he would never forget. With her wet cheek pasted to his, her teeth chattering, he realized she had trusted her life to him completely. Him, “the cripple.” It filled him with unexpected strength.

I cannot fail her.

"Ready?" he asked.

She nodded as if she understood, and in the next lightning burst, he threw. Aya caught the rope, and Ta dove into the torrent with the girl on his back. The river sucked them under. They rolled in the darkness, losing any sense of up and down. More driftwood banged off Ta's skull. He couldn't breathe. Spots filled his eyes. His lungs screamed for air. He felt the rope fibers splitting, and his palm grating on the rope, burning skin off. He wouldn't last.

Then another blue shock of light struck the world, and he slammed into the slope of ooze and knelt up into life-giving air.

"You did it, runt! You did it!"

Aya stood above him, cheering. Through blurry vision, he saw the girl crawling away on all fours, vomiting. Joy filled him. And another feeling. *Pride.* As life-giving as breath. He stood, reeled, and fell back down. Sour bile spewed over his lips. It didn't matter.

Alive. She's alive. And she wouldn't be, if I'd listened to them.

Another victory was a piece of him now. It could never be taken away.

13

After the storm blew on into the desert, the Akkadians crawled out of the lean-to and studied the beach in awe. It looked like a battlefield of the gods. In the blue moonlight beneath the dripping palms, Ta saw bushes uprooted, trunks flattened, and chunks of bank torn away.

"Enlil is mighty," Aya said quietly.

"He's got a temper to match yours," Ut said.

Astonishingly, food was everywhere. More food than they could have gathered in months. Fish flopped in puddles. Snakes lay draped over logs. Rats, herons, turtles, otters, frogs, and freshwater crabs speckled the beach as far as they could see. It was all there for the taking.

The companions looked at each other in disbelief.

We're saved.

"Turtle meat," Ut murmured. "I always wanted some. The chief hoarded it all for himself."

"Not anymore," Aya said. "That one's mine."

Uttering cries of animal joy, the travelers raced down the hill and fell upon the raw feast. Forgotten was the fact that they were in enemy territory. Everyone scrambled here and there, grabbing anything at hand and eating it raw. Even the new girl, who'd said nothing since coming ashore, pounced on the food with savage grunts.

"You did this, Ta," Aya called softly across the mud. "Your idea."

Ta was too hungry to answer. He just ate and ate, even biting into a random fruit he didn't know the name of, a bumpy-shelled thing as big as his fist. He ate so much that he finally fell back in the mud and stared up at the stars, gripping his swollen stomach. The night seemed to shiver with vibrant colors. The stars were bursting like yellow fruits in the sky. He felt young again, like after catching the gazelle.

An *idea* did this, he told himself. Who knew ideas could be so important? Yet one spark at the right moment had changed everything. A person rich with ideas would find great success. Could Ta learn how to make them?

Then he remembered the girl.

He sat up and looked down the bank for her. She was squatting at the water's edge, using a rock to crack open the shell of a freshwater crab. Her hands were shaking as if she hadn't eaten in ages. Lifting the dead creature in both hands, she attacked the meat inside with her teeth, spitting out shell bits like an animal. She wasn't exactly inspiring. Her black hair dripped messily over her face, tangled with twigs and river weeds. Her boarskin tunic was ripped, exposing a bony shoulder. She was of mating age, however, perhaps fifteen or sixteen, making her valuable to any tribe. And in the moonlight, something in her face pierced Ta's heart like a spear.

She was not typically beautiful. She was different. The shape of her nose, her more slender features . . . not Akkadian. Still, to him, lovely. Maybe the loveliest face he'd ever seen. Something about her made his breath catch. It was like he knew her, somehow. He recalled the warmth of her wet cheek pressed to his, her arms tight around him. It frightened him. He'd felt something for a girl only once in his life. Oona, a sickly girl back in Akkad. That had not turned out well.

He felt queasy as he remembered. For a brief time, even with his stump arm, he'd held out hope that the chief would pair him with a match. The season he came of age, at sixteen, a girl named Oona also reached the proper age for a female, fifteen. Nobody else seemed to want her. Ta began to harbor hopes. Oona was pale and endlessly ill. She suffered a hacking cough that rattled like wet bones in her throat. People kept away from her in case she was catching. She was considered a silly girl, too, rather useless and dull. She never spoke. Ta watched her from afar, noticing how her family scolded her and ignored her, expressing their shame. It gave him a secret dream. *We are both unwanted, Oona. It could be us against them all. I swear, if you are mine, I will work so hard for you, you'll forget your mate is a cripple.*

Then of course at the mating ceremony she was given to someone else—a young hunter who did not want her. A man who stood next to the home fire with Oona at his side, blue garlands around their necks, the priest chanting and shaking his sacred bead stick over them. The young man looked so miserable, doomed to a life with someone he despised. Yet Oona . . . Ta would never forget her look of joy. She'd landed a hunter, a real hunter, instead of Ta. It would mean more of everything good in life. More blankets, better garments, more food. More status. Extra cave space for her children. She'd escaped being stuck with a cripple, and her eyes shone with gratitude as she looked up at her new partner. Ever since, Ta had cut off such hopes. He'd accepted it like the severing of his hand.

Now, recalling this on the beach, he berated himself. Did you go into the water because you thought you could keep this girl? No. You went for her sake. Because she needed it. Because she was alone, and you know what that feels like. He grabbed his stump and twisted it painfully. She is alive and that is good. Don't ruin it with your selfish thoughts.

Still, he wondered why she was alone out here. Did she need a new tribe, too? Not only that, Ta thought with rising excitement. Maybe she knew this region, and where to settle.

He scurried over to Aya and whispered his idea.

Aya laughed. "I'm ahead of you, Ta. It will be nice to have another woman in the tribe."

She sat on a fallen log, Shulgi in her lap. She was feeding him chewed-up date mash on a finger. Shulgi, in baby fashion, was swallowing some of it, but spitting far more out onto his chin, where he patted it happily around on his cheeks, making a mess. Ta couldn't help smiling. Ah, baby life. He watched in bemused fascination as Aya, with motherly patience, scooped a chunk up and reinserted it back into Shulgi's mouth.

"What tribe is she, I wonder?" Aya mused.

"Long-range nomad. Mari region, maybe." Ut walked up with the pack on his shoulders, already stuffed with all the food it could hold. "It's her facial structure. Thinner, narrower than most Mesopotamians."

"How do you know?" Ta asked. He'd never met anyone outside his tribe besides these two.

Ut adopted a superior tone. "The legends. Didn't you listen to your tribe's storyteller?"

Aya peered at the girl warily. "Nomad! Ah, she's not safe, then."

Ta squatted on his haunches, considering. He knew the reputation of long-range nomads. The stories said they were thieves, disease-carriers, possessed by dark spirits, half-rats. Yet was it so? The girl's face was lovely in the starlight. She looked healthy, *normal,* unlike the rumors. His uncertainty deepened. I'm a thief myself, he thought. Have I a right to dismiss anyone?

Ut studied her. "Huh. She's pretty, for all her nomad-ness. Shall we recruit her?"

Ta looked up sharply, his jealousy automatic. It surprised him, yet he couldn't keep it down.

"Yes, I say we recruit her," Ut mused, answering himself. "Our tribe must grow."

Ta gulped. Ut was tall and handsome. Any girl would welcome his interest.

He clenched his teeth to control himself. Think of the girl, not yourself, fool. *Do what you admire.* It'll be good for her to join this tribe. Who cares if she prefers Ut? She was never yours.

Ut's voice took on a hungry edge. "I don't believe the nomad rumors anyway. Here, I'll go invite her to join."

"Excuse me," Aya said coldly. "Isn't this a group decision?"

Ut looked surprised. "Don't you want a female companion?"

"Disease is nothing to trifle with." Aya lifted her hand. "I say leave her." She looked at Ta expectantly, as if sure he'd follow her lead. "Ta?"

Ta said nothing. Disease was serious. The Great Plague had left a terrible impression on him. He'd never forgotten the stench of oozing blisters, and the pile of corpses outside the cave—his parents among them. Disease was impersonal and ruthless. Then again, who said nomads were diseased? Such ideas had come from the storyteller, who mimicked the propaganda of the chief. Neither was a reputable source. Ta was beginning to think they'd lied about everything. Even the *Enūma Eliš* might be tainted by their meddling.

Ta turned to Aya.

"Both our chiefs lied," he pointed out. "They said the Euphrates was free to settle. We *know* that's untrue, now. They could've lied about nomads, too." He pointed his stump at the horizon. "You said yourself they might've scared us just to keep us dependent on them. Maybe we should give this girl a chance."

Aya spoke impatiently. "Has she talked yet?"

Ta shook his head. "She might not know our tongue."

Ut was amused. "Maybe in the flood a log hit her skull and made her mute."

"Maybe a disease rotted her brain," Aya said harshly. "Maybe she's half-rat."

"I hope not. We need information." Ut stepped forward and waved. "Ho, girl. Over here."

The girl froze and looked up with the crab clutched in her hands.

Ut spoke slowly, as if to an idiot. "Us, Akkadian. You, who?"

The girl's posture remained tense, like a rabbit ready to flee a fox. She said nothing.

Ut laughed. "Well, she's not ugly. That's enough for me. A woman doesn't need to talk."

Aya fed Shulgi another finger of mash. "It's not worth risking disease. I still say no."

Ta prepared for battle. "I vote yes."

"Ta!" Aya cried as if betrayed.

"It's how I see it."

"I won't allow it," Aya said. "I have a child to think of."

Ut laughed and rubbed his hands together. "Hoho. Her voting system turns against her. See, Ta? She's not so pleased with it now."

"You've both gone mad," Aya snapped. "I tell you, I won't have her. Use your head, Ut. Stop being so woman-hungry."

"You're breaking the vote, Aya." Ut's lip curled. "Obey your own system. It's two-to-one."

"It's you, breaking common sense," Aya said. "This is unsafe. I don't have to listen to *you*."

A gleam came into Ut's eye. "Ahh," he said quietly. "Admit it. The vote only matters when it favors *you*."

"Don't be silly," Aya snapped.

"Oh, I'm serious. Know what I think? You don't care about the vote. You just want to control me."

"Friends, please." Ta glanced at the girl, alarmed. She was still watching them, taking everything in. "You'll scare her off," he whispered.

Ut seemed not to hear. Something had been building in him all day. "I've had enough of this voting stunt," he snapped. "The world's too dangerous to let just anyone decide our fate. From now on, we do the smart thing. Every time. Voting is over."

"The smart thing? You mean what *you* think is the smart thing," Aya said.

"In this case, yes."

"You're making yourself chief, then! Admit it."

"Call it what you like. I'll do what I must to keep this tribe alive."

"How noble!"

"That's right. No more *voting*. Or burning our food to *baals*, either. And Ta, no more diving into rivers after you're ordered not to." Ut stamped his foot, splashing mud. "In a word, no more stupidity."

"You plotted this from the beginning!" Aya cried. "You're power-mad, like our chief."

Ut's fist flew up as if he meant to hit her. "Never, woman," he snarled, "compare me to that man. What he did to me . . ." His face contorted. He was really going to strike. Aya gasped and hunched down, covering Shulgi.

"Go on. Do it. Show who you really are!"

But at the last second, Ut turned and shoved Ta instead, knocking him flat on his back.

"Ut!" Aya cried in surprise.

Ta slapped into the mud, stunned. The blow was totally unexpected. It hurt only a little, but he was so astonished, he could only look up in bewilderment as Ut planted his sandal firmly on Ta's chest.

"Ut, you fool! What are you doing?" Aya cried. "Get off him."

"I prefer not to hit women," Ut said. "It degrades a man. But I hate disobedience even more. Tonight, Ta broke an order. There must be consequences. Or none of us will survive."

Aya stood up and backed away. "I saw this coming. I predicted it."

"Order," Ut said. "That is what we need. We tried things your way, Aya, and even *you* couldn't follow the rules. Now we try it my way. And we *will* try." He looked at her coldly. "Or I'll leave."

"I knew it," Aya whispered. "Selfish. Prideful. Ambitious."

"Do you want me along or not?"

Aya's mouth snapped shut.

"That's right."

Ut looked down at Ta. "As for you, brother, you have a choice. Accept my leadership and whatever punishment I choose. Or I go."

"Beast," Aya breathed. But she didn't move, or speak again.

Ut bent lower over Ta. "Come, runt. I'm not angry at you so much. Just give in, eh?" He waved his hands generously and lessened the pressure of his sandal on Ta's chest. "This is for your own good. I just want to lead us to safety. You'll thank me later."

Ta's mind was swimming. He didn't know what to say. At the delay, Ut pushed his foot down harder, grinding his sandal into Ta's heart. And the girl was watching.

Shame filled Ta. It was just like back in Akkad, when bigger boys pushed the "cripple" around to show off and impress females. Ta shut his eyes.

Do what you admire. Care for your tribe.

What was that, here?

His gut twisted. Part of him wanted to resist Ut, throw his weight to one side, pull Ut over. But in the end, Ut would win, and it would only further divide their tribe and scare the new girl. Ta sagged. The choice was clear. For the good of everyone, he should get this over with as fast as possible. Let tempers calm. Later they could fix things.

"I'll take the punishment," he said quietly.

"Good fellow."

Ut looked almost relieved as he took his foot away. He didn't enjoy violence, Ta thought. The hairy fellow just wanted power. And he was willing to do ugly things to get it.

In that sense, Ta thought dryly, Ut *was* chief-like.

Shaking, he rose and brushed off his legs. Mud fell from his back. Aya hurried forward, holding Shulgi at her shoulder.

"Brother, are you hurt? Can I do anything?"

Ta waved her off. "I'm all right."

He couldn't bear to look at the new girl as he staggered to the river to wash. The shame burned in his blood like poison. You can travel across the world, make all the rules you want, he thought sadly. But in the end, you're just a cripple. And no woman will ever be attracted to that.

14

After that, Ta knew the girl wouldn't join. Indeed, when Ut beckoned her, inviting her into the desert in gentle tones, she retreated to the waterline, her legs tensed to flee.

"You scared her," Aya said in a satisfied voice. "Well done, Ut."

"Let her stay here, then," Ut said angrily. "We can't help her if she won't let us."

Yet it was not over. For once they marched into the starlit desert, Aya gave a soft cry, and Ta turned to see the girl on their tracks.

She was following quietly, holding up the ragged hem of her tunic, padding barefoot over the damp ground. When she saw them staring, she stopped and waited. But she did not run away. Ta realized she meant to shadow them at a safe distance.

Aya laughed. "She *must be* diseased, to follow us after that display."

"On the contrary, she sees strong leadership and she likes it," Ut said. "Smart girl."

But Ta was uneasy. If Ut's violence hadn't frightened her off, the girl might know of something worse back on the river. Maybe they should be worried about it, too.

"Ey, boys, stop staring," Aya said. "She's not a bowl of soup to drink up."

So they marched on, Ut whistling merrily, the girl trailing a hundred paces behind. Ta's heart lifted. A new recruit! Now they were four. Maybe this tribe had a chance after all.

After a long hike, they made it far enough into the waste to feel safe from the locals. There, with a little scouting, Ut found a dry wash to camp in, with high dirt walls to conceal their firelight from the river. They climbed down into it, and began preserving their food.

The mood rose, then. The haul was truly magnificent, and Aya began to sing with pleasure as she pulled items from the pack and arrayed them neatly side by side to prepare. They'd gathered enough to feed them for a month, and every piece would be used. There were otter bladders to make water bags from. Intestines, to dry into tying cords. Turtle shells to carve into bowls, or boil into precious gelatins and medicines. The bones, of course, could be whittled into buttons, fishhooks, sewing needles, game-call whistles, jewelry, and every other sort of tool. But they had to be preserved quickly, else they would rot and force them back to the deadly river. So they worked fast, and soon had six fires going. They set up a tripod of thornbush sticks above each blaze. And while the fires snapped and popped, they cleaned the carcasses with their stone knives, cut the meat and fish into strips, and hung the strips on the tripod poles to cure in the smoke. Even the girl helped, obeying Aya's stern hand signals swiftly, as if to mollify them for her presence. And when it was done, Ut and Aya spread their sleeping blankets along the base of the wash wall, and Aya patted down the empty pack, creating a hide nest for the girl to curl up on like a forest cat, to sleep on instead of wet gravel.

"But not you." Ut pointed at Ta. "You've still got your punishment to fulfill."

"I do?"

"Yes. You must stay up all night and watch the fires in case of foxes. And keep food from falling into the coals. It's a big responsibility, runt."

“All right,” Ta said dutifully.

“Good man.” Ut smiled. “Do this, and by sunrise you’ll be forgiven.”

Aya sighed. “Haven’t you done enough to him tonight, Ut?”

“Someone’s got to do it. Do you want to?” Ut smirked and waited. Aya said nothing. “Right. Didn’t think so.”

Ta sat down obediently. “I’m not tired.”

“Just remember to put the fires out before morning,” Ut warned. “Otherwise, the smoke will hang in the air, and the whole river will see it and know someone’s here.”

“Yes, Ta, that’s important,” Aya agreed. “Got it?”

“Got it,” Ta said.

Ut nodded. “See Aya? Learn from Ta. This is how to take a punishment.”

Then he lay on his blanket, turned his powerful back to them, and was soon asleep.

Aya and the new girl did the same. However, as the girl curled up in her cat’s nest, she sent Ta a probing look. Was there sympathy in it?

Before he could be sure, she also shut her eyes and began to snore. Ta was left alone by the wash wall, wondering what she’d meant.

The six fires crackled. Ta hugged himself. He felt a little cool in his hide loincloth now that he’d stopped moving. Other feelings were in him, too. Happiness, to see the girl there. Pride from the river rescue. And yes, pain from Ut’s sandal on his chest.

It was the old pain from Akkad, really. For years, people had mocked his stump. They pointed out how ugly and lumpy with gristle it was. They shouted, “Food thief!” when he walked by. In his cave corner under the stalactites, he grew used to eating alone, picking seeds from his half-empty bowl, sneaking glances at the happy blankets where families ate meat and berries. It wasn’t just their mockery that hurt. The ache of the stump—the ghostlike flicker of fingers no longer there—tormented him unpredictably, at inconvenient times. It was a permanent reminder of the barrier between himself and the rest of humanity.

You could make Ut feel that, a voice whispered. *Do it as he sleeps. That would be POWER. You could find a rock. Lift it. Smash his heel. Crush it to pulp. Make him a cripple, like you. Oh, he wouldn't be so arrogant, then.*

Ta glanced at Ut's blanket. Was it possible? Could he do such a thing? Part of him wanted to.

Then he remembered his code. *Do what you admire. Care for your tribe.* He let the anger go and hung his head. The day had been too overwhelming. He could sort through his feelings about Ut later. Besides, the heavy meal was hitting him hard. His eyes felt heavy. Exhaustion was stealing over him muscle by muscle, massaging his mind with soft, purple fingers.

Without realizing it, Ta slumped over, lay his cheek on the sand, and sank into oblivion.

15

It was morning when Ta woke.

He sat up stiffly. Sunlight was blasting into his eyes. After lying on pebbles and sticks all night, he felt terribly sore, and his head ached. Rubbing his face, he looked around—then leapt to his feet, his heart pounding.

The smoke!

The six tripods were still releasing white tendrils from the coals, allowing them to rise and mingle into a cloud that drifted slowly east on the breeze. Ta grabbed his stump in a panic. Just as Ut had warned, the entire Euphrates would see the smoke in the daylight and know someone was here.

Mistakes, Ta thought wretchedly. Back to them already, eh, fool?

Cursing under his breath, he rushed around kicking dirt on the coals. The fires died with angry hisses, and the smoke remnants drifted up and floated away.

Relieved, Ta sat in the shade of the wash wall to collect his thoughts. What did I expect? I invented two new rules, but I can't change just by *deciding* it, he thought.

No, to create a *new Ta,* he would need practice.

The realization calmed him. He was "in process," like a green fruit, not yet ripe. He must be patient with himself. He probably needed a mentor who could show him his weaknesses and light a new path. Where to find one, he didn't know. But he'd start looking.

His current mistake wasn't so bad, either. His friends were still sleeping in the shade of the wash wall, the food remained safe, and the river locals were most likely too preoccupied with repairing their camps after the storm to care about a bit of smoke in the waste. Thank the gods! This would serve simply as another lesson. Ta was determined, but not yet capable. Years wasted soaking in bitterness had left him unskilled. He must now develop skills, fast. Otherwise, he'd make a worse mistake, soon. One he couldn't correct.

Before long, the others awoke and ate. Then they broke camp and marched southeast, moving parallel to the river.

It was a great thing to be full, and the mood felt happier than it had in ages, despite what Ut had done the night before. The sky was as blue as a spring lake, and many colorful birds bathed in the puddles left over from the storm, singing and fluttering their wings, throwing off jewel-blue drops. The girl was there, too, traipsing along behind the group at her usual safe distance, wearing the fresh hide rags Aya had bound her feet in to protect them from the earth's rising heat. Simply seeing her made Ta happy, he wasn't sure why, and impulsively he waved his stump at her. To his delight, she gave a small smile and nodded back, and his heart glowed. A new friend.

Yes, it was a good morning. Even Ut's swelling pride could not spoil it.

"Ho, runt, go fetch me those yellow flowers." Ut pointed at a thornbush up ahead. "I'd like to chew on 'em as I walk. Refreshing, eh?"

Aya scowled. "Fetch them yourself, Ut. The runt stayed up all night watching the fires." She added sarcastically, "But, oh. Please forgive me. Should I address you as 'chief?'"

"Perhaps you should." Ut gave her a gleeful look.

"Ha! So you admit it."

"Why not?" Ut grinned. "Chief Ut. It sounds good, eh?" He pulled a toasted frog leg from his backpack, bit off a webbed foot, and grunted appreciatively. "But don't worry, I'm not a vengeful leader. Ta did well and he's forgiven. Our tribe is at peace. Right?"

Ta sighed. This wasn't worth a fight.

"I'll get 'em," he said, marching off to the flowers.

"See, Aya?" Ut gloated. "Following orders isn't so bad."

"I'd sooner follow a buzzard," Aya said.

Ut chuckled. "Give it time. Once I lead us to the river, you'll sing a different tune."

At noon, a canyon appeared. It wove south in parallel to the distant river, looking much like a tiny red river itself. In fact, Ta wondered if it might have been a true riverbed once, drying out over time. But it was quite small, just a stone's throw across. And it was no deeper than the height of an oak tree. Curious, the group stopped at the edge of it and looked down at the gravel bottom. Perhaps the new feature held some benefit.

Ut pointed down. "There's shade at the bottom, there. A nice strip of it. Maybe we could walk in it and be cooler. It's heading our direction, more or less."

"But once we get down, how do we get out again?" Aya asked. "We might get trapped."

Ut sighed. "Oh, woman. Why must you always—"

Then he froze. "Look out!" He threw himself to the ground and pointed into the canyon. "A giant!"

A giant? Ta thought. What in the name of the gods?

Ut's urgency scared them all, and they flopped to their bellies and looked where he pointed. Sure enough, across the gap, Ta saw it: a large man climbing the canyon wall. A giant, indeed!

Ta had never seen such a man. Though not quite a giant, he was certainly bigger than any human Ta knew—much bigger than his ex-chief. The giant's tiny loincloth did little to hide his bare back and legs, which bulged with rock-like muscles. Black hair fell over his shoulders, rippling like a stallion's mane. His hands were enormous, too, like bear paws.

"He's magnificent," Aya murmured.

"I bet he steals. Or eats other humans," Ut said sourly. "You don't get that big playing fair."

"What's he doing?" Aya asked.

No one answered at first. It was Ta who figured it out.

"I think he's hungry. Look, he's climbing toward that nest."

He pointed with his stump. Near the top of the canyon wall, a dead branch projected from the cliff face, its gnarled wooden fingers supporting a hawk's nest. Inside the nest were two red-speckled eggs, good eating.

"He's risking quite a fall for two eggs," Aya observed.

"He might be starving." Alongside his fear, Ta felt pity for the man. He knew what such hunger felt like.

Ut shot a nervous glance at Aya's chest-pouch. "How's Shulgi? If he cries and draws that monster up here . . ."

Aya hugged the baby close. "He just fed. He's dozing."

"Well, don't shake him too much."

"I'll care for my baby. You care for yourself."

The giant stopped climbing. He seemed to be trapped three-quarters of the way up. Ta watched him scan the final distance. One patch of smooth wall was all that separated him from the nest. The patch offered no clear handholds, however. If the giant hung there too long, his arms and legs would wear out. Indeed, his muscles were already twitching.

He *is* starving, Ta thought with pity.

Then, suddenly, he felt a bolt of excitement. He'd just had another idea.

"Let's recruit him," he whispered.

Ut recoiled. "Are you mad, runt? He'd rip our heads off."

Aya nodded. "Ut's right this time. We better leave before he sees us."

Ta kept silent. He saw things differently. This was the perfect recruitment opportunity. For one thing, the giant looked lost and in need of friends. For another, he needed food. And for once, Ta's tribe had food to offer him. All the giant could eat.

And what an asset he would be, Ta thought, his excitement growing. Why, the giant could be the foundation of their tribe. At present, Ta's group wasn't very attractive to join, being so weak and small. But with a giant along . . . who *wouldn't* want to fight beside such a fellow?

"We've got to try," Ta whispered. "He could deliver us a whole army."

"An army," Ut mocked. "Listen to him, the runt thinks he's a strategist now. Well, strategize this, runt. Hush up quick, or your chief will teach you another lesson."

"But Ut," Aya interjected, "you did say we need recruits. Fifty. Why not him, to start?"

"I don't have to debate," Ut retorted. "I'm chief and you two are nothing. Let's go."

"Wait," Aya interrupted. "Look, he's going to jump!"

The giant gave a loud roar and launched himself up the wall. His hand reached up, grasping for a rock knob that jutted above the sheer patch. For a moment, he seemed to float, suspended between life and death. If he missed the grab, he'd plummet to his death.

The Akkadians stared, mesmerized. Then, as if by magic, the man's fingers slammed onto the knob, making a red puff of dust. He had it!

One-armed, he pulled himself the rest of the way up and stabbed his feet into a crevice beneath the nest to secure his position. Everyone murmured in admiration as he reached inside the nest to grab his first egg. His big hand trembled as he cracked the egg on the canyon wall, slurped the yellow insides, then let the shell bits flutter to the canyon bed below. Ta was in awe. The man certainly deserved his breakfast. And it confirmed Ta's opinion.

"This is a once-in-a-lifetime recruit," he said with conviction. "If we don't try for him, we'll regret it forever."

"Did you not hear me?" Ut raised his fist threateningly. "Have you forgotten last night?"

"It's risky. You're right," Ta conceded. "So let's lessen the risk." He reached into Ut's pack and pulled out a blackened fish. "Hide safe up here. I'll go down alone and test him with this."

"A test," Ut said derisively.

"Yes, a test. I'll offer him just half this fish. If he takes it politely, and doesn't snatch the whole thing from me, as hungry as he is, it'll teach us something of his character."

"Or he'll eat your head," Ut said.

But Ta felt inspired. He himself had failed a hunger test just days ago, a good indicator of his character at the time. A night later, a second hunger test had come, but thanks to Shulgi, Ta had passed, revealing new growth. A hunger test was as good as any.

"Think of it this way," Ta said. "What's more dangerous? To start recruiting now? Or to continue marching day after day, with no warriors to protect us?"

"He's right," Aya said, also with growing excitement. "There'll always be *some* risk. So we might as well start."

Ut's patience was at an end. "We leave now," he said in a dangerous voice. "Last chance."

But something in his voice was strange. Ta frowned. Ut wasn't thinking of the tribe at all . . . but of his newfound power. That was it! Ut wanted to stay chief, two women all to himself. If the giant joined, that would change.

The selfishness of it filled Ta with fury. Moreover, it was stupid. Ut needed warriors to protect him as much as they all did.

Jumping to his feet, Ta waved the fish over the canyon.

"Ho, friend!" he shouted. "Up here."

"Runt," Ut hissed, grabbing at Ta's leg. "You're killing us."

But Ta danced aside and kept waving the fish. "Ho, friend! Ho!"

He hoped he wasn't making a terrible mistake.

16

Across the canyon, the giant turned and looked at Ta. Their eyes connected for what seemed like an eternity.

Then the giant let go and dropped through the air.

"He's fallen," Aya burst out.

"No," Ut said. "He's coming for us."

Halfway down the canyon wall, the giant's hands slammed onto a handhold. He caught himself and resumed skittering down, as fast as a lizard. It was an incredible athletic feat, but Ta didn't feel good about it anymore.

"Easy, friend. Don't hurt yourself," he cried. "I just want to talk."

But the giant kept going.

Three-quarters down, he let go again and plummeted the rest of the way to the canyon floor. He landed on all fours in a burst of red powder. Without hesitating, he reached behind a boulder, snatched out a spear and a pair of sandals, then sprinted toward the nearest bend. In an instant, he vanished around the rocky curve, leaving Ta reeling. It had been so fast.

"You've ruined us," Ut said, crawling back from the ledge.

"At least he can't get up here," Ta said.

"Oh, but he can." Ut pointed down the canyon rim.

And now Ta saw. Around the bend in the canyon, the rim looked indented. Part of the wall may have collapsed there, leaving a rubble slope. If indeed there was a slope there, the giant could run up it easily, without having to scale the canyon wall. Ta's skin turned cold. Why didn't I notice that? he thought in anguish. Reckless fool. He'd seized leadership, but his inexperience had plunged them into peril.

"He'll slay us now. It's over," Ut said dully.

"Find some courage, man," Aya said. "You're chief. Defend us like one."

"Oh, now you want me to be chief?" Ut exploded.

Ta stepped between them. This was no time for bickering.

"The plan can still work. He hasn't seen you, yet. Hide, and I'll test him. If it goes wrong, you can still get away."

"No, Ta. Don't go." Aya made a face at him. *I need you. I can't handle Ut alone.*

But behind her, the nomad girl was watching Ta intently. To his surprise, there was encouragement in her beautiful eyes, approval. *Go do this.* He felt a flicker of hope.

"I started this," he said. "I'll fix it. Goodbye for now."

And he raced off.

"Food thief," Ut snarled after him. "If he doesn't kill you, I will."

When Ta turned the bend, he found just what he'd feared. Part of the wall had collapsed, creating a slope of fallen rocks to the canyon floor. The giant was already halfway up it, bounding from boulder to boulder like a mountain goat without a trace of the weakness he'd shown before. Ta fell back, shaking. Thankfully, a glance over his shoulder revealed that his companions had scrambled behind a screen of bushes to hide. If they kept quiet, perhaps they could escape notice. Unless the giant tortured Ta for information.

Oh El, if you are still here, make me stronger than I am. I can't withstand torture!

A roar burst from the canyon as the giant leapt from the slope in a blur of muscle and whipping black hair. He landed in a cat's crouch paces away and lifted his spear to throw, the stone spearhead aimed directly at Ta's chest. Ta's mind went blank.

"SPEAK," a deep voice boomed. "What do you want?"

"I . . . I mean no harm," Ta squeaked.

"On the ground. Or I strike!"

Ta gulped. The giant spoke the common tongue, at least. He couldn't be a total savage.

"All right, easy."

Ta looked for a spot to lie down. The ground was so hot, it couldn't be just anywhere. He identified a shallow puddle that had not yet steamed away. He stepped into it and lay flat in the warm water, still holding the fish aloft to show his intentions.

"I just want to talk." He waggled the fish. "See? A gift."

The giant circled him cautiously, spear ready. His eyes took in the fish, then flicked to the desert for danger. He didn't answer. Ta watched every muscle twitch, hoping for clues.

The giant was not Akkadian, that much was clear. He had a broad, sunburned face with a jaw more square than any Ta had ever seen. His head was like a tree stump. He was perhaps thirty-five years old. He had long black hair, and a ragged beard that tumbled over his chest. The muscles in his shoulders were boulder-like. Veins in the thick forearms. Red, rugged hands. Tree-trunk legs. A warrior, indeed!

Yet already Ta was seeing beyond the muscles of the man. The giant looked weary from travel. Scorched. Dust-caked. His lips were as cracked as Ta's. Most of all, beneath the stony shelf of his forehead, his eyes were ready to fight, unafraid of death. Yet they seemed intelligent, curious. This was a human being, after all.

"What do you want?" the giant growled. "Where are your people?"

"I want to talk," Ta repeated.

"Talk." The giant laughed. "Out here, no one talks. Just this." He stabbed his spear at the air.

Ta grew bolder. "I'd like to sit up. May I?" He lifted the fish. "It's well-seasoned."

The giant glared at the fish. "Poisoned, I expect."

"No. I promise." Instinctively, Ta lowered the fish and bit off a small chunk and swallowed. "There," he said, spitting out a fish bone. "Now may I sit up?"

The giant stopped circling and squatted by his face, studying him. He seemed calmer.

"Any tattoos?" he demanded suddenly.

"Tattoos?" Ta was bewildered by the question. "No-o. No tattoos."

"You don't belong to Magog, do you?"

"Magog?" Ta frowned. "Who's that?"

"Huh." Another tense moment passed as the giant studied him.

"Your hand," he said sharply, nodding at Ta's stump. "Who cut it off? Was it Gog?"

"Gog?" Ta was lost.

"Quick. Don't lie."

"It was an accident. Rocks fell on my hand and crushed it . . ." Ta stopped. Somehow, he felt the giant would know it was a lie. He bowed, cheeks burning, and corrected himself.

"I'm sorry. I don't know why I lied just now. I'm a thief. I stole food. Long ago, in Akkad. The chief cut off my hand."

The giant looked away, considering. "So," he murmured. "A food thief. But an honest one."

At length, his shoulders relaxed, and he walked to a flat rock nearby and sat. With a gesture of his spear, he invited Ta to sit on a nearby rock, too.

"You're not Magog," he said crisply. "So, sit."

Ta dared to breathe again. It seemed he'd passed a critical test. Rising, he used his stump to brush damp sand off his chest. Then he walked to the rock, trying not to tremble too badly.

"Talk," the giant said. "That's what you want, isn't it?"

Ta nodded. He'd asked for this. So he gathered his breath, and talked.

A few hundred paces away, Ki lay behind a bush and watched.

Ta and the giant were sitting on stones now, gesturing, moving their hands. That was good. Their words were too faint to hear, but now and again the tone of their voices drifted to her like music. It was calm, no shouting. She breathed easier.

Ta, the one who'd saved her . . . he would be all right.

"What's happening? I'm afraid to look," Aya whispered.

"Why, they're just sitting on rocks, talking," Ut said in astonishment.

"That's good, isn't it?"

"Who knows?" Ut said. "Just keep that baby quiet, eh?" Baby Shulgi had begun to whimper, held too tightly in his mother's arms.

"Mind yourself," Aya said. She rocked her boy. "Shh, baby. All is well."

Ki kept watching through the spiny cover of the bush. Unlike the others, she'd expected this gamble to work. Even from here it was apparent—thanks to the giant's stump-shaped head and his size—that he was an Elamite. From her nomadic travels, she knew Elamites were a noble people. They were fearsome if crossed, but they had a warrior code of honor, which included showing hospitality to wanderers. Unlike Mesopotamians, Elamites never attacked long-range nomads without cause. Rather, they'd conference first to see if peace was possible, then exchange goods and news. Ki's nomadic tribe had encountered several Elamite scouts during its travels. They were always reasonable. Meeting one was a good omen.

Nonetheless, Ta had not known any of that. He'd seen a hard risk, calculated, and still gone.

Her admiration for him grew.

"What are they saying?" Aya asked.

"How should I know?" Ut said.

"Should we go over there?"

"Are you mad? We should flee."

"Abandon Ta? You traitor."

"It was only an idea," Ut said sullenly.

Ki kept watching Ta.

Until his appearance, her escape had been awful. During the last few days and nights, Magog's smoke signals had alerted the entire area, and time and again, as she rounded a river bend on her raft, fleets of grass boats had burst from the shore to catch her, shattering the air with bull horn blasts, war shrieks, and beating drums. Only her powerful wind device kept her free. That, and fashioning a second dart-thrower—which unfortunately she'd lost during the storm. But even her devices couldn't free her from the torment in her heart. *Where am I going? Why?* At least in Magog's pen, the voices of her people through the bars, and the question of how to escape Gog, had distracted her. Once on the river, however, with nothing but a wet raft to cling to and the vast unknown of Mesopotamia ahead, the emptiness bludgeoned her. *What do I do now?*

Then the storm came . . . and Ta.

She was asleep when the rain hit. Exhausted, she'd accidentally dozed off, drifting on the raft. The storm caught her unawares. A *crack* sounded, and opening her eyes, she found the world flashing and exploding above her. Before she could react, her wind-catcher snapped off the raft and flipped away on a gust, flying and spinning up, like a great black bird reclaimed by the gods, a thing too magic for this earth. It was the sign of her death and she knew it. Waves tossed her raft up and down. The world was spinning. The banks were bone-white in the lightning bursts. Her raft shattered against a palm tree, and she grabbed it but felt herself sliding lower down its trunk, the waters battering her. She felt almost relieved. She believed in nothing anymore. Not in her family's spirits surviving in *Kur*. Not in any god. Certainly not in the goddess Inanna, whose clay idol Magog had shattered. Yet out of sheer habit, Ki forced a prayer. *If there is any purpose for me in this life . . . or a god who cares for me . . . come now. I am still here. I will listen.*

And Ta came.

Not a cripple, as the others saw him, but as a force, something elemental. First as a word: "Here!" Then as a rope leaping to her out of the howling void. Despite her fear, Ki was tempted to reject the rope and slide off the tree into the black waters. But something about his blazing eyes reminded her of Asha, and she seized the rope and pulled herself in. She had called, and a god had answered: she felt an obligation. And Ta was there. His body joined with hers and he leapt off the tree, holding the rope, the torrent tumbling them over and over. The bank received them. Ever since, she'd been bound to him by a feeling she didn't understand.

The mark of a god was upon him, Ki thought. His companions clearly did not see it. But Ki did. It had been in him last night as Ut stepped on his chest and yelled at him—and Ta took it all, to keep peace. He watched the fires, fetched a yellow flower, suffered silently to keep them together. And finally took this risk, to recruit a giant. Ta embodied her father's code better than Ki ever had. *Do you love yourself more, or your people?* Ta loved his people.

He was sent to me, she thought again.

Why, she did not know. But she had something to cling to, now. Meaning lived in him. She needed to find out what it was.

"What's he doing now?" Ut whispered. "The fool . . . he's turning. Looking at us! He'll give us away!"

Aya gasped. "He's waving."

"Ah, the giant's looking too. What's happening?"

Indeed, Ta was waving his stump, and his voice was cheerful as he called faintly across the waste. "It's all right. He's on our side. Come see."

Aya looked at Ut in astonishment. "Well?"

Ut was tearing at his beard. "It's a trap. He'll eat us all."

Aya stood. "I think you're wrong, brother." And she went, clutching her baby tightly.

Ki also rose and followed.

17

Ta couldn't believe it. His gamble seemed to be paying off. He tried not to gloat as the group walked over and hesitantly sat in a semicircle around the giant. Instead, he busied himself playing the host, tenting two blankets across a nearby bush to cast a cooling rectangle of shade, then handing out fish for lunch.

"Pleased with yourself, aren't you?" Ut said as he received his fish.

"Shh, Ut," Aya whispered. "Try not to embarrass us, will you?"

It was like watching a beast eat up close. The giant's square brown teeth easily ripped off the fish's head. Scales, fins, and bones flecked the air as he chewed. The great knob in his throat bobbed up and down like a living creature. Yet the Elamite had manners, too, Ta noticed. After gulping the tail, the giant burped politely, as was proper, to show his appreciation for the meal.

"Here's another," Ta said quickly, pulling a second fish from the pack.

Ut glared, so Ta added, "The Elamites promised to tell us what he knows of the region."

"He better know a lot," Ut said. "Our food will be gone by nightfall, at this rate."

Aya shook out her long hair. "Nonsense. We've plenty to spare. Here, friend." She handed their guest the water bag. "Does the food taste all right? It's my seasoning, you know."

The giant accepted the bag with a bow. "It's remarkable, sister. Thorn flower juice, yes? And . . ." He pursed his lips, testing the flavors. "And redroot sap?"

Aya beamed, entranced. "Halfway there, stranger. It's my secret recipe—well, my mother's."

The giant grunted in respect. "Takes a talented cook to make redroot behave."

Aya blushed. "This is nothing. Let me forage in a forest, sometime. You'll taste marvels."

"If it's half as good as this, it'd be worth traveling for," the giant said.

Ta watched admiringly as the giant ripped into more fish. His big hands looked capable of crushing stones into powder, and cracking necks. Yet he was polite, deferential in his manners. Such a recruit would really boost their tribe. Ta scooted closer to hear every word.

"Where are you from, stranger?" Aya asked. "I don't mean to pry, but you're the second wanderer we've met out here after Ta."

"I hail from Elam," the giant said. "I am Rogg, son of Rogg. Honored to meet you."

"Pleased to meet you," Aya said. "We're Akkadians. I suppose Ta told you that?"

"He did," Rogg said. "He claims you're looking for a new home."

"We are. I'm afraid we've been walking so long, my feet are about to fall off. Do you know where we might settle?"

Rogg shook his head. "I'm a stranger here, too, sister. I know the river's crowded, but little more."

"Then what's this deal for?" Ut exploded, throwing his hands up.

Rogg held out his fish. "Take it back if you wish. But you're wasting a good deal."

"Keep eating!" Aya and Ta said together.

"Thank you. Then let me start at the beginning. It will make more sense."

Rogg chomped the final fish, then wiped his greasy fingers on his loincloth, sat back and began.

"Magog." He looked around. "Know of them?"

The Akkadians shook their heads.

"Good. I hope you never do."

Rogg's face darkened. "If you don't know, Elam is far to the east of here. A beautiful country, with many fine tribes. Susa and Awan. Bashim, Tash, and Der. And my village, Haz. It was a little one, just sixty people in all. But we were a good people, if I may say so myself. Upright and brave. Me, I had a mate and four younglings. I was happy in life. Happy, as I shall not be again."

"What happened?" Aya asked timidly.

"Magog."

As Rogg spoke the name, Ta noticed the new girl stiffen. She understood far more than she let on, he thought.

Aya clutched Shulgi tighter, her eyes fixed on Rogg. "Your family . . . did evil befall them? If it pains you, Rogg, you need not speak of it."

"The story is ugly, but it must be told. Else it will happen again." Rogg squinted into the distance.

"One day can change your life. My day was a year ago. One evening, after a daylong hunt, I returned to my camp to find it in smoking ruins, everything destroyed. Huts burned. Food and tools stolen. But most of all, the bodies of my tribesmen lay about dead, bloody and cut up. The women and girls, before they died . . ." He glanced at Aya and Ki. "I will say no more."

"Savages," Aya said.

"Just so. I knew it was outsiders right away. There are no such barbarians in Elam." Rogg's brow knitted together. "I ran through the burned camp looking for my family. Alas, I found them in the ashes of our hut."

The group stared at him, stunned. Rogg's voice tightened. He spoke in a detached way, intentionally keeping the story flat, at a distance from himself.

"There is no need to tell you how I felt. I buried them in the traditional way. Then, as is customary in Elam, I swore revenge."

The group scooted closer like rapt children at a fireside tale. The new girl, Ta noticed, had gone as rigid as a tree, her ears straining to catch every word.

Rogg wiped his greasy lips with the back of his hand. "That night I tracked the war party east. Without much trouble, I found them. Magog is arrogant and rarely conceals their tracks. Besides, it was a large party, a hundred men, marching straight into Elam. For a few days I followed, keeping far enough back to avoid being seen."

"Quite the hero," Ut said sarcastically.

Everyone glared at him, but the giant didn't seem to care.

"After days of watching their activities, I determined they were scouting for some kind of invasion. They kept hitting our local tribes, raiding them, killing them, resupplying off local plunder. They were also making otter skin maps of our terrain."

"How did you learn all this?" Ut demanded. "I doubt Magog volunteered it freely."

"I captured a Magog flank scout. He told me what I needed."

The travelers looked at each other with frightened eyes. Had Rogg tortured out the man's secrets? What roughness!

Even so, a tribe needed rough men, Ta thought. It was a rough world.

Rogg went on. "After I learned these things, I knew something had to be done. I could not let Magog send for reinforcements. So I ran to the neighboring tribes to unite them. Thank the gods, they accepted my word. I am known in those parts."

"Of course," Ut snickered. But no one heeded him anymore.

"In three days, we gathered a force of two hundred warriors," Rogg said. "We marched on Magog near the plain of Susa, ambushed them, and slaughtered them to the last man. Magog's hundred now sleep in the Underworld, if indeed they sleep at all. We cut their bodies into pieces and scattered them to the four winds without burial. If you believe in such things, their *emittus* will suffer greatly."

The group nodded in awe. All except Ut, who laughed.

"Well done, Rogg. The gods must favor you. You saved all of Elam by yourself."

"Not all of Elam," Rogg said quietly. "I did not save my clan."

Ut hesitated, then recklessly spoke again. "But one thing I don't understand, giant. If you won such a victory, why leave Elam at all? Surely its grateful tribes offered you pelts, a hut, even a mate to start a new life with." Ut's eyes narrowed. "It's a shame to see such a hero reduced to climbing a desert canyon for eggs."

"Shut up, Ut," Aya said. But Rogg soothed her.

"It is right to test strangers, sister. I welcome his questions."

He looked at Ut frankly. "Let me tell you why I am here. I swore vengeance upon those one hundred warriors, yes." His voice hardened. "But to fulfill my oath, I must chop off the head of the serpent that ate my family, not just its tail. The warlord of Magog. A man named Gog. He lives in Mesopotamia, some days north of here. My oath requires *him.*"

"For a warrior, you're very philosophical," Ut said.

But even he did not dare push further, and he quieted, scratching his hairy chest anxiously.

Aya sent Ta a significant glance. *See how even Ut is tamed? Rogg balances our tribe.*

Ta nodded in agreement. If she could recruit the Elamite, she should do so, by all means.

"Well, how has the mission gone so far, Rogg? Are you almost finished?" Aya asked.

Rogg picked a few glittering fish scales from his beard and shook his head.

"As I said, Magog's camp is several days north of here. Rumors tell me I'm close. But whether it is two days away, or ten, I'm not sure. As for the mission itself . . . it will be hard."

Aya shot Ta a worried look. "So you mean you won't . . . you can't . . . keep going our way?"

Rogg smiled sadly. "I would love to eat more of this delicious fish, sister. But I'm afraid this is our last meal together. I must continue north. And you, if you are sensible, will head south, as far from Magog's camp as you can go."

"Oh." Aya's eyes deflated. "I'm sorry to hear that."

Ta slumped too. No recruit after all. It was a blow. He'd risked much to be rejected so fast.

"But listen carefully, now, for this is the part where I earn my meal." Rogg looked at Ta. "Magog's patrols range far. Even down here. Their prime purpose is to gather information, but they also love to capture wanderers and toy with them for diversion. So if they find you . . ." He shook his head. "Bad news."

Ta gulped. He was beginning to realize how lucky they'd been, meeting Rogg first. It could have been someone far worse.

"How do we recognize Magog?" he asked.

"Simple. Tattoos." Rogg pointed at his face, his arms. "Gog has a system. He tattoos all his men black, head to foot."

"Seems like a lot of work," Aya said. "And a lot of ink."

Rogg nodded. "He has two reasons. One, the tattoos give his men unity. He needs this, for he captures them from all clans, all regions, so to rule them, he must destroy their identity and remake them in his image. Tattoos are Magog's uniform. Second, the tattoos prevent desertion. A man tattooed this way is hated by all the world and will find no safe shelter anywhere. His tattoos bind him to Gog forever."

"Clever," Ta said.

"Gog is no fool," Rogg said. "In fact, from what I've heard, he's a genius. Even a sorcerer. Some say his tribe is the biggest in the world."

"How big?" Aya asked anxiously.

"A thousand warriors," Rogg answered. "The same number in slaves. In all, two thousand."

"TWO THOUSAND?" the Akkadians cried.

Rogg nodded. "He's discovered a way to feed them all. I don't know how, but I'll find out."

Ta looked north. His old tribe had been just eighty adults. Against Gog's army, they'd have no chance. Gog could show up on a whim and turn them all into slaves. Ta shivered. He'd never imagined such monsters prowled just over Akkad's horizon.

Aya, for her part, wasn't finished with Rogg.

"Such a large army, brother," she said gently. "Isn't it better to let them be? Magog may fall apart on its own, no?"

Rogg shook his head. "Gog is a great warlord. He is undefeated. His numbers only grow, never diminish. If something doesn't change, he will keep growing and killing." Rogg bowed his head. "No other father should feel what I did that day. I will stop him, if I can."

"You plan to defeat thousands," Ut sneered. "By yourself."

"I don't have to kill thousands. Just Gog. Without him, Magog will fall apart. No other man has ever kept such a force together."

The group meditated on that, overwhelmed.

Then Ta had a sudden thought.

"Rogg, listen. In Elam, you defeated Magog a different way. You united many tribes into a great alliance. Why not unite Mesopotamian tribes the same way? Defeat Gog together? Surely others hate him as you do?"

Rogg shot him a look of respect. "Spoken like a true chief, Ta. I'd do that if I could. But I am Elamite, unwelcome here. And Mesopotamia is more divided than Elam. Every chief wants to be a little Gog. No one cooperates."

Ta sensed the truth of that. Akkadian chiefs hated each other. They refused to unite even to repel Gutians. An existential threat like Magog might start them talking. But by the time the clans could agree to gather at a *shura*, a clan council, it would be too late.

Aya still wanted to recruit Rogg. Supporting Shulgi's pouch in one hand, she combed her dusty hair aside with the other and scooted closer to him. And she was beautiful, Ta thought. Many a man would be tempted to stay, if such a woman showed interest.

"Rogg," she said, "must you really throw your life away for vengeance? Why not honor your family another way? You could burn offerings for them. Or win glory for their name in other ways. Why a suicide mission?"

"I swore an oath," Rogg said.

"An oath . . ." Aya said vaguely.

"We are not so different, sister." Rogg nodded at Shulgi. "You have your purpose. I have mine."

The finality in his tone quieted Aya, and she fell back, meditative.

"I still say you've told us nothing useful." Ut eyed the food pack. "This is all general, not specific to *us*. Forgive me if I feel cheated, Rogg."

"You are right to expect more. And there *is* more." Rogg faced Ta. "A Magog patrol is nearby."

Ta nearly fell backward. "Near *us*?"

"He's just scaring us," Ut said.

"I wish I was," Rogg said. "But I've been tracking them the last three days. Fifteen men. They're close. Less than a day's journey away. If they see you, they'll capture you, and that would be bad indeed."

Everyone scanned the horizon. It looked as empty as ever, but their footprints, freshly stamped in the earth, led straight back to the campsite they'd abandoned. Back to where I put up the smoke, Ta realized with a start. Why, if Magog saw the smoke and investigated the camp . . . they could follow the tracks *here*.

He looked at Rogg frantically, hoping he could forestall him, but it was too late. Rogg was already pointing at the pack of smoked fish.

"You must not smoke by day anymore. It's like blood in the air. Predators will come."

"Eh?" Ut said. "We didn't do any such thing. We're not fools. We killed the fires before dawn. Unless . . ."

His eyes widened, then rolled toward Ta. "You?"

Ta turned red. "I fell asleep before morning," he confessed.

"Runt!" Ut shouted.

"But the smoke wasn't up long," Ta cried.

Rogg was shaking his head. "I'm afraid every tribe for leagues saw it." He pointed at the river. "And they've been up to something. They've all been smoke-signaling each other the last two days.

Sending up puffs, messages . . . They may be in alliance. May even serve Magog."

"Yes, we noticed that," Aya said quietly. "Could you read the messages, Rogg?"

"No, unfortunately. But something's afoot. Not a good time to draw notice." He eyed Ta.

Ut was still enraged by Ta's mistake. "You'll pay for this, runt," he snarled. "I'm realizing it now. You're not a blessing from the gods, you're a curse. Why didn't you tell us about the smoke?"

"I'm sorry, I . . . I . . ." Ta gripped his stump and twisted. *Rule one: Do what you admire.* He'd failed his own code. He shouldn't have kept this secret. He hung his head.

"I was afraid," he mumbled. "I accept punishment. Whatever you say."

"An apology won't save us if we end up on stone altars, sacrificed to Baal," Ut snapped.

"What do we do, Rogg?" Aya asked.

"What does a gazelle do when it smells a lion?" Rogg asked.

"Run," Aya whispered.

"That's right."

Rogg pointed over the horizon. "Luckily, I can offer one last bit of help. I've come from the south. There's a forest of thorn trees there, not too far ahead. You can make it by the end of the day. Magog hates tracking in hard terrain, so if you can get inside that forest, Magog may not wish to pursue you there. After all, you are nothing special to them, just some random Akkadians . . ." He glanced at the girl. "And a nomad."

The new girl kept very still.

Rogg turned to Ta. "And from now on . . ."

Ta nodded. *No more daytime smoke.*

After answering a few more questions, Rogg rose and bowed.

"Here we part ways, my friends. Thank you for the fish. I wish good fortune to you. If I could, I would tell you more, such as where to settle. But this is a strange region to me. I can only advise continuing south, where Magog's patrols are less frequent."

"Are you sure you must leave, Rogg?" Aya pleaded. "We'd love to have you."

"I'm sorry, sister. I enjoy your tribe's company. And your little one . . ." His eyes softened as he gazed at Shulgi's round head. "But to Elamites, oaths are like stone. I must go."

He reached out and patted Ta's arm. "Just one more thing. This afternoon, push yourselves faster than you're used to. A little discomfort now may make all the difference later."

"Thank you, Rogg. Truly." Ta bowed.

"My pleasure, little brother. And my respect. It took courage, approaching me. You're on a worthy path. I suppose you're the chief of this outfit?"

"Me?" Ta laughed. He looked at Ut uneasily. "No . . . no chiefs here. We vote on things."

"Vote?" Rogg arched an eyebrow.

"Exactly," Ut muttered. "That's the first thing we agree on, giant."

"Well, it's not the title that makes one chief. Until we meet again, Akkadian."

Rogg stepped forward and clasped Ta's arm up to the elbow, in the typical handclasp of leaders. Then he turned to leave. Ta and Aya looked unhappily at each other. The Elamite's presence had been as nourishing as food. To think that now they'd have to face a Magog patrol atop their regular problems was depressing. To make matters worse, Ut looked furious. Once the big man left, Ut would surely deliver a hard reckoning for Ta's "disobedience." Ta was not looking forward to that.

But as Rogg bent to wipe his greasy hands clean in the dust, a new voice addressed him. An unfamiliar one—and female.

"Rogg, may I speak?" the voice asked.

The Akkadians looked at Aya. But it wasn't her. Slowly, the hairs on the back of Ta's neck stood up. It can't be. He turned to the nomad girl. Can it?

It was. She stood tall, her hair pushed aside like a raven's wing, revealing a shockingly beautiful face with olive cheeks and hard, intelligent eyes. Her shoulders, though narrow, were square and pulled back, giving her an aura of command. In her posture alone, she looked nothing like the bedraggled creature he'd pulled from the water last night.

"Why, you little sneak!" Ut cried. "You tricked us!"

The girl ignored him and bowed to Rogg. "Big brother. I have something to say."

Rogg chuckled. "This is a tribe of surprises! First, a chief who is not a chief. Now a mute who talks?" He bowed in return. "Speak, Little Enki. I am listening."

Ta couldn't help but smile. Calling the girl "Little Enki," after the god of cleverness and tricks, was a high compliment. Enki was a god to be reckoned with.

The girl spoke again. "Thank you, brother. My name is Ki, and I beg forgiveness for deceiving you all." She shot an apologetic look at Ta. "I didn't know who I could trust. You see, I just escaped Magog's camp myself."

Rogg's eyes bulged. "In truth? You swear this?"

"Upon my dead family's honor, I swear it," Ki said firmly.

"Hoho!" Rogg boomed. "Speak on, Little Enki."

"I thought you might be interested."

Ki put a hand over her stomach to indicate she spoke from her *emittu*. "May the gods strike me dead if this is not so. I spent days in a prison pen up there. I know the camp's quadrants. Its patterns and routines. I even saw Gog himself, and his heir, Prince Jakka. I'll tell you everything I know. You might use it for your attack."

Rogg gazed fiercely into her eyes for a long time.

"I believe you," he said finally. "You have seen Gog. Your face is the kind he leaves behind."

Ki nodded. "Magog stamped my people out like ants. I will be glad if you crush Gog's skull with a rock. But in return for my help, I want yours, too, brother. Guide us safely past this patrol, and I'll tell you all I know about their camp."

"By Baal!" Rogg laughed. "You're a bold one."

"Losing everything makes one bold, I suppose."

"Truly spoken," Rogg said.

The Akkadians watched the interchange, fascinated. Ki was half Rogg's size, yet she spoke to him like an equal. And when Rogg extended his hand to seal the bargain with an arm clasp, Ki took it as firmly as any chief, though her fingers could only halfway encircle his forearm.

"I accept this deal," Rogg said. "This meeting feels fated."

"I don't trust fate anymore," Ki said. "But I will trust you."

The two let go, and the deal was made. Ta murmured in appreciation. In one masterstroke, Ki had saved their group from both Magog and Ut. A "Little Enki" indeed. I could learn much from such a one, he thought, gripping his stump. Stay alert, Ta. Here are mentors of all kinds.

All business now, Rogg stooped to pick up Ut's pack. "Come, friends. Time to move. I will drive us hard today. You may soon regret this deal." He chuckled. "But if you're alive to complain of it tomorrow, my purpose will have been served."

He strode off, beckoning Ki. "Come, nomad. Up front with me. I will listen."

As Ki scrambled ahead to join him, the Akkadians followed in a daze.

"He's got our food pack," Ut muttered. "You two sanction this? Strangers carrying our hard-won food?"

Aya hardly heard him. "Ta, what a wonder you are. Two recruits in one day. And *what* recruits." She shook her head. "Not to mention the gazelle, and the river idea. Is this typical for you?"

Ta laughed. "Not at all, I'm afraid."

"Don't be so quick to celebrate him," Ut snapped. "He left that smoke up this morning."

"Pah!" Aya said.

"And he recruits troublemakers," Ut insisted. "We *know* the girl deceived us. I bet the giant has, too. A savior of Elam? I never heard of anything so ridiculous."

Aya waved him off. "What's wrong with you, Ut? A few days ago, it was just you and me, starving in the desert. Now look at us. The gods are helping, can't you see that? Ah, never mind. You're hopeless. Ta, hold Shulgi for me, eh? I want to hear everything." Unshouldering her sling, she handed the boy to Ta. "That nomad girl's clever, but she's not a real woman yet," she murmured, adjusting her skin robe. "Mark me. Aya, not Ki, will make Rogg stay in the end."

Ut scoffed. "That brute can have any woman he likes. It won't be you."

"We'll see."

Aya marched off, spitting on her hand and wiping the grit from her face to improve her appearance, leaving Ta and Ut to trudge behind.

"Don't think I've forgotten you, either," Ut said, glancing sideways at Ta.

"I know," Ta said quietly.

"Good." Ut glared at the front walkers. "In the end, those new ones will abandon us. And it'll be just us three again, like before. Then you'll remember your need for Ut."

18

Farther north, Jakka followed his warriors miserably down the bank of the Euphrates toward the village of Kish. Palm trees shadowed the dirt path they ran on, cooling the hot air. The warriors' sandals slapped the dirt, throwing aside pebbles and sticks. The men's breaths were steady and powerful. Soon the village of Kish appeared. Lifting his face eagerly, Jakka saw it approach in flashes of color between the trunks. Yellow reed rooftops. Brown deer hide mats over doorways. Green grass boats lined up on the mud beach in neat military order. Red fires guttering in dirt pits. Blue-dyed blankets hanging over window holes to honor Inanna. But no people. Why were the paths empty? This had better not be another disappointment.

"Be on guard," Nod barked. "Here is Kish. Remember, it is our vassal, so no violence."

The warriors rushed in silently, spears at the ready. Nod and Jakka followed at a safer distance, squinting as they emerged from the palm trees into the hot sharp sunlight of the village.

It had been an awful trip, Jakka reflected as he walked in. Village after village had failed to capture the witch. The recent storm had only made matters worse. For all he knew, it could have drowned her. Never had he seen such a storm. He and his warriors had sheltered far out in the desert, pounded and stung by rain for hours, cursing and gnashing their teeth in fear as the lightning flapped above them. Was Enlil angry at the *baru* for using his breath as a slave? Was he trying to kill her? Jakka needed her alive, and he didn't want to compete with a god to get her.

As they trotted between the empty huts, Nod tried to comfort him.

"I'm sure Kish caught her, Lord. It has the biggest fleet yet." Nod pointed at all the boats on the bank. "Not even a *baru* can dodge that many."

Jakka wanted to hit him. Nod had said similar things in every village.

Around him, Kish's huts crowded the waterline like brown animals herding to drink. Now Jakka saw the tribe ahead, at the far end of the path. A funeral ceremony was going on. There, in the shade of the trees, by a grid of dirt burial mounds, a priest was chanting before a sizable crowd. People were singing, beating drums. Women were ululating. However, as Magog ran up, the crowd panicked and tried to scatter, taken by surprise.

"Peace, Kish. You are our vassal," Nod cried, waving his hands. "No one will be harmed."

The warriors encircled the crowd, hemming it in with a prickling hedge of spear points. Mothers wailed and hugged their children. Fathers stepped in front of them, ready to sacrifice themselves. Old couples knelt and beseeched the gods. Jakka felt better. *This* was how the world saw him. He mustn't forget it.

The local chief, a bald man with a ratty beard, ran up and knelt before Nod. "Hail Gog! Hail Magog!" he bleated, banging his forehead on the earth.

Nod raised him to his feet and began to question him gently. But Jakka had come to hate these plodding interrogations. Nod didn't realize the urgency. If Jakka didn't recapture the *baru*, Father would make Hakka heir, and Hakka would do what Jakka intended to: eliminate all threats to the throne—starting with his closest sibling.

Jakka shoved Nod aside and snapped at the cowering headman.

"Ho, dog! I am Prince Jakka, so be quick. What news of the witch?"

The chief paled. "Prince Jakka? Truly? By Baal! If we'd known you were coming, we'd have prepared—"

"The *baru*, fool."

The headman nodded hastily and pointed at the boats on the beach. "Believe me, Lord, we did all we could. When we saw your smoke signals, we made ready at once. And when she rounded the bend two nights ago under the full moon, we put our whole fleet on the water for her, all banging drums and blowing horns."

Jakka examined the fleet with pleasure. Now he was getting somewhere. The boats looked narrow and fast. Their hulls were waterproofed in black bitumen, a tarry substance that seeped up from the ground all over Mesopotamia. It made the hulls sleek, further reducing drag. Impressive. Even a *baru* could not have evaded all these.

"Well?" he demanded.

"We closed in on her from all sides, Lord. Only . . . we did not anticipate her *speed*."

Jakka shut his eyes. In each village it was the same.

The headman trembled. "How do I say it? She enslaved the breath of Enlil. She swept around our flank faster than we could readjust, threading a narrow lane between us and that bank of rushes, there." He pointed at the reed beds. "Still, by chance positioning, our strongest warrior, Ashurbanipal, had a chance to hit her."

Jakka perked up. "Oh?"

"Yes, Lord. He paddled with all his strength and in fact was on pace to ram her straight into the reeds. Then, just a few strokes away . . ."

The headman hesitated.

"Go on," Jakka nearly screamed.

"She slew him, Lord. With magic."

The headman shivered, and the crowd murmured darkly.

Jakka was skeptical. "A girl killed your best warrior?"

"Showing is easier, Lord. Come."

Parting the crowd, the chief took Jakka to the edge of the graveyard where, at the edge of the mounds, a deep pit had been dug. Beside it, a dead young man, his skin cleaned, painted, and perfumed in high circumstance, lay on his back on a mat of rushes. This must be Ashurbanipal, Jakka thought sourly. The "best" in Kish.

He frowned at the corpse. It lay stiff, the hands crossed over the chest. The beard was oiled and curled; the toenails clipped. The eyes were painted darkly with kohl in the traditional manner of the dead. Meanwhile, personal artifacts lay in the pit, ready to accompany Ashurbanipal's *emittu* to the afterlife. A game board, a spear, a painted vase, a blanket studded with jade beads.

A woman also knelt beside the grave. A beautiful young thing, Jakka noted. She must be Ashurbanipal's mate. She wore a clean grass skirt, painted bone earrings, and colorful makeup for the burial ceremony. Jakka's loins twitched. She reminded him of the young Hittite girl he'd left back in the harem tent, an earth-skinned creature with dark frightened eyes. He'd intended to enjoy her the day of the witch's escape, but he'd been deterred. And he'd taken no female companionship since. He needed it, he realized now. He studied the kneeling girl. He felt a strong desire to leap on her and grab her body all over.

"See, Lord. The witch's weapon."

The chief handed over a dart. Jakka looked away from the girl with reluctance. He took the dart. One tip was pointy. The other was decorated with red bird feathers stuck on with tree sap. Jakka bent the dart. It snapped easily.

"A child's toy."

"Yet it made this death wound." The chief pointed at Ashurbanipal's neck.

Jakka bent to study the neck. Funny. He saw a hole in the throat. Tiny. As small as an ant. Hard to believe that could kill you. Yet a similar hole had been found in the neck of the officer slain in the *baru's* village, he remembered suddenly. The *baru* had a favorite murder method.

Fear touched him. How much magic did she have?

And gods, why did *he* have to face such a challenge?

The headman went on nervously.

"It happened fast, Lord. As Ashurbanipal's boat neared her, the *baru* threw this dart across the water and pierced his throat. He fell in the water. She slipped by." The chief shook his head gravely. "We did all we could, but how can we fight sorcery?"

Jakka glared at the broken dart in his hands. First the raft, now this. The witch's power seemed to be growing. What evil had he let loose?

More to the point, how much worse could this get?

He pulled Nod aside.

"What do we do?" he whispered.

"There is no fighting magic, Lord."

"And the storm?"

"It helped us, I expect. It likely destroyed her wind device and forced her off the water onto land. She will be easier to catch on foot."

Nod pointed south, into the desert. "We have a patrol down there, led by a fine captain, Ur-Baba. He leads fifteen men. Yesterday, he smoke-signaled us that he was tracking fresh footprints. It might be our fugitive. Ur-Baba could be catching her as we speak."

Jakka locked his fingers behind his waist and began to pace. He felt panic rising. But he needed to appear in control.

"Very well, Nod. Here's what we'll do. Restock our provisions from this village. Then smoke-signal our camp. Have the priests sacrifice ten slaves to Enlil on the stone altar—wait."

His excitement peaked. He had the *baru's* people!

"Now hear this, Nod," he said eagerly. "Tell the priests to take the witch's people and sacrifice them with flame and smoke. All of them. All forty." He rubbed his hands together gleefully. He could not disobey Father and hurt the witch. But her people? Father had said nothing about them. "Yes!" he said. "Put them all on stone altars. Order our priests to chant in a circle from sunrise to sunset, marching around the burning bodies without pause. Do it, Nod.

We will give Enlil the greatest sacrifice he's ever had. In return, the god will give her to us."

It was good to appease the gods. Jakka feared no entities in this world besides them. Well, he feared Father. But Father was nearly a god, himself.

He glanced at Nod, expecting approval. But Nod was staring at him, dismay in his eyes.

"Lord? Are you sure of this?"

"You question me?" Jakka asked in annoyance.

Nod gulped. "Your father meant to use the *baru's* people to manipulate her. If you kill—"

"ALL, Nod. Don't defy me again." Jakka glared into his face.

Nod paled. "Yes, Lord. All."

"That is better. Now tell me, which tribes lie farther south? Any bigger than Kish?"

It was admirable how quickly Nod composed himself.

"One tribe is bigger," he said quietly. "The village of Babylon. As you know, it is the biggest tribe on this river. It has three hundred people, a hundred boats. I'm sure they can catch her."

"But Babylon is not our vassal."

"No. Babylon is an ally. It serves our purpose just as well. Their queen will be glad to do Gog a favor."

"A queen?" That was interesting. A woman would be easy to bully. "Good, good," Jakka said. "Smoke-signal Babylon to make ready. In the meantime, I . . ."

His eyes returned to the kneeling young woman. "I will take a short rest."

Nod followed his gaze, then stepped forward quickly and lifted his lips to Jakka's ear.

"Lord, forgive me," he whispered urgently. "That is not our slave. She is our vassal. Your father made a treaty with these people."

"You would deny me?" Jakka was genuinely surprised.

"I mean there is an agreement in place. They send us monthly tribute. In return, we protect them." Nod stepped back, shaking his head slightly as if the matter was settled.

Jakka scowled. Nod's tone felt belittling, like an elder speaking to a child.

And suddenly all the rage and frustration of the last few days spiked in his chest.

"Answer me, Nod. In Father's absence, who is Magog's warlord?"

"You, my prince."

"Don't forget it."

Jakka spun and snapped his fingers at the kneeling woman. "Girl! Rise and go in that hut. Inanna favors you. Today, you will entertain a prince."

The woman looked up slowly. Her eyes were exhausted from crying, her cheeks drained of color. But she did not quiver like Jakka's harem women. Rather, she held his gaze, hard.

"I cannot," she said simply.

Jakka was fascinated. No one defied him! Except the witch, of course . . . It was strangely arousing. Of course it could not be tolerated. The Prince of Magog, defied by women? *No, no*. He glanced anxiously at his men.

"You misunderstand me, woman. Do you know who I am?"

"It is you who misunderstands, Lord."

The woman nodded at a bowl of date juice by her knees. Instantly, Jakka understood. Kish practiced the old customs, then. At the climax of the funeral the woman would drink the juice—poisoned, no doubt—and follow her mate into the grave with his trinkets to keep him company in the Underworld forever.

At this, Jakka's desire for her shriveled up. He wanted nothing to do with the Underworld.

Then he noticed his men watching, their eyes agleam with jealous desire. And Jakka realized that if he backed down now, he'd look weak.

"Last chance, woman," he said softly. "You can join your mate afterward."

"I will join him unspoiled," the woman said proudly.

Jakka cocked his head. Such defiance *was* more interesting than his concubines' submission. Desire stirred again.

"Oh, woman, you *will* go in the hut," he murmured. "Or I will cut your mate's corpse into a hundred pieces and scatter them across the desert for the crows to carry off. And my warriors will dig up all these dead," he nodded at the burial mounds, "and do the same to them. And the shades of your ancestors will haunt Kish forever, thanks to your stupid pride."

The woman whitened. Gasps burst from the tribe. Few threats could have horrified these superstitious savages more. They really believed the *emittu* of an unearthed corpse would haunt them, unable to find rest.

"Selfish girl!" one woman yelled. "Forget your arrogance and do what the prince requires."

She ran up and grabbed the bowl and dumped the poisoned juice out, splattering the earth and splashing the mourner's knees. The kneeling woman scooted back, astonished.

"Yes, girl," the chief yelled in agreement. "Join Ashurbanipal later. He gave everything for us. He will understand."

The tribe began to hiss and boo. The woman stared at them. She glanced at her dead mate. Then at the nearby hut. Her mouth twisted. But her people had crushed her. Her shoulders slumped. Ashen-faced, she gave a slight bow to the chief, then rose and trudged toward the hut.

Jakka followed, his heart pounding with delight. It was a total triumph. What do you think of me now, Nod? He smirked at the older man. I didn't even use my fighters. Just my wits. Meanwhile his warriors were all chuckling and nodding appreciatively. Jakka's heart soared. This would be the way of things from now on. Since the *baru* was dragging him across his future domain, he might as well sample a few local fruits along the way.

As he followed the woman into the hut, he didn't know what excited him more: the prospect of her in the darkness—her will broken—or his men's growing respect.

Fortunately, he could enjoy both.

19

As Rogg had promised, a forest soon appeared on the horizon, offering better concealment.

Unfortunately, the going also grew much harder, and their progress slowed. It seemed as if the earth goddess, Kishar, during the act of creation, had grown frustrated with this part of the world and smashed her fist down, throwing the landscape into disarray. Spiny vegetation sprang up and barred their way, slashing at them like claws, drawing bloody scratches, ripping their garments. There were also fresh gullies to cross. It forced the travelers to slide to the bottoms of deep trenches and pull themselves out by overhanging roots. Their muscles burned, and all the while, the afternoon sun blazed hotter and hotter. Worst of all, the jostling disturbed little Shulgi. Ta, still carrying him in the sling, noticed the boy kept whimpering and looking up at him with frightened eyes, as if pleading with Ta to fix the bumpy ride.

I dislike this, too, little brother, Ta thought sadly. I'm sorry. We'll rest soon.

Thankfully, Rogg was a great help. Whenever he was not dashing ahead to scout an easier route, he could be seen reaching down into a gully to pull someone up, or holding aside a branch to help them pass. With each instance, Ta's respect for him grew.

"Weren't you starving earlier?" he asked as the Elamite hoisted him out of yet another gully, pulling his stump. "I should be helping you."

"The strength is usually there," Rogg said. "It just takes the will to pull it out."

"That's it? Will?" Ta laughed.

Rogg grinned. "That, and years of hard training."

He marched off, his great tan back shining with sweat, and Ta watched admiringly. Rogg exhibited Ta's two new rules perfectly. *Do what you admire. Help the tribe.* The difference was, Rogg was capable of executing them. He had the aura of a finished man. Ta was just taking his first baby steps in that direction, and the gulf between them was wide. But if I study him and learn all I can, and push, Ta thought, maybe I can share in his magic someday. For magic it was. The big fellow made the trip feel less like a slog, more like an adventure. A trick worth learning.

Aya was also an admirer. "He's like a hero from the legends," she whispered to Ta. "He never complains. Never tires."

"He ate a heroic number of our fish, I'll give you that," Ut said sourly.

Aya dismissed him with a laugh. "Heroism may seem unrealistic to *you*, Ut. But keep watching. Even you may learn something."

Unfortunately, Aya soon began to struggle. In one descent, she fell and rolled her ankle—the same ankle she'd injured in the endurance hunt—and thereafter she needed a shoulder to lean on, to keep up. She also needed to rest more often. Time after time, she sat on the slopes and panted for air while the others stood about, waiting. And during one such rest, Ut lost his temper.

"If she wants Magog to catch us, she's doing a fine job."

Rogg knelt at Aya's side and reached gently for her foot.

"May I, sister?"

Aya gave him a pained look. "I'm sorry, Rogg. Never mind me. I can keep going."

"Here, let's see."

For a moment, Ta wondered if Aya was simply putting on an act to gain the giant's attention. But when Rogg removed her wrap, he revealed a foot so puffy and sour-smelling, so red and blistered, that everyone winced. Ta was amazed she could put pressure on it at all.

Rogg rewrapped the foot carefully. "You've done well making it this far, sister. Rest it as often as you need. Or soon we'll be forced to carry you."

"Bless you, Rogg." Aya shot Ut a vindicated look.

Ut glared back. But his demeanor changed when Rogg spoke to him respectfully, as if to a fellow warrior. "You have broad shoulders, brother. Will you loan her one?"

"Me?" Ut's eyes widened.

Rogg nodded. "It'll be hard. I've got the pack. No one else is strong enough."

Ut brightened. "Ah, well, sure, Rogg. I could do that."

They moved off again, Ut helping Aya now, draping her arm over his shoulder and saying authoritatively, "Easy. Watch that rock." Ta suppressed a smile. If Rogg could motivate even Ut, he *was* a magician. You'd actually want a chief, if they were like this.

Aya certainly agreed.

"You're wonderful, Rogg," she said shyly as Rogg held aside yet another branch to help her and Ut stagger past. "In all your travels, haven't you found a new mate yet?"

Rogg broke the branch off with a *snap* and handed it to her for a cane.

"I will never take another mate."

Aya's mouth dropped. "Never?"

Rogg shook his shaggy head. "My mate waits for me in the Underworld. When the time comes, I will rejoin her as I left her. Completely hers."

He marched off, and the group gazed after him in wonder.

"Now we know he's crazy," Ut laughed.

Aya sighed. "You'd never understand, Ut. Still, by the gods, I wish he was *less* perfect."

◆

At midafternoon, the group topped a bluff and looked around to get their bearings. A feeling of triumph filled Ta as he saw the thicker forest up ahead, the trees doubling in height. It was only a few leagues off now. They'd make it by nightfall, even with Aya's limp.

"Fine work, everyone." Rogg pulled out another fish, bit its head off, and chewed. "Push a bit more, and you'll earn your sleep." He spat out a mouthful of bones. "A deep sleep, too. That's how you know you lived a good day."

"Sleep," Aya sighed, sinking to the ground. "What I'd give to take it now."

Gathering themselves for the final leg, they drank water and lay under the bushes for shade. Ut picked at a blister while Ta handed the baby to Aya to feed. Then Ta limped to the rear of the hill to take in the view.

It was an intimidating one. The red desert still surrounded them on three sides, touching the blue rim of the sky at every horizon except the forested east, where the hills and trees awaited in brooding, hostile silence. In the south, the palm trees wove across the waste like a great black snake, glittering wherever the waters of the Euphrates peeped through. Smoke still hung above the trees every few leagues, barring entry, and Ta shook his head. If the whole river was like this, they'd be forced to join a local tribe—if the locals would accept them.

"Ho, Ta. What're you thinking?"

Ta turned. Ki stood behind him, her face glistening with sweat, her hair hanging in limp black rags about her face. She was holding a walking stick, leaning on it like an old lady.

"Oh." He gave an awkward smile. "I, uh . . . wasn't thinking of much. How're you?"

She looked exhausted, yet as beautiful as ever. Her brown eyes held such depths, complex with loss, that Ta felt childish and clumsy in comparison. He scratched his arm nervously, hoping she couldn't tell.

"I'm glad you stayed with us," he added lamely. "After last night."

Ki looked down at her rag-wrapped feet. "I wanted to apologize."

"For what?" he asked in surprise.

She gave him a guilty look. "You saved me. And I deceived you. Acting mute, and all that. Poor trade."

"No, that was clever," Ta said earnestly. "You didn't know us. It's understandable."

"I'll repay you somehow," Ki insisted. "I don't know how, but I will."

Ta was distracted. The memory of her warm cheek touching his as they dove into the torrent haunted him, making it hard to think of proper conversation. He shifted his weight.

"Really Ki, you repaid us plenty." Finding his senses again, he nodded at Rogg. "You got him." He laughed. "A pretty big repayment, I'd say."

Ki laughed, too. But her voice remained firm.

"Even nomads have a code, you know." She brushed a strand of hair out of her eyes and smiled to show she took no offence. "Can't let Elam have all the reputation for honor."

Ta grinned back. His stomach felt strangely warm and tight, but in a good way.

"We owe you an apology, too, I think." He glanced at Ut. "I'm sorry about . . . that. We're usually friendlier, I promise."

Ki tapped her walking stick on the earth as if it didn't matter. "I'm still puzzled. Why'd you do it?" She glanced at him curiously, before looking back down at her feet. Almost as if she, too, felt nervous. But that couldn't be, Ta thought. Someone like Ki couldn't be nervous around *him*.

"The river could've swept us away," she persisted. "You didn't know me. So, why?"

Ta shrugged. "We couldn't just watch you sink. Could we?"

She met his eyes, quizzical. "A lot of people could."

Ta remembered Ut's and Aya's votes, and grew embarrassed.

"I suppose," he said evasively.

Ki began drawing something in the dirt with her stick. “You just . . . appeared out of the dark. Threw me a rope. I thought you were some kind of spirit. Or something.” She laughed at herself, shaking her head. “I mean, is that common in Akkad? Saving people? Being . . . noble?”

Noble. The praise made him glow. No one had ever called Ta that before. But he couldn’t accept it. “You were right there,” he repeated. “We had to try.”

She looked across the desert, unsatisfied. “Do you think the gods send people, Ta? To help each other, I mean?”

Ta cocked his head, puzzled. “The gods?”

“I ask because . . . after my tribe was taken . . . I stopped praying.” Ki was hardly audible. “But clinging to that tree last night, I prayed again. I’m not sure why. I really don’t trust the gods anymore. Not ours, anyway.” She frowned. “I suppose, deep down, I still want life to . . . matter, somehow. Mean something.” She looked up. “But instead of a god, you appeared.”

“I’m glad I did,” he said, sincerely. “You’re wonderful, Ki.” Then, fearing he’d said too much, he added hastily: “A wonderful ally, I mean.”

She grinned. “You’re a not a bad ally, either.”

They both laughed.

“What’re you doing out here, anyway?” she asked. “You’re not from Ut and Aya’s tribe.” Her eyes dropped to his stump-arm. She was too polite to ask directly, but the question was there all the same. His heart plunged. And yet, he felt almost glad to get it out of the way.

“You’re wondering about this.” Bashfully, he lifted the stump in all its ugly glory. “I can’t really hide it. I wish I could.” He gave a rueful smile.

“I . . . I’m sorry, Ta. I didn’t mean . . .”

“I’m a food thief.” Ta breathed out heavily. “I stole.” He looked at his stump firmly, owning it. “But you know what? I think I’ve paid for it.” He felt relieved, saying it. “That’s why I’m here. To make a new start.” In a way, it was true.

"A new start." Ki's eyes brightened. "That's nice."

"It really is," Ta said.

Then, to his bewilderment, words flew from his lips that he didn't expect.

"This tribe we're making, Ki. It'll be a good tribe. No chiefs. Even women and cripples get a say." He rubbed his forehead with his stump, as if massaging the idea forth. "You know, maybe it's a tribe for lost people," he went on. "People drowning in rivers. People with stumps. People with nowhere to go." He nodded across the hilltop at Baby Shulgi, whose clubfoot was visible as Aya laid him out on a blanket to clean him. "Shulgi's tribe would've given him to Moloch. Not us. We're making a place for people like him. For people like . . . me."

Ta hesitated. But Ki's eyes were shining, and it gave him the courage to finish.

"Out here in the wastes, there could be many lost ones like us. Don't you think?"

Ki looked at him strangely. "That's beautiful, Ta. I've never heard of a tribe like that."

"Aya thought of it, for Shulgi."

Ta looked into the distance. The vision had not truly materialized before. Perhaps he'd needed time to see it. To let it grow. And grow it did. A vision shimmered in front of him like a dream. He saw it in a flash . . . the Euphrates clustered with huts . . . beautiful huts dashed with color over every doorway, as bright as bird feathers. On the bank, a host of people worked bare-backed under the palm trees. Women fished in the shallows. Men rowed grass boats. Children played and swam, splashing in the green water. Shulgi was among them . . . not as a baby, but as a young man, sitting in a boat and throwing nets out. On the bank, Ta and his friends sat on logs by a fire, roasting fish on sticks. From the huts a deep beating of drums came, overlaid by singing. Hundreds of voices chanted in praise of some brave deed. *Home. Home. We are home . . .* Then it was gone, melting away, and Ta was back on the hilltop with Ki, sweating in the sunlight.

Ki watched him curiously. "What was that?"

He wiped his face, clearing his mind. "Huh?"

"You got strange. Your eyes went to another place." Ki hesitated. "You saw something."

"Just our future tribe. It was . . . nice."

Ki's eyes pierced his. "Do you often . . . *imagine* things?" A strange urgency lit her voice.

"No. Never." Ta laughed. "I feel dizzy, actually. Maybe I should sit. This heat . . ."

Ki grew concerned. She came closer and examined his head for bruises. "Did something hit you in the flood?" she asked gently. "Or . . . ?" Her eyes darkened as she glanced at Ut. Ta winced. He wished she hadn't seen their fight.

"That was the first time that happened," he stammered. "We won't do it again. I mean, if you *want* to go with us—we haven't talked about it, but—well . . . you're certainly welcome to, if you like. We do need more people."

He clenched his teeth, wishing he hadn't spoken at all. But to his surprise, Ki looked happy and shy, the same as he felt.

"Ta, it's *good* to be with you," she said earnestly. "Traveling alone is awful. I'd much rather go with friends. Only . . ."

Ta's heart fell. "No need to explain," he said quickly.

"It's Gog I'm worried about," she said. "I must get away from him. If he catches me with you . . ." Her voice broke. "Ta, I can't bring more harm on people. You don't know Magog."

"Well," he said, trying to be polite and offer her a way out, "where were you going before the storm? On your raft, I mean."

Ki laughed. "It's funny. I'm not sure."

"If it's hard to speak of . . ."

"No, Rogg's right. We must speak of hard things, or they won't change."

Ki's frown deepened. "The truth is, I wasn't going anywhere. Just away from Gog. Not *to* any place." Again she hesitated, as if afraid to say something she shouldn't. "Just *away*," she finished. "And it's funny, because I always had goals in life. What to accomplish each day. Month. Year. But now . . . I've never felt so . . . directionless. I'm not sure where I belong or what I'm doing."

She studied the earth as if looking into it, toward the Underworld. As if feeling for guidance from her dead family. Ta understood. He'd felt the same after the Great Plague. To reorient after a catastrophic blow was one of the hardest things in life. One moment, your whole future was laid out before you, heading in a clear direction. The next, your hand was chopped off—or your tribe sacked—and you had no clue what new path to take. Or if there was even a path at all.

But she is searching, he thought. And that's something. In the cave I grew bitter and settled for the tribe's ways. I became what they called me. *Useless. Cripple. Runt.* I gave up. She hasn't.

"Ta."

To his surprise, she was smiling. And her smile was so pretty, it made his heart flip in a funny way that almost hurt.

"What?" he asked.

"I'm glad to be alive, Ta. I wasn't yesterday. But I am again, now. I think I have you to thank. You coming for me . . . it matters. I'm not sure how. But I know it does."

Ta felt happy. He wasn't sure what to reply. But he never got a chance, for Aya walked up.

"Excuse me, you two. I'm sure this is heartfelt, and all—thanking Ta for saving your life, eh?" She arched an eyebrow at Ki. "But this is more pressing." She pointed into the desert. "I think I see people."

"People?" Ta asked.

Aya sounded excited. "I think so. Could it be your old tribe? Should we signal them?"

Ta's mood plunged. His old people? Terrible. Korak would destroy Ta's reputation. It would ruin everything.

Squinting, Ta scanned the desert. "Where?" he asked, wiping sweat from his face.

"Don't tell Rogg yet. I don't want to look stupid if I'm wrong. There, see?" Aya pointed back the way they'd come. "It's bright, I know."

It really was so bright that Ta could hardly keep his eyelids parted, even shading his brow. Still, after a moment, the land came into focus. He saw the gullies and hilltops carpeted with thickets. Beyond lay the red desert and the canyon they'd found Rogg in, like a drizzle of blood across the waste. And there on the rim—

Ki pointed suddenly. "I see it."

Ta saw it, too. On the canyon lip was a blob. *Moving.* Ta's breath caught.

"Rogg, we need you," Aya said.

Rogg was there in an instant. His eyes followed Aya's finger into the distance.

"Maybe it's a herd of deer," Ta said hopefully.

Rogg shook his head. "Good work, Aya. It's Magog, sure enough."

"Magog!" Aya cried in alarm. "I thought it'd be Ta's people. How can you tell?"

"They're tracking us," Rogg said. "Moving fast, on the hunt."

Ta felt a chill. *Hunting.*

"Maybe they just want to talk," Aya said in a small voice.

"Magog never 'just talks,'" Rogg said.

"Why not?" Aya cried.

"Why do locusts pick the earth clean of life? It is their way. The death of grass means nothing to locusts. Our deaths mean nothing to Magog."

Rogg eyed the sun halfway down in the west. "But our plan holds. If we can hide in the thorn tree forest by dark, Magog may yet grow lazy and give up. They don't know we have their escaped slave, so they've no reason to work too hard." He looked at Ki. "Right?"

Ki said nothing.

Ut eyed Aya's ankle. "But she'll slow us down. They'll catch up before sunset."

Rogg nodded. "Unless we slow them down, too."

"How?"

"With a trick I've used before." Rogg pointed at a bluff to the north. "I'll run over there and build a fire, make smoke. Once Magog sees it, they may abandon the hard work of tracking and go straight for the smoke, giving you extra time to reach the forest."

He took the water bag and drank quickly, slopping liquid down his black beard.

Ut's eyes narrowed. "Suppose you don't mean to build a fire, though. Maybe you intend to break your deal and abandon us."

Rogg lowered the bag and looked at him.

"Before this day is finished, Ut, you will know my character. And I will know yours."

Ut colored and fell quiet. Rogg handed the water bag back to Aya.

"Push as fast as you dare, sister. But be careful. Don't injure yourself worse."

"Bless you, sweet Rogg."

"Bless you, too, sister. It is good to be near family again." He looked at Shulgi. "This was a nice day."

Then he was gone, leaving the thorn branches trembling. The group stared at the spot as if at the disappearance of a god.

"That's the last we'll see of him," Ut said.

"He'll be back," Aya said, hero-worship in her voice.

"Either way, we need to move," Ta said.

The group struggled on. As the red ball of the sun dropped in the west, the day's heat lessened, but at the same time the ravine sides grew steeper, the thorns thicker. Sweat gushed down Ta's sides. Rocks stubbed his toes. Occasionally, he slipped, bruising his knee-caps on the stones and tearing his skin open. Blood tickled down his shins. Nevertheless, the invisible pressure at his back drove him on, preventing a more manageable pace. It was an awful thing to be hunted. The gazelle must have felt something like this, he realized. *Forgive me, brother creature.* He began to hate the men following them. He cursed the terrain silently and tried to focus on his own steps. Rogg had spoken true. If the fugitives just fulfilled their roles, they'd reach the safety of the trees. Their own discipline was the test, not Magog.

A while later, his spirits lifted when smoke appeared in the distance. Rogg's decoy fire was up. Their chance of success had just doubled. The group gave an exhausted cheer.

"I told you," Aya cried, pounding Ut's back. "What do you think of him now?"

"It's something, I'll give you that," Ut said. "But he won't be back. We slow him down too much."

"You're wrong," Aya said.

Still, they had to suffer on. One foot after another. Grinding, mind-numbing work. There was no way around it, the distance had to be covered. Their sides ached; their feet blistered. Their tongues felt thick and foreign in their mouths. To live, Ta reflected, sometimes one had to suffer. So they suffered.

And then it happened.

On an especially steep slope, Aya gave a cry of pain. Ut reached for her, but she was gone, rolling backward into the gully bed, stones clattering after her.

"Aya!" everyone cried.

"Not again!" Ut roared.

She landed at the bottom in a heap. Everyone slid down to her, calling her name, but she wouldn't open her eyes. She just lay on her side, clutching her ankle, hissing through her teeth.

"My ankle," she gasped.

"Curse your ankle, woman," Ut said. "If you're lame, tell us now."

"I'll walk. Help me up."

"Don't make it worse," Ta warned.

Aya pushed herself up slowly. Keeping one foot off the ground, she clung to Ta's arm for balance as she carefully tested the other foot. "Ahhh." She collapsed again, holding her ankle with both hands as if she'd been pierced with a thousand splinters.

"You foolish woman! What have you done?" Ut cried.

Without permission, he knelt and ripped off Aya's foot wrapping. The ankle was even more swollen than before. It stank like a dead thing. Parts were yellow, others purple. Everyone grimaced and covered their noses.

"I'll walk," Aya panted. "Give me a moment."

It was clear her foot would not bear weight again for days. Everyone slumped on the rocks, defeat settling in slowly. It seemed surreal, Ta thought. They'd worked so hard, and now this? His rules didn't suffice, either. *Do what you admire. Help your people.* But how? He racked his mind, and no solution came. He was so dizzy, so tired. He lay back, muscles quivering. Aya was weeping. Shulgi, crying.

And suddenly, Ut came to a decision.

Grabbing the food pack, he climbed a few paces uphill, then turned, a strange expression on his face. "Why should we die, too?" he asked. "She made the mistake. Not us."

The others looked up, bewildered. To Ta's astonishment, Ut pulled a spear from his pack and leveled it at them. The wood tip was sharp and black, fire-hardened to a killing point.

"What're you doing?" Ta asked.

"Leaving," Ut announced.

Leaving. Ta tried to understand the word and couldn't.

"Just try to stop me." Ut shook the spear wildly, as if daring them to fight. "Don't look at me like that. I've got to live, don't I?"

"But Ut, this isn't *you*," Ta said. "You're our brother."

Aya touched his shoulder. "Don't waste your time, Ta. He's wanted to leave us for days."

"You can't blame me," Ut shouted downhill. "You think I want this? I've no easy options. Only hard ones." He stamped his foot. "I can't die! Why should I?"

"Go on," Aya said. "Leave us like you left your mate in the cave."

"How dare you!" Ut's eyes bulged. "She wasn't my mate. I didn't choose her. She was forced on me. Take it back."

Aya picked up a handful of gravel to throw. "Go on, traitor!"

Ta churned his mind, seeking a solution. But he was so hot, so tired.

"Rogg's coming back soon, brother," he sputtered. "He'll find a way. If we have faith—"

"Faith!" Ut laughed. "Gods help you, brother. You're dumber than you look. He's not coming back. Even if he did, he couldn't fight fifteen Magog warriors. Not with two cripples and a nomad girl."

"But we're a tribe," Ta said stupidly.

Ut ignored him and turned to Aya. "Admit it, sister. If you keep them here, you're the selfish one. They'll be slaughtered just to protect you."

"You'll never be a chief," Aya shouted back. "A chief doesn't abandon his people."

"A chief sees reality," Ut said. "He makes hard choices when others are too weak."

His voice quavered. It sounded like he was trying to convince himself.

"Ta, Ki, come with me," he said. "Bring Shulgi, too. Before it's too late." He sneered at Aya, "You won't even let your baby escape, will you?"

Aya's voice broke. "Please, Ut. Don't."

Ut's face contorted with several different emotions. Then something won out. He couldn't look at them anymore, and he spun and ran off through the bracken.

"Traitor!" Aya threw her handful of rocks uphill. "TRAITOR!"

But the rocks clattered off empty thorns. Ut was gone.

The group sat in stunned silence as the shadows deepened and the sky streaked with gold. It felt like the last moments of the world, Ta thought. The end of everything. The rocks cooled. The birds twittered mournfully in the canopy, as if singing farewell. Ta groped for an idea. But he needed skill and power. And he had neither.

"I knew I'd die someday," Aya said softly. "But I thought first there'd be a little happiness. I thought . . . someone might love me. Even for a short while."

"We do," Ta said. "He does, too." He handed her Shulgi.

Aya wiped her eyes and grabbed the baby tightly. "He'll have a good life. I'm still going to give it to him." She kissed him and pressed her cheek to his forehead, closing her eyes as Shulgi squirmed. "I'll bless him from the Underworld."

The Underworld. It was a place Ta didn't like to think about. According to the priests, *Kur* was a joyless place of dust and shadow. It was ruled by the goddess Ereshkigal, a queen with black wings, the body of a voluptuous woman, and a bird's scaly feet. All humans, whether virtuous or unvirtuous, went there after they died. There was nothing to savor in *Kur's* dim earthen chambers. No food, no drink, no true light. For eternity, the *emittus* of the deceased wafted past each other like mists, filling the air with moans of sorrow and regret. But this wasn't the time to dwell on such things, Ta corrected himself. If Magog killed them this afternoon, they'd have an eternity to ponder the nature of *Kur*. Now was the time for action.

He turned to Aya. "Let's not talk like this, sister. When Rogg catches up—"

"Ut was right." Aya shoved Shulgi back. "Take him and go. He can't die for me. No, my boy must live."

Ta was astonished. The baby wriggled as Aya let go, almost dropping him, so that Ta was forced to accept him. "Sister, we're not leaving you." He tried to give the boy back, but Aya folded her arms and shook her head rapidly.

"I made the mistake. I'll pay for it." She looked angrily at her swollen ankle. "All I ask is this." Hastily, she reached under her tunic and drew out a stone knife. "Don't let Magog touch me. Cut me, will you?" She tapped the nape of her neck. "Here, the spine. One swift cut. It's painless."

"Aya!" Ta was horrified.

"The cut stings, but the life goes out of you quick. My old mate said so. He does it to animals . . ."

Ta was crushed by the idea. Yet he saw the awful pragmatism in it. If they didn't leave her, they'd all die here, Shulgi included. Ta looked down at the suffering, round face, the little eyes shut tight against the heat. A black despair surged. Could I do such a thing? Kill a companion? Is it right?

Luckily, he didn't have to debate the question for long.

Suddenly Rogg burst into the gully with a loud crash. Breaking bushes apart, he slid down the gravel slope until he was beside them, his broad chest heaving, his face bright with sweat.

"Rogg!" everyone cried.

The giant's skin glowed. His face was as red as the earth. "Ho, brothers and sisters." He slapped the slope with delight. "I know my adversary, don't I? The lazy dogs. Anything to skip a little work. Magog took the bait." He looked north, where he'd planted the decoy fire. "They'll be snarling mad when they find out it's a trick. But we did it. They should be far off course by now. We'll make it."

He fell silent, gulping air. Ta studied him in awe. The man must have run nearly the whole way to make it so fast, a real feat over this terrain. Especially with his bulk. And after being so hungry, too. But most of all, he'd kept his word.

Respect filled Ta. And joy. There *is* honor. It does exist.

Rogg sat up. "Where's Ut, by the way? I thought we'd be farther along."

Aya told him. Her voice trembled, but Rogg grasped it at once and did not seem surprised.

"Bah, I suspected it. It was in his face all day." He waved the betrayal off as if such things happened all the time. "Never mind him. You're better off without a coward among you."

"Oh, Rogg," Aya wept. "I'm so glad you're back."

"Shh, sister, here, let me see." Rogg crawled over to examine her foot. "Ah. It must hurt like a hundred scorpion stings."

"It's all my fault, Rogg, just kill me and go on." Aya covered her face. "Do it quick."

"Don't be silly. We'll elevate this ankle and make a plan, shall we?"

Rogg helped Aya lie back and rested her puffy foot on a bush to drain. Not once did he wrinkle his nose at the foot's smell, nor utter a cross word. Ta watched reverently. "It's the law of war," the

Elamite kept saying. "The unexpected is what *to* expect. We must always be ready to adapt." He looked around, brow knotting up. "I'm just not sure how, in this instance. Bah! What I'd give for a good strategist."

"You mean you're not leaving us?" Aya dared to ask.

Rogg looked surprised. "I told Ki I'd stay, didn't I? An Elamite honors his word."

The Akkadians exploded in cheers. Aya blew him a kiss. Ta pumped his stump in the air. Even Ki leapt to her feet and whooped.

"Hooray, Rogg!"

"Thank the gods for Rogg!"

Rogg looked bashful. "A word's a word, eh? Let's not overdo it. Come, we must think."

"Of what, though?" Aya demanded.

"We must fight."

It was Ki who had spoken. She'd been squatting next to Aya, offering her the water bag. Now she set the bag down, folded her thin brown arms, and set her jaw firmly.

Rogg looked at her intently. "Fight, eh?"

Ki nodded. "We can't run, can't hide. So, we must fight."

"You're not leaving, either?" Aya asked timidly.

Ki looked at Ta. "I have a debt, too. And a nomad's honor matches an Elamite's."

Rogg chuckled. "I don't doubt it, little sister."

Ta beamed. *What a team.* How many in Mesopotamia were as noble as these two? Yet, from out of the vast world, they'd intersected *here*. It felt like destiny.

Are you helping us, El? Is this your work?

He tried to give Shulgi back to Aya. But Aya wasn't convinced.

"I admire your courage, everyone, but my baby must live," she said. "That's what matters. Fifteen Magog warriors are coming, and we are just four." She forced the words out. "You should still take Shulgi and go."

In response, Ki snapped a twig from a bush, knelt, and scratched a battle diagram in the dirt. Everyone crawled over. No one spoke until she finished. Then Rogg straightened and looked at Ki strangely.

"Perhaps you are a Little Enki. This might give us a chance." He pointed at the diagram. "You came up with this just now? Truly?"

"I pondered it all day as we walked. In case."

"In case." Rogg looked at her intently. "I see."

Aya was still puzzling over the diagram. "But where . . . how?"

Ta was confused, too. Ki touched his arm to show him.

"My tribe used to hunt bulls this way. It's dangerous work, for bulls can gore you with their horns, trample you, smash you. And they move in herds, like great black storms. Therefore, we use their size and numbers against them. We herd the bulls into a tight gully, just like this one, here." She nodded at the gully they sat in, at the steep slopes, the narrow funnel. "It's a natural trap. With their size, the bulls can't turn in the funnel and get out. In their panic, they stab each other with their horns. The rest we slaughter from above with a rock avalanche." Her voice turned as cold as a winter creek. "As we'll do to Magog today."

Ta shivered.

"But who will lure our 'bulls' into the trap?" Rogg asked.

Ki reddened, then turned to Ta. "I admit it isn't perfect. I wish I had a safer way."

At first, Ta didn't understand. Rogg tapped the diagram to help.

"We need bait to lure Magog in. Will you do it, Ta?"

Ta's mouth went dry. "Me?" He looked down at his stump. *Don't you see? I'm a cripple, I'll ruin everything.* "I . . . I can't," he squeaked.

Rogg spoke frankly. "Aya can't run. Ki and I have other roles. That leaves you."

Ta searched for his voice. It wasn't there.

"Listen, brother," Rogg said. "The whole plan depends on this position. If you have doubts, tell us now."

Ta swallowed. All the failures of his past rose up to choke him. But his friends were looking at him with need in their faces, and his rules echoed in his head. *Do what you admire. Help your tribe.* It came out before he could think it through.

"I'll do it."

Rogg squeezed his shoulder. Aya embraced him tearfully. Ki even kissed his cheek. At the touch of her lips, a strange warmth filled him. Suddenly he didn't care about the risk.

Rogg bowed. "You're worth ten of Ut, brother. Now, let's get started. Tonight, we become warriors. But first we must earn it with old-fashioned hard work."

Aya sighed. "We've been working all day, brother. I'm so tired."

"Between work and *Kur*," Rogg said, "I'll take work."

Ta handed Shulgi back. Aya grabbed him and kissed him. Then she looked at Rogg fiercely.

"All right. I'll work. Tell me what to do."

20

It was almost sunset by the time the trap was ready. Exhausted, Ta walked up through the cooling air to his appointed position atop the slope. A few hundred paces down, the gully bed looked like a great reptile, its stones glinting like scales. Thornbushes and gnarly trees provided cover to Ta's position. But certainly not enough to protect him. The sky flamed ominously, casting the leaves in an eerie light. Ta's hand was damp with sweat. Wiping it on his loincloth, he knelt behind a bush and looked around. Shadows from the boughs stretched over him, lengthening. His heart galloped. It seemed unreal that at any time, Magog could appear.

Rogg squatted beside him. "How do you feel, brother?"

"Not ready," Ta admitted.

Soon, tattooed men would run up the slope with clubs and knives to hurt him. How could total strangers want to do that? It didn't make sense. And Ta was exhausted. His hand was trembling. It didn't feel fair. For the biggest challenge of his life, he would start tired. He tucked the hand under his knee to hide its shaking from Rogg.

"I hope I don't disappoint you, brother."

"You won't," Rogg said confidently.

Ta didn't feel so sure.

"I wish Ut was here. He's a lot faster than me."

Rogg shook his head. "He'd scamper off like a rabbit at the first twig-snap. Wreck our plan before it began. No, we need someone here we can trust." He patted Ta's back. "Character first. The rest will come."

Ta brightened under the praise. "Thanks, brother."

"And don't worry. It's normal to be afraid."

Ta chuckled ruefully. "Are you afraid?"

Rogg laughed. "I'm flesh and blood, aren't I? But it's true, the more you do this, the better you get at it. You learn ways to lessen the fear."

Ta perked up. Rogg had skills he wanted, badly. Every moment with him helped.

"How?"

Rogg rattled off a few tips, speaking so casually, Ta sensed he'd trained warriors before. His final word, however, was not a statement, but a question.

"This may be the most important." Rogg faced him. "I've been meaning to ask. Why this name of yours?"

"My name?" Ta blinked. "You mean 'Ta?'"

"It has a meaning, no?"

Ta was impressed. Ut and Aya knew the old Akkadian tongue, so they knew "Ta" meant "cripple," of course. But the language was not spoken outside Akkad. Rogg shouldn't know it.

"How did you . . . ?" He grew suspicious. "Did Ut or Aya tell you?"

"I met some Akkadians in my travels. Even a brute like me can learn. So why 'Ta?'"

Ta held up his ugly stump and examined it. After so long, it still disheartened him. He could forget it for days at a time, but whenever he was forced to look at it . . . well. It was him. *Cripple.*

"After I stole, the chief renamed me," he mumbled. "The priest blessed it. So it's official."

"I see," Rogg said.

"It could've been worse. 'Rakka.' 'Thief.'" Ta hung his head.

Rogg gripped his arm. "You're more than a 'cripple.' I'll tell you, your chief naming people after their weaknesses seems poor leadership. As if that's all they are. Or can be." Rogg spat in the dirt. "Names matter more than people think."

Ta looked down. He wished Rogg didn't know so many bad things about him.

But instead of belaboring it, Rogg uncorked the water skin, drank, and handed it over.

"Go on. Drink."

"Shouldn't we ration it?" Ta asked in surprise.

"If you're too thirsty to run well, none of us will live to have any. Go on."

Seeing the wisdom of this, Ta lifted the bag and obeyed. The water was warm, but refreshing, and he drank deeply. His head cleared. His muscles flickered to life.

"It's good," he said, wiping his mouth.

"Here's what else is good. Tonight, you become a warrior."

Ta's heart rose. In Akkad, he'd often gazed longingly at the warriors as they left on scouting missions. The tribe honored them even more than the hunters. But Rogg was right. Tonight, Ta would join those lofty ranks, whether he performed well or not.

"But Rogg," he said, suddenly afraid again. "Have you killed many men?" He looked down the slope, wondering how he could bear to do it. Men, real men, would soon rush at him through the trees. "Is it like killing an animal? That simple?"

Rogg gazed meditatively down the slope. "I admit, it's an ugly thing. The ugliest there is. But remember, we didn't ask for this fight, Magog did." He met Ta's eyes firmly. "Don't trust their words. The only language left to them is force. That's all they value."

Ta couldn't comprehend it. It was still a human being. A person. "What if I can't do it?"

Rogg pointed back through the trees. "Think of your people. If you love them, you protect them. It's that simple." He waited for Ta to understand. "Do you love them?"

Ta nodded. I really do, he thought in amazement. Already I do.

A cool watery feeling went through him. He hadn't loved much, since his parents. It was strange to feel the difference.

"Right," Rogg said. "So when the fear comes, think of them. See their faces. Recall what will become of them if we fail. You'll find a way."

Ta's blood rose. If Magog touched his friends . . . put their filthy tattooed hands on Ki, Aya, Shulgi . . . then yes. He could kill.

Rogg saw. "Good," he said quietly. "And last of all, remember this: I envy you."

Ta laughed. "Me? You envy me?"

"Yes, you." Rogg's face darkened. "You still have your 'before.'"

He rubbed his beard. "What I wouldn't give to see my family again. My mate. My younglings. I'd break mountains, burn forests to see them. I'd slaughter nations of enemies. But no matter what I do, I am stuck in the 'after' of that day. But you, Ta. You still have your 'before.'" He seized Ta's shoulder. "So tonight, *keep* it."

Ta nodded. He'd always thought his "before" was losing his hand. Nothing good after. But that was wrong. Here, with his new friends, he was far happier than he'd been in Akkad. My life is just beginning, he thought in amazement. There is so much more to do, to see.

But tonight, he'd have to earn it.

"Rogg? You think we have a chance?"

"I do. But now I must go."

"I'm ready," Ta said.

"I know you are, brother."

Rogg pressed his forehead to Ta's and murmured a war blessing in the Elamite tongue. Ta did not understand it. But somehow, a sense of calm and strength flowed into him, filled his bloodstream. Then Rogg marched off, leaving Ta behind the bush in the dimming light, alone.

The gloom deepened. Flies nipped at Ta's ears. He lay flat, letting the flies eat, keeping his eyes on the gully bed. He was reluctant to make any big movements that might be seen. This was getting real, now. Incredibly real.

Birds cooed gently above him. Fireflies drifted by his face, blinking their green lights on and off. It was difficult not to think of what was coming. The fear began creeping in again, curling its black fingers around Ta's heart. Ta decided to try one of the tricks Rogg had given him. "When afraid, just work," Rogg had said. So, Ta worked. In his mind, he focused on the path he must run. He saw it over and over in his imagination. And Rogg was right. The more Ta worked, the more it blocked the worry. Time flew.

Then, in the gully bed below, a bird whistled.

Ta's body went as tight as a cord. That was no bird.

Holding his breath, he flattened even lower. There were gaps in the bush. He peered through them, looking downhill, scanning left and right. *There.* Crossing the bed, creeping up through the thorns, was a living shadow. It separated from the fainter shadows and flowed up the slope at a crouch. *Magog.*

Ta's blood began to roar. Rogg had described Magog perfectly. Tattoos darkened the man's body, giving him the aspect of a wolf. He crept low like a wolf, too, sniffing at the Akkadians' footprints as if on a scent. Even more strangely, a necklace swung from his throat, rattling against his pectorals. A string of dry human ears, Ta realized with revulsion. Trophies of murder.

So it was all true.

The man whistled again. More Magog warriors emerged from the bushes. Fifteen in all. They ran up after the leader in a pack, their eyes flat and cold. It was time to move. *Now.* But something was wrong. Ta's muscles wouldn't work. He was frozen in place.

He told his legs to stand. Nothing. The paralysis of a prey animal filled him. With horror, he recalled the last time this had happened. Crossing the Tigris with his fellow Akkadian exiles, his raft had capsized, and he'd unthinkingly splashed away to save himself, leaving a tool pack and an old woman to sink. Korak was forced to swim back for her. The pack was lost, and everyone scorned Ta for days. The same thing was happening now.

Ta tried not to panic. He wasn't in control of himself. All right. So what should he do? Was it too late to beg Magog for mercy? What had Rogg said? *The only language they understand is force.* No mercy. So, what, then? *See your people.* In a flash, Ta saw Shulgi dashed on the rocks; Aya, scalped with a stone knife; Rogg butchered, his noble flesh hanging in strips from a smoking tripod; and Ki thrown in the dirt, the men doing bad things to her.

NO.

For the first time in his life, Ta felt ready to fight.

In full view of the warriors, he rose and looked over the bush. Like a pack of hunting dogs, they froze and fixed their eyes on him, making no sound. I'm doing it, Ta thought breathlessly. No turning back now.

For what felt like an eternity, he stared. They stared back. A drop of sweat tickled down his temple, the world achingly vivid. Then, slowly, the biggest warrior lifted a tattooed hand in a greeting. "Ho, friend. You look hungry." He turned and beckoned to one of his hulking companions, who carried a shoulder pack. "We have food. Meat." At the human gesture, Ta's resolve wavered. What if Rogg and Ki had been mistaken about these people?

Then he looked closer. The speaker also wore a necklace, he realized. Not of ears, but of yellow bones. *Finger*-bones. Ta's *emittu* flipped over. Then, indeed, it was easy to turn and run.

Shouts erupted. "Stay, friend!" Ta ignored them. He raced along the ridgetop. Logs, branches, and thorns leapt out to trip him. But thanks to Rogg, he'd run the path in practice, then again in his head, many times. Anticipating every dip and turn, he shot through the understory.

Crashes erupted behind him. They were coming. Ta turned sharply downward. At the crotch of the two slopes was the chalk-white bed. Access to it was given at only a few points; farther on, the walls grew tall and steep. Ta slid down a groove and hit the gravelly bottom and raced on, drawing the pursuers after him. The plan was working. The sheer walls rose higher on each side. Soon they stood over twelve paces high, just as Ki wanted.

"Stop, friend! We have food, water," the voices shouted after him down the funnel. Ta checked his pace a little. He could not get too far ahead. Just far enough to evade capture. But slow enough to keep them chasing—

Something whizzed past his leg. A spear? Yes. It struck the wall ahead, throwing up a white cloud of dust that coated his knees as he charged through it. They were trying to lame him.

Then he was around the turn, into the dead end. Relief hit. Whatever happened now, his part was done.

He looked around the trap. A pile of debris blocked the exit ahead. It stood higher than a man: logs, rubble, thorn matter, and other junk. The group had dumped it there on purpose to close the area. It looked natural enough, if Magog didn't inspect it too closely.

"Ta, you made it! Here!"

Ki leaned over the gully lip, waving. "Quick, I hear them coming. Rogg, the rope."

Rogg appeared and tossed a noose down. Ta needed no urging. He ran to the noose, stabbed his stump in, and grabbed the rope higher up with his good hand. "Go." Instantly the rope went up. Rogg heaved it mightily, jerking Ta higher with each pull, lifting him out of the death trap. Ta felt exhilarated. *It's working. Almost there. Go!*

Then a *snap* exploded in his ear, and he was falling. All the way down!

Shocked, he hit the rocky bed hard, striking his hips with hammer-blow force. Hot pain shot up his spine. Above, Ki and Rogg pulled out of sight, yanking the snapped rope with them. Ta sat up dizzily, holding his end of the rope. The broken end. A stunned despair filled him. So this is how it ends? A stupid rope-break? He lifted his eyes to the violet sky. *Gods, are you against me? What did I do wrong? Worship yourselves now, pitiless idols. I'm done with you.*

The crunch of footsteps filled the funnel. Ta turned. Magog was streaming into the trap. Just in time he jammed the broken rope under his thighs to hide it, but it hardly mattered, everything was over. He was like a baby bird trapped in a nest, watching a big black snake slither toward him. The warriors slowed to a walk. They filled the gully wall to wall, just as Ki had hoped, four men abreast at the widest point. The rear ones had to hop up and down to get a glimpse of him. Some were laughing. All were panting, out of breath from the chase.

"Ey, Akkadian. What happened, twist your foot?" A big one knelt at Ta's side. The leader. His finger-bone necklace glinted red in the sunset. "You shouldn't have run." He shoved Ta in the chest, knocking him back with surprising force. Ta slammed flat onto his shoulder blades and lay still, paralyzed with fear. With indulgent slowness, the leader knelt on Ta's chest and ground his kneecap into Ta's sternum, screwing pain into the bone. It suddenly hurt to breathe. Hot waves of agony radiated into Ta's core. His voice croaked out pitifully.

"What've I done?"

The man bent closer, inspecting Ta's face. His breath was nauseating, his body odor foul. Sour urine. Oily sweat. No bath for days. He laughed gently.

"Done? What has he done, brothers?"

"He did that fire," one said. "Had us chasing all over Mesopotamia."

"He did," another said. "Cut his face, Ur-Baba."

Ur-Baba grunted in agreement. In a swift motion, he grabbed Ta's beard and yanked it up, putting a knife to Ta's throat. Beneath the stone blade, Ta's jugular vein fluttered thinly, struggling to carry its flow of blood. Ta's mind went empty of all but the knife. One slash, and his life would gush out forever. *Start the attack,* he pleaded silently. But nothing happened.

Ur-Baba's knife lowered and tapped Ta's stump. "Look here, brothers. He's a cripple."

The warriors pressed in, murmuring. The plan had gone all wrong. Ta forced himself not to look at the gully lip. If he looked for his friends, he'd give them away.

There was no mercy in Ur-Baba's eyes. "Now wait, brothers. Didn't those Akkadians a few days ago mention a cripple?"

"Yes, yes," the warriors agreed. "Must be him."

"How many cripples wandering our desert? Not many, I'd wager."

Ta's heart dropped. *Akkadians?* Could Ur-Baba mean his old companions, Korak and the others? Who else would know about Ta?

"How many were there?" he burst out.

"Oh, ten, eleven."

"Are they all right?"

Ur-Baba's eyes gleamed with humor. "In a sense. Nice and peaceful, now."

The blood drained from Ta's head. His fellow exiles. "You killed them?" he whispered.

"You should be glad. They betrayed you readily. We didn't even have to torture them."

Ta felt as if a club had broken his chest. He lay breathless, the world spinning. He had not expected this. So, my old tribe is gone, he thought. Korak, brothers, sisters . . . we never got along, but you did not deserve this.

And if I'd stayed with them, I'd be dead too, he realized.

Ur-Baba's voice snapped him back to the present.

"Found new friends, though, didn't you, cripple? Better ones."

Ta shook his head. "N-o . . ."

"Meet a nomad girl, by chance?"

"No," Ta said in alarm, perhaps too quickly.

"What about a giant?"

"No!"

"Lies!"

The tattooed hand slapped Ta's face. Sparks burst in his head. The warriors cheered.

"You didn't make that decoy fire," Ur-Baba shouted. "A bigger slave did. Man-feet made those tracks. Not your little-boy feet. So where is this man now?" The knife traced the line of Ta's mouth. "He's got a lying tongue. Should we cut it out?"

"Cut him, Ur-Baba. Give him pain," a man shouted.

"Or is this closer to home?" Ur-Baba seized Ta's good hand and slammed it flat on the gully bed. He pressed the knife to Ta's wrist-vein with a dark smile. "We value things we've lost." He bent lower, bone necklace swinging. "How much do you value this?"

Under the knife, Ta's wrist-artery throbbed. His hand! His only remaining hand! The pounding of blood in his ears grew deafening. "Cut! Cut!" the warriors screamed, hopping in delight. "Make him a double-stump!" The knife pressed harder. Ta's eyes fixed on his left hand. He knew Ur-Baba could do it. If he could execute Ta's friends, eleven people, a hand would be nothing to him.

"Please," Ta begged. "I'll do anything."

"Your big friend," Ur-Baba said patiently. "Where is he?"

Ta wavered. The ambush had failed. The others had abandoned him. He was alone. He had to save himself at any cost or—

He froze. *At any cost?* Even betray my friends? No. That was too far.

Do you love yourself more, or your people? Rogg had asked. Ta did. Already they meant far more than a hand. They'd given him life again. If he betrayed them, he betrayed himself. And he'd done that enough in Akkad.

To his surprise, he met Ur-Baba's eyes.

"Join me, Ur-Baba."

The warriors fell quiet. Ur-Baba sat back, his jaw slack. He tried laughing, but he was so puzzled, it came out like a choking sound. "Did he say *join,* brothers?"

"Maybe his head is diseased," a warrior suggested.

Ur-Baba leaned farther back, scanning Ta for clues of plague. But Ta's confidence was rising. His trail might end here. But he was himself, at last. It made things rather simple.

He nodded at the tattoos. "Why do you obey Gog? He brands you. Uses you. Kills you. He cares nothing for you. You're his slaves."

"I am no *slave,*" Ur-Baba scoffed.

"I was a slave myself." Ta's conviction grew. "A sort of one, up in Akkad. So I know what it's like. That's why I'm here, starting a new tribe. No chiefs. Every member gets a say. It's a place for starting over. Thieves. Cripples. Runaways. Anyone, really . . . with no place to go."

Something stirred in Ur-Baba's face. His warriors, too, looked dumbstruck, and kept glancing at Ur-Baba for guidance.

"By Baal." Ur-Baba forced a laugh. "Did we catch a philosopher?"

"Call it what you please." Ta lifted his stump. "If I can start over, you can, too." He nodded at their tattoos. "Why not be free of those, brother? Be new."

Ur-Baba looked at him. Had a break in the mask appeared? A puzzlement?

Then his warriors exploded into laughter, mocking Ta. And Ur-Baba's eyes hardened.

"How the slave yaps," he exclaimed. "Yaps and yaps! He'll disease all our heads."

"Cut his noisy tongue out."

"I will." Ur-Baba yelled into Ta's face: "Gog is great!"

"GOG IS GREAT!" screamed the warriors.

"But doesn't it sicken you?" Ta cried, frustrated. "Hurting people all the time? What were you *before* those tattoos? Don't you remember?"

Ur-Baba waved his knife in contempt. "Pah. You speak like a woman because the pain is coming to *you*. But the pain does not come to *us*. Only the pleasure."

"Pleasure in killing?"

"Oh, cripple." Ur-Baba grinned like a boy with a dirty secret. "Weak ones never know this, do they? The pleasure of walking down the main path of a village and saying, 'Ah, that one there.' And taking any woman you please. Taking her there in the path, shattering all custom." His grin widened. "And afterward, when I cut her mate's and children's throats in front of her while she weeps, and watch her *emittu* drain out forever . . . *that* is pleasure. To shatter a person's hope in life, to drink their despair—that is to become their god."

Ta listened, dumbfounded. A black feeling seemed to flow from Ur-Baba into him. Ur-Baba lowered his face to Ta's, as if to kiss his lips. "And tonight, cripple," he whispered, "I will drink *your* despair. Do you have a woman in your tribe?" His eyes searched Ta's. "Yes. I see you do. Tonight, she will scream for help. And you will listen as I cut her apart like a rabbit, piece by piece. Your *emittu* will come out of you, and I will sip of it. Then, cripple, believe me—I will be *your* god."

Ta wasn't sure what Ur-Baba meant. But now he understood Ki's hatred for these people. They might have been human, once. No longer. So Ta braced himself to die.

"It's a pity we can't be brothers," he said quietly. "The world is uglier for it."

"You can still save your woman. Tell me where your big friend is."

Ta shook his head.

"Well. Perhaps you are a man after all." Ur-Baba set his knife back on Ta's wrist joint and prepared to cut. "So pay like a man."

Ta tensed and shut his eyes. *Help me bear it well, El. Don't let me shame myself.*

But then it happened—the thing he'd given up hoping for.

BOOM.

A crash filled the gully. An explosion of dust and noise that shook the ground.

"YAAAH!" Ur-Baba sprang back as if he'd been stung.

Ta sat up, panting. The attack had begun!

The crashing went on and on. It was a great roaring, a cacophony of rumbling and *cracks* that split the air. The warriors all spun, spears raised. Debris was avalanching into the entry funnel, closing off the only escape. "Keep back," Ur-Baba yelled. He stepped on Ta's arm in his haste to get away. But there was no escaping the white dust-fog that filled the area, blinding and choking everyone below. They didn't leave me! Ta could have wept. My dear friends!

Some warriors scrambled deeper into the trap, stepping on Ta. Others pressed against the walls for safety, shouting at the avalanche as if to challenge it. Still, it kept coming, closing off the funnel. The rubble piled as high as a man's chest, shutting the gully in. And hidden in the fog, Ta seized his chance.

He leapt up and ran to the wall. Above him, Ki appeared on the lip. She dropped another noose, and this time the rope held. Up Ta went. Up. And once he reached the lip, he slapped both arms along it and struggled to heave himself over.

"Where can you go, cripple?" Ur-Baba shouted from below. "The whole world is Magog's! Every corner and hole! There is no place to hide."

Ta rolled over the lip. As he did, Ur-Baba threw his stone knife. It struck Ta's hip and sliced open his skin, hurting terribly. But luckily it struck the hardness of Ta's hip bone and ricocheted off into the bracken. And now Ta was safe, Magog trapped below.

"Is it bad?" Ki bent over him, looking at his wound.

"It's fine," he said. "What happened?"

"The platform stuck," Ki said in frustration. "But I fixed it. It all works now."

"Thank the gods," Ta said.

"Now it's our turn." Ki's eyes blazed. "Time to hit back."

Below, Ur-Baba screamed in infantile rage. "Kill them! Kill them all!"

In obedience, his warriors launched a hail of spears at the gully lip. Not a moment too soon, Ta and Ki fell flat. A hot wind overshot them as the hail of wood flew past. The spears went up into the thorn branches and clattered off harmlessly, sending a faint shower of chips down onto Ta's back. Rogg was right, Ta thought. They're overconfident, sloppy. Magog had just lost half their weapons.

He crawled back to the lip in time to hear a scream of pain below. The area still smoked with dust, too murky to make much out. But by the avalanche wall, a Magog warrior had been struck by a spear. It stuck out of his back, wobbling as he screamed and turned in a circle, trying to reach around and yank it out.

The culprit was Rogg. He stood behind the avalanche wall, a bundle of fresh-cut spears on the ground beside him. He bent down, selected a second weapon, and took aim for a second throw. Past the barrier, Magog was crammed into a tight pack. Rogg could hardly miss. With a roar, he hurled his second spear into their ranks. A second cry of agony resulted. Now two men screamed. They writhed, blocking the progress of the others who struggled to push past them to the barrier.

"There he is. The big one," Ur-Baba shrieked. "Get him! I will eat his heart!"

The warriors threw their wounded companions aside and charged. Behind the chest-high barrier, Rogg was ready. "For my village!" he bellowed. A third spear flew. A third man fell back into the crowd, both hands gripping a spear in his stomach.

"Platform two," the giant yelled at Ki.

Ki nodded. The plan was entering its middle phase. She ran off toward the second platform as Ur-Baba's men continued to toss hatchets.

And Rogg was a marvel. He kept up the distraction admirably. He ducked behind the barrier, let the hatchets bang off it and flip away into the dusty fog, then stood up again and hurled a fourth spear into the crowd at point-blank range. A fourth shriek rose as a fourth body fell. "For my dead mate!" Now he grabbed a club. A man trampled his hurt companions to get over the barrier, waving his stone knife—and received a *CRACK* in the face from the club that spun him limp back into his fellows, adding to the wall of injured flesh. Ta slapped the ledge in exultation. *Yes, Rogg. YES.*

"Second drop," Ki yelled. "Here I go."

At a second platform, she yanked a rope, and there was no delay this time: the platform's front two supports collapsed at the tug, and its fore edge banged down. It created a slant that unloaded a second pile of rocks, sticks, and debris—this time onto the heads of the astonished warriors.

"Go, Aya!" Ki shouted across the gully.

On the opposite lip, Aya knelt by a third and final platform. Nodding at the command, she yanked a rope of her own, initiating a third avalanche. It hit the warriors even as Ki's load did, obscuring the kill-pit in dust.

"Keep it up!" Rogg roared. "We've got them!"

Now the final phase of the fight commenced. Sticks and stones sat in piles along the gully lip for the friends to throw. And throw they did, hurling the objects willy-nilly into the roil. Some projectiles missed and clattered uselessly off the bed. But others hit, audibly cracking bone and mashing flesh. Ta, for his part, threw with a red fury he'd never experienced. Ur-Baba's ugly words had changed him, sickened something inside. He screamed like an animal as he threw. Rogg, meanwhile, was a vision of the death god, Nergal. Behind the barrier, he danced side to side, throwing, ducking, bobbing up to throw again. His eyes flashed with righteous fury. His long hair flowed out like liquid flame. His throws were quick but not rushed. Each flew with precision. Each delivered death. The warriors wanted none of it, and shoved each other to get away from him, clutching their wounds, red blood squirting through their fingers.

"Ho, cripple! I want *you*!"

Ta looked down. Ur-Baba stood directly under him, covered in gashes.

"Look in my eyes, cripple! I will bite off your face!"

With that, the warrior grabbed a thick root that clung to the gully wall and began to climb, pulling himself up toward Ta, hand over hand. His front teeth gnashed the air, chomping for Ta's flesh. His finger-bone necklace rattled. Ta shrank back. All his life he'd wavered before such power—before the chief in the Akkad, before Korak in the desert.

But no more, he thought suddenly. No more.

Leaning back over the lip, he raised a rock and heaved it down. It flew directly into Ur-Baba's face. The *crunch* was awful. Ur-Baba went limp and tumbled back into the gully. He landed with a *crack* that surely broke his back. Twitched, went limp . . .

And the battle went on.

Ta wasn't sure how long it continued. But suddenly Rogg roared, "STOP," and Ta went still, abruptly drained. So did the others. It was strangely quiet in the gully.

Ta looked around blankly. His tongue was gritty with dust. His ears rang. It was so quiet, he heard soft broken groans, and the scratchy sounds of the enemy crawling through the dusty fog.

Rogg climbed over the barrier, holding his club. "Ki, watch my rear."

Ki nodded.

"Akkadians, you may not wish to see this," Rogg warned.

Obediently, Ta and Aya shut their eyes. But Ta still heard it—the awful *crunch* of Rogg's club crushing bone—as he strolled among the survivors, ushering them off to the Underworld.

21

When Ta finally permitted himself to look again, the ugliness in the gully numbed him.

He saw eyeballs glazed with grit, and mouths ajar, filled with bloodstained teeth. He saw bent limbs poking from the piles of rubble. Bones protruded from flesh like white sticks poking out of red mud. Horror filled Ta's *emittu*, and he clutched his stomach. What had they done?

Only one warrior remained alive. He crawled slowly away from Rogg, groaning as his broken leg dragged behind him.

"I must question him." Rogg stepped in front of the man, lowering his club to block the man's crawl. "You all should return to camp."

"You mean to torture him?" Aya whitened.

"Not if he answers honestly. But there are things I need to know. For instance, has he any friends in the area?"

"No, no," the warrior groaned.

"We will see." Rogg looked upward. "Go."

The others obliged, and soon the gully faded into darkness behind them.

The camp wasn't far. This was good, for both Aya and Ta were injured. They had to lean on Ki, arms around her shoulders, hopping to keep their damaged limbs off the ground.

"You've strong legs, nomad girl," Aya said. "For one so skinny."

"Nomad legs are strong," Ki said. "They have to be, to walk all over Mesopotamia."

When they arrived, Ki helped settle Ta and Aya on their blankets beside the fire pit. Shulgi hung in his sling-pouch from a tree branch, high up for safety from predators. He was irritated—hungry—and seeing Aya, he began to babble, waving his pudgy hands. Aya laughed softly.

"Really, son? After all your mother's just done for you?"

Ki smiled and took him down. Aya rocked him and hugged him, shutting her eyes. Ki knelt to prepare the fire. Ta lay flat on his blanket and buried his face in his arms.

He felt more and more sick. He kept seeing the tattooed bodies twisted in the rubble. Kept hearing the *snap* of Ur-Baba's back as it broke on the rocks. This didn't feel like the victories from the legends. No. Ta's gut felt raw, as if a sharp stone had scraped it hollow.

The others seemed to feel it, too. Night descended quickly, and in the firelight, their faces looked dull and empty, like wooden masks. Aya crawled over and pressed a poultice to Ta's hip, stinging the cut. Ta hardly noticed. The firewood snapped and hissed. The night felt thick around them. Ta wondered where his enemies' *emittus* were now. In *Kur?* Had their lives mattered? Did anyone's?

Only when Rogg stepped from the trees did the mood change.

"Ho, friends. Dinner, courtesy of Magog."

Rogg was carrying three Magog packs. He dropped them in the dirt proudly. "We got some nice plunder in there. Trinkets and things. Food. Rummage in 'em. I bet you find something you like."

He looked around eagerly. Then he saw their faces, and his tone softened.

"Ah, forgive me. I forgot. It is your first battle."

He knelt beside Aya and wrapped his great arms around her, like a father embracing a daughter. Aya began to weep, and Rogg nodded.

"Weep, sister. There is no shame in it. Your *emittu* is merely sick. We were not made to kill each other. Even if it is Magog."

He hugged Ki, then. And Ta last.

"Don't forget, *they* asked for this," he said, patting Ta's back. "If they'd won, you and I would be dead right now. And the women . . . worse. Who wishes that?"

The others shook their heads.

"Good!" Rogg smashed his fist into his palm. "Remember, in life sometimes you *must* fight. And fight you did! Ki, what a plan. Aya, those throws!" He clapped Ta on the shoulder, nearly knocking him over. "And brother, you kept faith under the knife! Many warriors would have broken. Not you. You were ready. I knew it."

He crushed Ta in another hug, and his touch was so powerful, it flooded Ta with warmth, pushing away the black emptiness inside. Ta sat up straighter.

"Thank you, Rogg."

"No, thank *you*. Today is a rare thing. Magog seldom loses." Rogg faced the group. "So come, lift yourselves up. Don't disrespect your work. Honor it."

Then he did something wholly unexpected. Turning his shaggy face to the sky, he spread his arms, opened his mouth, and roared into the blackness. "RAAAHHHH!"

The others watched in astonishment. But Rogg kept at it, thumping the drum of his chest.

"RAAAAAAAAHHH!! RAAAAAAAHHHH!"

His voice shook the air like a lion's after a kill. Every emotion was in it. Joy and pain, rage and pride, love and sorrow, and a hundred more feelings besides. Hearing it, something primal in Ta awoke, an animal joy at being alive. And before he knew it, he joined in.

"Raaah! Raaaaah!"

Then they were all screaming together, beating their chests, howling as if they'd gone mad. Ta's throat hurt, but each cry expelled a host of bad spirits into the night. And when he quieted at last, he felt almost like himself again.

Rogg grinned.

"Better, eh? Now let's eat. Nothing like a battle to give you an appetite." He pointed at Magog's packs. "As you'll see, they eat only the best."

The mood lifted after that. The group ate heartily, laughed, drank, and recounted the battle in detail. Everyone had done something praiseworthy, and the more they talked, the happier they grew. Setbacks like Ta's rope snapping only made them more giddy at their victory. Magog's bags held fresh spices, too, and Aya added them to the feast with great effect. Gulping a bite of smoked rabbit down, Ta wiped grease from his lips and looked around the fire at the proud shining faces. He felt very close to them. Battle had bonded them like nothing else could.

I'd do anything for them, he thought suddenly. And I truly believe they'd do the same for me.

Ki reached out, testing Ta's poultice. "Forgive me, Ta. When that first platform didn't work, I really thought . . ." She blew out a long breath. "I thought I'd killed you. How's your hip? It's not too painful?"

"It's nothing."

The warm touch of her hand satisfied Ta more than all the food in the world. He felt like he was floating, every throb of pain from Ur-Baba's knife cut a blessing.

Drawing their attention, Aya lifted her water bag in a toast.

"To Ki and Rogg. You are no longer strangers, but honorary Akkadians. From this day forth, your troubles are our troubles."

"Hear! Hear!" Ta cried, pumping his stump in the air.

"If you ever need help, just ask," Aya said. "Ta and I will answer."

"Yes!" Ta agreed.

Ki and Rogg bowed deeply, almost shy. Rogg's voice grew solemn.

"Elam is your home, too, brother and sisters. If you ever visit my country, you will enjoy a feast you'll never forget." He patted Ta's arm. "The finest goat meat. Rich *ibil* leaf paste." He pointed at Aya. "And fire ant salad. It's better than it sounds, I promise you. In fact, you might get ideas for a new recipe."

The others laughed.

"Of course, you're honorary nomads, too," Ki said. Then she winced. "That is, if you wish it."

"We wish it," the group cried. "Hear! Hear! To nomads!"

Then, right there, Aya urged Ki to stand and do a nomad dance. Ki hesitated. But they cheered her, and banged sticks together, and slapped time on the ground. And soon Ki's black hair was flying, dust puffing up under her bare heels. A strange wild chant flew from her lips. It was a tune of far hills and mountains, of vast deserts and yellow plains unseen by Mesopotamian eyes. The others loved it, and they howled and clapped as she leapt around the fire, until Rogg stood and joined in awkwardly, stomping the earth so that it trembled. Everyone burst out laughing. Finally, Ki fell to the ground exhausted, her face glowing with sweat in the red firelight. Ta could not look away. She was so beautiful.

Intuitively, he drank from the water bag in a symbolic gulp of alliance. The others murmured assent and drank too, sealing their pact of friendship with the gift of precious water.

"Good gesture, Ta," Aya said. "You're coming along. You really are."

But once Rogg finished his symbolic gulp, he lowered the bag and rebuked Aya gently.

"Come, sister. Does he not deserve a better name than 'cripple?'"

Aya covered her mouth. "Ah, forgive me. I didn't even think of it. But what can I call him?"

"I don't mind," Ta said quickly.

"I do," Rogg said. "Names matter. We'd be in *Kur* right now if you'd given us up to Ur-Baba. But you didn't. Is that the work of a 'cripple?'"

Ta gripped his stump uneasily. "But the chief . . . and the priest—"

"Bah!" Rogg roared. "No priest can shake his bead stick and make you a man. It's deeds like tonight's that do it. Nothing else. Believe me, brother. The more you do, the more you'll change. One day you may even welcome these battles, for the greatness they summon in you."

The women flickered their tongues in ululations of support. But Ta lowered his face. I'll never welcome such things, he thought. I hope everything is easy and peaceful from now on.

But Rogg wasn't finished.

"In Elam, a warrior wins his name in his first battle. This was Ta's. I say he's earned a name."

"Yes, Rogg," Aya said.

Ta was shocked. He was used to his name. But everyone looked so excited, he didn't want to spoil the mood.

Rogg scratched his beard. "I admit, I'm not good with names. And I don't know many Akkadian ones."

"I do." Aya sat up, looking excited. "I know one that fits perfectly." She faced Ta. "It comes from an ancient legend. Every Akkadian knows it. The legend of Sargon the Great."

Ta laughed. "Really, Aya."

However, both Rogg and Ki seemed interested. Rogg was nodding. And Ki leaned forward, shadows dancing on her face, her hands folded in her lap. "Go on," she said. "I never heard it."

Aya bowed.

"Here is the short version. Many generations ago, a woman fell in love with a man who wasn't her mate. They got a child in secret, and when he was born, she put him in a grass basket and floated it down the Tigris River, entrusting him to the goddess Inanna. The goddess took pity on the babe. She guided the basket to a friendly tribe, and they raised the boy as their own. His name was Sargon, and he rose to become their chief.

"He was not just any chief, either," Aya said, smiling at Ta. "He beat back five Gutian invasions. Led his tribe to prosperity. Most of all, he united Akkad into a peaceful alliance of tribes, the only time this has ever happened. He did it not by conquering them, but by convincing them to live by a code: the 'Code of Sargon the Great.' The code protected everyone equally. Strong and weak alike. Of course, after Sargon died, the Akkadian tribes went back to fighting each other. But we still look back on this period as the peak of our greatness. All Akkadian tribes sing songs in Sargon's memory."

Rogg nodded. "In Elam we know of Sargon. Everyone respects him, even his enemies."

Aya brushed hair out of her eyes. "And what of Ta? Has he not shown traits of Sargon lately? Taking risks for his people. Saving strangers from rivers. Calming Ut. Recruiting giants. Defeating Magog tonight. That is the way of a hero. He deserves the name of one. 'Sargon!'"

Ta laughed, embarrassed. "Dear sister, this is a kindness beyond words. But really."

However, Rogg and Ki were nodding.

"It is fitting," Rogg said. "Let it be done."

Ta's voice rose in protest. "I can't take such a name. It is for a great man, not me."

"All the better," Rogg said. "You will be forced to live up to it."

It seemed they really meant it. Panicked, Ta looked for an excuse to get away. But the women noticed and pointed their fingers, laughing. "Quick, grab him! Before he tries to run." So Rogg grabbed Ta's shoulder and restrained him on the blanket.

"Now kneel, brother, if your hip will permit it. And receive your blessing."

Bewildered, Ta knelt and bowed. Rogg reached into one of the stolen Magog packs and drew out a fist-sized purse, one a priest might store holy aids in, such as frankincense resin, or waxy gums for incense. Lifting it, he opened it over Ta's head, and a cool oil flowed down his brow into his beard, smelling of myrrh. Ta trembled. Myrrh was a rare and precious purifying ointment, reserved for honoring the highest ones in a tribe, chiefs or priests. Not a cripple.

Rogg didn't stop.

"Brother, you did a great thing today. You sacrificed yourself to save the tribe. For this, we honor you. And we give you a name. No longer shall you be called 'Cripple,' or any such foolishness. Forthwith, we dub you, 'Sargon, Highly Praised One.'" He poured out the whole purse, and when he finished, he shouted: "Welcome, Sargon. Live long and become great!"

"Sargon!" the others echoed. "Live long and become great!!"

Even Shulgi giggled on his blanket and waggled his clubfoot, as if to agree.

Then, one by one, they approached and kissed the anointed one's damp head, saying, "Welcome, Sargon."

Ki kissed his forehead last of all. Pulling back, she gazed at him with such pride and warmth that he blushed. He did feel different. For what woman had ever looked that way upon "Ta?"

After the ceremony, the group went back to eating, drinking, and discussing the battle. But Sargon just sat there in a daze, amazed at what had happened. He was afraid to move, lest he wake up and find it all a dream. He'd never felt so happy.

PART

II

22

The morning after the battle, Ta sat up and looked around the campsite, relishing the feeling of being alive.

The site was peaceful. Sunlight dappled the bushes, and red birds chirped among the leaves, filling the air with pleasant music. A rabbit hopped by, wiggling its whiskered nose. Ta yawned and stretched. Yesterday, the odds had been all against him staying in this world. Now every sensation was a gift, something he had no right to expect.

He checked on his companions. They were still slumbering on their hide blankets—all except Rogg, whose place was empty. The big warrior was probably up scouting the perimeter. Ta smiled. Always impressive, that fellow.

Then, suddenly, he gripped his stump. He'd called himself *Ta*. He was *Sargon* now. Anxiety struck. What if he couldn't live up to it?

He wasn't sure why, but he felt a desire to be alone in a high place. Heeding the feeling, he limped stiffly uphill through the trees, favoring his knife-cut hip. It was hard work, for the wound was only fresh-knitted, and even the slightest jerk threatened to rip it open. Maybe this was a reckless idea, he thought. He grew winded, and when he was only halfway up, he had to stop and lean against a trunk, panting as he rested his throbbing hip. Nevertheless, he reached the ridgetop eventually. And there he found a warm boulder to sit on from which he could look out over the gullies and hills.

El, thank you for this day, he thought, folding his arms. *I will not take it for granted.*

The view here was even more beautiful than the one below. Red birds zipped here and there in the canopy, and small black squirrels scurried through the overhanging limbs, scratching the bark with their tiny claws. Once again, Sargon felt a rush of joy at being alive. In a burst of gratitude, he lifted his nose and breathed in the warm air that blew over the forest. A medley of odors came to him. Bird dung and acacia sap. Einkorn and emmer wheat. Wildflower and shrub. And above all, the complexity of the red soil itself, enriched annually by snowmelt from the Zagros Mountains. This was the glory of the "land between the rivers," a layering of minerals incomparable in the known world. Year after year, the floods poured their wealth across the alluvial Mesopotamian floodplain. And it was all Sargon's to enjoy.

A sense of peace filled him. He still felt the weakness of "Ta" in himself, interwoven through his body like rotten fibers through fresh cord. But his triumphs were there, too, and he shut his eyes and thanked "the One Who is here." Too many things had fallen into place to make this an accident. Something new was occurring in this desert, he was sure of it, and he intended to keep his heart open and see what came.

I beg your help, oh El, he prayed. *I have been both Ta and Sargon. And Sargon is life. And Ta is death.* He clenched his fist. *Help me be Sargon! Help me never go back to Ta! I swear I will burn much meat to you on the stone altar once we find a home. And I will be faithful to you all my life. And treat you as separate from other gods.*

He sat praying like that for a long time. And when he was done, he opened his eyes and watched the new day come, spreading gold and red over the land.

◆

"Ho, brother. We're not interrupting, are we?"

Rustles in the understory announced the arrival of his friends. Sargon turned and smiled as Aya waved up at him through the trees. She was still limping, her arm around Ki. But Rogg was there, too, carrying Shulgi in one arm, a satchel of food in the other.

"Thought we'd join you for breakfast," Aya said. "You mind? It looks nice up there."

"Just in time," Sargon said. "I was getting hungry."

Rogg rested the satchel beside the rock and spread a hide rag to set the food on. Sargon's mouth watered. There was fish, duck meat, berry paste, and a bowl of crushed tubers and seeds.

"Magog's a good host," Rogg said, sniffing it happily. "Aya put it together while you were taking it easy up here. She crawled around in the bushes for magic herbs. Fixed things nice."

Aya shook her finger at him. "You tasted it already? It was supposed to be a surprise!"

Rogg grinned.

"I tried some, too," Ki confessed. "The fish rub is delicious, Aya."

Aya grew bashful. "Well, in a forest, there's more variety, you know. Even a thorn forest."

They sat and passed the things around, and Sargon marveled at how delicious they tasted. Indeed, the fish had a mix of three flavors he'd never experienced together: earthy, fruity, and sweetly sour at the same time. The only one who didn't love it was Shulgi. He fussed and spat out everything Aya gave him until she surrendered and fed him his usual fingerful of date mash, which he gobbled up victoriously.

Rogg, however, was fully impressed.

"Where'd you find fruit flavor out here, Aya? By Enki, it's good."

"Bushes have berries, Rogg. I thought you were more observant," Aya teased. "Perhaps your eyesight is getting weak in your old age."

Rogg grunted, chewing on a fish tail. "Maybe."

"Truly, how old are you?" Aya insisted, her eyes flashing playfully.

Rogg scowled and grabbed another fish. "I forget."

The group laughed.

Their future was uncertain, however, and their conversation grew more serious. Two of them had injuries and would need to heal before they could travel. Magog's supplies would dwindle each day. And they still didn't know where to go.

"What about that warrior you questioned?" Aya asked Rogg. "Did he mention a free site?"

Ki and Sargon glanced at each other. Rogg hadn't mentioned what he'd done to the fellow, and in truth, nobody wanted to know.

Rogg showed no remorse. He casually jerked his thumb toward the battle gully.

"He told me one useful thing. A big tribe controls this area. Supposedly it's the most civilized tribe on the Euphrates."

The group grew curious.

"Civilized," Aya repeated. "What's that mean?"

"I agree, anything might seem civilized compared to Magog," Rogg said. "But I've heard of this village before. It's called 'Babylon.' Know of it?"

The group shook their heads.

"Ba-Babylon?" Aya struggled to form the word.

"It's a Sumerian word," Rogg said. "This is the region of Sumer now. The tribes are strange. 'Babylon.' 'Eridu.' 'Ur.' Odd to pronounce. But the good news is, we've left Magog's territory behind us. This far south, Gog controls no more vassal tribes, so the smoke signals chasing Ki should end."

Ki blew out a stream of air. "That's almost too good to believe."

Rogg looked north. "Gog doesn't rule everything. Not yet."

"But what is Babylon like?" Aya insisted. "What if they're as bad as Magog?" She added under her breath: "You think they caught Ut? I wouldn't mind that."

"Well, when I talked to the warrior," Rogg said, "he told me that Magog destroys, but Babylon builds. According to him, Babylon has beautiful dwellings. A great fleet. Three hundred people. And a wise queen to rule them."

The group listened closely. This might be promising, Sargon thought. We're desperate.

"Should we send a scout in?" he asked.

"We might," Rogg conceded.

"Isn't that dangerous?" Aya asked.

"Maybe. But some tribes like helping wanderers. In return for offering food and shelter, the tribe gets news of the world." Rogg pondered it. "Babylon has no cause to harm us. They don't know we fought Ur-Baba."

"But Magog is still looking for me," Ki pointed out. "What if they're waiting in Babylon?" She looked at Sargon, then hung her head. "I'm sorry, friends. You need this, and I'm making it more troublesome."

"Nonsense, sister," Aya said. "We're alive because of you. Here, hold Shulgi, he's not grumpy anymore and he'll make you feel better, eh?" She handed over the baby, a gesture of great trust.

It worked. Ki's tense expression melted instantly. As she settled him in her lap, Shulgi grabbed a strand of her hair and pulled, making her laugh. She stroked his head gently, returning his babyish grin, so bright and full of joy. Longing filled her face. It was intimate, seeing her like this, Sargon thought. He was glad she wasn't just a fighter, but a family person, too.

"I could go in alone," Rogg suggested. "Come back and report."

"It's too risky, even for you," Aya scolded. "You heard her, Magog might search there."

"They're looking for a girl, not an Elamite. Besides, if they cause trouble, I can, too."

The others shook their heads in amusement.

Sargon patted his arm. "Brother, you've fulfilled your deal. You needn't risk more for us."

"No more talk of deals, brother. We're battle family now. 'Your troubles are my troubles,' remember? It goes both ways. I'll stay until there's a good plan."

The group looked at him in admiration. Sargon patted his back. "You're a good brother, Rogg."

"It'll help me, too," Rogg said gruffly. "Babylon will know things about Gog."

After that, they talked on, debating the risks. But they'd only just finished breakfast when a shout from a neighboring ridge shot across the gully, stunning them.

"Ho! Strangers!" it called. "Don't be afraid."

The voice echoed off the rocks, making them turn and stare. There! On the nearest ridge, a figure stood waving. A woman. At that distance, she was about the size of Sargon's hand. But her features were clear. She looked slender, and young—perhaps twenty-five—and wore sandals and a reed skirt. Unthreatening.

"What a creature," Aya muttered. "Is it human?"

In truth, the woman had a strange hairstyle. Her head was shaved bald, as smooth as an egg, making it glint in the rising sun. Perhaps it was a sign of rank, Sargon thought, for in the trees behind her, a pack of men stood waiting, all with long hair down past their shoulders. Like a mosaic, their bodies flashed in the gaps between the trunks—grass skirts, painted spears, red war masks, brown chests—warriors! At least thirty. His throat tightened as the woman's voice rang again through the clear air.

"Peace, strangers. Good morning."

"It's not Magog, is it?" Aya asked nervously.

"No, Magog would have tattoos." Rogg squinted. "Babylon, I bet. Scouts. By the gods, what brought them here?" He looked up at the sky. "Did vultures draw them? Last night I covered the bodies with rocks to keep birds from circling and giving us away. Maybe I didn't pile enough."

Sargon shook his head, scanning the blue sky. He hadn't seen a vulture since the gazelle.

"So how'd they find us?" Aya asked.

But the figure was shouting again.

"Fear not, wanderers. I come from Queen Ishtar, ruler of Babylon. This is her territory, and she bids you welcome. Will you come peacefully? I am Nisaba, right hand of the queen. I carry the authority to protect you. But answer quick. My queen's generals are impatient men."

Rogg stood to answer. Showing no fear, he lifted his spear and shook it above his head.

"Careful, Babylonian," he roared across the void. "Believe me, this weapon will find your heart one way or another, if you mean us harm."

"What a handsome fellow!" Nisaba laughed back. "I am sure those muscular arms could do many things to me. But you'd better put that stick down, or we'll be forced to pluck it from you. The queen has instructed me to bring you peacefully; but if you will not come, I must invite you in other ways."

"Is Gog your master?" Rogg demanded.

"Don't insult us, giant. Babylon has no master. Certainly not a pack of tattooed savages like *that*." Nisaba spat into the gulf. "I suggest you practice your manners before we reach Babylon. Ishtar is readier to spoil pretty things than I am."

Rogg gave a low growl, and his muscles tensed. Sargon feared he would do something rash, starting them down a bad path. To forestall this, he quickly touched Rogg's leg.

"Brother, this might be good. We need help, remember?"

"Yes, Rogg," Aya begged. "Please, let's surrender."

Across the pass, Nisaba taunted him. "Listen to your harem woman, giant. It seems the gods gave you strength, but not wits. Whatever she's saying, it's wiser than your attitude."

"I am no harem woman," Aya shouted back angrily. "Though what you are, bald one, I can't tell. Man or woman?"

"Oh, very much woman," Nisaba called back. "Rogg knows. Don't you, Rogg?"

Sargon interrupted quickly. "If you're truly friendly, Nisaba, may we confer first?"

"Certainly," Nisaba replied. "But do not mistake courtesy for weakness."

The group turned and discussed it. Sargon was most concerned for Ki. If Babylon learned who she was, they might trade her to Magog. Luckily, Aya had an idea.

"We'll fool them. Gog expects a girl alone, not in a group. We'll pass Ki off as Akkadian."

"You can't risk it," Ki protested. "Anything could happen—"

"Hush, silly," Aya said. "Your troubles are our troubles, right?"

"Right!" the others said.

Ki's eyes misted, and she bowed.

"Thank you, friends. I won't forget this."

"Stop that. We'll call you Eshnunna." Aya pulled her upright and brushed her forehead off. "That's a good Akkadian name." She grabbed Ki's hair and began tying it into a braid, an Akkadian style. "Yes, much better. We'll say you're Sargon's mate, too, eh?" A mischievous light twinkled in her eye. Ki and Sargon both laughed, embarrassed.

"Right," they all said. "Eshnunna."

They put their heads together and hugged, and Rogg stood to face Nisaba.

"Do you promise us safe passage, Babylonian?"

"Ishtar's word is good, giant. Be at peace."

"Very well, bald one. Let us see what Babylonian honor is worth."

Rogg lifted his spear in show. Then he set it down, indicating peace. The Babylonian warriors advanced down the slope into the gap. Sargon gulped. It was a funny feeling. A moment ago, they'd been as free as the squirrels in the trees. Now their fate lay in the hands of Queen Ishtar.

23

Sargon's pulse pounded as the Babylonian warriors guided Rogg and "Eshnunna" ahead down the slope. It was unnerving to feel so powerless. The smell of so many warriors all around him was primal and dense, making it hard to focus. And when they lashed spears into two makeshift stretchers for Aya and Sargon to ride on—and carried the stretchers down a well-trodden hunting trail toward the Euphrates—there was much bumping and sudden swerving, making Sargon clutch one of the side-poles for safety. Nevertheless, he decided to hope. Soon he would see Babylon, the "most civilized tribe on the Euphrates." What an opportunity that would be! If he studied Babylon the way he studied Rogg, he might learn valuable things for his future village.

They reached the village at noon, and as they humped out of the trees, Sargon sat up eagerly on his stretcher to see better.

The village bustled with activity. A dirt path ran along the bank. On each side of it were huts, eighty or more. Women squatted in small groups in the shade of doorways, mixing grain in bowls, scraping skins, tending fires. Along the waterline, more villagers washed clothes and mended nets. In the river, naked men stood in the prows of grass boats and threw tridents of hard *quasab* reed into the water. The men laughed and called to each other, and the mood seemed pleasant as they pulled their tridents back on ropes, often with sparkling fish attached to the spikes. In all, Sargon's first impression was one of order and prosperity.

Yet more impressive still were the domed huts, made of yellow reeds. Never had Sargon witnessed such sturdy-looking structures. Animal-hide flaps hung in the doorways, some tied open to permit airflow. In the walls, small holes had been cut to admit light. Pillars of bent reeds formed the domes of the structures. Bands of paint wrapped around the domes, creating a colorful array of greens, reds, and blues. From a distance, it resembled a flock of giant birds, reminding Sargon of his vision in the desert.

Then he saw it another way, and he laughed with delight.

"Why, they're little caves," he said. "And everyone gets their own."

Nisaba smiled. "You lived in a cave? Akkadians really are barbarians."

Sargon was so used to being insulted by his "betters" that he shrugged the insult off easily.

"They're lovely huts, Nisaba. But how did they survive the storm? They're just reeds."

At the compliment, Nisaba eased up. "I suppose you can't be a true barbarian with such manners. Look." She pointed at the bank, where reedbeds packed the river shallows. "Good lumber is hard to work with. And limited on this river. But reed is light and firm. It bends easily to a desired shape, and we have an infinite supply of it. We can build our structures as big as we please. Take our *mudhif*."

She pointed at the end of the path. Sargon gasped. There, a golden hill loomed over the village, the largest structure he'd ever seen. It was so big that at first his mind had dismissed it as a thing from nature. But now, as Nisaba described its construction, he saw the craftsmanship in its tall, bundled pillars. Deep holes rooted the pillar bases. Arched tops formed a great tube.

"'*Mudhif*' is an old Sumerian word," Nisaba explained. "It means 'home tent'; but as you can see, we upgraded from tents generations ago."

Sargon understood at once. "Yes, every tribe needs a place to gather, or it has no *emittu*."

Nisaba nodded with approval. "Just so, Akkadian. What was your *mudhif* back home?"

"The cave chamber. We used it for speeches and story times." Sargon was already imagining a *mudhif* in his future village. A place for public discussions would be essential to tribe life, especially if they lacked a chief.

"Are they hard to construct?" he asked.

"Yes, very tricky to build," Nisaba answered. "It's a Sumerian skill. Gog tried once, but his *mudhif* kept collapsing, and he slaughtered all his builders in a rage."

"Now that is barbaric."

"Hoho! The queen will like you." Nisaba winked at Rogg. "I'd let him do the talking."

Rogg glowered, but Ki interjected politely to keep the friendly mood up.

"Nisaba, I'm also confused. How do you prevent flooding?"

Indeed, the flood seemed to have bypassed Babylon entirely, Sargon noticed. Of course, some huts showed wind damage, and fallen branches lay piled between the structures, ready to be used for kindling. But otherwise the village looked untouched.

Nisaba eyed Ki curiously. "Very observant, nomad. Who knew your breed was so clever?"

Ki noticed the trap. "I'm Akkadian, actually. Eshnunna's my name. We northern Akkadians are often mistaken for nomads."

"Mmm, yes, the shape of your nose, your skin color. I can see why."

"We're mates," Sargon chimed in from his stretcher.

Ki shot him a crooked smile.

"Well, I meant no insult," Nisaba said. "Eshnunna makes a good point. Floods hit us regularly, so we take precautions." She pointed at a trench that encircled the village. "Who can guess the purpose of that?"

Sargon studied it. The trench was wide and deep. A wood gate at each end separated it from the river. But if the gates were opened, the river would pour through and fill the trench, flowing water around the settlement.

"A flood channel," Ki exclaimed.

Nisaba arched her eyebrows in surprise. "Impressive. You've seen one before?"

"Never, but it makes sense. If you divert the excess flood water, the huts won't swamp."

Nisaba looked at her probingly. "You're right, Eshnunna. Without this trench, floods would wash away everything, forcing us to rebuild each season. We'd never be able to construct anything big. Certainly not a *mudhif*."

A narrow plank platform crossed the trench into the village. As the warriors carried Sargon's stretcher over it, he looked down and marveled at the stout pillars of palm trunk that supported the planks, permitting hardly a creak. In the dry bed, villagers in grass skirts worked diligently, cleaning up wreckage from the flood. The trench had clearly saved Babylon from heavy water flow, keeping it high and dry while flotsam whooshed around it.

Thank you, El, for showing us this, Sargon prayed. *We will build a trench, too.*

His faith grew. This visit was already proving critical to their future.

"And the river god?" Ki asked. "Enbilulu? Does he punish you for diverting his waters?"

Nisaba smiled. "He doesn't seem to mind. We burn extra offerings to him each month."

Sargon grunted admiringly. "The gods favor Babylon. Akkad has nothing like this. We have fallen behind."

"Save your flattery, Akkadian. It is the queen you must impress, not me."

◆

Leaving the footbridge, they marched through the domed huts toward the giant *mudhif.* Villagers ran up, pointing and shouting, but Nisaba waved them away. "Yes, yes, the giant is pretty to look at. But mind your manners. Remember, they're the barbarians, not us."

She pushed aside the grass entry-mat and led the group in. Sargon blinked in the cool space. It took time to adjust to the dimness. He made out a swept dirt floor, stout reed pillars supporting an arched ceiling, and clay pots lining the walls. In each pot, grass burned to deter mosquitoes and fill the area with a pleasant scent. In the center of the room a fire flickered in a pit, sending smoke up through a hole in the roof. The circular opening was black and shiny from years of such outpouring, and the great walls must have fended off countless storms. A sense of grandeur and tradition pervaded the room.

Just like a cave, but better, Sargon thought. He shook his head in admiration. If he'd stayed in Akkad, he'd never have learned such wonders existed. It motivated him. What else could be out there? Right then, he promised himself to see as much of the world as he could.

As the guards helped Sargon and Aya down from their stretchers, a large figure marched forth from the gloom. Two shirtless boys followed, energetically flapping palm fronds to cool her off. This had to be the queen.

"She approaches," a guard shouted.

The warriors pressed spear tips to the prisoners' napes, making them bow. Queen Ishtar stopped a few paces away and surveyed the line of them with cold eyes. After bowing, Sargon snuck a glance upward to see who they were dealing with.

Ishtar was an enormous woman. She had large masculine hands, a broad forehead, and a healthy wobble of fat hanging over her waist-belt. Her breasts hung almost to her belly button, and her thighs bulged, giving her an air of prosperity and vitality far beyond any woman in Akkad. Her head, like Nisaba's, was shaved as bald as an egg. But more impressively, Ishtar carried a staff with an emerald stone at the top and wore a leather band on her brow studded with a red opal. She looked like a queen. When she pointed her staff at Ki, her voice, too, was blunt and powerful.

"Your name, girl?"

"Eshnunna," Ki said. "Of Akkad."

"You don't look Akkadian. More like a rat nomad."

Ki paled.

Ishtar pointed her staff at Rogg. "What is her real name, Elamite?"

"Eshnunna, queen."

The emerald swung to Aya. "You agree?"

"Eshnunna, Great One."

"All liars!"

The queen strode to Sargon and gazed into his face. "And here is a cripple. Take caution, young man. I will ask one more time. But first, know that I am Ishtar, ruler of Babylon, and liars do not prosper in my *mudhif*." She pointed her staff at Shulgi, who peeped out from Aya's arms like a tiny ferret, black eyes glinting. "Do you wish that child cut in half with a battle ax?"

"No," Sargon cried.

"Then answer truthfully. What is the correct name of this rat nomad?"

Sargon's mouth went dry. How could he choose between Shulgi and Ki?

Luckily, Ki spoke up, relieving him of the burden.

"Forgive me, queen, I deceived them. You are correct, I am a nomad. Ki is my name."

The queen grunted and returned to her. "So nomads do speak a human tongue. I thought your kind communed mainly with mice and other vermin."

Ki smiled politely. "Have you ever met a nomad, queen?"

Ishtar leaned on her staff and laughed. "Tell me, rat," she said, ignoring the question, "how did you meet these folk?" She bent closer. "Was it in the storm, two nights ago?"

The friends looked at each other in astonishment. Aya burst out, "How can you guess all this, queen? Are you some kind of *baru*?"

The queen smiled. "Ah. Beautiful Aya, of the famous temper."

Aya gasped. "You know my name? And ho!" she flared. "*Who* says I've got a temper?"

Rogg nodded. "This morning you knew just where to find us, too."

The queen turned. "Mighty Rogg. Your reputation also precedes you."

She waved her staff, and from another corner of the *mudhif* two warriors dragged forth a man in a leather gag. They shoved him to his knees paces away and tore the gag free, making drool run down his beard. Sargon felt pity for him, whoever he was. His knees leaked fresh blood, and red welts covered his arms. He looked as if he'd been recently caned. Yet there was something strange about him, too. He was hairy, almost animal—

Sargon gasped. *Ut!*

"You!" Aya cried. "I should have guessed."

"Ho, everyone." Ut rubbed his sore jaw. "Believe it or not, I'm glad to see you."

"Traitor!" If not for the spears, Aya might have sprung at him and clawed his face to ribbons. "Once was not enough to betray us? You gave us to her?"

"They tortured me. What could I do?" Ut showed her his welted arms.

"Viper!" Aya cried. "The gods will rip out your forked tongue and choke you with it, or I will."

The guards restrained her. The queen walked over and looked gravely into her face.

"I don't blame you, Aya. I despise traitors, too. But in my *mudhif*, I will have order, do you hear?"

Aya shrank down. "Yes, queen."

"Good. Now I will speak. We caught Ut sneaking along the river last night, and he told me everything, so there is no point lying anymore, is there?"

She looked at Ki pointedly. "Nomad, I will ask a last time. My scouts have been watching the river, and they tell me Gog has been smoke-signaling his vassal tribes for days. We can read these signals, and by our interpretation, he has been chasing an escaped slave. A nomad witch. Is it you?"

Ki said nothing. Everyone leaned forward, staring at her.

A witch? Sargon frowned. Ki had never mentioned that.

"This *baru*," Ishtar went on, "evaded Gog's tribes using . . . well, some kind of magic." She sniffed as if she did not believe it. "Now Ut tells me you were pulled from a raft during a storm. And you admitted to escaping Magog. So."

Ishtar bent forward, eyes afire. "What is so special about you? What is this 'magic?' And why should Gog—who hates to be embarrassed—alert the whole river to his incompetence by throwing up so many smoke signals? You must be important."

Everyone looked at Ki expectantly, including Sargon.

Nervously, Ki cleared her throat.

"Queen, I might speak better if spears were not hurting my friends' necks."

"Fine, fine."

Ishtar impatiently waved the spears away, and Sargon straightened, relief flooding his spine.

"Thank you, queen." Ki rubbed her neck. "I will tell you everything. In return, I beg your protection for my friends. Not for myself," she emphasized.

"You are in no place to bargain, child. Besides, what good are words? I could promise anything and change my mind later."

"I thought the words of a queen were worth something," Ki said.

Ishtar smiled with amusement.

"Very well, girl. Your friends have my protection for now. But push me no further."

"Thank you, queen. I understand."

Ki bowed and took a breath, gathering herself. Sargon and Aya glanced at each other. *A witch?* Aya mouthed. Sargon shook his head. It was Ki. She couldn't be evil.

"I am not a witch," Ki said. "But I am the last survivor of my tribe. And we had a . . . a . . ." She gulped. "A weapon. That is what Gog wants."

Ishtar's eyes fiercened. "A weapon. Mmm, go on."

"It is a good weapon. I will die before letting Gog steal it, but I could give it to you, if you like. Especially if you use it against Gog. His enemies are my friends."

The queen's fingers tightened on her staff. "How soon might I see this weapon?"

"Today. At sunset." Ki's expression was brave, even queenly, and Sargon's heart stirred. It didn't matter who she faced—a giant, a queen—Ki held her own. He knew of no girl like her.

"I hope this is not too bold, queen," Ki said. "To prove my weapon's worth, I challenge Babylon to a water race. Pick your strongest paddlers, and let them face me in my boat, alone. I will outpace them all. You'll see how I evaded Gog and his river of vassals."

"You have a flair for showmanship, child." Queen Ishtar chuckled. "A race it shall be. Nisaba, feed these travelers, tend them, and give this nomad all the help she needs."

Her staff lingered over Ki. "As for you, I hope you are not trying to make me look foolish. If so . . ."

"I'm not," Ki promised.

"I hope so. For the sake of your friends."

At sunset, all of Babylon assembled on the bank for the race.

The sky was burning red, and the huts gleamed gold, casting their molten reflections over the water. Ki's palms were sweating. A mob of over three hundred Babylonians in grass skirts lined the shore, cheering and pumping their fists. "HAIL BABYLON," they screamed. "CRUSH THE NOMAD!" They sounded savage, Ki thought. Like they wanted not just victory, but blood.

"Take your places," a herald cried, waving his staff.

With a shout, Babylon's six strongest warriors paddled their boat out into the river. Ki paddled quietly after them in her own craft, trying to ignore the taunts they shouted at her, and their big flexing arms. The Babylonian craft was far superior: a war canoe built long and sleek, raised in prow and stern. She, meanwhile, paddled a bulky fishing craft built for stability not speed. In addition, it was weighed down with five bodies not allowed to paddle. Sargon, Rogg, Nisaba and two guards sat on the gunwales, adding extra weight. Ishtar had demanded this, and Ki could understand why. The queen desired a "true test" of Ki's weapon. Ki accepted this. But she also knew her wind-catcher was still in its early stages of development. It might malfunction at a critical moment, like her avalanche platform at the gully had, losing her the race. If that happened, Ishtar would hurt her friends.

Ki gazed wistfully at the domed huts, sleeping mats inside. Would life ever slow down? Nonstop danger was exhausting. She had another worry, too. What if her device worked?

She glanced uneasily at Sargon. The first time she'd demonstrated her wind-catcher at the Tigris River, her people hadn't taken kindly to it, not at all. How would Sargon respond? Her hand lifted automatically to her throat, where the black pendant had once hung. Would he act like her tribe had? Call her a *baru* and shun her?

"Make ready!" the herald called from shore.

Using their paddles, the two teams pointed their boats downriver and waited. The Euphrates flashed pink. Mist rose from the reedbeds, and palm trees stretched shaggy purple shadows out from the bank. The world felt ancient and mystical, unchanged since creation. Ki's anxiety built.

"Ho, nomad. I hope this thing performs better than it looks." Nisaba looked skeptically up at the wind-catcher blanket, rolled up and hanging from the crossbeam. "Will it capsize us? I dislike to get wet."

The two Babylonian warriors snickered.

"You better not be bluffing, nomad," one said. "Ishtar's got nasty tortures if you fail."

"Hoho, she does," said the second one. "She'll slather you in gore and toss you in the insect pit, let them burrow through you for days. They chew tunnels through your organs and eyes and belly before your *emittu* escapes."

"Creative," Ki muttered.

"Better yet," the first laughed, "we'll slit a hole in your belly, drag your big intestine out. Tie it to a tree twenty paces away. Let the birds fly down and peck it clean while you watch."

They burst into laughter and slapped each other's shoulders. Ki pretended to ignore them, though imagining a bird eating her intestines made her bowels feel watery. She glared at her wind-catcher. *Don't stick on me.*

Sargon, however, was fed up with the men. He turned to Nisaba. "I thought Babylon was civilized. This feels more like Akkad."

Nisaba frowned, her bald head glinting. "He's right. Shut up, you two. You are low, indeed, to be scorned by a cave dweller."

The guards shut their mouths, and Ki looked gratefully at Sargon. He gave her a slight nod. But he and Rogg looked so uneasy, she began to feel even worse. How can I explain myself to them? she wondered. How, if even I don't understand what I am?

Still curious, Nisaba stood up and shook the mast.

"So what is it, anyway? Some kind of nomad superstition?"

"Magic," Ki said angrily. "Don't break it."

"Forgive me, goddess, I didn't realize it was sacred to touch." Nisaba made a face and sat.

"On your marks," the herald shouted from shore.

Ki raised her paddle. The other boat did likewise. The crowd fell silent. Ki's heart pounded . . . Then, to her surprise, Sargon reached out and touched her kneecap.

"We trust you," he said quietly.

Ki looked at him in bewilderment. "Why?"

He smiled. "You're 'Little Enki.'"

Rogg nodded in agreement. "Show 'em, sister. Like you showed Ur-Baba."

Strength rushed through Ki's arms. Her heart swelled. Who were these good men? And how had she gotten so lucky, to find them in this vast ugly world?

Onshore, the herald commenced the countdown. "Three . . . two . . . one . . . GO."

A warrior blew a ram's horn, giving the starting signal, and with a shout, the Babylonian warriors dug their paddles into the water and shot ahead, churning up a golden froth with their blades. "ISHTAR! ISHTAR!" they chanted, paddling in rhythm. But Ki just sat there, drifting. Everyone looked at her in alarm.

"Um, the race has started, 'Little Enki,'" Nisaba mocked.

Ki wiped sweat from her face. "I want them to get a lead."

"A lead?" The warriors burst into laughter. "That's nomad logic for you. Oh, the insect pit will be noisy tonight!"

Nisaba shot a pitying look at Rogg. "Handsome one, you can't blame me for what happens next. I did what I could. You are in Ishtar's hands now."

Rogg and Sargon were both looking confused. Ki felt sad that she hadn't briefed them. But they might not have trusted her to do this, if they'd known. As the waves tapped the boat, they looked at each other, then back at her, uncertainly. Ki gripped the paddle shaft so tight, her hands hurt. "I need a gap between us. For perspective," she tried to explain. "That way, when the gap closes, Ishtar will see how fast I'm really going."

It sounded strange, but she knew this course was right. In the past, she hadn't shown her people properly. Hadn't babied them. Now she knew better. Humans could be as blind as mice pups when something new appeared; it was her job to help them *see.*

Asha's voice echoed in her heart, reassuring her.

Trust yourself, Ki. It's time to accept what you are. Not a witch. A gift.

Rogg spoke. "There is such a thing as overconfidence, sister."

"This is strategy, not arrogance, I promise," Ki said, her heart tearing apart.

Rogg studied her closely. "Then do it your way, just as you see it."

With that, he sat back, trusting her completely. Sargon did likewise, relaxing against the gunwale in full support of her method. Ki could have hugged them both. Instead, she tightened her mouth and gave a slight bow, in gratitude. All right, she thought. All right.

She was ready to show them her true self. They deserved it. If she didn't, their bond would always be a lie.

Onshore, the crowd was cheering more madly than ever. Ahead, the Babylonian boat was far in the lead. It was time. Taking a breath, Ki set her paddle in the trough and turned to Sargon.

"Dip a finger in the river and stick it in the air."

Sargon looked confused, but he obeyed and put his wet finger up.

"What do you feel?" she asked.

He frowned. "Enlil's breath, cooling my finger."

"Just so. And it is Enlil, not any human, who will win this victory today."

With that, she yanked on the ropes, unraveling the blanket skin with a loud *clap.* Wind bellied it out instantly, and a great force seized the craft and thrust it forward like a dart.

"Ho!" everyone cried and grabbed the reed gunwales for safety.

"What's this?" Nisaba shouted. "*Baru,* what's happening?"

Ki didn't answer. She just tightened the ropes further, feeding speed to the craft. Soon her hair was flying, the world streaking past in purples and golds. Nisaba yelled for it to stop, but Ki only pulled the ropes tighter, shooting the boat ahead so fast that water hissed beneath the hull, and waves thudded into the bow, throwing spray up in their faces.

One of the guards, beard whipping back in his mouth, screamed: "She *is* a witch!"

And the other cried: "Throw her over! We will fly away into the sky!"

But Rogg turned and blocked their path, roaring, "You will do *nothing,* dogs. You hear?"

And the guards huddled down, cowed.

Onshore, the cheers turned to cries of alarm. People raced along the bank, trying to keep up with Ki's pace. In response, Ki pulled the ropes still tighter, the joy of her power rushing through her. Her secret was out now, no hiding it, so she might as well do this all the way, and *crush* Babylon. *Baru* or no, she was *good* at this.

"Faster," she urged the full-bellied device. "Come on, you fat fish of reeds. Faster!"

Within moments, she'd pulled even with the other boat. Then she passed it. Six astonished Babylonian faces, crimson with effort, watched her shoot by. Their paddle blades churned up froth, and their muscles bulged and strained, yet Ki glided ahead without any effort. Soon her crew was looking back in awe, watching the war canoe shrink.

"By Enlil's breath," Rogg roared. "It's magnificent, Ki. Glorious!"

Ki was too connected to her craft to answer. What a craft it was! It didn't matter that it was wide and shallow-bottomed, she realized. It was a true boat, whereas before she'd been limited to wooden rafts, square, clumsy and resistant to water. This boat, on the other hand, was coated with slick bitumen that lubricated its underside and shot it faster through the water than she'd ever gone. It even began to tilt up on its side, as if to capsize. Ki had to yell at her crew to sit up on the opposite rail just to balance out the weight, and with the enthusiasm of the panicked they obeyed. The shift created an equilibrium that permitted the craft to fly stable, despite just one side touching the water. More spray flew up as it slammed faster into the little wave caps. Drips from its exposed underbelly speckled the river underneath. The sullen river heat was gone. The wind was delicious and cool. And suddenly, embracing the strangeness of it, Rogg roared, "RAAAAAHHH! RAAHHH!" And Nisaba, laughing with delight beside him, grabbed his stout arm and cheered too. And as they crossed the appointed finish line, they were all yelling like that, whooping and pumping their fists—even the two warriors—while their competition remained a little blob, far behind.

Angling the boat toward shore, Ki relaxed the sail and turned to Sargon, anxious of his reaction.

His eyes were shining, his beard damp with river water. He opened his mouth to speak, and for a moment Ki's heart teetered on the edge of a black pit. What would he say?

He gave a joyous laugh. “Ki, that was amazing. We need to do that again.”

“You don’t think I’m a witch?” she asked timidly.

He looked at her as if she’d uttered the craziest thing in the world.

“Why, Ki, you’re *magnificent.*”

“Oh. Well . . . thanks.”

Tears stung her eyes. She turned and fiddled with the guide plank, pretending to be busy, lest she give her feelings away.

24

Sargon felt dazed as the tribe swept him into the *mudhif* for the victory feast. Ki had amazed him before, but this was something else, something *beyond.* There was no time to sort out his thoughts, though. Nisaba quickly seated the travelers in a place of honor beside the fire pit, which forced them to socialize with the elders as the room bombarded them with colors, smells, and sounds.

Over three hundred adults sat around them in concentric rings extending back to the reed walls. Everyone was discussing Ki's triumph and speculating how it could benefit Babylon. Adding to the noise, musicians in one corner blew reed flutes and tapped skin drums incessantly, while from another corner, children in grass skirts ran forth carrying trays of delicious-smelling food. The travelers gawked as the children set the trays down on the grass mats before them. There was blackened fish, steaming waterfowl, a clay bowl of roasted dates, sweet bean paste wrapped in edible *etu* leaves, and much more. Mighty was the abundance of the Euphrates! After subsisting in the desert for so long, Sargon and his friends had to struggle not to fall upon the food and start gorging themselves right then. Luckily, Aya had the presence of mind to give them a warning look, and they remembered their position and mastered themselves. They were still prisoners, subject to the whims of their powerful hosts.

Aya leaned close to Sargon, her cheeks pink with excitement.

"How was the boat?" she whispered. "Is Ki really a witch? Are you witched now, too? It was so fast, we couldn't believe it. I've never . . . well, how should I feel? Excited or terrified?"

"She's Ki," Sargon said firmly. "She's our tribe-sister."

"Yes, but what *is* she?"

Sargon shook his head. Ki would explain it when she was ready. What mattered now was how their position had changed. Before the race, they'd been prisoners about to be tortured. Now they were spectacles, everyone looking at them and pointing, including the elders. This could be used. *Rule two: Help your people.*

"We must ask for a map," he whispered.

"Good thinking, brother. Let's ask the bald head." Aya nodded significantly at Nisaba, who sat on the mat adjacent Sargon. "She knows things."

"Would she respond better to you? You're a fellow woman."

Aya laughed. Sargon had merely spoken out of nervousness, and they both knew it.

"You're 'Sargon,' now, brother. Time to live up to it."

Sargon smiled grudgingly. "Fine. But next time you get the fancy name."

He turned to Nisaba, formulating his approach. A map could fix everything. It would point them in the right direction, help them avoid conflicts with the locals, and predict how far they still had to go. A whole future awaited them, if he did this right.

But before he could begin, a strange ritual intervened.

More children ran forth carrying clay bowls. One was placed before each person in the *mudhif*, the guests included, and Sargon looked into his, puzzled. Inside the bowl floated a mysterious red juice, as thick as blood.

Nisaba leaned over to explain. "Our mealtime ritual. Everyone drinks it. Guests too."

"How?"

"Watch."

One mat away, Queen Ishtar raised her bowl above her bald head. The crowd did the same, creating a forest of lifted bowls. Nisaba nodded at Sargon, so he and his companions lifted their bowls, too.

"Enbilulu, Lord of the River," Ishtar shouted. "Send us POWER. Spill the blood of our enemies."

"POWER!" the tribe echoed, and drank their bowls empty.

It was an eerie toast, Sargon thought. Uneasily, he recalled his pledge to El that morning to be faithful to him alone. However, it would be impolite and dangerous to reject their hosts' customs, so he drank his bowl quickly, promising El he meant none of it. His friends did the same. Aya wiped her mouth in disgust.

"Is it a weird cult?" she whispered. "It's not blood, but it feels . . . close to it."

"At least it's not our own blood," Ut said.

Aya shot him a cold look. He was still an outcast as far as she was concerned, even though the Babylonians had released him and placed him on the mat with the guests.

"Nobody asked you, traitor," she snapped.

"What're you complaining for?" Ut said. "Look at this food. I brought you here."

"By turning us in."

"I was tortured. I'd like to see you do better."

"Just wait till after dinner, I'll torture you myself."

Sargon sighed and shook his head. This was not the place for disunity.

"Ey, fight later," he whispered. "For now, let's get a map, right?"

To his relief, Ishtar waved her ivory scepter, allowing everyone to eat. Then even Ut and Aya forgot their anger and dove in.

What a feast it was. There was water blossom stew, sweet *idu* salad, and palm fowl basted in white sauces. Also bowls full of wheat berry, mixed with red flower petals. How had Babylon found so much wheat? Sargon wondered. A vast territory range would be needed to gather this much. Moreover, he noticed a platter of flat brown stones that sent up an irresistible odor of barley. He abandoned his half-eaten slice of fowl and reached for a stone, curious.

Nisaba noticed and smiled.

"Good eye, Sargon. That is our specialty. We call it 'bread.' Babylon is famous for it."

Sargon lifted the almost weightless stone and sniffed it in confusion.

"It looks like a rock," he confessed.

"Drizzle it with honey and bite it," Nisaba laughed. "See how like a 'rock' it tastes."

Not wanting to be rude, Sargon politely drizzled honey on the stone—a rare treat in itself, since some poor forager must have endured countless bee stings to secure the honeycomb—and forced the stone to his lips. He expected to break his teeth. That first bite, however, would stay with him for the rest of his life. As soon as the warm bread crumbled in his mouth, a delicious flavor flooded his taste buds, stunning his mouth with pleasure. Overcome, he swallowed the bite and found that it filled his stomach more pleasantly than any food he'd ever tried. Before he knew it, the entire stone had disappeared into his mouth, and he was reaching for another.

Nisaba smiled. "Told you."

"It's a miracle," Sargon said.

"So say all who try it. In fact, according to legend, it was Anu, god of the sky, who gave it to the Babylonians. They were lost and starving in the waste, and Anu took pity on them. He dropped a trail of bread stones along the ground and led them here to settle."

Ut tore into his own stone. "This is living," he cried, mouth full. "Akkad doesn't know a thing like it. Eh, Aya? Even your best-seasoned meat can't beat *this*. Hoho, bread!"

The Babylonians laughed and slapped their bellies in approval. Ishtar smiled.

"Eat all you like, dear guests. Ki has earned it for you."

The friends obliged happily, and when the first tray of warm stones was finished, children ran forth with more. Sargon was in ecstasy. Crumbs stuck to his fingers, and golden honey dripped into his beard. Nothing seemed to matter but the next bite, and the next. He forgot the map entirely.

"Is bread easy to make?" he asked Nisaba. "Could you teach us? Or is it a secret?"

"No secret," Nisaba said, "but it requires a great quantity of grain. Baskets of it."

"Baskets!" the travelers cried, looking up.

"How can you fill *baskets* with seed?" Ki asked sharply.

"Yes," Aya agreed. "In Akkad, our women would forage for months to gather that much."

Nisaba nodded. "We keep foraging camps across our territory, days apart from each other, which do nothing but gather seed and send it back here. Babylon also happens to control one of the most abundant seed grasslands in Mesopotamia. Even so, it is difficult to get so much. That is why we make bread only on special occasions. Like today."

"Hail, Babylon! Hail, bread!" Ut cried.

Nisaba leaned close to Sargon. "But perhaps tell your friends not to, ah, eat with their left hands." She pointed at his companions, who were all hunched over their meals in their ragged animal skins, gobbling food with both hands. "In this part of the world, the left is reserved for dirty tasks like wiping up after the latrine."

Sargon prickled with embarrassment. Back in Akkad, eating with both hands had been considered good manners, for it implied enthusiasm for the meal. But here he noticed that the Babylonians ate in a more refined way, sitting erect and eating with just one hand at a measured pace. In comparison, his companions did look barbaric.

As for Sargon, he only *had* a left hand. But that was another matter.

He quickly leaned over and whispered the message. His friends reddened and dropped their left hands at once. Thankfully, few in the *mudhif* seemed to have noticed the error.

"Thank you," he said.

"Not at all," Nisaba said. "Customs are different everywhere, we know this."

Eager to move past it, Sargon searched for a new topic—and remembered the map. Before he could lose his nerve, he mentioned it, then quickly added, "Forgive me if I'm being rude again."

"Not at all. All wanderers wish this." Nisaba snapped her fingers. "Girl. Fetch us a map."

A child ran to the corner of the *mudhif* and returned carrying a rolled otter skin. Sargon's mouth dropped. After all their fear and blind wandering, might they really see where they were?

As the girl spread the map out, weighting the corners with clay bowls, he and his companions pushed their food aside and drew close to the picture like freezing people crowding a fire.

"Thank you, Nisaba," Aya said. "Stay back, Ut, don't touch me."

"Just trying to see," Ut grumbled.

The map was incredibly detailed. It seemed to contain all Mesopotamia, with two blue squiggles running across it, one for the Tigris River in the north, another for the Euphrates in the south. Dots marked the locations of each tribe, mostly along the rivers.

"Here is Babylon," Nisaba said, tapping the center of the map. "As you can see, we occupy a prime location on the Euphrates. The whole world flows past us with news, making our maps the best-informed in the world."

"Best in the world," Aya repeated reverently.

Nisaba nodded. "Here is Magog's camp, north of us. Here are its vassal tribes. You, *baru,* dodged this gauntlet with your wind-catcher, a thing no one has ever done." She kept tapping the dots. "Farther south you find more tribes, a few marshes, the great desert."

It was a good description, but as Nisaba talked, Sargon frowned. He saw no free spaces.

"Where could we settle?" he blurted.

Nisaba shook her head. "The whole river is taken."

Sargon's heart dropped.

"Nowhere?" he asked stupidly. "Not even one place left?"

"It is a busy world. Has been, for a long time."

Sargon sat back, breathless. The news sank in. *Nowhere.* He looked at his companions, who appeared just as crushed. *It can't be true. It can't.*

"You mean," Aya asked timidly, "if we hadn't stopped here, we'd have kept walking forever?"

"I'm afraid so," Nisaba said.

In desperation, Sargon pointed at the map again, at a gray patch devoid of dots in the south. "What is this shading, here?"

"Oh that." Nisaba grimaced. "The Great Marsh."

"Is it free?"

"Believe me, you won't like it. It's a swamp. A mire lousy with leeches, flies, snapping turtles, and snakes."

"People?"

"Barbarians. Marshmen, they are called. All of Sumer looks down on them."

"Even nomads?" Ki interjected, half-humorously.

Nisaba returned a flat smile. "Yes, marshmen rank even below nomads."

She tapped the gray patch. "They are savages, always raiding and squabbling. Sometimes refugees flee there, but they simply disappear. The marshmen kill and enslave them. We put no dots in the area because it's unchartable. The channels are constantly flooding, changing course. Mud islands sink and reform in other places. It is an unfinished land. One the gods gave up as irredeemable. No," Nisaba said decisively, "the Great Marsh is no place for you."

"If you haven't charted it yourself, how can you be sure?" Sargon asked, grasping at any hope. "Forgive me, but we've been misled before, by our old tribes."

"I understand. But you see, I am marsh folk myself."

"You?" Aya's eyes widened. "But you seem so civilized."

"Thank you, sister." Nisaba's face grew wistful, and she ran a hand over her bald pate, as if to smooth out old terrors. "It is a testament to Babylon's greatness that even I, of such low blood, can be improved . . ."

She glanced at Ishtar, who was listening closely. The queen nodded, giving permission to continue.

"I don't mind telling you," Nisaba went on, "I lived in the Great Marsh until the age of thirteen, when another marsh tribe conquered us, as is their way. But I was lucky. They didn't kill me. Instead, they sold me to Babylon, where Ishtar noticed my potential and promoted me year after year until I became her top adviser. Now my life is better than any marshling chief's. Monthly, my marsh blood grows thinner. I drink of the nightly bowl. I praise Enbilulu. One day, I may even become a true Babylonian."

Queen Ishtar smiled. "Nisaba is the best adviser on the river. I couldn't manage without her. I have decreed that my son, when he comes of age, will take her as his mate. Once they are joined, Nisaba will be my true daughter."

Ishtar rubbed the head of a chunky boy, perhaps twelve years old, who sat eating bread at her side. The boy was so focused on licking honey from his stubby fingers that he seemed not to hear this pronouncement, and Nisaba's face tightened. Sargon pitied her. Clearly, she would give up a chance at love for power and safety. A hard trade.

I would not make it myself, Sargon thought.

He glanced at Ki, wondering how she felt about it.

"So," Aya prompted, "there's really nowhere for us to go?"

"Not on the Euphrates," Nisaba said.

The friends looked at each other vacantly. *All this way. For nothing.*

It was crushing. Their dream of a special tribe was dead almost before it had begun.

As the bad news sank in, the noises of the *mudhif* seemed to fade away, and the "black feeling" Sargon had lived under in Akkad returned. A feeling that crushed your chest, paralyzing you. Sargon sat motionless, gazing emptily into the fire. *Nowhere to go.* What a world. Strong ate weak. And the weak had nowhere to be.

He bowed his head. Maybe El is not guiding us to a better life, he thought. Maybe my vision was a delusion, and we are on our own.

"Sargon."

He looked up foggily. To his surprise, the queen's brown eyes looked into his.

"Sargon, I have a proposal for you."

"For me?" he repeated stupidly.

"For all of you." Ishtar looked at his friends. "You've assembled quite a tribe. Babylon could use such talent."

Sargon's mouth went dry. What was happening?

"As you know, a leader strengthens her tribe all she can. When she finds quality, as I do here, she would be a fool to let it slip away." Ishtar lifted her ivory scepter. "Sargon, I officially invite you to join Babylon."

Sargon and his friends sat upright, astonished.

"Queen!" Aya cried.

"I mean it," Ishtar went on calmly. "Join us. Rest your tired feet by our green waters and see what Babylon can offer you."

Sargon couldn't breathe.

Aya lifted her baby fearfully. "Even him? With his foot?" Shulgi wriggled in her hands, giving displeased grunts. His clubfoot shone red in the light. Ishtar smiled.

"Even him, yes. Enbilulu provides for all. Even 'unfit' ones, and women. You two, take note." She nodded at Ki and Aya. "Babylon is unique on this river, for I require no woman to take a mate without her consent. You will not find another tribe with that policy."

Aya hugged Shulgi tight, muffling his cries with her hand. "Praise you, queen! Bless you!"

Ut fell on his face and banged his forehead on the mat. "Great One! We will serve you forever!"

Sargon looked around the *mudhif*, speechless. Could it be? This mighty place would now be his home?

It seemed so. The entire tribe was smiling, nodding, and patting their stomachs, even the elders. He knew he should feel triumph.

Yet oddly, he felt flat and empty. It puzzled him.

Why do I feel no joy?

The queen was still looking at him. A smile curled her lips.

"Sargon, you seem troubled. You dislike my offer?"

"No, queen," Sargon said. "I am too grateful to speak."

"Yet you hesitate. Why?" The queen cocked her head. "Perhaps you desire no ruler at all?"

Sargon's eyes snapped to Ut. The hairy man's guilty expression confirmed it. He'd told Ishtar about voting. Sargon's gut twisted. This could ruin everything.

But the queen didn't seem angry. Merely interested.

"Come, Sargon. Tell me this idea," she said.

A tense silence filled the room. Sargon looked at his friends for guidance. Aya and Ut were shaking their heads rapidly. To debate the cons of rulership with a queen in her own *mudhif*—and before all her people, too? It was reckless.

Babylon's elders were also glaring at him. One whispered to Ishtar:

"Such ideas should not be discussed publicly, queen. The tribe may be disturbed."

"Are Babylon's methods not defensible?" the queen snapped. "Should we fear fair argument?"

"Of course not, I only—"

"Then be silent."

The queen adjusted her headband as if to remind him of her position. "Sargon, you are an honored guest under my protection, so speak freely. As you see, I am not surrounded by deep thinkers." She shot the elder a cold look. "I would enjoy this."

The elder shriveled, and Sargon knew he'd just made a firm enemy.

"You really wish this?" he asked reluctantly.

"I do."

Sargon shot his friends an apologetic look. But maybe this could prove beneficial, he thought. Ishtar was an experienced leader. Her wisdom might sharpen Aya's voting idea into something even better.

Sargon wiped sweat from his face.

"Very well, queen. It is simple. Our old chiefs were bad. We want no such rulers again."

"So instead of a chief, you'll give everyone a 'say?'"

Sargon nodded. "As Ut told you."

"How has it worked so far?"

"Not well," Sargon admitted.

Indeed, they'd broken Aya's system from the start.

"No, not well," he repeated sadly.

The queen's eyes flashed. "Yes, Sargon. Even you couldn't obey the system. But in my opinion, you were right to ignore the vote to rescue Ki from drowning. You acted like a good ruler. You saw what had to be done, and did it. Let the mob squall." She waved a hand. "You see, having a ruler is not bad. Just having a stupid ruler."

She spread her arms to encompass the *mudhif*. "Ask my people what form of government they prefer. Here is the best of all worlds. A queen who loves her people like blood. I put no babies out to die. I fill every belly with bread. I let women pick their mates. I destroy our enemies. These are my children, I am their mother, and all my power flows out to them."

"HAIL, ISHTAR! HAIL!"

The *mudhif* exploded with cheers. The tribe had bent forward to listen, and now their voices shook the air so mightily that Shulgi wailed in fear, prompting Aya to shush him.

Sargon was impressed.

Ishtar waited for the tumult to die down, then smiled.

"Come, Sargon, are you to be beaten so easily? That is not the Sargon who slew Ur-Baba. Please, do not fear my rank. In dialogue, the only authority is reason, not position."

Sargon nodded, appreciating her graciousness.

"Very well, queen. I'll say it. One person's conscience is a flimsy protection for a tribe."

Ishtar smiled. "Go on."

Sargon held up his stump as an example. "Even I, in a moment of weakness, stole food." He looked at Ut apologetically "Not just in Akkad. But from my fellow outcasts in the desert."

"I guessed as much," Ut said. "I knew there was a reason you were alone."

"Voting," Sargon persisted, "helps this. It gives better protection than a single conscience. When all members have a say, they'll protect their own interests and block anyone too selfish."

"Well done, Sargon. I am enjoying this," Ishtar said. "But let us probe further. Voters can be selfish, too. Remember how Ut and Aya voted to let Ki drown? What is the difference between a selfish tyrant and a selfish majority of voters?"

Sargon nodded. She had good points.

He struggled for a moment, digging his fingers into his stump. Maybe I am out of my depth, he thought. Who am I to argue big ideas? He'd never done it before.

Then, inspiration hit. *Your name,* a voice whispered. *Sargon the Great. Think of that.*

He sat up eagerly.

"You're right, queen. Voting isn't enough protection. More is needed."

"Such as?"

Sargon's excitement built. "In Akkad, there was a famous ruler. Sargon the Great."

"I know of him," Ishtar said. "Any educated person does."

"He was a wise ruler," Sargon said, "so wise, he didn't trust himself completely. He created a code, the 'Code of Sargon.' Even he could not break it. That is what our tribe needs. A code of laws to protect it from its rulers, whether they be a chief or a majority." His pulse quickened. "Thus, rulers could pass away, but the code would live on. And a tribe would retain its core character, even decades later." He sat back, panting. The inspiration flickered in his blood like lightning. *Thank you, El.* This was it, the missing piece.

Even the queen looked impressed.

"What would this code consist of?" she asked after a while.

Sargon nodded. "Wiser heads than mine would need to fashion it. But in spirit, the code would be based on . . ."

He frowned, searching. But the answer was in front of him. It was in the way Aya held poor Shulgi, the clubfooted boy. Thanks to her love, he was alive, not food for Moloch.

"The code is like a parent who loves her children," Sargon said. "*All* her children. She loves them fiercely, no matter if they are strong or crippled, male or female, infant or old. To the code, they are all her blood. And she will do anything to defend them." He finished earnestly. "The code says we are all family, worth protecting. Its rules stem from that."

The queen looked at him keenly. "Well done, Sargon. I must think on this."

She sat back and folded her hands across her belly and shut her eyes. The fire crackled softly. Sargon looked around, feeling suddenly exposed. Indeed, the elders were sending him looks of pure loathing. But many others seemed fascinated. Ki and Rogg, for starters. Nisaba, too. In fact, the whole tribe. With a thrill, Sargon realized he'd just orated to hundreds of people, the biggest audience of his life.

After a while, Ishtar spoke.

"So, it is ugliness you hate, Sargon. That seems to be part of it."

"Yes," Sargon said, uncertain where this was going.

"I admire this, I do. It is beautiful." Ishtar frowned into the fire. "Unfortunately, ugliness is necessary in this world."

"What do you mean?"

The queen touched her stomach with a sad smile.

"I feel a kinship with you, Sargon. We are both leaders, despite our obstacles. I, as a woman. You, as a cripple. Therefore, I will caution you, one leader to another. Do not be too idealistic. No leader can avoid ugliness. It is futile to try. You will cripple yourself far worse than losing a hand."

"I'm not sure I accept that," Sargon said cautiously.

"Hear me. The more you lead, the more ugliness you will do. This is a truth I learned early, as a young queen."

Ishtar's eyes grew sad, as if remembering terrible past events. "It is a hard truth. One's followers often remain blissfully ignorant of the ugliness that is necessary. But a queen must be strong, *take on* ugliness for her people. Else they will suffer. And that, I will not allow."

A murmur of support rose throughout the *mudhif.*

"I'm not convinced," Sargon said.

"Will you submit to a test?" Ishtar asked.

Sargon nodded.

"Very well, then." Ishtar looked into the fire. "Imagine your tribe is starving to death in the wilderness . . ."

Sargon smiled thinly. This took no imagination at all.

"Your hunger is at its peak. Then, one night, you spy a fire glimmering in the distance." Ishtar's eyes watched his. "You sneak up, and drawing near, spy another tribe, a smaller one, roasting meat over the blaze. Enough meat to save your people. Thus, you face a choice." The queen lifted a finger. "You can chase off this smaller tribe and take their food and survive. But you will make them starve." She looked at him frankly. "Would this be ugliness?"

"It would," Sargon said, a heaviness growing in his stomach.

"So, what do you choose? Steal and live? Or keep your code, but lose your people?"

"I'd ask the other tribe to share," Sargon said quickly.

Ishtar laughed. "A sweet sentiment, Sargon. But few in this world share. So, for argument, say this tribe will not share. What then?"

She leaned closer. "And before you answer, think of the cost of nobility, here. Think of your people starving to death over the following days. I mean, really *see* it."

She looked at Ki. "Imagine cradling this special young woman in your arms under the burning sun. See her cheeks growing hollow from hunger. See her lovely eyes fading to dullness. See her skin grow tight on her ribs, and her teeth protrude. With a little ugliness, you could save her. But no. You have a vague idea about nobility. You will let her die."

Sargon's stomach tightened. Ishtar was no fool. She had gone right to the tension at the heart of his code. *Do what you admire. Serve your people.* What if serving his people meant feeding them in ways he did not admire? Stealing? Was this conflict irreconcilable?

Ishtar's mouth hardened. "Look at her, Sargon. Tell her to her face that you'd let her starve for a code. Do it."

Reluctantly, Sargon glanced at Ki. His heart wavered. How beautiful she was, with her brown skin and her deep, intelligent eyes. She had already suffered so much. How could he ask her to suffer more? For an idea?

To buy time, he asked, "What would you do, queen?"

Ishtar raised a fist above her head. "I am Babylon's mother. Before letting even one of my children suffer, I would drench all of Mesopotamia in blood."

The response was instantaneous. A roar exploded across the *mudhif.*

"HAIL, ISHTAR!" the tribe roared. "HAIL! HAIL!"

Warriors thrust up fists. Women gave a shrill ululation. "HAIL, BABYLON! HAIL!" Sargon felt buffeted as if by a great wind. It took a long time to die down. And all the while, the queen waited, her eyes blazing on him. Only when it passed did she finally lift her chin in expectation.

"Well, Sargon?"

Sargon swallowed. His ideas were abstract. And Ki was right here, flesh and blood.

"I . . ." he stammered. "I . . ."

Luckily, Ki interjected with help. And her voice was strong and unwavering, hardened by experience. "Queen, forgive me for answering," she said with a bow. "But I have been a prisoner of Magog. Thus, I know what the path of power looks like, walked to its furthest end. And I tell you here and now. I would rather die young than live even a day on the trail of ugliness."

"Hear! Hear!" Rogg cried. "Well-spoken, Little Enki."

Sargon's heart filled with joy as she rushed on.

"What is more," Ki said, "any chief who felt the same, I would gladly serve. And by the gods! If there was a code that did this? Why, it would be even better. Like an oasis in the waste, it would give hope to the world."

She turned to Sargon. "With all my heart, I wish this tribe existed."

Rogg banged his fist into his palm. "Well spoken, little sister. Just so. We all go to the Underworld, eventually. Let it be with clean hearts and bright *emittus*."

Hearing this, Sargon's *emittu* rose up, overflowing with pride and kinship. This was exactly the kind of people he wished to live and die among. *Do what you admire. Serve your tribe.* He agreed with his friends: it was no service to let a tribe degrade into ugliness.

Ishtar spoke.

"Mighty Rogg. Clever Ki. You have given worthy answers. But you forget one thing. Your families are safely dead. So, tell me. If they were still alive, and ugliness could save them—would you not do it? Even a little?"

She looked piercingly at Rogg. "Imagine your younglings were here, about your feet. And you, Ki. You had siblings, did you not? Perhaps a sister?" Ki nodded. "Imagine your sister with her arm around you, celebrating your success. Alive, instead of dead. And just a little ugliness could make it so. What then?"

Rogg and Ki sat back, shaken.

Ishtar nodded. "You see, my people are alive. And whatever it takes to keep them so, I will do."

25

After dinner, two warriors in grass skirts walked the travelers up the main path to the guest hut, sheltering them from the villagers who trailed after them in the warm dark, whispering and pointing. The Babylonians were no longer focused on Rogg or herself, Ki noticed, but on Sargon. It seemed his talk with Ishtar had stirred them, and their voices filled the night, debating his idea. She walked in the rear of her group, listening intently. Something significant had happened tonight. It had awoken her black spirit, filling her with energy. But she still wasn't sure what it meant.

"Well, that was stupid, Ta. You nearly ruined everything," Ut said, trudging at Sargon's side. "What were you thinking, debating the queen like that?"

Rogg shot him a hard look. "His name is Sargon, now. Not Ta. Remember it."

Ut laughed. "You can't scare me here, giant. We are under Ishtar's rule." He spread his hands grandly, preparing to say more, until Rogg's expression made him think better of it. "Anyway," he muttered, "don't tell me what to do." And he fell silent, scowling.

Outside the guest hut, the tallest warrior held aside the entry mat. "I will be here all night if you need anything," he said as they walked in. "Tomorrow you'll get a tour of the village."

Here all night? Ki thought dryly. So we're still prisoners.

But it was a commodious hut, with all the basics provided for, and the group's mood lightened as they entered. A fire painted the reeds with orange light, while rolled-up hide blankets and reed mats lined the far wall, ready to use. Also present were clay ewers of water, bundles of kindling, their supply packs from the desert, and stone mortars and pestles to grind seed with. The familiar odors of sap and whittled wood calmed Ki, undercutting her concerns. Still, as the others unrolled their blankets and prepared to sleep, they began to argue. Ki sat cross-legged on her mat by the far wall and listened. It appeared Ut and Aya were still furious at Sargon for challenging the queen.

"Of course we must accept Babylon's offer," Aya said angrily. She was washing her injured foot in a clay basin. "There's nowhere else to go, you heard Nisaba. So what's the debate?"

Sargon was wiping Shulgi's bottom with a skin rag. The smell was sour, but the baby giggled and cooed, and Sargon smiled as he dipped the rag into a jar of water to clean it. Ki found herself smiling, too. It made her feel warm and peaceful to see Sargon like that.

"But shouldn't we discuss it?" Sargon asked. "We've come too far to be hasty."

"I want a better life for Shulgi. That's why I left. And I've found it." Aya pointed at the grass mat hanging in the doorway. "Look out there. Life doesn't get better. This is the most wonderful tribe we've ever seen. It's got everything we want. Huts. Warriors. Bread. *Mates*." She looked at Ut significantly. "That's why he left the cave, anyway."

"I always admitted it," Ut said angrily.

"I want the same, actually. I've changed my mind about that. I want protection. And here we've got it. If we leave, we'll have to build it all from scratch. We could work our whole lives to acquire a fraction of what's already here. For what? To 'give everyone a say?' The queen's convinced me of the value of *that*. Even if we recruit enough members to feel safe, the tribe would grow out of our control. The newcomers would form a majority, and outvote us at every turn. They'd change our home into something we can't possibly foresee."

"The code fixes that," Sargon said.

"The *code*."

"Yes. It will keep us on track, even if we get outvoted." Sargon set the soiled rag aside, poured water from a pitcher into a basin, and began to rinse his hand and stump in it. "Voting was your idea in the first place, remember? You created it to protect Shulgi."

"I say we get rid of it. It was a brand-new idea. It failed. The code will work no better."

"Sargon the Great used it."

"A legend. It may have been exaggerated over the decades." Aya set her swollen ankle on a mat to dry. "The whole point of government is to make life pleasant. It's pleasant *here*. So, starting now, I'm Babylonian."

"Me too," Ut said. "I'd like to add—"

"Nobody asked you, traitor," Aya said. "You shouldn't even be in this hut with us."

It went on like that for a while. At last, Aya grew tired. She took Shulgi and lay down on her grass mat to sleep. The others did likewise.

Not Ki, however. Her mind was abuzz, and she needed to talk to Sargon alone.

As Rogg crushed the fire into embers, dropping the hut into reddish darkness, she waited. Not until Ut and Aya began to snore did she creep around the hut, listening at the reed wall for eavesdroppers. Finally satisfied, she crept up to Rogg and Sargon and tapped their arms.

They were awake. Somehow both had anticipated she'd want to talk, and they rose and joined her in an isolated corner of the hut, knee to knee, heads close, so as not to wake the others. Their pupils reflected the crushed coals, glittering redly.

"Something wrong, Ki?" Sargon whispered.

"I'm sorry, brothers. I know we need sleep, but . . ." She glanced at their sleeping companions.

"We're here," Sargon said. "Whatever it is."

Ki breathed out slowly. "I think we should leave Babylon."

Sargon nodded as if he'd expected this.

"You were quiet, earlier," he said.

"This tribe you spoke of tonight . . ." Ki pressed her fingers to her temples, concentrating. "It's the finest vision I've ever heard. A code against ugliness. Why, a thing like that . . ."

"It's not my idea. It's Sargon the Great's."

"Yes, but the world let his vision die."

Ki looked into his eyes. The way he looked back so steadily reassured her.

"My people were nomads. We traveled all over Mesopotamia, passing one tribe after another. I tell you, Sargon, there is so much unhappiness in this world. So many people with nowhere to go. But if your tribe existed, why, it would be like a bonfire on a black night. All the little ones suffering in dark places could see it glimmering from afar, and whisper of it, and dream of fleeing to it one day." As I would have, if I'd heard of such a place, she thought. "Mesopotamia needs such a tribe. It needs hope."

"I want this, too," Sargon said earnestly. "But there's nowhere to build it. Nisaba said so."

Ki took a deep breath. The time had come to tell him *what she was.*

Suddenly her black spirit leapt up in her, protesting. *Foolish girl. They'll turn on us, just like your tribe did.* But Ki pushed it down. She had to tell the whole truth. Friendship demanded it.

"Sargon, there's one more thing I've kept from you. I . . ." She clenched her fists. This was the moment. "I have a black spirit," she forced through her teeth. "I am a witch, like they say."

Silence met her. Ki waited tensely in the darkness. For the first time, the men didn't answer, and her heart dropped. They *would* shun her. Just like her old tribe!

"Let me explain . . ." she stammered.

Before she could go on, though, a confident chuckle emitted from the dark. It was Rogg, his voice deep and rumbling. His strong hand patted her arm.

"Little sister, no. You don't have a black spirit."

“I really do. I wish I didn’t,” she said, half-pleading.

“You may think so, but you don’t. You see, in Elam, we had one such as you.”

“One like me?”

Rogg nodded. “Some called him a sorcerer. Others called him a Thinker. And that was the correct view.”

“A Thinker!” Ki repeated, stupefied. She’d never heard such a term.

“Yes,” Rogg said firmly. “This man had a brilliant mind. He invented things, philosophized, planned great military strategies. All Elam respected him. We called him a ‘son of Enki.’ But he was a Thinker. Not a sorcerer. And that’s what you are. A Thinker.”

“I’m a blasphemer! I have a black spirit!” Ki cried, twisting her hands. “The gods punished my tribe for what I did.”

“Never utter such foolishness again,” Rogg said. “No, you have the ‘lightning mind.’ Solutions strike just like that, don’t they?” He snapped his fingers. “Quick as lightning?”

Ki sat back. *Lightning mind.* Yes, that was what it felt like when the ideas came. Zaps of lightning, bursting out of nowhere into the darkness of her head. Ever since childhood, she’d felt it.

She nodded hesitantly.

“Black spirits do evil,” Rogg said. “But what evil have you done? You have *good* ideas. Ideas so powerful, they scared your tribe. But that is natural. Everyone fears what they don’t understand.”

Ki touched her temples, bewildered. This was unexpected, but it felt . . . true. In her gut, the black spirit scrabbled frantically, trying to get deeper into her, away from Rogg. But he squeezed her arm harder. And suddenly, to her surprise, the black spirit wasn’t there.

Ki lowered both hands to her pelvis, stunned. Yes, the feeling was gone.

“How do you know this?” she whispered.

“Your strategy in the gully,” Rogg said. “It’s not normal, what you came up with. Especially you being so young, and lacking military experience. Right then I guessed what you were. And after today’s wind-catcher, there is no doubt. You are a Thinker.”

Ki's hands shook. She stuffed them under her legs to hide it.

"Tell me," she said urgently. "This Thinker of Elam. What was he?"

"He was a great one," Rogg said. "Like you, he tried to help his tribe, make life better for his village. But his mind was so powerful, the other chieftains grew jealous and wanted his gift for themselves. They tried to capture him to make him their slave, and a great war began. The Thinker was killed. And no one in Elam benefited from his brilliance." Rogg shook his head in disgust. "Behold the waste we make of our gifts."

"I see," Ki said softly.

"Tell no one else, sister. If people learn your nature, they'll try to capture you, use you for their own greedy ends. I'm not surprised Gog is after you. He must know what you are and want you to grow his power. If Ishtar realizes, she'll snap you up, too." Rogg glanced at the door flap. "That wind-catcher. It's not a thing of your tribe, is it? You came up with it yourself."

Ki nodded.

"I thought so. Ishtar must not learn that."

Again Ki reached for her black spirit. Again it was not there. It was just her. Alone.

She felt strangely light, as if a great weight had lifted.

But what was left?

"So . . . I'm really not a witch?"

Rogg shook his head. "Who knows where your power comes from? Perhaps the gods gave it to you. Perhaps you really are a 'chosen one of Enki.' But an evil spirit? No. Your actions say otherwise."

Ki looked at Sargon. "What do you think?"

"You're Ki. That's what matters."

Ki covered her face, overwhelmed.

"You were about to tell us something," Rogg said. "We interrupted you."

In a rush of gratitude, Ki nodded. This was the second big moment. *The wheat.* She'd almost forgotten it, the reason Jakka was chasing her, the reason she was still alive. But her friends' attentiveness encouraged her, and soon her words were flowing, pushing the story into the world.

And what a story! Food. The end of starvation. She winced to think how close she'd come to killing herself and robbing this from humanity. It shamed her. *Forgive me, family*, she prayed. *This is our legacy, my way to honor you. I'll never consider killing it again.*

" . . . that's why Gog's chasing me," she finished. "He wants me to grow 'magic' food for him and fix his supply problem. But I won't, I swear."

The others were listening in open-mouthed amazement.

"You can *create food*?" Sargon whispered, dumbfounded.

Rogg grunted. "Perhaps you'd better explain it again, Ki. Remember, we aren't as quick as you."

Ki nodded, and tried again, slower.

"Do you believe me?" she asked nervously.

"I can hardly grasp it," Sargon said. "But it's you, Ki. Of course I believe you."

"You don't think I'm odd?"

"Odd," Sargon exclaimed. "Why, Ki! Have you . . . *solved hunger*?"

Ki's excitement rose. He got it. He was the first person besides Asha—and Gog—to see its potential.

"I think so," she admitted bashfully.

Rogg stroked his beard. "Mmm. I see why Gog is so intent on you, now. This solves his food problem. He could feed as many warriors as he wants, two thousand, ten thousand. There'd be no stopping him. He'd grow big enough to conquer all Mesopotamia." His voice stumbled. "Even . . . take Elam."

Ki's heart was pounding. She felt so relieved to be trusted, she suddenly couldn't help herself. She leaned forward and hugged them both tight.

"I never thought . . . I mean, after my tribe was . . . I never thought I'd share this," she said awkwardly, pulling back. "But Sargon, I had to tell *you*, because this could give a tribe much power. More power, maybe, than any tribe has ever had. If it made evil men strong, I would hate myself. But if it strengthened a good tribe—one with a code against ugliness—I'd die happy. As soon as you spoke tonight, I knew what I'd been missing. Do you see? I need *your vision* for mine to live. My dream only matters . . . if it's paired with yours."

Sargon's eyes shone in the darkness. He hugged her again, and she felt his heart beating against hers. She felt breathless until he let her go.

"I want this too, Ki. But we still don't have a place to settle."

"I don't see a solution for that," Ki admitted.

"And there's another problem," he went on. "Aya and Ut want to stay. Shulgi needs a safe place to grow up, too. How can we drag them back into the wild? All for an idealistic mission that could easily fail?"

"Ishtar won't let us leave anyway," Rogg said.

"No?" Sargon asked.

"Certainly not. She'll make Ki build her a fleet of wind-catchers. During that time, she may realize what Ki is."

"And if we three try to escape," Sargon said, "she could hurt the others in revenge. Remember what she said? To protect her people, she'd willingly 'shed oceans of blood.'"

Ki shivered. "Lovely."

The conversation sputtered after that. It had been a long tense day, one twist after another. Their minds were exhausted. They agreed to sleep on things and regroup tomorrow.

However, before returning to their blankets, Sargon and Rogg both hugged Ki again, and promised not to share her secret. Ki felt very close to them. And her black spirit was quiet.

"We're tribe," Sargon insisted. "Don't forget it."

"Goodnight," she said happily.

"Goodnight," the men said. "See you tomorrow, Ki."

In the red dark she lay down on her mat, her stomach aswirl with emotions. She didn't expect to sleep, there was so much to think and feel. But her body had other ideas. The moment she pillowed her hands under her cheek, she began to dream.

26

The next morning, the travelers ate breakfast in the guest hut, then followed their warrior escort on a tour of the village. There was much to see, but Sargon was so preoccupied with the question from the previous night, he couldn't focus. When the tour finished, he sat under a palm tree by the river and rubbed his eyes.

What do we do?

The others seemed happy here. Indeed, they were already participating in village life. Down at the water's edge, Ut was regaling two young women with stories of his adventures—much embellished, Sargon noted with amusement—while farther up the bank, Aya sat with three young mothers, shelling nuts as their infants played on a grass mat. Out on the river, Ki and Rogg spearfished under the tutelage of a white-bearded Babylonian. Ki's trident splashed into the water and returned with a fish wriggling on the spikes, and the whole boat burst into applause. Ki drew it up with astonished delight, and on the bank, Sargon smiled. How content they all seemed. To abandon this seemed madness. Why should they "help" Mesopotamia? What had it ever done for them?

Looking up and down the bank, he shook his head. It was all so lovely. Yellow birds perched on the bending reed stems. The water drifted by in green-gold ripples. The sky was blue, empty of clouds.

What was it all for? Why shouldn't he stay here with his friends for the rest of his days, delighting in bread and honey? Did life require more than that?

At noon, the queen invited them into the *mudhif* for another meal.

This time, just a few elders and advisers joined, and as they waited for the food, they were entertained not by a group of musicians, but by a song-girl with a lyre.

The sophisticated Babylonian instrument was overlaid with lapis lazuli, soft beaten copper, and mother of pearl. Sargon and the others sat entranced as the girl's long elegant fingers plucked the gristle strings with hypnotic skill. In poetic verse, she sang out a classic tragedy they all knew: of Dumuzi, ugly god of rams, and of his yearning for the beautiful Inanna.

"This is my favorite," Aya whispered, nudging Sargon with her elbow.

He nodded, remembering how Ut had once told it in the desert. How the beautiful goddess, trapped in the Underworld, tempted the infatuated Dumuzi down to her with promises of love—then tricked him into taking her place. Ignoring his cries of despair, she abandoned him in the darkness while she rose back to the land of the living, singing joyfully. Ut had told it well. But now the girl's husky honeyed voice sang it better than Sargon had ever heard it. And when she finished, he, along with everyone else, wiped his eyes and applauded wildly.

"Truly, they are more civilized here," Ut murmured.

Sargon nodded. Everything in Babylon seemed superior to Akkad. It made him feel sad—both for the backwardness of his people, and for his own plight. It made him want to shelter in Babylon's cool river huts forever and never experience hunger or fear again. And perhaps this is Ishtar's intention, he thought. To coax recruits to settle, rather than to aspire.

Across the mat, the queen smiled as if she could guess his thoughts.

"That was a fine conversation last night, Sargon. Most intriguing. I still feel refreshed by it." She waved the lyre girl away. "You had all night to consider my offer. Are you ready to join?"

Sargon's gut tightened. He'd hoped to have until dinnertime to decide.

"Well." He cleared his throat. "Actually, ah . . ."

The queen frowned. "Do you mean to refuse me?"

Aya and Ut both erupted in fury. "No, Great One!" they cried. "We accept!"

"I asked him." The queen held eye contact with Sargon. "He is my favorite."

Sargon flushed, embarrassed, and bowed.

"I'm sure I don't deserve it, queen. I thank you, but . . . we haven't finished discussing it yet."

"Then you wish to leave," the queen exclaimed.

"No, it's just . . . with so much information to take in—"

"The heart knows faster than the mind," Ishtar said crisply. "Your delay says it all. Your heart is waiting for your mind to catch up. You will decline."

The Akkadians were shooting him furious looks. Sargon knew he had to fix this.

"Please, queen, we take our oaths of loyalty seriously. May we wait until dinner to say them? I mean no disrespect."

The queen gave him a strange glance. "You are an interesting man, Sargon. Very well. Let us eat."

She clapped her big hands and children in grass skirts ran out carrying more bowls of sacred juice. Like the previous night, the queen lifted hers in both hands and cried: "To Enbilulu, Lord of the River. May he send us POWER." The elders echoed her and drank, prompting the guests to follow. And they all did—except Sargon.

As he put the bowl to his lips, he felt the queen watching him intently . . . like a cat watching a squirrel in a tree, waiting for it to fall. And suddenly, he felt strongly that he must not drink.

Surprised at his own boldness, he sipped the red liquid, but only pretended to swallow. Instead, he let it sit in his mouth until the queen glanced away to confer with an elder. Then he spat it quickly into a bowl of fish soup at hand, and set the bowl aside, determined not to touch it again. It was probably just a stupid feeling, he thought. Still, he felt strangely relieved.

After the meal, Ishtar ordered pillows of ox hide brought forth. The singer was summoned back, and once more her voice and lyre filled the *mudhif* with magic. This, along with the comfortable pillows and heavy meal, made Sargon lightheaded and drowsy, and his lids were just beginning to droop when he heard a strange *thud* nearby. Looking over, he saw Ut slumped on the mat, asleep.

Sargon sat up quickly. "Please forgive us, queen. We don't mean to insult you."

The queen waved a hand to quiet him. She was reclining on her side, a peculiar smile on her fleshy face. *Her* eyes were not tired, he thought in alarm. No, they were sharp and bright. Hungry.

"After a rich meal it is proper to sleep. Your friend compliments us, Sargon. You might do the same."

Sargon felt his arms growing strangely heavy. Turning, he found his other companions nodding off, too. Aya slumped flat on her pillow, her mouth slackly open. To Sargon's alarm, Baby Shulgi rolled from her arms onto the dirt floor and lay on his belly making small grunts of displeasure, kicking his tiny clubfoot, until a girl attendant picked him up. Farther off, even big Rogg was rubbing his forehead as if he'd forgotten something.

"I feel . . . so slee . . . shy . . . shleepy," the giant said. "As if . . ."

Suddenly he crashed like a felled tree, landing amidst the platters and scattering food everywhere.

Ki burst out: "The sacred juice, Sargon. It's drugged! Enki root. Run—!"

Then she, too, slumped, leaving Sargon alone.

"What is the meaning of this?" He faced the queen. "We are guests! You promised us safety!"

The queen watched and said nothing.

"Last night you promished . . . pwomishd . . ."

He could no longer speak properly. He hadn't swallowed it, whatever the drugged juice was, but a little must have penetrated the lining of his mouth before he spit it out, for now his tongue was tingling.

The queen encircled her twelve-year-old son with her big arm and pointed at Sargon.

"Look, dear." She sounded far away. "Their ideas seem beautiful. But see where they lead."

"Yes, Mother."

"A leader must live in reality, not fantasy. Else this will happen to him and his people."

"Yes, Mother," the boy repeated, wide-eyed.

Talk wouldn't fix this, Sargon realized. There had been talk last night, and this was the result. His only advantage, then, was to pretend to be drugged too, and figure out a plan.

Shutting his eyes, he flopped over as the others had, striking his head painfully on the mat.

It worked. Footsteps surrounded him. Strong hands hoisted him into the air. As they carried him out, he hung utterly limp, knowing that even the slightest twitch would give him away.

Nisaba's voice followed him faintly.

"He intrigued you, queen."

"He is an idealist. As I was, when I began."

"A long time ago," Nisaba said.

"Yes." The queen sighed. "A long time, indeed."

27

Sargon kept his eyes shut as the warriors set him down in the guest hut on his back. Heavy *thumps* told him the others were being laid out the same way. He heard Rogg's loud breathing, so he knew they were alive. Still, as the warriors stomped out of the hut, he felt a rising dread. *Magog.* It had to be. Ishtar must have calculated the risks and decided it was safest to give her guests to Gog, who would take them north to a life of slavery.

Sargon's stomach clenched. Had they come so far for this? Ur-Baba's gnashing teeth filled his mind. He imagined dirt pits, whipcracks, and hideous laughter. His friends screaming as red flames leapt from stone altars. Magog feeding on Ki's wheat. Black-tattooed hordes spreading across the earth . . . marching on Akkad.

Unless I do something.

But what? He wasn't special. Ki could think, Rogg could fight. But "Sargon" was just a name pasted over "Ta." And "Ta" had never—

Stop, he thought sharply. Rogg would hate this. He'd tell me to spit this from my mind and work. And that was right. He couldn't afford to sulk. His friends had no one else.

So Sargon gritted his teeth, focused his thoughts, and worked.

◆

An hour later, a ram's horn blew in the distance, starting a commotion in the path. Feet ran by the hut and mothers screamed at children to get indoors. Window flaps dropped. Gradually, the village grew still. Then came the heavy tramp of feet. Many feet, marching in time. *Tramp, tramp, tramp.* Sargon's blood hammered. He still had no plan.

The door flap whipped inward. Footsteps entered. Sargon risked opening his eyes to slits. He saw four Babylonians—Ishtar, Nisaba, and two guards—march inside, followed by five men tattooed as black as wolves. Magog.

"As promised, Prince Jakka." Ishtar walked to the bodies. "Magog signals. Babylon delivers." She pointed at Ki. "Here is your *baru*, no?"

She looked like another person entirely, Sargon noticed. She was pale and strained, though dressed in even more regalia. She wore a beaten copper band on her forehead, studded with a ruby, and a heron-feather cape that hung from her shoulders as white as ivory. She adjusted the cape nervously, and went on.

"They are drugged with Enki root but unharmed. They'll sleep past dark."

A shriek of triumph filled the hut. From the tattooed pack, a young fellow raced to Ki and knelt over her. "By Baal, it *is* her. Filthy nomad rat! Fitting, eh, Nod? She is felled by Enki root just as she felled her guards."

This had to be Jakka, Sargon thought. Ki had described him well. He sported a manly beard, but appeared fragile, ready to snap into a tantrum at the slightest pressure. The spoiled child's face beneath his tattoos made him even more terrifying.

"Filthy rat. Oh, she'll *feel* what she put me through." Jakka swung his hand and slapped Ki's face, making it flip sideways in sleep. Sargon nearly leapt up and struck Jakka back. But that would ruin everything, so he mastered himself and kept still.

An older Magog man spoke. "Our thanks, queen. Gog will not forget this. You will be rewarded."

Sargon studied him through half-cracked lids. This had to be "Nod," the one Ki truly feared. Indeed, he looked the opposite of the prince. His face was wooden and expressionless, rippled with creases and scars. His eyes were cold, vacant. But intelligence lurked in them as they flicked over each body in the hut, including Sargon's. Processing, calculating, giving nothing away.

Queen Ishtar addressed him. "Thank you, Nod, but our alliance is reward enough. I hope it is as strong as ever."

"It is." Nod's pleasant tone contrasted with his awful eyes. "Of all our allies, Babylon is most valued."

"Wait, Nod," Jakka interjected angrily. "They captured the *baru* yesterday, yet waited to signal us until today. Why?" He glared at Ishtar. "Did they consider keeping the witch themselves, perhaps?"

His brazenness made Nod wince. But Nisaba stepped swiftly between the parties, speaking in a light, humorous voice to diffuse the tension.

"Forgive us, prince, we delayed because we didn't want to disturb you with trifles," she soothed. "You must know we smaller tribes tread lightly around Magog. The instant we felt sure it was her, we smoke-signaled."

Jakka snickered under his breath, but before he could speak, Queen Ishtar picked up the thread in a pleasant voice. "What now, prince?"

"I'll take them," Jakka snapped. "What else?"

"All?" Ishtar asked.

Jakka laughed. "Why not?"

"You want the girl, of course," the queen said gently. "But what interest are these others to you? It might be tedious to march them all north under guard. Especially him." She pointed at Rogg. "I know you wish to return swiftly. I could dispose of them, if you like."

Sargon felt a flicker of hope. Was Ishtar trying to help?

Jakka gave a screeching laugh, quashing it.

"Don't insult me, woman. If Magog knows anything, it is how to herd slaves. Let the giant try and misbehave. I'll slice his friends' noses off one by one until he settles down. Besides," Jakka rubbed his hands together greedily. "He is a real bull of a fellow. Made for the battle pit. I'll toss him six opponents at a time. I bet his big hands rip 'em all apart." He grinned at his companions. "Would you like to see that, brothers?"

Three hideous bursts of laughter turned Sargon's bones hollow.

"Meanwhile, we are tired," Jakka went on. "We'll rest here tonight. Got bread?"

"Yes, but it will take time to prepare," Ishtar said. "Please, relax in our *mudhif* until we dine at dusk. Our singer is unparalleled."

"Fine." Jakka stretched his arms. "Meanwhile, fetch me a woman. Not now, I am tired. But after dinner I'll want amusement."

Ishtar looked taken aback. "A woman? I did not expect . . ." Sargon had never seen her so off-kilter. "Forgive me, prince, but our women are not slaves. All Babylonians are my children."

"But I want one." Jakka spun toward Nod like a spoiled son turning between parents. "It's been ages since the last village."

Nod whitened. "Forgive me, Lord," he said under his breath. "But you took a woman in Kish, Sippar, *and* Isin. That was unusual enough, they were vassal tribes. But Babylon is an ally. The whole southern river follows its leadership."

"What do I care for that? I want a woman."

Nod gulped. "Lord, truly—"

"A woman, Nod. I WANT A WOMAN."

Sargon was horrified. How could such a child wield the power of Magog? Madness! Nod seemed bowled over, too. He struggled to find words.

"But Lord, this is . . ." He shuffled close and tried to speak quietly, so the others could not hear. "An insult to an ally is long remembered, Lord. Technically, the queen is your equal. I suggest—"

"Equal? Bah! Magog is ten times her size. I want a Babylonian female, Nod. I lust!"

Nod shriveled, then turned to his hosts apologetically. They were staring at him in wide-eyed disbelief. Ishtar spoke sternly.

"Nod, five years ago when Gog and I made this treaty, you were present. You heard the terms promised—"

"MY FATHER IS NOT HERE."

Jakka's face turned bright red. He strode to the queen and began to pace around her, as if inspecting a slave. "You treat with ME, woman," he screamed, shoving his face at hers. "WHO AM I? Tell me."

Sargon watched in awe. He couldn't believe one ruler would treat another this way. The Babylon sentries couldn't, either. Their fingers gripped their wooden spear shafts, and they kept glancing at their bald queen. Ishtar, meanwhile, had emptied her face of all emotion.

"You are the future ruler of Magog. We hail you, prince—"

"Just so. And in decades to come, you will deal with ME, ME, ME."

The queen gazed emptily ahead, taking it. Sargon was in awe. To so casually shame the mightiest queen on the Euphrates, Magog must be powerful indeed.

Jakka rounded on Nisaba. "And who is this pretty egg? Perhaps I will take her and teach Babylon a lesson. I've never had a bald one." He peered at her greedily. "Yes, she'll do."

Ishtar nearly laughed. "Prince, she is my top adviser, not some common—"

"A curious specimen." Jakka eyed Nisaba's bald head. "Is she Babylonian?"

"Not quite," Ishtar said uneasily. "I bought her from the Great Marsh."

"A marshling!"

Jakka paced around Nisaba now, tattooed fingers twitching. His worm-pink tongue emerged and wetted his lips. "Another new fruit to taste. When I am warlord, I will conquer that silly marsh and take many such creatures to my tent. Yes, perhaps this creature could be useful to me, advise me where to attack. Father has no marshling slaves, does he, Nod?"

"Not that I know of, Lord," Nod said warily.

Suddenly, Jakka grabbed Nisaba's head with both hands. Digging his fingers into the smooth dome, he cried: "How strange it feels! How often is it shaved?"

Nisaba twisted free and backed away, glancing at Ishtar in terror.

The queen appealed to Nod with a desperate look, but Nod had gone rigid, eyes on the dirt, as if he'd witnessed this scene too often before. Jakka took this as permission. Giving a cry of delight, he rushed at Nisaba and slapped at her long legs, laughing. She scampered farther backward, grass skirt rattling, as Jakka's warriors roared with approval. "Queen!" Nisaba cried. But Jakka pursued her to the reed wall, leaving her no room to escape. There he began grabbing her all over, pushing aside her skinny flailing arms, feeling her body ruthlessly.

"I will have her, Nod. Magog needs wombs. Wombs to bake sons in, as the kilns of Babylon bake bread. Haha! We will take her to Magog with us when we go."

Jakka roared insanely, and his men roared too, stamping their sandals on the dirt floor.

"Nod, you'll see." Jakka gripped Nisaba by the throat and stared into her eyes, so that she turned her face in revulsion. "She will give me a son, a half-Magog, half-marsh son, to rule as my puppet when I conquer the Great Marsh. How's that for strategy, old goat?"

Nod stood slack-jawed. Ishtar shot him a beseeching look, then faced Jakka.

"Prince," she begged. "How did we offend? I implore you, do not joke of this. Let her go."

"You dare command me?" Jakka turned on her. "Do you weary of our alliance, woman?"

Queen Ishtar froze. She studied Jakka carefully, probing whether he was serious. Her eyes swirled with calculations. But gradually her pupils dimmed, until her face crumpled completely.

"You know I value it, Lord."

"Then you will not toss it away over a marshling whore."

Turning again, Jakka grabbed Nisaba's face in both hands and kissed her fervently on the mouth. Nisaba struggled, gripping his wrists. But Jakka kissed her long and hard, then released her and marched out of the hut. "Send bread and honey to the *mudhif*," he shouted over his shoulder. "And make haste. I must get my energy up before I enjoy my marshling snack."

All but two of his party followed him out. The remaining pair grabbed Nisaba and forced her onto her belly, making a triangle out of her body as they tied her hands and feet. Nisaba cried out in pain. But her focus was on the queen.

"We can fix this, Mother. Let Jakka rest. After he is calmer . . ."

"Then what?" Ishtar said quietly.

"Then . . . another woman, perhaps."

Ishtar looked drained. "My clever Nisaba," she said softly. "It is no good."

"Queen Mother," Nisaba cried. "Your son! I belong to your son!"

Ishtar absorbed this, then wiped her face and looked off at the entry flap.

"Queen!" Nisaba said.

For a long moment, Ishtar did not speak. Her warriors waited, staring at her. When she finally spoke, she sounded flat, dull.

"You know what Gog is, Nisaba. It was you who taught me."

"Give me time, Queen Mother. I will find a solution, I will." A vein bulged in Nisaba's round forehead. "I can't see it yet, but please, if I just think . . ."

"How?"

"I . . . I will find a way," Nisaba spluttered.

Ishtar waited. And when Nisaba still struggled, the queen said sadly, "My sweet political sorceress. My dear one. If even you cannot figure it out, who can?"

Ishtar was resigning herself to it, moment by moment. Defeat was filling her face. It was remarkable how quickly she accepted it, Sargon thought. With a sigh, she reached out and stroked Nisaba's bald head fondly, as if in a final blessing.

"Babylon will not forget you, Nisaba. Morning and night, we will sing for you in the *mudhif*. A legend will be made for you. Your name will be lifted up on the lyre."

"I don't want a song! I want to stay in Babylon," Nisaba cried. "Queen!"

Ishtar did not answer. She had a look of terrible despair, one Sargon recognized too well from Akkad. It was the look of submission to the black feeling. To the *way things were.*

Fight, queen! Treasure your dignity! he wanted to shout. *Don't surrender it so cheap. It won't come back easily.*

But the queen was already trudging out, leaving the grass flap swinging in her wake.

28

Only the two Magog guards remained. They sat throwing bone dice on a wooden game board they'd found near the wall, cursing with each toss. The dice clicked noisily. The hut seemed smaller, crowded with their sweaty bodies. Sargon struggled to breathe calmly. How horrible this all was! And yet . . . could it be used?

He peeked sideways at Nisaba. She lay quietly, her face in the dirt. He wished he could see inside her mind. She might know a secret way out of here.

After a while, one man turned to Nisaba. "Ey, marsh worm. We're bored. What're these peg-holes for, eh?" He tapped the game board. "Give us the rules."

Nisaba lay still in her ropes, ignoring him. The man looked surprised.

"Ey, worm. You think you're too good for me?"

Nisaba didn't move.

Rage twisted the man's face. He jumped up as if to kick her, but his companion restrained him. "She's not yours, brother. Let the prince tame her."

"I suppose," the first grumbled.

"That's right. You just sit and keep watch. In fact, I'm tired, I need a nap. Spell me, eh?"

"I'm tired too," the first one complained. "What about *my* nap?"

"After."

The second man curled up on his side and was instantly snoring, leaving the first alone. With a resentful muttering, the first crossed his legs, sat back against the reed wall, and stared at Nisaba. His eyes began to glow. Sargon's stomach turned.

"You should be nice to me, marsh worm," the man said at length. "I'm a sub-captain. I got two slaves already." He cackled. "Maybe when the prince is done with you, you'll be my third."

No reply.

"Save your breath, then," he said angrily. "You'll need it. The prince wears his pets out fast."

The afternoon dragged on. The air grew stuffier in the confined space. Sargon's bladder began to ache. Eventually he let the urine run freely down his leg, raising a sour smell that mingled with the sweaty odors of his drugged companions. It was humiliating to lie flat in his own wetness. Yet an image kept replaying in his head, the image of Ishtar's face, crumpled in defeat. It drove him to think harder. That's not me anymore, he told himself. It *will* not be.

He lay there, alternately thinking and praying. And gradually, the prayer calmed him. And amidst the calm, a fresh idea stirred. It was an old Akkadian saying: "The enemy of my enemy is my friend." And here was Nisaba, freshly an enemy of Jakka. What if he recruited her?

The hut dimmed further. Sargon clung to his idea, struggling to squeeze life from it. Recruit her. Recruit her. But how? To speak to her, he needed the guard to leave. Then, he'd need a real plan to tempt her to his side. But what?

Under the door flap, the strip of light faded from white to gold. Smells of dinner floated in, along with laughter and singing from the *mudhif*. Sargon began to panic. Time was running out, and still a real plan evaded him. If only Ki was awake instead.

Yet he'd had ideas, too. He should replicate that. In the desert he'd used the cover of the storm to forage safely at the river. How had it come to him? By going over the facts. By reviewing them slowly, without emotion. The facts suggested things.

He reexamined what he knew. Soon dark would fall. Then the village would gather in the *mudhif* for dinner. Music would play. Children would run in with bowls of sacred juice. Queen Ishtar would lift her bowl in a toast. She'd shout, "Hail, Enbilulu! Send us power!" Everyone would drink. And then—

His breath caught. The juice!

The scheme was so wild, it felt like a fantasy. Yet it was better than nothing.

Now he needed the guard to go away.

Luckily, the guard had been sipping from the water skin all afternoon. As the line of daylight beneath the entry flap turned purple, he stood up, scratching his loincloth with tattooed fingers. "Ho, worm. I got to make a puddle outside. Behave till I get back, eh?" He nudged her with his toe. "Or I'll kick your chest to mush."

Nisaba spoke sharply. "Your master wants my chest in good condition, I think."

"Careful, slave. I don't like back talk."

He nudged her harder. Then, giving a pleased chuckle, he tramped out, leaving the door mat flapping. Sargon's throat tightened. It was now or never. And he had to be *good*.

Taking a breath, he gathered himself . . . and spoke.

"Nisaba."

The bald head snapped around. The intelligent eyes stared at him as if he was a ghost.

"You're awake!" Her mouth fell open. "How?"

"Shhh." Sargon nodded at the sleeping guard. "Don't wake him."

Nisaba glanced at his friends, then back. "You didn't drink?"

He shook his head.

"Who warned you?" Her eyes flicked to the path as if to tell Ishtar. "Who betrayed us?"

"No one. I just guessed. Now listen, Nisaba, we must—"

"By Enbilulu! You're cleverer than you appear. It was Ishtar's expression, wasn't it?" Nisaba groaned. "I've trained her and trained her."

"Please listen, sister. There is no time."

"For what?" She laughed. "You want to mock me now for sharing your fate, I suppose." Her voice hardened. "Go on, Akkadian. Taunt me. The gods do have a sense of humor."

"Just the opposite," Sargon said. "I want to recruit you."

Nisaba gave a barking laugh. "Recruit!"

"Shhh, please." Sargon glanced at the sleeper again. This wasn't working. Outside the hut, the other guard's urine was striking the reed wall. Sargon had to hurry.

"When he comes back in," he whispered, "you distract him. I'll do the rest."

"The rest? You?" Nisaba rolled her eyes. "Fifty Magog warriors are outside. Not to mention all of Babylon. What can a cripple do?"

"Not give up," Sargon said sternly. "For a start."

Nisaba shut her eyes. "You don't understand what these people are."

Sargon tried to keep the frustration from his voice. "I *understand*," he said, "that we've lost everything."

"Wrong, Sargon. There is always more to lose. Torture, for instance. I cannot endure that."

"There'll be no torture if we get away."

"I'm not as optimistic as you, Akkadian." Nisaba twisted in her ropes as if to prove her point. "And your optimism cost you. The queen liked you. If you'd accepted her offer, she'd have hidden you before Jakka got here. But you were greedy, you wanted better. Now look at you."

"You'd have helped Ki?" Sargon demanded, already knowing the answer.

Nisaba hesitated. "Well. The *baru* was a necessary sacrifice."

Sargon dug in, hard. This was the clincher to his argument.

"Our tribes are different, then. Mine doesn't abandon its people."

Taking his point, Nisaba fell quiet and looked away.

Sargon collected himself. He had to see it from her point of view. From where she lay, things seemed impossible. He had to inspire her, or she'd never join. What would Rogg say?

With that, the Elamite's voice spoke through him.

"Think ahead, Nisaba. Months from now, when you're suffering in Magog's camp, you'll look back at this moment and wish you'd had the courage to try. This is your *before*. The *after* may destroy you. That's what Magog does, they drink your *emittu*. Even if you survive in their camp, you won't be yourself anymore. Can you give that up without a fight?"

Nisaba said nothing. Outside, the guard's stream of urine was getting weaker. Sargon's frustration boiled over. "Talk!" he said, surprising himself with his tone of command.

"I had a 'before,'" she murmured at last. "In the marsh. With my family."

Sargon nodded, listening as hard as he could.

"Then the neighbors attacked." Nisaba studied the arched ceiling. "I knew them personally. Nice people, I thought. They traded with us sometimes." She laughed bitterly. "And one morning they came with spears and clubs. It's been 'after,' ever since."

Despite the need for urgency, Sargon found himself pitying her. "I understand, sister. Believe me, I thought my 'before' was before they cut off my hand." He lifted his stump. "But I was wrong." He nodded at his friends. "Thanks to them, I'm happier than I ever was with two hands. Turns out I'm still in my before. You can be, too."

"You just want to use me, Akkadian." Her eyes closed again. "That's all people do. Use me. I am weary of it."

"Babylon used you," Sargon pressed. "But you were an outsider to them, as I was an outsider to my tribe. But here, we're all outsiders." He gestured at his friends. "A baby with a clubfoot. An Elamite. A nomad. That's the difference. When everyone's an outsider, no one is. So join us, Nisaba. Never be an outsider again."

"Pretty words."

Sargon clenched his teeth. The guard's feet were tapping back around the hut. Time was up.

"I can't force you," he said. "I can help. But you have to ask."

Nisaba eyed him doubtfully. "Just out of curiosity, what's your plan?"

Sargon told her in one breath. Then he lay flat again, as if drugged.

Nisaba's mouth dropped. "You *are* mad."

"Mad?" he said out of the side of his mouth. "Mad is giving up your life without a fight."

Then tattooed hands shoved the door flap inward, and Sargon shut his eyes. Had the guard overheard them?

The guard went straight to Nisaba. He kicked her in the hip, twice. Sargon heard every blow.

"You been a good worm, like I told you?" He kicked her again. "There was noise in here."

Nisaba didn't move. The warrior kicked her a third time. "Eh? Eh?" Enjoying it.

Nisaba still did nothing. The man laughed uneasily. Finally restraining himself, he stomped to the wall and sat.

"Fine, worm. Rest your voice. The prince will have you singing plenty, believe me. I will enjoy the sound."

Sargon breathed out slowly. He'd failed. Nisaba didn't trust him. He'd done all he could, but it wasn't enough. *So move on*. That's what Rogg would say. *Never mind the failure. We all fail. Just get working.*

He tried to refocus. However, a moment later, a voice broke the silence. Nisaba's! It surprised him so much that he nearly twitched, giving himself away. Had she reconsidered?

Nisaba cleared her throat. "Forgive me, brother. I didn't catch your name."

Sargon parted his eyelids to slits. The guard had been fiddling with the game board again, trying to figure it out. He lowered it and stared at Nisaba, then broke into coarse laughter.

"By Nergal, the creature speaks. What does it want? Not my name, I know that."

"My bonds. They're too tight." Nisaba pushed on her ropes. "My hands are rotting off."

"Well, well," the man jeered. "How the bird sings when it wants something. You should've been nicer earlier, bird."

Nisaba ignored this. "I can't feel my fingers," she said flatly. "If they fall off, how will I attend to the prince?"

"Oh, he won't be needing your hands." The man guffawed.

"Just loosen them a bit." Nisaba twisted her ropes, making them creak.

Sargon's breath quickened. She was doing it; the plan was starting!

The warrior shook the game board. "If you'd told me the rules for this, maybe."

"Very well, I'll tell you the rules."

"Too late. This is more amusing."

"Something better, then," Nisaba said. "Let me praise you to the prince."

The warrior straightened. "Prince Jakka?"

"The same."

The man scoffed. "As if he'd care what you think. He takes a woman in every village. What do female opinions matter to him?"

"That's the difference, brother. They stay slaves. I don't. I entered Babylon a slave. But I became right hand to a queen." Nisaba let that sink in. "When I do it again, Jakka will know your name. Will it be with praise? Or something else?"

The warrior shook his head in wonder. "The worm! How it slithers and slithers!"

Sargon's excitement grew. *Well done, Nisaba. Keep it up!* She was maneuvering the guard just where she wanted him. A true negotiator!

Nisaba spoke again. "Tell me your name, warrior."

Her voice carried the ring of authority, the arrogance of one used to being obeyed. The warrior's face wrinkled with confusion. He glanced at his sleeping partner for help. Finding none, he gave in.

"Akshar," he said grudgingly. "After my father."

"An Assyrian name," Nisaba observed. "Gog captured you from some hill tribe in Assur. Near the Tigris River, I expect."

Akshar said nothing. His past—a human past—flitted up in his eyes. Sputtered. Died.

"So Jakka will hear it all," Nisaba said quietly. "That *Akshar* is to be relied upon. Promoted. Given new robes and quarters. Or . . ." Her voice chilled. "Akshar is a blunderer. A thief. A spy."

"Careful, worm," Akshar said.

The ropes creaked. "Just free my hands, brother. It costs you nothing."

Akshar hesitated. Then, with a groan, he rose and crouched in front of her.

"If it'll shut you up. You swear you'll be grateful?"

"I'm already grateful, brother."

Akshar snorted skeptically. But he bent and began to loosen the knots.

"I want a promotion to captain, at least. You hear?"

"It is done."

Akshar's back was to Sargon. It was time. Sargon felt fear, as always. It crushed his chest like a boulder. But it was only fear, he'd beaten it before, and he forced himself up through it and rose and tiptoed to the reed wall where the mealtime tools were kept. There, from a bowl, he grabbed a stone pestle, grainy and thick, the bulbous end made for crushing seeds into powder. Then, weapon in hand, he turned, evaluating his next move.

Akshar's back was still turned. Greasy hair flowed over his shoulders. His spine was lodged in a valley of muscle. This would not be easy. If Sargon misplaced his first strike, the warrior would overwhelm him and destroy the plan. Not only that, it felt a terrible thing to strike a man from behind. But Sargon hardened his heart. Magog would show no pity to his friends. Sargon could show none in return. He had to be rough, like Rogg.

For my friends, he thought, raising the pestle.

He charged.

Akshar heard him coming as the pestle struck down. "Ho!" He turned, his eyes flying wide. Too late. The stone bulb struck the round top of his forehead. A dark liquid spurted out, and he collapsed sideways across Nisaba's body, as limp as a sack.

Nisaba kicked him off, hissing: "Again! It's not over!"

So Sargon brought the pestle down again and again. It was hideous. The skull crunched. More hot blood splashed out. A sweet-smelling liquid covered his hand. Still he kept bashing until brains fell out, as pale as fat. Only then did he recoil, trembling. Death had never been so intimate.

"The other, before he wakes," Nisaba said.

Sargon turned, raising the slippery pestle once more. It seemed even worse to kill a sleeping man, his tattooed face peaceful in repose, a gleam of drool sliding down his beard. But a barrier had been crossed, and Sargon's body carried him forward in a red tide of violence. Again the pestle struck. Again the foe lurched upward, raising his powerful hands to ward the pestle off. But the critical damage was done, and with a few more blows, the fighting hands dropped.

Sargon retreated, shaking, the queen's voice echoing in his head. "The more you lead, the more ugliness you will do." Looking at the mess, he feared she was right.

But there was admiration in Nisaba's voice as she stood, rubbing her wrists.

"Ishtar was right about you, Akkadian. You're more dangerous than you appear."

"You too, sister."

"Just get to know me. You have no idea." Nisaba went to the nearest body and grabbed its feet. "Come. We must hide these."

They pulled the corpses to the wall and covered them with grass mats, then wiped themselves clean. Nisaba dragged over more mats to cover the blood on the dirt floor. Finally, they crept to the entry and peeked under the door flap into the path. Sargon's heart was still pounding. Once again, a single idea had changed everything.

And if my little mind did that, he thought, imagine what Ki's can do.

Dusk lingered between the huts. The domes threw purple shadows into the empty lane.

"Where is everyone?" Sargon asked.

"Inside the *mudhif*, as you hoped."

Sargon looked toward the golden hill. Indeed, from it came a muted babble, the whole tribe inside for the feast.

"Is there any Enki root left?"

"In the storage hut." Nisaba pointed down the path. "It holds the leftovers from the batch we used on you today, already ground into powder."

"Enough?"

"Should be plenty. It's sitting in a basket next to the tub of sacred juice." Nisaba gave a dry laugh. "Honestly, I'm surprised no one's tried this prank before."

"What if you're seen?"

"As far as the village knows, I'm still Ishtar's right hand. She wouldn't have told anyone yet. It'll embarrass her too much." She looked at him. "Sargon. This may work."

"Good fortune, sister."

Gripping her bald head in both hands, Nisaba muttered a prayer to whichever marsh gods she worshipped. Then, with a last glance at the *mudhif*, she pushed aside the flap and strode into the path as boldly as if she was free. Sargon watched in admiration. Nisaba was brave, skilled, and ruthless. Ishtar's loss was his gain.

Not a bad streak of recruits, he thought. First Ki and Rogg. Now Nisaba. His tribe was fast becoming one to reckon with.

When Nisaba returned, she refitted her ropes in case anyone should enter the hut to check on them. Then she lay back in the dirt.

"Things like this don't happen, Sargon. Not since the legends. If it works, all of Mesopotamia will sing of it around their campfires. The name of 'Sargon' will have influence."

He lifted an eyebrow. "Now who is optimistic?"

"Politics is what I do." Nisaba shrugged. "True, we'll most likely fail and be tortured to death. But I'd rather dwell on the upside, wouldn't you?"

Sargon chuckled grimly. "I see your point."

The gap under the door-flap went dark as night fell. The noise from the *mudhif* grew louder. The toast was coming. Nisaba had completed the operation just in time. Sargon strained his ears, trying to catch everything. But even he wasn't ready when the village suddenly went silent, and the queen's muffled voice burst into the path.

"Enbilulu, send us power," she cried.

"POWER," the masses answered.

Silence descended as they drank.

"Was there enough drug?" Sargon whispered.

Nisaba's eyes glittered in the darkness. "I put in all there was. It shouldn't kill anyone." She hesitated. "I don't think."

"How long until it takes effect?"

"Same as at lunch."

They waited, sweating profusely in the blood-smelling dark. Sargon tried not to imagine all the ways the plan could go wrong. The drug could hit at different times. Magog might not participate in the toast. Extra juice might dilute the bowls, making the drug ineffective . . .

Then a scream burst from the *mudhif*, and his breath caught.

"It begins," Nisaba said.

Shouts poured into the street. Curses. Wild prayers to the gods. Inside the hut, Sargon and Nisaba lay as rigid as wood, listening to footsteps hammer past in the path. They heard *thuds*, too, bodies hitting the dirt. The plan was working.

Then the flap whipped aside, and a tattooed hand thrust a torch in. Red light burst across the reed walls. Following it was Jakka's enraged face, his teeth bared.

"Guards!" He swept the torch before him, spraying the dirt floor with sparks. "Akshar! Krekk! Where are they? I'll skin them for this."

A warrior ducked in after him. "Perhaps they're at the latrine, Lord."

"This is *her* doing, curse her."

Jakka ran to Ki and kicked her legs, hard. She was still so drugged, she didn't move.

"She sleeps," Jakka cried in astonishment. "So who . . . ?" He lifted his nose, sniffed. "Smells like blood in here. You whiff that?" He spun toward Nisaba. "Marsh worm, I'll have the truth out of you, by Baal. Talk!"

He thrust the torch flame at her face as if to blind her, and Nisaba cried out in fear. But then Jakka wobbled, and the torch struck the dirt. The prince slammed down beside it. By the door, his companion also buckled and fell. The Enki root had worked just in time.

Sargon leapt up and snatched the torch away from Nisaba's face. "You hurt?"

Her eyes were fixed on the flame. "I hate him," she whispered.

Outside, the screams had vanished. The footsteps, too. All that remained was the pulsing music of the night bugs. Free! Sargon thought. Free!

The torch was nearly out. He threw it into the fire pit to catch on the embers. In the yellow flare-up of light, he saw the stone pestle lying in its mortar. He grabbed it and crouched over Jakka's body. The man was his age, but far more muscular. Even in his drugged state, he looked ugly, terrifying. Sargon's rage surged. How dare this man kick Ki! His evil must stop now. Sargon positioned the killing pestle over Jakka's temple. He might have struck, too, if not for Nisaba's voice.

"Wait, brother. Think."

Sargon kept the pestle raised. "Let me do it, sister. We can end this here."

Nisaba shook her head. "This ends nothing. If Jakka dies here, what will his father do? See *further,* Sargon."

Sargon blinked. The blood was thundering in his face. He hadn't considered Gog.

Nisaba's voice grew urgent. "If you do this, Gog will be forced to destroy Babylon to save face. He'll bring unimaginable suffering here. Children and elderly will die. Is that your wish?"

Sargon shook his head slowly. Children were not the enemy.

"Afterward, Gog will chase you to the ends of the earth. For what? What do you gain? He has more sons, more heirs. Probably wiser ones." Nisaba kicked Jakka's leg. "If we must fight Magog someday, let this fool lead the tattooed horde."

Sargon clenched his teeth. Everything in him wanted to strike Jakka, punish him for what he'd done to Ki. But Nisaba's voice was clear and steady, the voice of an adviser who had counseled a queen. Sargon knew she was right. Slowly, he lowered the pestle.

Nisaba slumped in relief. "You are wise, Sargon. Wiser than many."

"And you still care for Babylon. Even after they betrayed you."

Nisaba looked toward the entry flap. "They were like family. For a time."

Sargon grasped her forearm, gripping it up to the elbow in the handclasp of chiefs, as Rogg had taught him. "You are one of us, now, Nisaba. Your troubles are our troubles."

Nisaba gave him a strange look. She didn't believe him, he could tell. But perhaps a piece of her wanted to.

She gave a weak laugh. "I have nowhere to go, now. May I come with you?"

"I hope you will." Sargon released her arm and walked to the doorway. "We'll need supplies for the journey, though. May I steal some?"

In answer, Nisaba walked over and pushed the grass flap aside.

"Enter Babylon, Sargon. You have conquered it."

29

Sargon waded into the river. The water was cool, the mud sticky under his bare feet. He put his shoulder to the stern of the boat and pushed. After a brief resistance, it jerked loose of the beach and glided over the black shallows toward open water. The craft rode low, heavy with the bodies of his drugged friends. Sargon threw a dripping leg over the gunwale and heaved himself in. Settling in the stern, he seized the wind-catcher rope and held his breath. Here was the moment of truth.

"You sure you can work this thing?" Nisaba sat in the prow, paddling slowly, her bald head glinting. "I hope so," she added uneasily to Baby Shulgi, who slept in her lap. "Muscle won't get us far with all this weight." *Especially since only I can paddle.*

"It will work," Sargon said with more courage than he felt.

He pulled the rope. The wind-catcher dropped and filled with breeze. The sudden force nearly tipped the boat, causing Nisaba to gasp and grab the gunwale for safety. Loosening the rope, however, Sargon steadied them, and the boat slid forward smoothly.

"Hoho! Feel it go," he cried.

Behind them, Babylon's fleet burned, illuminating the shore as brightly as if it was day. Before leaving, they'd waded along the beach applying torch flames to the reed hulls. Now each boat—waterproofed with flammable black bitumen—whooshed redly up into the night. There would be no pursuit by Babylon for a while, Sargon thought with satisfaction. The boats were roaring and gushing flame, tossing up sparks and red-glowing grass which spiraled into the water and hissed out. One ember landed on Sargon's arm and stung his skin, making him brush it off. But so far, the huts seemed safe, despite the smoke billowing back into the village.

Sargon was glad of that. He and Nisaba had taken great care not to let the drugged villagers be hurt. They'd turned the sleepers onto their bellies so they wouldn't choke. And finding several children who hadn't drunk the juice, they'd settled them in a hut to tend the babies. The children were nervous, but Nisaba reassured them it would be all right. Now a few stood on the beach holding water bags in case the fire spread, their faces proud with importance.

"That's Morak, there," Nisaba said wistfully, lifting her paddle in farewell to a boy onshore. The boy smiled and waved back. "That's Mitala." A girl in an otterskin tunic ran up and waved, too. "When they're of age, they're to be mates."

Sargon barely heard her. A black force filled his blood, fixing his attention on the red glow. *Power,* it whispered. *Why stop? Burn all fifty Magog men, as they deserve. Let the name "Sargon" be feared.* Images stabbed him. Hundreds of tattooed men knelt in rows, chanting his name. Babylonian women fanned him with palm leaves. Jakka and Ishtar lay on stone altars, begging for mercy. *This can be yours,* the voice whispered. *All you need is the will.*

Sargon shuddered and shook himself. That was not a voice he wanted to listen to.

Under blue moonlight, his friends awoke one by one, splashing river water on their faces to snap out of their stupors. Aya was angry at first and looked back toward Babylon, long out of sight by now. "I'll swim back if you don't turn us around!" But Sargon explained it patiently, and when his friends understood, the boat rocked with their efforts to crawl to him, pound his back, and cheer. Most affected was Ki, who held him so tightly, he thought she'd never let go. She, more than any of them, understood the fate they'd so narrowly escaped.

"Sargon, indeed." Rogg laughed. "He's living up to his name. At this rate, he'll need more honorary titles."

"More?" Aya asked, clutching Shulgi.

Rogg nodded. Elamite warriors often took new titles after each battle, he explained. "One, before he died, got to be called, 'En-Men-Gal-Ana-Mesh-Ka-An-Gasher.'"

"Just 'Sargon' is plenty, thanks," Sargon said hastily.

Through it all, Nisaba sat quietly in the prow, looking nervous. Sargon introduced her as generously as he could, saying, "Without her help, we wouldn't be here. I gave her my word she could join."

"For you, brother . . . all right." Aya faced Ut. "But him I won't forgive."

Until this point, Ut had been as excited as the rest of them. Now his hairy body, black against the moonlit river, seemed to shrink until he was almost a shadow. Aya raised her hand.

"Who else votes him off?"

Ki and Nisaba raised their hands.

"That's a majority," Aya said, keeping her hand up. "Throw him over, Rogg."

Ut gave a frightened laugh. "Don't I get a say?" He glanced frantically at Sargon and Rogg. "Think, brothers. If you put me ashore here, they'll catch me. It's murder!"

"I don't care." Aya banged her knee. "You betrayed us in the desert. You'll do it again."

Ut turned desperately to Sargon. "I'm Akkadian, brother. You can't want this."

Aya laughed. "You beg *him*? The one you thrashed at the river?"

Sargon watched uneasily. Ut looked like Ta in the desert, begging Korak. And if I needed second chances, Sargon thought, I owe some, too. *Rule Two: Do what you admire.*

"Aya," he said. "Aya."

"I don't want to hear it." Aya stood up in the boat, rocking it. "Not this time. No!"

"What kind of tribe will we be? Harsh or merciful?"

"Neither. We'll be *just*."

"I needed mercy." Sargon held up his stump.

"You never *took over the tribe*."

Sargon held her gaze, waiting. Aya shut her eyes, battling within herself. "He'll betray us one too many times, brother." But when Sargon held firm, she slumped, and finally gave a sigh.

"For you, brother. And only you." She glared at Ut. "But it's clearly a mistake."

Ut gawked at Sargon as if he couldn't believe it. In answer, Sargon scooted forward and hugged him, remembering how after the battle in the gully, Rogg's touch had pushed the emptiness away. "Fresh start," he said, pulling back. "Brothers again." Ut nodded. But he crawled away and huddled under the mast pole, and didn't speak for the rest of the night.

"Well," Aya grumbled, "now that we've made that mistake, what's next?"

"I've been pondering this, actually." Ki nodded at Sargon, and explained her vision for making food. The others listened in astonishment. "The only problem is, we need access to water," she finished. "Since the whole Euphrates is taken, we can't settle anywhere without a fight. But what if we make *more* river?"

"More river?" Aya laughed.

"Yes, more." Ki pointed north. "Babylon already does this in miniature. When their trench fills with floodwater, it becomes a little river."

"I suppose that's one way of looking at it."

"We'll dig a trench just like it, only on a much larger scale. We'll channel water from the Euphrates into unclaimed desert, where no one competes for territory. Then we'll camp there and grow plant-food."

"Fascinating," Rogg said slowly. "But such a dig would take a long time."

"And thousands of diggers," Sargon agreed.

"Unless we find a pre-dug trench," Ki said. "One made by the gods."

Sargon's jaw dropped. "Like a canyon."

Ki smiled at him proudly, then turned to Nisaba. "Know any canyons? Dried-out riverbeds?"

Nisaba looked at her strangely. "One comes to mind. Uruk Canyon."

She grabbed a piece of charcoal and a skin rag. Then she began to sketch, propping the rag on her knee. "Uruk Canyon was probably a riverbed, ages ago. Then the north end silted up. It dried the bed out, and the overflow created a marsh. But if we dig the silt away, water might refill the canyon, restoring the original river." She held the rag up for all to see.

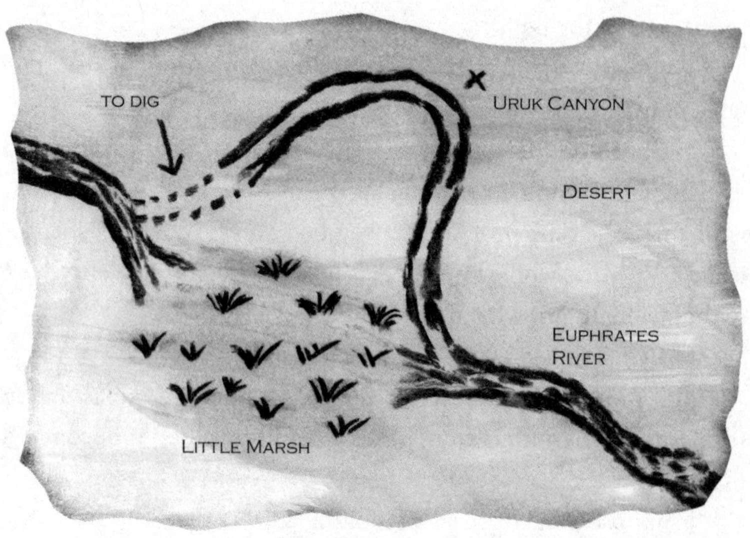

"Nobody lives out there?" Ki asked.

"It's desert. You could camp uncontested. And nobody lives in the Little Marsh, either—the air is too toxic—so you won't steal water from anybody."

Ki tapped the gap between the Euphrates and the mouth of the canyon. "How far is this dig?"

"A quarter league," Nisaba estimated.

The group sat quietly, trying to imagine it.

"*We* can't dig that," Aya said. "It'd take a lifetime."

Ki touched Nisaba's knee. "We'll recruit marsh tribes. You said life is miserable in the Great Marsh. If we offer them a life at Uruk . . ."

"It's almost mad enough to work." Nisaba rubbed her forehead. "But the marshlings are a backward people. Their blood feuds span centuries."

"But if we could unify them . . ." Ki turned to Sargon. "I know it won't be easy. But if we can dig Uruk, we'll build something amazing. Our own tribe, with a code." She pressed his stump tightly. "What more could we ask from life?"

Sargon was too happy to speak, so he just nodded. This was the vision he'd seen in the desert.

"Hear! Hear!" Rogg said. "This is a fine plan."

"But you're leaving us now," Aya said sadly. "You have to hunt Gog."

Rogg shook his head. "Your troubles are my troubles. Until you've decided this question, I'll stay and help. Who knows? Maybe this tribe will hurt him more than I can."

"Rogg!" the passengers cried and flung their arms around him.

"It's nothing, friends."

Rogg turned away, wiping at the corner of his eye. Tears, Sargon realized with surprise. The giant must have suffered greatly, traveling the world alone, haunted by his dead family. He was a mighty warrior. But even warriors needed friends.

Sargon felt a rising joy as the boat sailed on, the stars glittering above the palms. Destiny seemed with them. Hours ago, all had appeared lost. Now they had freedom, supplies, a boat . . . and a real plan at last.

30

They sailed south for several days. It felt nice to make progress without effort for a change, and spirits were high. They napped, drank water, rested their sore feet, and fished over the side. Aya cooked a stew that had everyone smacking their lips, a delightful concoction of water lily flowers and duck feet. Rogg offered lessons in trident throwing. Ut, for his part, recited the Epic of Gilgamesh—the full version. It took half a day, but he performed it so well that Aya grudgingly admitted, "Well, even a traitor's got some use."

Nisaba demonstrated her worth, too. They passed several villages with fleets of fishing boats out in the water. These passings always made the Akkadians nervous. But each time, Nisaba stood up in the prow and shouted a password. And the local fishermen parted their fleets to let the wind-catcher glide by, pointing at the sail and babbling excitedly, as if witnessing the characters from a legend. Once, Sargon even heard "*Baru! Baru!*" floating across the water.

"Why don't they attack?" Aya asked. "Hasn't Magog smoke-signaled them about us?"

"These tribes are free," Nisaba replied. "Jakka can smoke-signal all he wants."

"May they remain free, then," Sargon said.

"And may Uruk have a hand in that," Rogg said.

They glided on. The weather remained calm. The breeze held. And finally, days later, they came to the Great Marsh.

It didn't seem like much at first. The river simply began to widen. Yet it kept widening and widening, until the banks receded over the horizon, leaving them in a gray boundless sea. Threads of smoke lifted at the watery rim of the world, indicating other tribes. Reed islands began to appear, splitting the sea into channels. When Nisaba led them down one, still more reedbeds appeared, dividing the way again and again. The passages grew ever narrower. By midafternoon, the fugitives found themselves gliding down a sluggish lane hardly ten paces wide. The true marsh had begun.

Now Sargon understood why Nisaba had warned them against it. It was not pleasant. Giant *ihdri* reeds arched over the boat like trees, creating shadowy passages of stagnant air that hummed with flies and stank of ancient ooze. The sail went slack due to lack of wind, and they had to roll it up and use paddles and punt poles to keep moving. Flies bit. The sun roasted their arms. The easy part of the trip was over, and there was much groaning from Ut and Aya.

"Gods curse it," Ut said. "I was just beginning to enjoy the sailing life."

"Do the flies ever stop biting?" Aya asked, waving a cloud of them from poor Shulgi's face. "At this rate, we'll have no blood left by nightfall."

"At least Jakka will struggle to find us in here," Nisaba said. "He may not even dare to enter. Magog is much hated in this marsh."

They were all glad of Nisaba's company now, for she knew the tricks of the swamp. At her bidding, they rubbed mud on their exposed skin to create a thin barrier against the mosquitoes. She also pointed out small markers in the reeds—lopped off reed stumps—that announced the territory of different tribes. "If we trespass beyond those marks," she warned, "we'll be attacked. That's how outsiders get into trouble."

"I didn't trust you at first, sister," Aya said. "I'm sorry."

"Don't be," Nisaba said. "Trust must be earned."

Hour by hour, the channels grew more sluggish. Fogs of flies wafted up, biting terribly, and welts arose on the travelers' eyelids, ears, and lips. Sometimes the ooze-water grew so thick, it formed a sludge impossible to pole through. Again and again, the group had to hop out to raise the boat's draft and push it ahead out of the stick. Sargon hated this process especially. To sink into filth up to his chest, his feet going down, down into blind blackness . . . to push and groan, sloshing forward in the sticky heat . . . until finally he climbed back into the boat—only to find himself covered with leeches.

"Ugh." Ut ripped a fat gray one off his knee. "Disgusting." Ut's blood dripped from the leech's mouth. He tossed it into the water with a curse. "No wonder you hate it here, Nisaba."

"This is nothing, I'm afraid," Nisaba said.

"It gets worse?"

"Beware the snapping turtles. Poke your paddle into the mud each time you get out. You don't want to step on one. They grow so big here, they can rip off your foot."

"Great."

"We haven't encountered the locals yet, either." Nisaba peered into the reeds. "Nor the red vipers, whose venom kills with one bite. Nor the nightly mosquito storms—"

"Enough," Ut said. "I'm starting to wish I was back in Babylon."

"Don't let us stop you," Aya muttered.

Ut shot her an angry look. But beneath it, Sargon could see he was hurt. Leaning forward, he nudged Aya with his stump. Aya glowered but sighed.

All right. But Ut doesn't deserve you.

They paddled on. On through the heat, the sludge and the flies. On through frogs croaking in the slime. On through the marsh birds honking among the rushes, crying out mournfully like the ram god, Dumuzi, trapped in the Underworld, calling for his traitorous lover, Inanna, who'd abandoned him in darkness forever. It was the sound of the "black feeling" from Akkad, Sargon thought. The sound of giving up. Of sorrow and defeat. In the desert, he'd sworn to reject it. Now he hoped he could persuade the marshmen to reject it, too.

At sunset, they endured a terrible storm of mosquitoes, then spent a hot night crammed in the boat, trying to sleep. But in the morning, they noticed smoke a league off, and decided to recruit their first tribe.

"You sure you want to do this?" Nisaba asked. "Marshmen are unpredictable."

"We're sure," Sargon said.

"Then we must request permission to visit." Nisaba turned to Rogg. "Blow thrice on the ram horn. If we hear three blasts back, we're invited."

"And if we hear nothing?" Rogg asked.

"Then they're not at home. Or . . ."

"Or what?" Ut asked sharply.

"Or they're planning an attack."

"Lovely," Ut grumbled.

Nonetheless, Rogg blew, and soon three blasts came back.

"So it begins," Nisaba said. "Whichever gods you pray to, start now."

The group journeyed in. It took much longer than Sargon expected to navigate the maze of channels. But at noon they entered a gray lake with a village at the far end.

"Be polite," Nisaba warned. "Marshmen are proud and will fight. No insults, no matter how childish they act toward us."

"Fine by me," Aya said. "There's only one person here I'd like to insult."

Ut gave her a wounded look. "That goes both ways, sister—"

"We must also show unity," Nisaba interrupted. "If they sense weakness, they'll exploit it."

Sargon was curious as they beached their craft and climbed out. This village was nothing like Babylon. Dumpy grass huts cluttered the mud, guarded by hostile-looking villagers in grass tunics. They stood along the shoreline, pointing sharp reed stakes at the travelers, giving them black looks as if to drive them back into the lake.

"No sudden movements," Nisaba said.

The crowd encircled them. Surprisingly, all were women. Not a single male. Several eyed Nisaba's bald head and muttered: "Babylonian whore." But more stared at Rogg, marveling at his big muscles. In fact, this relaxed the mood, for a few ran up to touch Rogg with a fingertip, then scampered back, pointing and giggling, prompting a spatter of laughter. It gave Sargon hope. These poor folk looked so bedraggled and sickly, with sunken eyes and shocks of lank hair dripping like weeds into their faces, that perhaps they'd happily trade this soggy prison for Uruk.

Nisaba bowed. "Is your chief here? We bring gifts."

"Gifts?" a voice shouted. "Why didn't you say so, you bald-headed snake?"

A man rushed out of a nearby hut, an otterskin pelt flapping about his knees. He had a greasy beard, ropes of knotted hair down his back, and inflamed, pink-rimmed eyes. He also carried a long reed, which he slashed viciously at the females, scattering them.

"By Baal's gut! It's Nisaba!" he cried. "What brings such a lofty bird down in the muck?"

"Oh no," Nisaba muttered.

"Is he bad?" Sargon asked.

There was no time to explain. To avoid being rude, Nisaba stepped forward and bowed.

"Chief Adad, it's been too long. How was the annual clan meeting? Ishtar regretted she could not send me this year."

Adad spat dismissively. "A disaster of a *shura*. I've done my best to forget it. But I ask again, why are you here? You should be upriver, getting fat with your queen. You must have angered her greatly to be sent back here among your old people."

"Remember, it was marshmen who sold me to Ishtar. I never chose to leave."

Adad looked her up and down. "Well, if you're ready to come back, I'll buy you. I offered Ishtar heaps of otter pelts for you at the *shura* two years ago. She wouldn't sell. Now you're older and will soon be wrinkled, so my price must be less." He looked hopefully at Rogg. "Who do I negotiate with? You, big warrior?"

Rogg growled softly in warning, but Nisaba interrupted before things worsened.

"Chief, we bring bread. May we speak in your *mudhif*?"

"Bread! I haven't tasted it in ages. Come, come." Adad marched off. "Fine time for lunch."

While Aya and Ut stayed to protect the boat, the other guests entered Adad's *mudhif*, a tiny affair, smaller even than the Babylonian guest hut. It looked ready to collapse, Sargon thought. Snails, ants, and beetles crawled on the reed walls, while smoke from the fire pit clouded the air, forcing everyone to cough. Nevertheless, as Sargon sat on a damp grass mat, he tried to remind himself that this unpleasantness meant Adad had plenty of reasons to consider a move.

"Now, who are these people?" Adad eyed Sargon's stump. "A cripple? That's bad luck, you know. And by the gods." He recoiled from Ki with distaste. "You bring a rat nomad into my *mudhif*?"

Nisaba let the insults pass and produced a bread stone from her pack, which she broke into two pieces. One went to Adad, the other to Sargon, their elected spokesman for the meeting. Sargon was so nervous, he set the bread in his lap, unable to eat a bite.

"Honey?" Adad asked, eyeing the pack greedily.

"None, I'm afraid," Nisaba said.

"Huh, we marshmen don't rate fine Babylonian honey, I suppose."

Nevertheless, Adad lifted the bread and attacked it. Four women stood behind him, watching with longing as he chomped the bread until it was gone, spilling crumbs down his grizzled beard into his lap. "Ahhh . . . ahhh . . . so good," he moaned as if he'd been waiting for this meal all his life. "No wonder your queen is so fat." Sargon watched in amazement as Adad plucked the crumbs from his beard. Compared to the mannered Babylonians, this man was barbaric indeed.

Do we even want such a person in our tribe? he wondered.

Still, he began politely, trying to make small talk.

"Thank you for hosting us, Chief. I hope we come at a good time. Where are your men? I saw none outside. On a hunt, maybe?"

Nisaba shot him a warning look too late. Adad was already laughing, spitting crumbs.

"Boys? I hate boys. Nasty, violent creatures, boys. They grow up to murder their father, take his women. As soon as we birth 'em, we put 'em under water, if you know what I mean. Give 'em back to Ningikuga."

Sargon's mouth dropped. Adad was a child murderer! He glanced at Nisaba to see if it was a joke, but her stony expression revealed the horrible truth. Instead of sacrificing babies to Moloch, this tribe gave its sons to Ningikuga, goddess of reeds and marshes.

Sargon nearly rose and walked out of the hut right then. He wanted no murderer for his tribe brother. Yet behind Adad stood the four women, looking morosely at the dirt floor, and he stopped himself. Uruk is for them, not just their chief, he thought. For them, I will stay.

Adad finished eating and wiped his fingers dry on his otter robe.

"Now, cripple, tell me your story. And tell me of the wider world, for I miss it. You may not believe it, but I used to travel upriver before Gog trapped us all in this hole, terrorizing us with his raids and his world greed. By the gods, how I miss the blue skies and red deserts. The giant aurochs bulls, and the black forests choked with pines. Tell these dumb creatures what it's like." He smirked at the women. "They've only lived in muck, so when I talk of the old places—the lions and elephants, the cliffs and mountains, the wind that sweeps the reedless plain—their frog-minds do not believe it."

Sargon took his cue, and quickly related their whole tale, starting in the desert and ending with Babylon. And at first it went well. Adad and his women hooted with delight at the story of Magog's defeat in the gully. Then, hearing of Babylon's embarrassment with Enki root, they burst into cheers. "Hoho! The fat queen gets hers at last!" But when Sargon started on Uruk Canyon, Adad's attention drifted. He stared at a fly buzzing around the hut, no longer listening at all.

Sargon tried to make his pitch more interesting. He waved his stump, talked louder, but to no avail. Adad suddenly snapped out his rod to hit the fly, missed, and struck a woman's face, making her cry out in pain and grab her nose. Adad burst into raucous laughter. "Miss one pest, hit another," he shouted. "Serves you right, woman."

Reddening, Sargon glanced at his companions. The disappointment in their eyes confirmed it. He was failing.

Adad dropped his rod and clapped. "The cripple tells a good story, doesn't he, harem? Clap, now. Be polite. He'll be on his way. Unless . . . ?" He eyed Nisaba's pack hopefully. "There is more bread?"

Sargon tried a last time. Giving his chunk of bread to Adad's gnarled hands, he said urgently, "It is bread I speak of, brother. At Uruk there will be heaps of it for everyone. Won't you like that?"

"Go on." Adad laughed and slapped his knee, his mouth spraying crumbs. "Unlimited honey, too, I suppose?"

"Are you content here?" Sargon asked, frustrated.

"There is no life out *there*. How dare you insult my marsh? In my *mudhif*, too!"

"I only mean," Sargon said earnestly, "that I, too, was stuck back in Akkad—"

"Enough! What have you brought me, Nisaba? A child to lecture me on life?"

"Please, chief, I only—"

"No, child. Now you listen. I will teach."

Then Adad began a story, one more bewildering than any Sargon had ever heard.

"Once," Adad began, "there was a hunter out looking for honey. Suddenly a lion sprang at him from the high grass. Fearing for his life, the hunter jumped down a nearby pit to escape."

Sargon looked at Nisaba in confusion. Nisaba shook her head slightly. *There is no telling with this man.*

"Listen, listen," Adad cackled. "I heard you. Now you hear me, eh?"

Sargon bent forward, ready for anything that might help.

"Falling down the pit, our hero saw something even worse than the lion," Adad said. "A mass of red vipers wriggling at the bottom. Fearing their poison, the man turned in midair and grabbed a vine that, by chance, hung down the pit wall. He caught it, and there he dangled, surrounded by death. Vipers below. A lion above. And now the vine itself began to stretch under his weight."

"Bad day," Sargon said, at a loss.

"It gets worse," Adad said gleefully. "The vine shifted, disturbing a honeycomb lodged in the pit wall—honey, just like the man wanted. Unfortunately, a swarm of bees burst from the comb and attacked him. But something fortunate happened, too. As the bees stung, a golden drop of honey leaked out and trickled down the vine. It slid all the way to the man's lips. Hungry, he stuck his tongue out and enjoyed a brief taste of sweetness. And there he hung, savoring each drop of honey before the vine should break and drop him to the snakes."

Sargon understood at last. "Ah. I see."

"Then you're not as stupid as you look. Come, prove it."

Sargon nodded. He'd lived this way in Akkad, chasing tiny bits of sweetness amidst the pain, ignoring the larger picture.

"It's the story of your life, Adad, isn't it? The lion symbolizes Magog, keeping you in the marsh. The fraying vine is age, shortening your life day by day. The bees are daily sufferings: boredom, bugs, bad food. Yet drops of honey exist, too. Mates. Status as chief. This *mudhif*. You will settle for these small drops, rather than risk fighting for a full life at Uruk."

"Quite right, Akkadian. I've been out there. I know what it holds. So, thank you, I'll hide in my honey pit, and let you face the lions." Adad smiled thinly. "You young pups always dream. But we old dogs survive."

He sat back, looking pleased with himself. "Eh? Eh?"

Rogg was shaking his big head. "He who tells small stories will live a small life, Adad."

"You tell yourself big stories and become big, I suppose?" Adad eyed Rogg's muscles. "No thank you, Elamite. You meaty warriors are good for one thing—dying for your chiefs. You can have it."

As a last resort, Sargon turned to the women. Surely they didn't want to remain here?

"Uruk will be different," he urged. "We'll have a code. One that protects everyone, even women and baby boys. Don't you want . . . ?"

Nisaba was tugging at his elbow again. The women, rather than showing interest, had gone rigid. Adad was swelling up in rage. Sargon realized his mistake. He'd just challenged Adad's authority over his women! Unforgivable in any culture.

Adad jumped to his feet. "Trying to steal my old crows, eh? They're worth a lot more than a stone of bread, I'll tell you! Bring otter pelts if you want 'em, Rich, soft pelts to trade. Else, go away. Adad's women are not free!"

"Chief, I did not mean to—" Sargon tried.

"GO NOW! Or I'll throw you to the snapping turtles."

It was a direct threat, and Rogg stood swiftly, bumping his head on the low ceiling, making the entire *mudhif* shudder. "Careful, marshman," he warned, flexing his massive arms. "Sargon is more forgiving than I am."

Adad sulked and pointed at Ki. "Well, what do you expect? You come here, tell me a nomad rat can move the Euphrates? That's blasphemy, by the way. No wonder her tribe died. Enbilulu must've cursed 'em."

Ki stood, pale. "Come, Sargon. This man has given up on life. He will never hear us."

Adad's face turned purple. "A woman, back talking in my *mudhif*? OUT!"

His shouts chased them from the hut. "Rat! Cripple! Bald snake! Never come back! Not that you'll be able to . . . ha! Gog will see to that!"

31

"Well, *that* didn't work," Ut groaned as they paddled away. "Sargon, forget this code. People hate it."

"Maybe you're right." Sargon felt sick. He'd been so ineffective as a spokesman, he'd almost started a fight.

"Don't worry." Ki touched his arm in gentle encouragement. "That was our first try. There are many other marshmen to recruit. Right, Nisaba?"

"I warned you about my people," Nisaba said.

"They aren't all this bad, are they?"

Nisaba said nothing.

"We'll improve," Sargon said fiercely. "We'll do better."

But in the days that followed, he began to wonder. More chiefs rejected them. None believed Ki could move the river. Nor in a code that would, after all, limit their power. Village by village, the group's spirits dwindled.

The swamp became more difficult, too. The channels grew ever shallower and narrower. And to make matters worse, they frequently had to portage.

This was a new kind of torture. Portaging meant cutting a tunnel through the forests of reeds, then carrying the boat through the passage on their heads to the next water channel. Sometimes it was only a short portage. But sometimes they spent hours wading through the stinking muck, cutting reeds. And shortly after a sixth chief rejected them, they faced their longest portage yet.

It was already hot and bright. They'd portaged just the day before, and their hands were raw, their energy low, when they came to the dreaded sight of yet another dead end. Indeed, the forest of reeds was so thick and deep, they could not see through it to the next waterway. Rogg had to wade in to scout it, and he disappeared for such a long time that even before he returned, they knew this cut would take a day or more.

"We could paddle back and try another route," Nisaba suggested.

"We'd end up portaging anyway, wouldn't we?" Ut asked.

Nisaba nodded. "Probably."

"Great. I'd rather put my head in a snapping turtle's mouth."

A lump rose in Sargon's throat. The morning sun was already oppressive. Nobody wanted to wade in the slime and chop a tunnel. But there seemed no alternative. Resigned, they got to work.

It was a low point of the trip, no doubt about it. Clouds of flies beset them, and hacking at the wood-hard reeds with stubby stone knives made their hands bloody. The slime rose to their knees, meaning they were constantly yanking leeches off their ankles. Sargon grimaced as he ripped off an especially big one, fat with his blood. He held it up and looked at the gray bag of its body. Like the swamp, it was draining him one drop at a time.

Thankfully, Rogg was still Rogg. He volunteered for the point position and attacked the reeds with his stone knife as if they were Magog warriors.

"Fight on, brothers and sisters! I spit on Adad's drops of honey. I'd rather portage! It pushes us past the edge of what we can do. That is how to become great."

"Who wants to be great?" Ut ripped another leech off his arm. "Give me a mat under a shady tree. That's greatness enough for Ut."

Morning became noon, then late afternoon. Still there was no end in sight. The group flagged. Ut fainted and had to recover in the boat, holding the crying Shulgi. Up the tunnel, Aya sat in the muck and began weeping.

"We'll never get to Uruk. We just struggle and struggle and never arrive."

"We've made so much progress," Sargon said to encourage her. "You brought Shulgi all the way across Mesopotamia. If we can just recruit—"

"But every tribe rejects us. Why will the next one be any different?"

And Sargon had no answer.

Near sunset, Ki took over the challenging point position, giving Rogg a rest. Sargon joined her, and while he chopped ahead, Ki worked close behind, widening the pathway with her stone knife. It was one of those days you just had to get through, she told herself. Just push and push, like Rogg said, and after a good night's sleep, things might look different in the morning.

Then, disaster.

As Sargon reached for a cut swath of reeds, an evil hissing arose near his fingers. A viper! They both froze. The reptile lay coiled in shallow water by Sargon's hand. A red viper—the kind that killed with one bite. Its black tongue flicked in and out. The gold orb of its eye, slit by a black pupil, was pure reptilian death: no negotiating with *that*. It must have been hiding here from the heat of the day, sleeping, until Sargon chopped down its shelter. Now its head wove back and forth, preparing to strike.

"If you move, it attacks," Ki whispered.

Sargon's eyes never left the snake. "Stay back."

Black terror rushed through Ki. If this good man died, her world would shatter just as it was coming back together. She couldn't bear that. Be perfect, Ki. Perfect!

Slowly, she picked up two chopped reed stalks. Holding one in each hand, she reached around Sargon and lowered the first stalk toward the viper. The snake immediately focused on it. Carefully, Ki moved the stalk to the side, drawing the reptile's attention away from Sargon's knees. Sensing danger, the viper coiled tighter, rubbing its scales in a terrifying rasping noise. Ki brought forth the second stalk, the one that meant business. She took a breath, muscles tightening. Careful. Not one slip . . .

She lunged. Her second reed stabbed into the viper's coils, pinning it in place. As expected, it lashed around as fast as an eyeblink and sank its long translucent fangs into the stalk, injecting a clear poison. Now Ki's first reed struck its head—once, twice, thrice. It was over.

Sargon fell back, trembling. Ki was, too. Lifting the dead snake by the tail, she rammed through the final stretch of reeds to the channel beyond, and tossed its body in, breaking the calm water into ripples. The sky was streaked with sunset, the water pink, reflecting the sky. The viper sank slowly, pale underbelly turned up as it disappeared into the murky depths. The beak of a giant snapping turtle rose to receive it.

Ki shuddered. I almost lost him. What a meaningless tragedy that would have been. What was life, that such things could happen?

But he's alive! Alive!

Splashing back, she hugged him. He hugged her, too, and neither let go until their blood slowed. Finally, she pulled back, and they both started laughing with relief.

Impulsively, Ki tapped the side of her cheek. "Reward, please."

Sargon leaned in and kissed the spot—then pulled away, looking startled. She blushed. His lips were strong and warm. An electric heat had shot down to the roots of her stomach. She'd never felt that way before. Suddenly her *emittu* was very afraid.

Why did I do that?

Breathlessly, she laughed to hide the weak feeling. "Thirsty? I need water. I'll bring some."

She marched down the portage tunnel, her heart booming. Sargon looked after her, silent.

◆

They did not finish the cut before dark as they'd hoped. But Ki didn't mind. For, as the evening mosquito storm descended, everyone crawled into the boat to hide under the skin blankets, and she found herself pressed close to Sargon.

There was much grumbling and scratching in the dark heat. A great humming arose as the mosquitoes battered the blankets, sensing blood. The group held the blanket edges down, but many bloodsuckers got in, and it was difficult to breathe, and Shulgi was crying, and their bodies stank. But Ki's shoulder pressed tight against Sargon's, and a strange contentment filled her. He felt like home.

She'd never imagined she would feel this way again. In the pen in Magog's camp, it had seemed impossible. Yet now, after the mosquito storm departed—and Sargon stood up and folded the blanket and handed it to her, glancing at her in a way that was both shy and tender—she looked back the same way. Even here in the swamp, she was happy. Because of him.

I don't deserve it, she thought. I abandoned my people, yet I get to be happy. How is that right? Fear gripped her. Somehow, she sensed the gods would not permit such a thing for long.

The next day, another tribe rejected them. And that evening, they camped on an abandoned mud island feeling more defeated than ever.

The island had little to recommend it, besides being the only dry ground in range. Flies whined in their ears, and frogs surrounded them in a thunder of mating calls. But Ki had something bigger on her mind—the ghosts of her clan.

That afternoon, Nisaba had told her the terrible news. In Babylon, Jakka had boasted of burning the rest of her tribe. Every man, woman, and young one, roasted to death because of her.

Ki bowed her head. She'd known this might happen. Yet she'd risked it anyway. For the rest of her life, she'd carry that guilt.

She glanced across the fire at Sargon. He was all the home she had now. If the past had taught her anything, it was this: she must give him everything. All her power, all her care. Hold nothing back. As she'd failed to do for her people.

Aya passed out the soup bowls. Murmurs of appreciation rose at her skillful use of fresh marsh ingredients. She'd done wonders mixing turtle meat, frog legs, freshwater crab, and crunchy lily leaves into a dense broth. Still, even their praise could not stop Aya from grumbling.

"Maybe that fool Adad was right. Maybe this is all the honey we will ever find." Aya looked around the island and sighed. "To get so far, only to settle for this . . ."

Ut was glum, too. "I feel rather like that poor creature," he observed. A moth had just plunged into the cookfire, and he watched it flutter on the coals, its wings erupting in flame. "It wants something not meant for it. Maybe we do, too. Even if we make it to Uruk, we'll be out in the open, exposed. Gog could hear Ki is there and come capture us."

"We're recruiting fighters," Sargon countered.

"We can't even recruit cripples. No offense," Ut said, eyeing Sargon's stump.

Sargon shrugged. He never took offense, Ki knew. He was the opposite of Jakka.

Aya was feeding Shulgi a finger of mush. "I hate to say it, but the traitor's got a point. Magog's got a thousand warriors. We'll never recruit that many. If we go out there, will we ever feel safe?"

Ki thought of her dart-thrower. She'd hoped to give it to her clan in atonement. But that was no longer possible. Should she mention it here?

She looked around the camp. It reminded her too well of the pit in Magog. The rushes hemmed them in like cage bars, and the giant brown moths kept singeing their wings and falling onto the coals, sizzling and dying like tiny sacrifices to Baal. No, she couldn't stay here. But what of her dart-thrower? Her fingers lifted automatically to her throat, where the black pendant had once been. She swallowed. She wasn't sure she wanted to start all that again, either.

Then, to her surprise, Asha's voice whispered, *All, Ki. Hold nothing back.*

And with a look at Sargon, Ki knew.

As usual, sister, you're right.

She lifted her hand for attention. "Sorry to interrupt, everyone. But I have an idea."

She wasn't sure how they would respond. But by the time she finished, Rogg was beaming.

"Little Enki! Do you realize what this means? It will change warfare forever."

Ki felt bashful. "I only tested it a few times."

"Trust me, sister. Wait and see."

"One more thing." Ki turned uneasily to Sargon. "I think Ut should speak at the next village."

Ut jumped up, rubbing his hands. "Yes, sister! Put my storytelling to use."

Aya turned on him. "Ey, traitor! Nobody likes you. We don't want your help."

"You don't want it, but you need it," Ut countered. "These marshlings care nothing for abstractions like a code. Logic won't move them. You need their emotions. And for that, you need dazzle! Glory! Magic!" He pointed at Ki. "And here we have a *baru*, ready and waiting."

Ki glanced at Sargon, unsure how he'd take it. But Sargon was nodding, and her *emittu* warmed at the sight of this good-hearted man who always put his people above his pride. Father would approve of him, she thought sadly. I wish they'd met.

Sargon spoke. "Aya, we need help, no matter who gives it. We've heard Ut's stories. We know what he can do. Let's give him a try."

Everyone but Aya lifted their hands in agreement. Sargon bowed to Ut, his voice grave.

"Brother, if this works, you'll atone for quite a lot."

"Then it will," Ut said fiercely. "I'll make it!"

A day later, they tried their eighth tribe. This time, however—as the usual crowd of hostile villagers ran from their huts to the beach—it was Ut's voice, not Sargon's, that greeted them.

"Ho, friends! We are entertainers from faraway Akkad!" Ut leapt out of the boat waving a stone of bread. "We bring magic, games, and prizes. Who wants to play?"

At the sight of the bread, excitement filled the crowd, and every hand stuck up.

"Me! Me!"

"Beat our champion to win." Ut pointed at Ki. "Surely this bag of bones can't toss an object farther than you? Step up! Throw any object you like." He drew a line in the mud with his toe.

A tizzy of laughter exploded as the villagers ran up to examine Ki, pinching her arms, looking for the trick. Everyone wanted to try. Children, elderly, even the chief lined up to throw. Soon rocks, spears, darts, and clumps of mud were flying down the central lane of the village between the huts. Farther in, protected by the hut walls, Nisaba and the elders stood marking the distances to make sure no one cheated. Everyone was cheering, laughing, and taunting each other. The mood was completely different from every previous attempt, and Ki's hopes rose.

Anxiously, she glanced at Sargon. He was watching intently, clutching his stump, a pained look in his face. She nudged him with her elbow.

"You all right?"

He chuckled ruefully. "Ut's much better."

"He wouldn't be here without you. Everyone knows that."

"Flattery, Ki?" He looked at her sideways.

She grinned. "What's wrong with a little flattery?"

When the throwing was done, Ut paced up and down, shouting in a prophetic voice.

"Marshmen, behold! A *baru* of the north! A nomad despised by men, yet chosen by the gods to punish Magog for its greed. The day of judgment is at hand!"

It was Ki's turn to perform. She approached the dirt line with her dart-thrower. As the crowd watched, she drew a dart back and pointed the tip at the sky, making the bow a beautiful arched extension of her body. A murmur rippled through the crowd. She shut her eyes, praying that this didn't go wrong.

For you, Asha.

The goat gristle cord *twanged.* A gasp rose from the villagers as the dart soared over the huts, the island, the lake. Up, up it went, like a bird with a life of its own. It fell at the far edge of the lake and splashed and floated there, turning in a circle, sending out small ripples. No one spoke.

Ki turned to Sargon. For a moment, her old fear of rejection rose up in her chest. Would he think her strange? But no, only pride and loyalty showed in his face. *Well done.* Ki grinned back, her heart pounding. Whatever happened, he was with her. It was enough.

The crowd roared with amazement and surrounded Ki, battering her with questions.

"Are you a real witch?" a girl cried half in fear, half in wonder. "Can you teach me?"

"*Baru*! Chosen of the gods!" said another.

"A miracle," cried a young man. "Think of the enemies we could slay. Viper Clan would stand no chance."

"*Baru,* can you turn my mate handsomer?" an old woman laughed.

"Hoho," her mate cackled. "Grow her teeth back, too, please, while you're at it."

Now Ut began to pace again, lifting his fists. The tribe turned to him.

"Are the gods great?" he asked.

"The gods are great!" the village shouted.

"Then praise them! For I tell you, they will liberate you from this marshy prison. Cast all evildoers into pits. Crush Gog's skull under your heel. Feed Magog's intestines to the birds of the air. Scatter tattooed corpses across the mountains and wadis!"

The crowd cheered, loving it. "THE GODS ARE GREAT! HAIL! HAIL!"

"They will move rivers. Heap you with bread. Banish hunger from the bellies of the faithful!"

"HAIL THE GODS!" the village yelled.

Nisaba drew closer to Ki, a funny expression on her face. "Some men have a natural gift with crowds," she murmured. "Ut is one."

"You've seen this kind of thing before?"

"Yes." Nisaba seemed uneasy. "A prophet is useful. As long as he's on your side."

"He's on our side," Sargon interjected.

Nisaba looked at him. "Let's hope he stays that way."

Ut shook his fists at the gray sky. "The gods will send signs! A *baru*, to give us power! A giant, to lead us in battle! A crippled chief, to guide us! One pitiful in the eyes of men, so that all may know it is the gods, not *lullu*, who do these things!"

"THE GODS ARE GREAT!" the crowd roared.

Aya huffed. "I told you to be wary of him. Hear that? A 'cripple, pitiful in the eyes of men.' That wasn't in rehearsal, Sargon."

"As long as it works," Sargon said. "I just wish he'd mention the code. It feels dishonest, hiding it."

"After the river is dug, brother," Aya said. "Then do anything you want."

They fell quiet and listened. The more Ut talked, the more inspired he became. Waves of cheering buoyed him. He threw his head back and banged two sticks together. His hairy body contorted and danced. From his lips poured phrases far more poetic than any he'd tried in camp. Ki thought: he does have a gift. If I didn't know better, I'd say a black spirit was helping him. But the villagers' dirty faces shone in a way they never had before, and Ki knew he was giving them hope. The source might be hollow. But the hope, that was real.

As Ki herself knew, few things were more powerful.

32

"Halt, dogs! That's far enough."

The Great Marsh shimmered with morning heat. Jakka held up a fist, and his warriors dug their paddles into the ooze of the channel and dragged his boat to a stop. Ahead lay yet another divide in the reeds. Jakka stood up in the bow and shaded his brow with his tattooed hand. Right or left, each route led deeper into the heart of the swamp. The way was already narrow. Soon he'd be able to reach out with both hands and brush the reeds sliding by on each side.

How am I supposed to find the witch in *that*? he thought miserably.

"What is your wish, Lord?" Nod asked in a dull voice.

Jakka stared wretchedly down the two gray liquid pathways. Which to take? The water glittered and hurt his eyes. A mist of mosquitoes wafted over him, biting, making him slap his face. By Baal, this was the worst place he'd ever been. Yet the witch was in there, hiding in the unnavigable reeds, and he couldn't go home until he plucked her out. Father would declare Hakka heir unless Jakka got her back.

CURSE HER. I just want to be back in the harem tent! Why don't you help, Baal? Haven't I burned you enough slaves? What good are you if you don't come when I need?

Jakka turned around. Ten boats floated behind him, prows bumping sterns. The Babylonians had built the boats hastily for him, eager to see him on his way. Now his men floated there silently, spears across their knees, tattooed faces grim and sullen. Most refused to look at him. Those who did had a surliness, even a contempt in their faces, that they'd never have dared back on land. Jakka hated them even more than the witch.

Trying to appear confident, he faced Nod.

"Make two groups. Twenty-five and twenty-five. We'll cover more marsh that way. Nod, you come with me. Ur-Gasim will lead the other pack. We'll meet up tonight."

No one moved. What was happening? His skin prickled. Why didn't they obey?

Nod rose unsteadily in the trough and stepped forward until he could speak in Jakka's ear.

"Lord, a word, if I may. These men know better than to go in there. It's—"

"But I TELL them to," Jakka snarled. "I COMMAND."

"Yes, Lord. But, you see, the marsh is packed with enemies. On open ground we can destroy anyone. But in there, the marshmen have the advantage. It is their home terrain. They can spring ambushes, tempt us into mazes, starve us. They hate us, you know. Your father—"

Jakka grabbed Nod's beard and yanked the older man's face close.

"If you mention Father again, I'll rip your tongue out. You hear?"

"Forgive me, Lord. I only—"

"I can't wait for her to come out. She might die in there. I must *get* her."

"Lord, I merely—"

"Just do your job. WIN."

Soon after, Jakka's team was lost. Every route turned into a dead end. Flies bit and stung. The air stank, making him dizzy. Worse, the boats kept sticking in the mire, forcing his men to climb out and slog them forward. He kept thinking of home. When another wall of reeds confronted him, forcing a portage, he lost his temper.

"You keep leading us into traps, Nod. Stop!"

Nod kept his head down. "I wish I could. I'm just a land-dweller."

"Figure it out," Jakka screamed. And in his head, he thought: When we get home, Nod, you will be first upon the altar. But until then, Jakka needed him.

At noon, a smoke signal went up a league away. The second squad was requesting help.

"They're lost, too." Nod failed to keep the *I told you so* out of his tone. "What shall I reply, Lord?"

Jakka groaned. "I didn't think Ur-Gasim was so incompetent. Get him back here."

But the maze was so impenetrable, the two teams couldn't reconnect, no matter how they tried. Every channel led them deeper into the swamp. At dusk a mosquito storm struck, leaving them cursing and slapping, too demoralized to go on. Jakka reluctantly let them bed down for the night in their boats. It had been one of the worst days of his life.

But it was nothing compared to what followed.

As the warriors dozed in their boats under the starry sky, a fleet of black-painted canoes shot suddenly out of the rushes on all sides. A marshling ambush!

"Attack! Attack!" Magog's sentries cried.

Before the warriors could form a unified defense, the enemy rammed their boats at high speed, capsizing several and separating the rest, making them more vulnerable. Jakka came sharply awake to screams of, "For my village!" and "For my dead mate!" He ducked low in the trough as the *swish-swish* of sharp reed javelins filled the air. The speed of the attack was devastating. The enemy craft had shallower drafts, enabling them to glide over the muck with astonishing speed to ram, then maneuver away—only to shoot in and ram again. Jakka found himself fending off club-blows in the dark. Pure terror, disorienting animal fear, gripped him. Now he understood Father's obsession with overwhelming odds.

A fair fight wasn't *fun*. Not at all. Jakka never wanted to feel this way again.

Only luck permitted him to escape. A club-blow knocked him out of his craft, and when he came up in the water, his chest bruised and buzzing, he realized he had to flee if he hoped to survive. He swam away from the slaughter and hid in the reeds. Submerging himself in the scum like a frog, only his eyes, nose, and ears above it, he listened to the cacophony of hacking, screaming, and cries for mercy going on around him. Jakka would never forget it. These were his men, their deaths his fault. But he was too scared to help. All that mattered was his life.

At dawn, the survivors found each other by secret Magog bird whistles. Nod was among them, a fact Jakka was grudgingly thankful for. Counting Jakka, only ten remained. Their boats, however, had been towed away by the marshlings, leaving his men up to their chests in slime. They were stranded.

Jakka forced a sickly grin. "Go ahead, Nod. Say you were right."

"Bad luck, Lord. No one could beat that ambush." A leech was clinging to Nod's ear like an ornament, fat with his blood. Jakka hated him too much to pull it away. "May I suggest, however . . ." Nod gulped. "That we stop chasing her and go home?"

Jakka spat water out of his mouth. "Permission granted."

They were utterly lost. They sent up a smoke signal to beg the second party for rescue, but no signal returned. A similar misfortune must have befallen them, too. It left only one option. To wade out of the marsh on their own.

Days of misery followed. Days of leeches and sunburn, of fever and eating raw frogs. Jakka and his team slogged blindly northwest, hoping to hit the edge of the marsh. It seemed infinitely vast. It killed two men of snakebite. A third died from his battle wounds. A fourth stumbled through the reeds into the nest of a wild boar, where the beast tore his stomach open with its protruding yellow tusks. The boar escaped, and Jakka's team slew the screaming man to eat his flesh and abate their hunger for a few days. But how long could this continue?

Another awful morning came. As ever, the sun was hot and bright, coaxing steam from the slime. Jakka waded numbly through the reeds, pushing his chest through the filthy water. It felt like he'd been doing this since the beginning of time. Ahead, his four surviving warriors led the way in animal silence, snapping reeds aside, batting at mosquitoes. Their pupils gleamed with the intensity of starving men, which they were—until Nod suddenly lifted a fist.

"*Marshmen*," he hissed.

Jakka's heart lurched. His men, as one, sank into the muck in attack stances, leaving only their black-tattooed faces exposed. Jakka pushed forward to Nod's position, lily pads and reeds tugging at his long trailing hair.

"What do you see, old goat?"

The adviser pointed through the screen of reeds. Ahead lay a middle-sized lake. Across it was a mud island with a village on it.

"*Saved*," Jakka whispered. "About time, thank Baal."

"May it be so, Lord," Nod agreed.

Jakka bent forward, scanning the island for options. Only a few shoddy grass huts crowded it. Six grass boats were pulled up on the beach, however, more than enough for Jakka and his surviving men to paddle out in. The only obstacle was a group of marshlings in the center of the village. Twenty sat around a fire pit, roasting fish on sticks and singing. Twenty obstacles between Jakka and freedom.

"What are our odds, Nod?"

"Half are women and won't fight," Nod whispered. "Our six can take the rest."

"I won't be fighting." The terror of the ambush still lingered. "I'll come after."

If Nod felt any contempt, he masked it perfectly. "Five, then."

"Can you do it?"

"We've no choice. So we will," Nod said.

"Good man."

The warriors swam into the lake with excruciating slowness. They made no sound but the tapping of ripples against the far bank. Jakka followed much farther behind. Even if his men died, he intended to grab a boat in the chaos and get away. But he'd have to time it right.

Arriving at the beach, Nod gave the signal. His hand chopped the air, and the warriors' shiny tattooed bodies burst from the water and sprinted up the mud paths between the huts. Their victims didn't realize what was happening until too late. Women screamed. Spears flew. Clubs cracked bone. Blood flecked the air. This was what Magog was good at, and within moments, the battle was over.

Most of the surviving women surrendered and lay face down, wailing as Magog's warriors herded their children together at spear point. After all Jakka had suffered, it was most satisfying. Still, he was too anxious to enjoy it, and he pushed Nod toward the prisoners.

"Make them talk, Nod."

"Gladly, Lord."

Nod yanked a ten-year-old boy free of his mother, grabbed his hair, pulled his chin up, and pressed a stone knife to his jugular vein. The woman shrieked, but a warrior held her back while Nod calmly gave her the terms.

"The gods won't help your son, woman. Only you can. So answer truthfully."

"Anything! Anything!" the woman cried, eyes fastened to her son.

"You know the way out?"

"I do."

"You'll take us?"

"By all the gods, yes."

Jakka could have wept. This horror was coming to an end.

Wiping slime from his face, he shoved Nod aside and grabbed the lad and pressed his own knife to the slender throat. The little pulse fluttered under the stone blade. The control felt good. Jakka never wanted to lose this feeling again.

"One more thing," he told the woman. "I seek a nomad traveler. A *baru*. She is in this swamp. Hear any word of her?"

He didn't really expect anything, but to his amazement, the woman nodded vigorously.

"The whole marsh speaks of her, Lord.'"

The knife nearly fell from Jakka's hand. "Wha . . . at?" he sputtered. "*Who* speaks of her?"

"The whole marsh. The tribes claim she is the handmaiden of the gods. The anointed one, who will drive Magog from Mesopotamia—" The woman stopped short, sensing she might have gone too far. But seeing Jakka intently listening, she rushed on. "Did you not know? The witch performed magic here, on this very spot. I thought that's why you came."

Jakka stared at the mud beneath his bare feet as if it was cursed. "Here?" he whispered.

"Yes, Lord. Three days ago several tribes came to hear her speak. Many joined. Half my tribe, as well. That is why so few remain." She laughed bitterly. "I thought it would be safer for my boy to stay here until the river flowed at Uruk. But now . . ." She looked in anguish at her son. "See what happens when you try to outthink the gods? Ah, son! Your mother failed you."

She broke into sobs, and Jakka glanced at Nod incredulously. *The witch has an army now?*

Nod just shrugged. *Your father was right. She was the best slave we ever captured.*

Jakka barked at the woman. "Uruk? You mean Uruk Canyon?"

"Yes, Lord. She will move the river there and defeat hunger. The hairy prophet says so."

Prophet? They had a prophet now, too? Jakka's panic rose. And what else did she say? *Move the river.* This kept getting worse.

"How many joined her?" he demanded.

The woman looked at the sky, thinking.

"At least three hundred," she said finally.

Three hundred. The earth seemed to tilt under Jakka's feet. *No. NO.* This was madness!

He had to get her back *now*, before it got any worse.

Shoving the boy aside, he faced his men.

"We finally know where she is." He waved his knife south, toward Uruk Canyon. "We will strike before she gets stronger. Forget her stupid three hundred, we are Magog. They are just marsh worms. Without reeds to hide in, they will be as helpless as children!"

He got no reply. His blood-splashed men turned their tattooed faces to Nod, and a silent communication passed between them. With a sinking feeling, Jakka remembered how far from home he was. How very alone. If he pushed them too hard out here in the wilderness, with no witnesses, they might . . . No, they wouldn't dare. Would they?

When Nod spoke, he was like a father soothing a child.

"It is time to be practical, Lord."

"Practical," Jakka repeated.

"Yes, Lord. If we go to Uruk now, the witch's three hundred will kill us. Then no word will return to your father. The nomad rat will win." Nod let that settle, his eyes meeting Jakka's with a steadiness he'd never have dared back in the real world.

I won't forget this, old goat, Jakka thought.

"But you can still triumph," the adviser went on. "If you return to camp, you can gather your warriors and march swiftly to Uruk with overwhelming odds. Remember, Magog has never been defeated in open battle. You'll capture her easily. And three hundred slaves, besides. Your father will call you *wise*, prince. He will respect you."

Jakka shut his eyes. He wanted the witch NOW. He wanted to feel her wriggling in his hands, screaming in anguish as he caused her a hundred times the pain she'd caused him. Oh, he WANTED it. But he could not deny Nod's points, either. Nor the icy way his men looked at him, sending shivers down his back. In this unreal marsh world, everything was upside down.

Slowly the resistance drained out of him. He tore a gray leech off his foot and distractedly watched the hot blood release. Fine, he thought. I'll leave this wretched swamp and take a bath. Eat. Relax in the harem tent. Once I return here with all my power, the witch will be mine.

Still, he would never forgive Nod for this lack of faith. Never.

"So be it, Nod. Home it is."

His men's relief was palpable.

"Long live Lord Jakka," one shouted hoarsely.

Jakka walked away, hate brimming in his eyes. *You win for now, Nod. Enjoy it. Once this is over, my torture-knife will find you. And then, dear goat, I will take my time.*

33

The sun was at its zenith, pouring down a dazzling white fire, as Nisaba sheltered under a palm tree to watch the marsh tribes land. She dug her fingernails into the bark to steady herself as over a hundred boats fought through the reedbeds and slid up onto the mud beach. Just a few years ago, tribes like these had sacked her village and sold her into slavery. Now she was back among them, forced to be their ally.

If I succeed, she thought grimly, I'll be as much of a *baru* as Ki.

The air burst with sound. Warriors banged skin drums, boys pounded the sides of their boats with paddles, and priests chanted, "*Baru! Baru!*" as women in grass skirts formed circles on the beach to dance their wild marsh capers, hair flying, hands clapping. It was a joyful moment, for many had never left the marsh. But Ut's prophesies had worked almost too well. Nine tribes were here. Over three hundred adults. Almost overnight, Uruk had become one of the largest tribes in Mesopotamia. Unfortunately, Nisaba thought dryly, no two marsh tribes in history had ever stayed friendly longer than a few days.

The tribes, already skittish, gave each other wide berths as they marched into the palm tree forest to set up their camps. A fight could break out at any moment. Nisaba drifted camp to camp, watching closely. It was no accident that the spears the boys planted beside their chief's tents were mounted with barbaric trophies. The bleached skulls, children's scalps, and flags of clattering human skins were not just decorations, but warnings. Women set up the huts while warriors stood sentry between the camps, facing off against each other. Their faces were hard with hostility. Yet there was opportunity here, too, for a politician skilled enough to seize it.

You've prepared your whole life for this, Nisaba thought. If anyone can do it, it's you.

As the tribes continued unloading their boats, she conferred with the nine marsh leaders. Thanks to her experience under Ishtar, she knew these men, and how to coax them. Within hours of the landing, she had them cooperating on larger projects. Two clans mounted sentry patrols to secure the perimeter. Others cleared a beach area along the bank, cutting the reeds with stone knives. Some dug latrine trenches. A team foraged for dinner in the Little Marsh. Nisaba also sent envoys to the local tribes with messages of peace. The marshmen were here to dig Uruk Canyon, then leave—not start a conquest.

Once things were going in an orderly fashion, she strolled back to the tenth camp, her home. The execution made it seem simple. But she knew that without her experience running Babylon, none of it would have happened.

Arriving at Sargon's camp, she sat on a log by the fire pit and watched her companions work. *Home*, she thought absently. The word hadn't much meaning anymore. Home was simply a place she could live and not be a slave. She liked Sargon and the others. But liking was not home. Nisaba knew the difference.

"Ho, why isn't she helping?" Ut asked.

"She's doing more work than you." Aya pointed at the nine other camps going up. "You prophesied well, Ut. But this is all Nisaba."

"Excuses," Ut grumbled, breaking sticks into kindling with resentful *snaps*.

Nisaba passed a hand over her bald head and gathered herself. Look at me, she thought with a sad smile. A onetime handmaiden to a queen is now adviser to . . . what? In Babylon she'd had everything. Her own luxurious reed hut, servants, platters of rich food. This place was a cluster of savages calling itself "Uruk."

But it wasn't slavery to Jakka, at least. The memory of him made her flesh crawl. If she shut her eyes, she could still feel his hands on her body, grabbing her ruthlessly, slapping her legs, choking her. It was not the first time a man had done that. She'd never forgotten the feel of slavery—especially in the days before Ishtar bought her. The stink and exhaustion of it. The beatings with canes. The things done to her by cruel men in the dark. She could not endure that again. So Uruk had to succeed, even if the odds were against it. Nisaba had nowhere else to go.

Waving a hand, she beckoned her friends over.

"I hate to interrupt, but I need your permission for something important."

The group gathered quickly, pulling up logs to sit on. "Good work so far, sister." Sargon nodded at the other camps. "It'd be chaos without you."

Nisaba forced a smile. Their friendship gratified her, but Ishtar had offered that, too. The only reliable thing was self-interest. For Nisaba to feel safe here, she needed her new people to see her as indispensable. This next measure should ensure it.

"I agree, the plan is going well. I'd like to keep it that way." She rubbed the back of her neck. "I need your permission to recruit spies."

"SPIES?" The group looked shocked.

Nisaba stared fixedly at the fire pit, waiting for them to process it. Regular people didn't understand politics at all. You had to baby them into it. She'd learned that in Babylon.

"What's so bad about spies?" she asked finally.

"Well, in Akkad, our tribe had spies," Aya said. "Everyone reported on each other, and it was awful. We don't want that here."

"A person can't live without eyes," Nisaba responded.

"Eyes?"

"That's right." Nisaba covered Aya's face with a hand. "What do you see?"

"Nothing."

"Exactly. You could bump into a tree or walk off a cliff." Nisaba pulled her hand away. "Spies are eyes, that's all. To see what's coming. To learn what tribes are plotting. To look ahead and scheme for peace. Plotting for peace is even harder than plotting for war. If you want peace, I must recruit eyes."

The Akkadians looked uneasy. But Rogg nodded. The most war-experienced, he knew.

"But they seem so peaceful," Aya said, scanning the camps.

"I'm sorry to disappoint you. But since leaving the Great Marsh, these nine chiefs have fantasized about one thing—ruling Uruk themselves. Believe me, I know my people. They'll try to take over, soon. Without spies, we will not see it coming. It will destroy everything we've built here. It means murder and rape among the huts. Slavery of children. Pure ugliness." She looked at Sargon. "So, what's uglier? That? Or a little spying to prevent it?"

"I don't believe you," Ut said suddenly. "You just want power."

"Hush," Aya chided him. "She advised a queen. Have you?"

"I mean it. Just now I talked to a woman from Heron Clan. She was so friendly, I can't believe she intends evil."

Nisaba laughed. "The marsh *shuras* always start this way. Ishtar used to dread them, fearing the tribes would unite into a rival power on her southern border. But I knew it would never happen. And I was right. Each year, within days, the tribes start fighting, ruining the *shura* and sending everyone back to their villages. That will happen here unless we head it off. Remember, we're only six people surrounded by three hundred. We can't be careless just because we have a *baru*." She looked at Ki. "In fact, they may try to steal her for themselves. As happened to the Thinker in Elam."

Ut sighed. "Then why did we even come here?"

"Spies give us a chance. If we anticipate trouble, we can exploit it."

Sargon rubbed his beard. "How will you recruit? We've no resources to pay a spy."

"Leave that to me. I was spymaster for Ishtar. I have my ways."

A long debate followed. Nisaba listened quietly. She trusted Rogg, Ki, and Sargon to see reason. Sargon, in particular, seemed keen to learn. He reminded her of a young Ishtar, watchful and hungry to grow. Maybe she could work with such a one. Train him, as she'd trained Ishtar. In time, Sargon might make a decent leader. Uruk would need one. And Nisaba needed Uruk.

When the debate finished, Sargon bowed to Nisaba.

"You saved us in the marsh, sister. We'll trust you here, too."

Nisaba bowed back. "I swear on my dead family, you won't regret it."

Sure enough, over the following days, things played out as she expected.

At first it went well. In the morning, Rogg blew the ram horn, and Ki led the tribes into the desert to begin the dig. Some went down into the canyon bed, where they used sticks to stab up the hard, dry dirt. Others sledded the dirt away, using switchbacks carved into the canyon sides. A large team remained near camp and chopped a path through the palm forest, cutting the trees down with stone chips called "hand axes" to create a lane to connect Uruk Canyon to the water. They made fine progress, and that night at the campfire, the friends cheered Nisaba, calling her a *baru* of organization.

Of course, the next day it all went downhill. But this, too, was in her prediction.

34

They were eating breakfast in camp when the commotion started. It began at the southernmost edge of the settlement. A distant shouting turned their heads. When it continued, groups of onlookers left their lean-tos and walked over to see.

Here it comes, Nisaba thought.

Aya was feeding Shulgi small soft water berries, putting them into his mouth one at a time so he could try his new baby teeth on them. She looked south through the trunks in annoyance.

"Who has the energy to fight this early? It's just rude, really."

A mob of people ran past on the beach, grass skirts rustling. Aya's annoyance turned to fear. She glanced at Nisaba. "Is it a battle?"

"Not quite. This is a trickle. The flood comes later."

"You're so dire!"

"You had peace all yesterday. That's better than most marsh *shuras*. Be proud."

Rogg grabbed his war club. "I can break a few skulls if it's needed, sister."

"It may come to that, dear Rogg. But for now, we must not overreact. Remember, we need these tribes. Without their help, the dig dies."

"I'm ready any time," Rogg growled, slapping the club against his palm.

Rising, the group hurried down the beach. When they arrived, they found two clans—Otter and Turtle—standing in a face-off across a space of dirt, shouting and shaking their fists.

"What's going on?" Rogg asked a young bystander.

The boy was delighted to talk to the giant warrior.

"It's some fun, eh? The brutes. Otter Clan stole food from the common store. Turtle Clan caught 'em. Lowly crabs! Let 'em rip each other apart, I say."

And so it was. The Otter chief was yelling desperately at the booing crowd, trying to defend himself. "Why shouldn't I keep a little boar meat for myself?" he shrilled, white beard flapping. "It's payback! Turtle Clan sold me ten cracked shells last year."

"And two years ago," the Turtle chief yelled back, "you sold me a bag of rotten pelts! Where's my compensation?"

People began to shove. Handfuls of mud flew. Someone kicked over a lean-to. Aya was horrified. "Will it be war?" she asked as Shulgi hid his face in her breasts, trying to burrow away from the noise. "This is no place for a baby. I wish I was back in Babylon in the mother's hut."

"Foolish people," Ki said sadly. "If they'd just dig, they'd have all the food they could eat."

"If only, if only," Nisaba said. "Men have uttered such words since the dawn of time."

She nodded to Rogg, and the giant grabbed a drum from a nearby camp and marched between the two clans, roaring: "To work, to work. The chiefs will settle this tonight."

Thankfully, his size did the trick. He scattered the crowd, and the clans trickled back to their work sites, grumbling to each other.

Unfortunately, once there, instead of working, they stood around hollering obscenities at each other, listing various outrages throughout history. The companions dug steadily, hoping to set a good example, but no one followed it. Compared to the first day, nothing was getting done.

"Nisaba?" Aya begged. "This is your domain. Any help?"

"We mustn't appear to pick sides," Nisaba advised. "That would kill what influence we have. We must keep calm, lead by example." But the fighting went on, and the clans continued to sit around, wasting time.

Finally, at midmorning, Aya lost her temper. She threw down her digging stick, gave Shulgi's sling pouch to Sargon to wear, and marched over to a pack of men to confront them.

"Don't let anything bad happen to her," Sargon told Nisaba.

"Right."

Wiping sweat from her hot face, Nisaba rose and followed Aya into the shade of the canyon wall. There, a pack of Heron Clan men stood at the mouth of a switchback, jeering at passersby. Aya walked right up to them. Her temper was leaping out of control. She hadn't come all this way to let a few dumb brutes ruin her baby's future.

"Ho, brother." Aya tapped the biggest man's arm. "Why don't you work?"

The fellow turned, angry at first. But seeing the beautiful young woman, he grinned.

"Ey, sister. You're Akkadian, huh? What's it like up there?"

"Do you want to go back to the marsh?" Aya asked. "Get rid of that smile."

Nisaba watched patiently, knowing it was better to let this play out.

"Don't you see you're ruining your own future?" Aya pressed.

The warrior laughed. "Why pick on me, pretty tulip? Shrew Clan hasn't moved a pebble."

"So make a good example. Shame 'em into working."

"Those dogs have no shame. And if they don't work, we won't, either."

"Right," said another, leaning in. "We're not their servants."

Aya began shouting, waving her hands, stamping her feet. At first the men just laughed at her. But finally they grew annoyed and lumbered away, leaving her alone by the switchback, shaking her fists at the white sky. Dropping her arms, Aya stared after them in despair.

"Thickheaded fools. If they won't listen, how can you reason with them?"

Nisaba nodded. "Now you understand my people."

That night, Sargon began to see, too. He sat with her at the council of chiefs, listening to the leaders argue, his eyes tightening with disgust. "Some leaders," he whispered. "They're worse than their followers."

"Isn't it always so?" Nisaba asked.

She understood his contempt. Followers might intentionally shirk work, but at least they knew they were being lazy. These bearded leaders actually believed that shaking their staves and beating their hairy chests counted as labor. Indeed, the more they insulted each other, the more accomplished they seemed to feel. They'd proudly report every insult back to their people. Ego stroking was far easier than work.

Enmerkar, chief of Heron Clan, was the worst. His clan was the biggest, at sixty people. It made him critical to the dig's success, and he knew it. He loved stamping his feet, shaking his staff, and roaring like a bull. "Brothers, why should we break our backs digging?" he yelled, lifting his staff. "This is a fine stretch of bank. Let's settle here."

Sargon leapt up, alarmed.

"You know we can't, Brother Enmerkar." He pointed south toward the nearest tribe. "This is their territory. We promised we'd leave for Uruk Canyon as soon as the dig finishes. If we stay, it'll mean war."

"What of it?" Enmerkar lifted a thick red fist. "War is good! We have three hundred bodies. Our neighbor has sixty. Let's fight! We'll win plunder, slaves. Harem women, for our tents. A home right here on the water. Who *doesn't* want war?"

"Hear! Hear!" shouted several chieftains.

Sargon sank down in despair. Poor man, Nisaba thought. He still believed the chiefs could be reasoned with. Enmerkar knew better. He had a great belly, furry brows that made his eyes pop, and a deep voice that boomed across all ten camps, spreading greed and division into every ear. Many chiefs seemed intrigued by his idea. Some put their heads together, whispering excitedly.

Sargon leaned toward her. "If this idea gains favor, it will destroy the dig."

Nisaba nodded. "I warned you about my people."

"Any help from your spies?"

"Not yet," Nisaba said. "But soon."

Thankfully, the following day at dusk, it came.

Nisaba was on her usual walk around camp when she saw it—a warning signal scratched at the base of a palm tree, just where she'd asked for it. A white gash, made by a stone knife, like a white caterpillar on the bark. The back of her neck prickled. The emergency was here.

Quietly, so as not to raise any alarms, she went back to camp and tapped Ki on the shoulder. Ki nodded, and they gathered satchels filled with dirty garments and marched down through the trees to the portion of beach reserved as a laundry area. There, disrobing until they were naked, they stepped into the water to pretend to wash while they waited for Nisaba's spy.

It was a beautiful evening, Nisaba thought. A fine contrast to the trouble that was coming. She felt wistful as she waded into the warm water and stopped, waist deep, her toes sinking into the soft mud. The sky was ablaze in yellow-purple glory. A soft breeze blew across the river's surface, sending ripples against her belly. This was Nisaba's river. It was in her blood, and she loved it. The breeze shook the palm branches and rattled down a scattering of ripe dates, clattering them *click-clack* in a musical percussion across the dead fronds. A flock of ducks passed overhead, honking and beating their wings, on their way to sleep for the night. Nisaba followed the flock with her eyes. It was pretty to watch as they splashed to a landing among the reed beds. To listen to their honking . . . and the easy chatter of the marsh women washing garments around her, enjoying a moment of freedom unsupervised by their men . . . even to feel Ki at her side, eager for her first meeting with a spy . . . it was good. Life was worth fighting for, Nisaba thought. And fight one must, or evil hands would snatch it away.

"How will we know the spy?" Ki whispered.

It was the washing hour, and at least thirty women stood around them in the water, naked and working busily, scrubbing hide clothes.

Nisaba teased her. "What should a spy look like?"

Ki laughed. "You're right. I suppose if she looked like a spy, she'd be bad at her job."

Nisaba patted her thin arm. "I'm sorry you have to be here. But this spy asked to meet the *baru*. As Sargon pointed out, we've no resources to pay her with. So today, my resource is you."

"I don't mind. It's exciting." Ki looked around. "But is it safe here? Among all these people?"

"Nowhere safer. In plain sight is usually the most invisible of all."

Ki smiled. She liked sayings like that.

"Now we wait," Nisaba said. "When she feels safe, she'll come."

They began washing. Nisaba lifted a dirty garment from the satchel hanging on her shoulder and dipped it into the river. And it was good to empty her mind for a moment, give herself to the work. She scrubbed the rag for a little, then twisted it, splattering the river's surface with dirty brown drops. Then she hung the clean garment over her shoulder to drip-dry, and lifted out another. Laundry was a female task, considered lowly. Yet compared to politics, it felt a pure, noble thing. At least a rag could get clean. The nightly clan meetings just made things dirtier. And Nisaba's work was dirtiest of all . . .

Then a voice spoke, and she knew the spy was here.

"Ho, Nisaba. I hoped I'd find you here."

A tingle went up Nisaba's spine as a middle-aged woman waded past them, carrying her own satchel of laundry. She stopped just ahead of them, took out a garment, and began to wash it, acting as if the two women weren't there. She addressed the water, hardly moving her lips.

"It's an honor to meet you, *baru*. You won't remember me, but in the swamp I saw your magic. I admired it."

Nisaba intervened coldly, getting things proper. "You speak to me, Tau. Like always. The *baru* is here, as requested. But she's too important for you."

The shoulders of the woman stiffened. She was in her mid-twenties, with high, proud cheekbones, dark skin, and beautifully slanted eyes that made her look more like a woman from the Zagros Mountains than a marshling. Her back was broad and strong-looking, too. But a patchwork of fat purple scars on her shoulders indicated her master beat her often. It was those scars that had first prompted Nisaba to recruit her. They'd hinted correctly at Tau's bitterness, her readiness to betray her clan. Self-interest, as usual.

Tau's voice grew cold. "Ho, bald head. I'd say it was an honor to see you again, but that would be a lie. I'll speak with the *baru*. Or not at all."

"Insolence," Nisaba said under her breath.

"You're not Ishtar's right hand anymore. You've nothing to offer me. Your worth's declined, while mine's increased."

"What mush your head's become since I last used you. Stupid woman."

"Am I?" Tau glanced around. "Enmerkar is more valuable than ever out here. Can you deny it? In fact, I'd wager I'm your most important spy in this whole camp. Am I wrong?"

"Enmerkar?" Ki glanced at Nisaba, her eyes excited. *We have a spy under the most troublesome chief? Wonderful work, sister.*

Nisaba smiled thinly. Ki was smart enough to appreciate Nisaba's worth. Good.

She bowed to Ki slightly. "I'm sorry for Tau's rudeness. She was a fine spy when I first recruited her for Babylon. But now her head's swelled too fat to be sensible." She turned as if to go. "We needn't put up with this."

Tau shook her head. "You won't leave. You need this."

"And *this* is?"

"Not so fast. What do I get in return?"

"After the channel is dug," Nisaba said stiffly, "there will be rewards aplenty. You know my word is good. I always paid you well."

"You never gave me what I really wanted."

"Which was?"

Tau's voice grew strained. "To come to Babylon."

"I never offered that!"

"I know," Tau sulked. "I was too valuable to you in the swamp, spying on Enmerkar. You were content to leave me there forever. So here I am, still in misery. And now it's too late. You couldn't get me to Babylon if you wanted to."

"Uruk will be better than Babylon," Nisaba lied.

Tau snorted. "This place? Better than Babylon, greatest village on the river? Ha, even you can't sell that, bald one."

Nisaba had no reply. Tau was right, and it hurt. Ah! To exchange the most civilized tribe in Mesopotamia for this Uruk desert! She struggled to reply.

"Besides, when you hear my news," Tau went on, "you'll see Uruk won't last the month."

Nisaba might have lashed back. Luckily, Ki spoke first.

"You've suffered, Tau. I'm sorry. But you're why we're here. This place . . . we're building it for everyone."

Tau softened. "I know it, nomad. I heard about your family. I heard what Magog did. I'm sorry. I lost my family too—"

"Enough small talk," Nisaba snapped, losing her patience. "Why'd you cut the signal in the tree, Tau? Just to insult me? Speak up. If you've nothing useful, the *baru* and I have work elsewhere."

"You have nothing to offer me, Nisaba, yet I will spy," Tau said. "Not for you, but for the *baru*. You're lucky you brought her, or I'd tell you nothing."

Ki frowned. "Why me, Tau?"

Tau bowed slightly. "Do you not know, *baru?* The other concubines and I . . . You are a good woman, leading the dig. You lead it well. True, you're a nomad, but we can forgive that. We pray for you nightly. If you succeed, maybe you'll win us women a little respect." She chuckled. "Even if not, it's fun seeing you make the chiefs so nervous."

Ki's fingers tightened on her washing. "Thank you, Tau."

Tau smiled back, then shot a dark look at Nisaba. "But be careful, don't let selfish ones corrupt you. In the end, they care only for themselves."

"Deep wisdom, thank you," Nisaba said sarcastically. "Now the news, eh? You said it was urgent. Well?"

A moment later, Nisaba and Ki waded ashore, stunned. Even Nisaba felt shaken. Tau's news was worse than she'd feared.

Drying themselves off, they slipped into their robes and hid their laundry bags under a bush for safekeeping, then hurried south into the deepening shadows under the palm trees. There was no time to waste, even to warn the others. If Tau's word was true, Uruk was about to collapse.

"Maybe you shouldn't come with me," Nisaba said as they ran into the trees. "If anything happens to you, this dig will fail."

"The dig will fail anyway if we fumble this," Ki said fiercely. "I'm coming. You need more ears. Don't you?"

Nisaba nodded.

"Then the choice is easy."

They ran faster, palm fronds crackling under their sandals. And Nisaba couldn't help admiring her companion just a bit more. Sentimental, but brave, she thought, stealing a glance at the bony little nomad beside her. And a genius as well. Yes, Nisaba could have fared worse after Babylon than this.

They arrived in the glade just as the sun went down. In the last red flash, they saw the clearing, and it was as Tau had described. A burned area opened before them in the trees, a stretch of blackened stumps and scorched earth where a bolt of lightning had once struck the ground, starting a fire. Dense ferns and bracken stood all around the clearing. But within the oval area, there was no groundcover to hide in. Nisaba and Ki stopped and surveyed the area.

"Where now?" Ki whispered.

"I hate hiding," Nisaba said. "I manage spies, I don't like doing it myself."

Ki pointed up at the palm canopy. "What about there?" The scorched ground offered no cover, but the branches might. The two women could hide in the treetops on opposite sides of the clearing, and thus be sure to overhear the conspiracy, whichever side of the area it took place in. It was a good idea, but Nisaba winced.

"Bad things in trees. Scorpions. Bats. Snakes. Tarantulas," she muttered.

Ki nudged her arm, teasing her. "Come, spymaster. What's worse? A coup, like you always say? Or a little scorpion bite?"

Nisaba chuckled. "You're right, as usual, *baru*."

"Good fortune to you," Ki said. "See you shortly."

She ran to the opposite side of the glade, and Nisaba found a tree nearby and began to climb. The bark was sharp and hurt her skin, and even as light as she was, she shook the tree, making dates fall *clickety-clack* onto the frond carpet below. I'm getting too old for this, she thought grumpily. Mid-twenties? Yes, and my hands soft from years of high living. Still, the tree was sloped, not impossible, and soon she was up it, squashing herself in among the sharp-bladed fronds.

A scorpion was right there.

Nisaba froze, forgetting all about intertribal politics. The scorpion was perched on a bending frond just an arm's reach away. Its segmented tail curled over its armored back with a venomous stinger dangling from the tip. Its black pincers looked capable of snipping her pinkie off. And to her surprise, riding on its back were several milky-white scorpions—babies! Nisaba had disturbed a mother carrying a family.

Easy, Mother Scorpion. I've no quarrel with you.

Nisaba reached out carefully and rattled the scorpion's branch, hoping to shake it off. Instead, the scorpion skittered deeper into the fronds and vanished, not far from her face. Nisaba gulped. *I see we'll be neighbors tonight. Truce?* She kept still, trying not to think of all the biting things—scorpions, tarantulas, bats, lizards, ants, tree rats—in the packed fronds around her, hunting and murdering each other in the shadows. *Hunt away, neighbors. Just leave me out of it.*

Dark fell quickly. Nisaba waited. She couldn't see Ki across the glade in the tree anymore. Nor the ground below her, over twenty paces down. She tried not to think what would happen if she fell. Would she snap an ankle? Break her back? Crippling herself now, as the world was about to burst into carnage, would not be ideal.

Then footsteps approached, and she heard Enmerkar's voice growling through the blackness. Nisaba focused. It was time.

"Where's everybody?" Enmerkar's big voice complained. "I can't see a thing."

"We're here first, chief. They'll be coming soon."

"Fine, wait for me. I need to make a splash."

A black shape shuffled to the base of Nisaba's tree. It pulled aside its loincloth and began to splatter the trunk with urine, raising an ammonia stink that made Nisaba wrinkle her nose. Disgusting. That was one thing about spying—you got up close to everyone's filth.

Then more crashes approached, and voices hissed, "Here they come, chief. You ready?"

Enmerkar grunted and finished his toilet and marched back to the group, wiping his hands on his thighs. Nisaba relaxed.

"Ho! What's the password?" a voice called out.

"Gods above! It's me, Enmerkar," the chief snapped. "Get over here, Rat Clan."

The groups gathered close to Nisaba's tree. And now she saw the wisdom of Ki's positioning, for their hushed tones were surely inaudible to Ki's side of the glade, while Nisaba heard every word. She leaned forward, hardly able to stomach it. But hear, she did. Bad things. Ugly things. Things accompanied by cruel laughter and foul jokes. By the end of it, she felt ill.

"Never fear, brothers," Enmerkar chuckled. "By tomorrow night, Uruk will be ours."

"But once it is, will you honor the deal?" another chief asked.

"I say I will," Enmerkar snapped. "You've got my word."

A third chief laughed. "His word, brothers. Thank the gods."

Mocking laughter responded.

"Listen, fools," Enmerkar said. "This only works if we're unified. You want Uruk or not?"

Suddenly, something skittered across Nisaba's knuckles—a scorpion? She was so startled, she gasped and shook her hand wildly. The thing fell off, not stinging her. But the palm branches rattled, and several dates fell and struck the frond carpet near the men.

They went silent.

"What was that?" someone asked.

"Could've been the wind," another suggested. "Or a bat."

"Something's up," Enmerkar said.

Nisaba's heart began to pound. Footsteps marched to her tree, crackling all around its base. She held her breath. Suddenly Enmerkar hugged the trunk and shook it, nearly knocking Nisaba out. A fresh host of dates pattered down, striking a few heads.

"Ow," someone said. "You hit me with a date, chief."

"Climb this tree," Enmerkar said. "I think something's up there."

"But, chief, there's scorpions and rats up there."

"Gimme a torch."

"We didn't bring torches, chief," the voice complained. "You wanted this dark and secret."

"Then a flint, you dog. Just spark something. I want to see."

Nisaba couldn't think what to do. With light, she'd be caught. And with what she'd heard, they'd have to kill her. Her mind raced, seeking a solution. Then—a miracle.

Across the glade, more dates clattered down. Ki was throwing them. A diversion! *Baru, indeed!*

"See, chief, it's everywhere," the warrior said. "The dates are ripe and ready to fall. They've been falling all day whenever the breeze blows."

"That explains it," another chief said. "Good. No need to light a fire. It's suspicious looking."

"Fine," Enmerkar said. "Back to camp then, I'm hungry. And remember, brothers—no talk of this to anyone. Even your concubines."

"Right, right," the chiefs grumbled. "We're not children, eh?"

Nisaba shut her eyes as they marched off. I hate being a spy, she thought. I hate it! Whatever she paid Tau for this awful job, it wasn't enough.

Not that Nisaba would tell her that.

Back in camp, the two women collapsed by the fire pit, relieved to be alive. Nisaba was slippery with sweat. The *baru* wore the bewildered, stunned look typical for new spies. Nisaba rubbed her shoulders, comforting her. She wasn't sentimental, but her heart was full for Ki. She's like me, she thought. Lost her clan and family, yet still she fights.

"Not bad, *baru*." She patted Ki's bony arm affectionately. "Not bad at all."

Ki gripped her hand. "It's evil, what they are. Evil."

"Don't worry about them. We'll figure something out."

The others emerged from their lean-tos. They'd already finished dinner and wanted to know where the pair had been. They seemed worried. Aya was even angry, like a flustered mother.

"You can't go off without telling us," she scolded. "Bad *baru.* Bad spymaster." She held up a bowl of stew. "My new recipe is cold now."

Nisaba bade them sit. They obeyed, and their eyes widened as she told them the news.

"It's a few days sooner than I predicted. But Enmerkar's ready. He's built a big faction to support him. Tomorrow at the council meeting, he'll demand a vote to name him *lugal.*"

The group was outraged—and confused. Only Rogg knew what a *lugal* was.

"Enmerkar's no *lugal,* I'll tell you." He shook his big head at the other campfires winking under the trees. "Takes a real leader for that."

"What's a *lugal*?" Aya asked, frightened.

"In old Sumerian, it means 'big man of big men,'" Nisaba explained. "A council of chiefs votes to elect one. If over half agree, their pick becomes *lugal.*"

"King?"

"Not quite. But he can veto council votes, so he drives every decision."

"How many votes has Enmerkar got so far?"

"Five out of ten. He needs one more."

"Will he get it?"

"I think so. The size of his faction will tempt some to seek his favor. Then Uruk will be his."

"Not if I stop him." Rogg gripped his war club so tightly, his face turned red. "It's a long dark night. He may have a nightmare coming."

"It may come to that, brother," Nisaba said sincerely. "But first we must be subtle. Or we could start a civil war."

Rogg set the club down. "True, sister. In war, the innocent suffer most."

"What will Enmerkar do as *lugal*?" Aya asked in a small voice.

"That's no secret. He tells us each night at the council meetings." Nisaba picked up a stick and prodded the fire embers, stirring up a funnel of red sparks. "He wants to stop the dig, settle here, and conquer the neighbors. But he won't get to." She laughed. "He'll start irritating everyone, and once he does, the chiefs who hate him will sneak back to the Great Marsh in the night. His faction will bicker. Enmerkar will overreact. Soon, the rest will leave him, too."

Ut was skeptical. "You see it that clear?"

Nisaba nodded. "Rogg is right, only a great *lugal* can keep a coalition together. Enmerkar will wind up alone. Then the locals will attack him and drive him back to the marsh, and he'll be what he always was. A small-timer stuck in the swamp, nursing lost dreams."

"Why can't he see this?" Aya cried. "He's ruining it for everyone."

"He lacks a Nisaba to guide him," Sargon joked.

"I happen to agree," Nisaba said seriously. "Greed makes men stupid. Always has."

"So Uruk falls," Sargon said. "Unless . . ." He looked at her. "What would Ishtar do?"

Nisaba was pleased. Sargon was always listening, asking questions. Essential for a leader.

But she replied simply: "If Ishtar was here, she'd make 'invisible war.'"

Aya recoiled. "War on her own people?"

"Not real war," Nisaba reassured her. "Ishtar saw all Babylonians as her own children, so she'd hate to inflict that on them. Here's what I mean."

She bent forward, trying to frame it properly. This was the tipping point. Her friends wouldn't like it. But if they let her work this black magic, Uruk could be saved. If not . . .

"Study Ishtar's early days," she began. "When the young queen took the throne, no one believed she could continue her father's legacy, so a Babylonian faction tried to assassinate her. They slipped a red viper into her sleeping blankets. Luckily, she caught it and called a council meeting. But we all knew the assassins would try again.

"Her generals advised her to start a program of interrogations and public executions. I alone was against this. I knew it would scare the Babylonians, make them hate her, and undermine her even more. In fact, I suspected the generals themselves were the assassins. So I ran an 'invisible war' for the queen." She looked from face to face. They were listening intently. "This was a series of secret operations that, without anyone seeing it, wiped out every threat. It worked. Within a year, Ishtar's power was undisputed, her generals were dead of 'natural' causes, and her hands remained clean of her own people's blood—as far as anyone knew."

She fell silent. The group was staring at her in wide-eyed fear. Nisaba felt a chill. Saving Ishtar's reign was one of her proudest achievements. But not everyone could appreciate that.

Thankfully, Sargon didn't seem stuck. "How would it work here?" he asked quietly.

Nisaba nodded. "It means hunting for weak joints in Enmerkar's faction. Applying pressure. Seeing what snaps." It would be nothing traceable, she explained. For instance, Enmerkar's prized cup might be found in an ally's hut, leading to a dispute. Or a chief might suffer food poisoning, keeping him from a key council vote. Or Enmerkar's concubine might be caught having an affair, depressing him. Anything to keep him off balance until Ki dug the river.

"That's our chance," Nisaba finished. "If Ki moves the river, she'll win real power. We must keep this project alive until then."

Silence met her. Everyone looked deflated—except Rogg, who was nodding.

"Anything to keep us from war, Nisaba."

Nisaba lifted her palms innocently. "I offer tools. You decide how to use them."

"Invisible war," Sargon repeated.

He was thinking deeply, clutching his stump. Nisaba watched, curious to see what he would do. He was idealistic, like Ishtar when she was younger, and the uglier options grated. But Ishtar had gotten over that, quick. Assassination plots had that effect, Nisaba reflected dryly.

Suddenly Sargon turned to Ki.

"Little Enki, you always have ideas."

"Not this time," Ki said. "I wish I did."

Sargon banged his stump on his knee. "I just wish we didn't have to hurt anyone. Even these awful chiefs." He rubbed his forehead. "It's getting us off on the wrong foot. Who knows where it will end? All these marsh folk. They fight and squabble . . . but they're like us. They just want safety and good lives for their families. It's greedy chiefs who ruin everything."

"That's true," Nisaba conceded.

"If we could tame the chiefs, somehow . . ."

Ki stood up. "Tame the chiefs, you said?"

Sargon's eyes brightened. "You see something, Little Enki?"

"Why . . . it's almost . . ."

Ki began to pace around the fire pit, rubbing her temples furiously. Nisaba's heart quickened. The Thinker in Ki was springing to life. Lightning flashed in her eyes. Nisaba had never seen this process before, but it was obvious to them all. The group watched, breathless, as Ki began to mutter to herself. Ishtar did not have this, Nisaba realized. A true Thinker.

Ki stopped suddenly. "It sounds mad. But it could work."

"Well, what?" everyone demanded. "Don't keep us waiting."

Ki looked embarrassed. "We let Enmerkar win. We make him *lugal*."

"No, Ki," Aya cried.

"I know." Ki lifted her hands. "But listen. Maybe this is a blessing after all."

35

That night, in a wash of blue moonlight, the four chiefs still unallied with Enmerkar met secretly at the bottom of Uruk Canyon.

They kept their bodyguards close as they walked up to Sargon and Nisaba. One chief thumped his spear angrily in the dirt and pointed the tip at her.

"If this is a trap, Babylonian," he warned, "my tribe is armed and waiting. One shout from me, and they'll run out here and crack your skulls."

Nisaba rubbed her bald head and nodded at Sargon. "He called this meeting. Ask him."

Sargon stepped forward. She knew he was nervous from the way he cleared his throat. But he'd been practicing all evening with Ut, and his voice was firm but gentle. He bowed just as Nisaba had taught him to, and gestured politely with his stump, making his points. His unthreatening manner caught the men off guard, and they listened.

"Enmerkar!" they burst out when he was done. "Curse his wretched hide!"

"The sly dog *would* bite our heels. I'll skin him!"

"What do we do, eh? Send Rogg?"

"Use the *baru*," urged another. "Pox his lying tongue!"

"Peace, brothers," Sargon reassured them. "His faction numbers five. Now ours is five, too. The advantage of surprise is ours. We'll hit him tomorrow, hard."

The next morning, they marched boldly to Enmerkar's camp and found the burly chieftain sitting alone at the mouth of his shelter, sipping broth from a clay bowl. He was looking quite pleased with himself, Nisaba thought, humming and gazing blissfully at the sky—no doubt imagining himself *lugal* of Uruk—when the delegation startled him. Spilling his soup, Enmerkar leapt to his feet, eyes popping.

"Hoho, what is this, bald head?" he roared at Nisaba. "A Babylonian ambush?"

Nisaba deferred to Sargon again. Stepping forth, he bowed amicably.

"We bring no weapons, brother, unless you count words. I've plenty of those for you."

"Words indeed." Enmerkar beckoned to his warriors, who were running over in states of half-dress. "I see you've formed a faction. Conspiring outside the council is cause for war."

"We've only conspired to honor you, brother. May we? Uruk needs a leader."

Enmerkar gaped at him. "A leader?" A . . . ?" Suddenly the message sank in. "You mean me? Well, of course. I . . . I have many ideas for Uruk."

"We'd like to hear them. Summon your faction. Let's talk."

It was amusing how ready he was to believe such flattery. In his excitement, he even forgot to deny he had a faction, and within the hour all ten tribes were sitting at the council fire, negotiating his appointment to *lugal*.

During a break, Nisaba sat beside Aya back in camp and explained how it would work.

"Maybe I'm not as smart as you all, but I still don't see it." Aya was burping Shulgi, holding him against her shoulder and patting his back as the baby dribbled bubbles down his chin. "Why will Enmerkar negotiate? His faction has more warriors than ours."

"Enmerkar's greedy," Nisaba explained. "If he fights, he may win. But valuable men will die, and many in Uruk will flee, cutting his prize in half. On the other hand, this deal places him over three hundred people, making him one of the top rulers in Mesopotamia. Few leaders can pass up that prestige."

"But then he's *lugal* of Uruk. What do we get?"

"The code."

It was a brilliant compromise, Nisaba thought. Only a true Thinker like Ki could have seen it.

"Enmerkar gets to be *lugal.* But we get the code, to check him. And we'll make it so powerful, *it* will rule Uruk. Not Enmerkar."

Aya saw it at last. "And Shulgi will have a home."

"That's right."

Aya burped Shulgi anxiously, thinking it through.

Nisaba waited. Green goo dribbled down the baby's chin, and she leaned over with a hide rag and wiped it up. It felt strange, doing that. Shulgi giggled, and Nisaba found herself smiling back. It made her wonder if she still wanted children. But no. That dream had vanished long ago.

"It sounds almost too clever to work," Aya said finally, wrinkling her brow.

Nisaba folded the rag. "It better not be. Or all this," she nodded at the camp, "goes away."

But it did work. Later that afternoon, the council voted on the code of Uruk, and every chief's hand shot into the air to approve it. Nisaba breathed a sigh of relief. Not only was this the most complicated political maneuver she'd ever managed, but she'd worked it from a position of far greater weakness than in Babylon.

A celebration day was declared. In each camp, tribes feasted. Bonfires burned, and drumming, singing, and bead-rattling filled the palm forest. But Nisaba wasn't finished. She and Ki went down to the riverbank. And there, together, they molded five tablets out of river clay. Using a sharp reed, they cut pictures into each tablet, one for each rule of the code. Then they dried the five tablets hard in the sun, and set them in a row by the council fire, leaning them upright against a log so that any Urukite could see.

"Now no one can 'forget' these rules," Nisaba said, looking at the pictures. "Though our *lugal* will certainly try."

The others came up, and they all stood quietly for a time, admiring what they'd done.

THE CODE OF URUK (told in picture symbols):

1. No Urukite may harm another.
2. All may seek justice by trial.
3. The council shall elect a *lugal* each year.
4. The *lugal* may veto any council vote.
5. Three-fourths of the council may alter the code.

Nisaba shook her head in admiration. Nothing like this had existed in Mesopotamia since Sargon the Great. Chiefs did not willingly give up such power. But thanks to fear of Enmerkar, the marsh chiefs had conceded it for protection. Now Sargon had it all. A unified Uruk, and a code.

Sargon chuckled. "We should thank Enmerkar for this."

Everyone laughed. "Thank the gods for Enmerkar!"

"Still, it's not perfect," Ki said. "Slaves and concubines like Tau aren't full Urukites."

Nisaba nodded. No chief, not even in Sargon's faction, would have voted to free slaves or concubines. Forcing it would have sunk the deal. However, embedded *in* the code was the power to change the code itself. So, in time . . .

She pointed at Tablet Five. "Look, Ki. Dig the river and grow wheat. You'll become so influential, you can add any rule you want."

"Hear! Hear!" the others cheered. "Hooray for Nisaba."

Nisaba bowed. Their support couldn't be relied upon forever. No human support could. But today, for now . . . it was nice.

36

The next morning, the dig progressed as it had the first day. And that night, Sargon sat at the council meeting amazed at how far they'd come. The channel was lengthening. A path to the river was being cut through the trees. And now the opposing factions were even laughing together around the fire, secretly mocking Enmerkar for yet another self-aggrandizing speech.

The big fellow was banging his staff and bellowing into the night.

"For my next deed, I wish a stone *stele* set up on the beach in my honor. I want my likeness carved in it, so that all visitors will know it is I—first *lugal* of Uruk—who moved the river."

The chiefs smirked and rolled their eyes. They did not love him. Even those in his faction had merely been using him for power. But now, thanks to the code, they all had a way to become *lugal*. Sargon smiled. *Politics.* They were flattering each other instead of fighting, drumming up votes for the following year. They'd even begun flattering *him*. It was all false, of course. But far better than civil war.

Unfortunately, the peace was not to last.

As the meeting ended, a man burst from the darkness. He ran into the firelight and threw himself at Enmerkar's feet, causing everyone to murmur in shock. The firelight illuminated a face stained with dirt and tears, his beard matted with mud.

"*Lugal*, I seek justice," he wept, banging his forehead in the dirt. "Justice, I beg you!"

"By Enlil, what is this?" Enmerkar said, stepping back in alarm.

"My daughter . . . ah, my family name!" the man cried. "Please!"

More people ran out of the trees. A lot more. They surrounded the council in a wall of red-glittering eyes, shouting, waving torches, and stamping their feet. Some even climbed the palm trees to get a better view. Half of Uruk was here!

Enmerkar was outraged. "How dare you interrupt this council, dog?" he shouted at the prostrate man. "You bring a mob, too? I should whip the skin off you."

"*Lugal*, forgive me," the man begged. "I would never interrupt, if not for . . . oh, gods! My daughter . . ." It seemed he could hardly speak through his sobs. "I am from Otter Clan, *lugal*, but I seek justice from the code of Uruk." He pointed at the five tablets standing against the log. "Tablet Two. 'All may seek justice by trial.'"

Enmerkar glanced at the tablets in irritation, then at the other chiefs. He clearly wanted to go to his tent and sleep. But the crowd was shouting, and the chiefs looked frightened.

"Let him speak, *lugal*," one murmured.

"Yes, yes," the others said. "The people seek it. The code requires it."

Enmerkar glared at the supplicant. He had crawled to the fire pit, snatched ashes from it, and rubbed them into his hair and beard, making them gray like an old man's. It was a traditional display of grief. The crowd moaned louder in support.

Enmerkar threw up a hand in exasperation. "Fine, dog. We will hear you this time. But from now on, I want forewarning, eh? Nothing so late at night."

"Council, hear me," the man begged. "I am Warad, of Otter Clan. I speak for my eldest daughter. She is beautiful and precious to me, the jewel of my heart. Just now, when she went to the river to fill our water bags . . . she . . . she went alone, despite her mother and me warning her to take her sister for protection. The beach was empty, dark . . ."

Sargon stopped breathing. He sensed where this was going. The chiefs did too, and everyone drew closer. The sap bursting in the fire sounded very loud.

"Forgive me, High Ones," Warad said. "At the waterline, a man sprang at my daughter from the rushes. He wore a reed mask. She couldn't see his face. He . . ." Warad beat his forehead with his fists.

"Out with it, wretch," Enmerkar said.

"In the dark he covered my darling girl's mouth with his hand. He held a stone knife to her throat. He . . . he shamed her, *lugal.* Oh, gods, he shamed her. She is ruined forever. Help us!"

The crowd murmured darkly. Sargon's stomach twisted into a knot. Nisaba had warned him of this. Woman-trouble! More than any other kind, woman-trouble could rip the clans apart.

He scanned the trees for help, but Ki was out at the dig site, making preparations for the next day. Nisaba was with her. Sargon had to manage this alone.

Sensing power in the crowd, Enmerkar softened his tone. "Speak, Warad. Your *lugal* is listening."

"Thank you, *lugal.* Please don't think my family is dishonorable. Even under attack, my daughter showed virtue. She bit into the hand that covered her mouth and made the wicked dog let go. Then, in her instant of freedom, she screamed for help, and behold! Good people from all the tribes of Uruk came running." Warad pointed at the crowd. "These fine ones! And on the way to my girl, they found this fellow hiding in shallow water. This beast . . . one called Togg!"

Two warriors dragged a new man into the firelight and tossed him onto his knees. The crowd began spitting and shaking their fists. "Pig!" they shrieked. "Viper!"

Sargon's blood stirred. Togg was tall, strong, and had an arrogant-looking face, bearded and square-jawed. He was the type of hunter who always got his way. Sargon imagined the poor girl's terror in the dark—her pain and dishonor—and his rage boiled over. Wretch. How dare this man hurt a girl-child and throw the work of hundreds into peril? He must pay.

"Stone him dead," the crowd howled.

The chiefs also cursed and spat. For the first time since arriving, they seemed responsive to their clans. The mob was growing out of control. More people were running up. The palm branches shook as the climbers screamed and shook their fists. Sargon had never seen them this worked up. The chiefs' bodyguards drew closer to them, clutching spears and clubs. Enmerkar, however, basked in the attention. Head high, he walked over to interrogate the prisoner.

"Well, Togg? Is it true?"

Togg bowed frantically, muddying his forehead. "Please, *lugal,* I didn't do anything. I was just washing my dinner bowl in the river."

"Why hide in the reeds, then?"

A bitter laugh. "A mob ran toward me, shouting, 'Catch him!' What would you do? I hid."

"Only guilty dogs hide." Enmerkar faced the crowd. "Shall we stone him?"

"STONE HIM!"

The words struck Togg like physical rocks. He looked around wildly, as if to escape. Then his eyes lit on one of the tablets, and his face brightened.

"The Code of Uruk! Tablet Two!" he cried. "It says, 'All may seek justice by trial!'"

Silence fell over the clearing. Sargon's blood froze. How dare this wretch use the code to defend his evil?

As if hearing his thoughts, Togg faced him directly. "Akkadian Chief, it is your code. Will you honor it?"

Sargon blinked, paralyzed. "Me?"

"I ask for a trial! Do you believe in your code or not?"

Sargon didn't know how to answer. "I . . . eh . . . " he stammered. This man was wicked! Protecting him was not the purpose of the tablet!

Luckily, Nisaba appeared out of the crowd and ran up. She grabbed Sargon's arm and whispered, "I came as fast as I could. Do not take up this cause. If it were any other issue, perhaps. But not this one. Marsh tribes value their women's honor too highly. You hear?"

Sargon nodded. Her reasoning made perfect sense. Tempers were so high that people might go from loving the code to hating it if Togg used it to escape justice. And why not ignore it, just this time? It would be so easy. The mob wanted blood; the chiefs wanted to please the mob. Even the *lugal* was eager to flex his power with a public stoning. So why not?

Yet something felt off. Sargon looked up at the waving palm branches, trying to see what.

Strange, he thought. I feel like when I stole food.

Yes. That same subtle voice seemed to be whispering: *Just do it. Who'll stop you?* But he was "Sargon" now, and he had his two rules. *Serve your tribe. Do what you admire.* So what did he admire?

With surprise, he realized he admired . . . the code!

It was a good code, he thought. Crafted carefully, with the help of Ki, to get the whole truth out and prevent hasty mistakes. Indeed, in Akkad his chief had often delivered unfair punishments motivated by politics. A trial stopped that. And if Sargon wanted that protection for himself, he had to give it, too. Every time. It wasn't true fairness otherwise.

Besides, if Uruk broke the code now, when would the breaking end? The code would become nothing but a bit of dirt. A joke any *lugal* could kick aside.

Yes, Sargon thought, clenching his fist. If we want a code, we must keep the code. Now and always.

Gritting his teeth, he walked across the open patch of earth and grabbed Tablet Two. Holding it up, he turned slowly in a circle, showing the tablet to the crowd. Nisaba's eyes swelled. *No, brother.* Sargon ignored her.

"Hark, brothers and sisters," he shouted. "Our code promises a fair trial for all. Even him. So let's do it properly and get it over with. After the verdict, his punishment will be the same. And we will keep our integrity."

He expected everyone to agree. To his dismay, the night exploded with fury.

"Akkadian savage!"

"Men care only for men!"

"Fool!"

"Traitor!"

The crowd began to spit and throw pods of dirt. A lump struck Sargon's shoulder, bruising him. Astonished, he ducked and rubbed the sore spot. They were acting like he'd *pardoned* Togg's attack. But he hadn't, he'd just suggested a fair trial. Maybe they didn't understand.

Dodging more earth clumps, he waved the tablet at the crowd and shouted again.

"It's to protect you, too. If you're ever accused, you'll want this rule yourself, eh?"

No effect. Feet stomped; spit flew. Curses struck him like a hot wind.

"Fool!" they screamed. "Helper of barbarians! Go join Magog!"

They didn't trust the code yet, he realized. They'd seen big fellows get away with this again and again, and they believed the same was happening now. The larger vision escaped them.

As for Enmerkar and the other chiefs, the mob's rage delighted them. It meant a shrinking of Sargon's influence and a rise in theirs.

Enmerkar roared gleefully. "Some code, eh? It helps bad men. We should destroy it. Smash the bits of clay and be done with it."

"SMASH THE TABLETS," the mob screamed. "SMASH! SMASH!"

Nisaba shook Sargon's arm urgently. "Stop this, Sargon. It's the excuse he needs to undo everything. You're giving it to him. Why? For Togg, that wretch?"

"It's not about Togg." Sargon waved the tablet. "This is Uruk. This."

Seeing his resolve, Nisaba sighed. "Very well, brother. You decide. I only advise."

Enmerkar was still laughing, rubbing his hands with glee.

"Have your trial, Sargon. Help this pig you love. We pass judgment at moonrise. Meeting adjourned."

He dismissed the crowd with a wave, and still shouting and booing, they dispersed to wait in their camps. Nisaba ran off for help. Sargon, meanwhile, sat morosely by the council fire and brooded. Togg certainly looked guilty. His square head and big arms were like every hunter's in the cave who'd bullied "Ta" and gotten away with it. Yet Sargon couldn't see another way. The code either mattered, or it didn't.

And it does. I believe that.

So he clutched his stump and hunched over and waited, hoping he wasn't terribly wrong.

After what felt like an age, the moon popped above the trees, and a cry burst from the darkness. "The trial is on!" With a great thundering of bare feet, the tribes ran back.

All of Uruk came now, even elderly folk and children. Everyone was eager to see the stoning. The palms creaked and swayed as people climbed up in them to see better. They were so excited, their shouts hurt Sargon's ears, and people were booing him, calling him a lover of savages and dogs. The chiefs, meanwhile, returned slowly and with much dignity, heads raised high. They sat on their favorite logs and jeered the prisoner, while Enmerkar grinned across the flames at Sargon. *It's the code tonight, you tomorrow,* his eyes said. *My thanks, cripple.*

Finally, Sargon's companions appeared. Heart pounding, he stood and waved. It felt like he'd been waiting forever to see them.

Ut reached him first. "We can't leave you alone for a moment, can we, brother?" he joked, surveying the mob.

"You did the right thing, Sargon," Aya said, striding up. "Don't you listen to Ut."

"Did you investigate?" Sargon asked. "What'd you find?"

Ki stepped forward, ready to answer. But before she could, Enmerkar cut her off.

"Speak, witch. Defend this dog of yours, if you can."

Ki turned, and with deliberate slowness, took her place in front of the fire. The crowd quieted. Even now, the *baru* was feared and respected. Ki knew this, and smoothing her boarhide tunic, she locked her hands behind her waist and began to pace, intentionally building suspense. Sargon watched her closely. Ki kept her head down, a lock of hair falling over her olive cheek. But she cast a quick glance at him, and there was a keen light in her eye that told him she knew something. His heart beat faster. If anyone could bring good out of this, she could.

Ki lifted her voice.

"First, let us state the facts," she said, speaking loudly so everyone could hear. "By all accounts, a tragedy occurred tonight. Not long ago, a masked man attacked Warad's daughter at the river. She bit her attacker's hand, then screamed for help. The attacker fled. The question is, who was it?"

Ki looked at Togg. "One suspect is here. He has asked for a trial. Therefore," Ki raised a slender finger, "the obvious first step in any investigation would be to check for a bite mark on his hand." She faced the chiefs. "Did you do this?"

Silence met her question. Ki swiveled to Enmerkar. "You wanted to stone him. Did you check his hand?"

"I . . . uh . . ." Enmerkar looked uncomfortable.

"Hmm. Please do so now."

Under the mob's gaze, the chiefs had no choice but to obey. Scratching their beards and muttering, they surrounded the prisoner and forced his hand up to the light. Their faces fell. One by one, they backed away.

"Is there a bite mark?" Ki asked.

"No," admitted a sullen voice.

"Aha!" Ki said.

A murmur rippled through the crowd. Sargon's heart boomed. What did this mean?

Enmerkar snorted. "This proves nothing. A bite could be soft and leave no mark."

"Perhaps."

Ki resumed pacing. "Or perhaps this is the wrong suspect. Either way, it is worth further investigation."

Enmerkar stamped his feet in fury, but the crowd muttered against him, and he fell silent.

Ki went on.

"To investigate further, Rogg and I visited the attack site. Unfortunately, we didn't find much. Even under torchlight, the area was too dark and trampled by footprints for tracking. But something puzzled me."

She frowned at the earth. "When the girl screamed, a mob ran toward her from camp. They caught Togg halfway to her, hiding in the reeds. That means . . . if Togg was the attacker, he abandoned his victim and ran *toward* the oncoming mob. Who would do that?"

She shook her head. "No one! Running toward the mob ensures you get caught! You or I would run *away* from the crowd, farther south into the empty dark. Once alone, we'd sneak back to camp through the trees to avoid notice."

Her question met silence. Enmerkar didn't like it.

"Frightened men are fools," he snapped. "Togg lost his nerve and ran toward the mob, it's that simple. He dodged into the water once he realized his mistake."

"I disagree. Even a rabbit runs from a wolf. And our attacker is not an empty-headed rabbit. He had foresight. He made a mask. He waited for the girl at her usual watering spot. I think he planned an escape route, too."

"Theory," Enmerkar said.

"Yes, theory. But Rogg and I followed up on it. We searched south of the attack site, farther from camp. And behold. Among the palm trees, we found this."

Ki beckoned to Rogg, and the tall Elamite stepped into the firelight and handed her a grass mask stained with mud. Sargon's heart jumped. The mask of the attacker!

Ki walked around the fire pit, showing the mask to the crowd. Fingers pointed. Excited gasps and whispers rose. Ki was no fool.

She knew the real judge here was the mob, not the council. And she was playing to them accordingly.

"Note the stains," Ki told the crowd. "River mud, hardly dried. This was worn tonight."

She gave the mask back to Rogg.

"To make sure, I showed this mask to the victim, and she confirmed it was her attacker's. So, I ask you. How can Togg be the culprit? Could he run fast enough to drop this mask in the forest, then run back to the beach, pass the girl, get near the mob, then hide in the reeds—all in time to be caught there? Is that likely?"

No one answered.

"I asked Rogg to run the course himself. Sure enough, even Uruk's greatest warrior couldn't do it in time. Therefore." Ki raised her finger. "Togg is not the man!"

The mob went wild. They whooped, shrieked, and shoved each other in giddy excitement.

"WITCH! WITCH!" they screamed. "TELL US MORE."

They were *entertained*, Sargon thought in disgust. They'd almost stoned an innocent man, yet now they showed no hint of remorse. They were just eager for their next victim.

Togg was let go. He staggered away, weeping with relief. Sargon felt wretched for him. And furious at himself for judging the man so quickly. He'd been one of the mob himself, for a moment. *Forgive me, Togg*. But thanks to the code, no real harm had been done.

Nisaba came close. "Turns out you were right, brother. But now we have another problem."

Sargon nodded. "The attacker is still among us."

"Right. If we don't find him, it will stir up distrust among the clans."

"But we saved an innocent man," Sargon pointed out. "And we proved the code is worth defending."

"Let's hope it's worth it."

"Worth it?" Sargon faced her. "If it was you down there, Nisaba, would it be worth it?"

Nisaba looked at him strangely. "I see your point."

Meanwhile, Ki resumed pacing.

"So!" she said. "We had a mask, but no further clues. And Enmerkar had given us only until moonrise to solve the mystery. Not much time to save an innocent man."

The crowd laughed, enjoying Enmerkar's discomfort. He glared at Ki, hating her. Sargon wondered if she was taking this too far. The *lugal* would hurt her if he got the chance. Indeed, there was murder in Enmerkar's eyes, and Sargon wondered how many lives the big fellow had stamped out in the secret corners of the marsh for far less than this.

"That was a nice trick, witch," Enmerkar snarled. "But in the end, your investigation failed. I doubt the attacker will ask for his mask back. All you've done is leave us more confused."

"Oh?" Ki lifted her chin. "You forget one thing. As you say, I am a witch."

The crowd sucked in its breath. She *was* a witch. This trial kept getting better!

"All marsh folk know that if a witch finds a personal item like that mask, she can curse it," Ki said. "Even leagues away, she can stick it with bone needles and cast a spell on it to make the owner suffer."

"Yes, that is so," the mob agreed.

Sargon smiled. In his brief time with the marshmen, he'd learned how superstitious they were, even more than Akkadian folk. Ki was playing to her audience perfectly.

Enmerkar paled. "You can curse a mask? Pox its owner?"

Ki shrugged. "I visited each camp, threatening to do just that if they didn't help."

Enmerkar was genuinely frightened now. He might hate Ki, but he'd seen her dart-thrower and wind-catcher, and he respected her power.

Sargon, however, saw the real trick. *You're brilliant, Ki.* And he shouted:

"You set a trap!"

Now the crowd saw it too, and they began hopping up and down in excitement.

"Of course!"

"A trap!"

"Little Enki, in truth!"

Ki nodded. "Yes, I set a trap. As I rounded the camps, I let it slip where the mask was—that I'd left it back in my hut, ready to be cursed—in hopes the attacker would hear my threat, fear a curse on him, and sneak there to retrieve it. Sure enough, while I was out, someone entered my hut to snatch the mask. And Rogg was hiding in the dark, waiting for him."

"A true *baru*!" Roars of excitement filled the air. "Our *baru*!"

Ki turned to the darkness. "Rogg, bring out the prisoner."

On cue, Rogg marched into the firelight shoving a bound man. The man collapsed on his knees with a cry. His hands were tied in front of him with heavy grass rope, and his long hair swung over his dirt-stained face. A cheer louder than any before burst from the crowd.

"Ki, you did it!" Sargon cried, running to her.

But now Ki faced him, her expression grim.

"Forgive me," she whispered. "I didn't know."

"Know what?"

A cry of anguish cut her off. "My son!"

Sargon turned, his face prickling. The shout was from Enmerkar. He looked ready to rip his beard off his chin. His own son knelt before him, bound, bruised, and muddied.

The son looked just like his father. He had the same manly beard, bushy eyebrows, and even the beginning of his father's rounded belly. He shouted like his father, too. "Get away, giant! How dare you touch me?" he yelled at Rogg. "I am the *lugal's* heir. Father, execute him!"

Rogg simply grabbed the lad's bonds and yanked his hands up to the firelight.

"Behold. The proof!"

The crowd leaned forward eagerly. Sure enough, a bite wound was visible on the son's left palm, a crescent of bloody teeth marks, still fresh. Enmerkar stared in shock.

"Son, oh, my son," he moaned. "What have you done to me?"

"The girl was asking for it, Father," the son cried. "She tempted me for days. I only—"

"Silence!" Enmerkar roared.

The boy shut his mouth, astonished.

Sargon interjected quickly.

"The code benefits you, too, Enmerkar. Your boy is entitled to a trial, same as Togg."

"No," Enmerkar groaned. "He has confessed. I will fix this."

He turned from his boy, unable to look at him. Everyone waited tensely. The *lugal's* response could be fatal, Sargon realized. If he decided to protect his son from justice by summoning his faction to fight, then Uruk could be ripped apart.

At last, the *lugal* spoke.

"My clan is shamed. I will set this right."

A sigh of relief came from the onlookers. The worst would be avoided.

"Your *lugal* is not without honor." Enmerkar raised his face proudly. "My son will take Warad's daughter as a mate. No shame shall be upon her. She will live as a full member of our clan. For the rest of her life, she will stay with us. Furthermore, a mate-price shall be given to Warad. A rich price of . . ." Enmerkar winced, as if peeling up a fingernail. "Thirty otter pelts."

The council murmured in approval. The offer was generous, far more than a low-status family like Warad's could usually expect. Sargon knew Enmerkar was only doing it to preserve his position. Still, the result could have been much worse.

All eyes flicked to Warad to see if he would agree.

Suddenly a woman burst from the circle and threw herself on her knees beside Warad. Her hair, too, was streaked with ash. Her eyes were red-rimmed from crying.

"Shame." She grabbed Warad's arm. "Shame! Our daughter lies bleeding in our tent, and you sell her to her attacker for *otter pelts?* Coward!"

The crowd stirred. Many women flickered their tongues in agreement, their anger rising.

Warad lifted his hands helplessly. "Our girl is ruined, dear. What man of honor will take her? Is this not the best she can hope for?"

"No bargains." The woman faced the council, eyes gleaming. "Give us justice! Like the old customs."

The ululations rose higher. Sargon's gut sank. He knew what justice according to the "old customs" meant, here. *Castration.*

"An eye for an eye! A tooth for a tooth!" Warad's mate shouted. "This beast took my daughter's womanhood. Give us his manhood in return. Otherwise, Uruk is just another corrupt tribe where the 'high ones' never pay."

Sargon clutched his stump. Enmerkar would never agree to castrate his own son. Uruk was on the verge of civil war once more.

As expected, Enmerkar stamped his foot and spat into the fire. "The council will not consider this," he roared. "It is outrageous. I order you to take my deal, Warad, else my faction will leave Uruk this very night." He laughed. "Try to finish your dig *then.*"

It was all happening so fast, Sargon could hardly think. The mother was weeping. The chiefs were shouting. Enmerkar was shaking his fist. His son continued to wail for help. Overwhelmed, Sargon turned to his friends for guidance.

"An eye for an eye," he whispered. "It is so ugly. Is there a better way?"

Nisaba folded her arms. "Take the *lugal's* deal. It's the only way to peace. If you choose the other way, an eye for an eye, a war will start. All we've worked for will be lost."

But Aya grabbed his arm and shook him.

"I respect her, Sargon. But this time you cannot listen. A tribe needs justice. In Akkad our chief never punished hunters for what they did. Many women suffered. Bad things were done in the dark corners of the cave. That will happen here, too, if our justice lacks teeth."

Looking into her face, Sargon wondered if such things had happened to her, and his heart felt sick for her, and for the whole race of humans, who did this to each other over and over.

He shut his eyes. *What do I do?*

The custom was awful, awful. And Enmerkar's son was screaming at him, pleading with him to show mercy.

"You are kind, Akkadian. I know it," the lad yelled. "Ut got a second chance after he betrayed you. Yes, I heard that story. So why not me, too?"

But in the darkness behind his eyelids, Sargon imagined Warad's daughter again, struggling in the mud with a knife to her throat, and his stomach twisted. She had lost something even more profound than a hand. For her, nothing would ever be the same.

Rule Two: Serve your tribe. Aya was right. Uruk needed teeth.

Steadying himself, Sargon raised his stump.

"Uruk must protect its little ones," he told the crowd. "My vote is . . . let the custom be done."

The crowd gasped. Enmerkar sputtered in rage. "Preposterous. He's lost his head."

Then he made a fatal mistake.

"I am *lugal* of Uruk," he roared, stamping both feet. "I, and no other! Who are you, cripple? Nothing. A fly. I could slap you dead, if I cared to notice you."

He beckoned his warriors. "This trial is over. Free my son. Send these fools to their huts. As for Warad? I give NO otter pelts. NOTHING. *That* is what his defiance gets him!"

Sargon listened in astonishment. Enmerkar had just overstepped, gravely! He'd insulted the council and all the tribes. It could backlash, if someone would seize it.

Raising his stump, Sargon ran to the fire and shouted: "Hark, brothers! Do you hear that? He calls you 'nothing.' Is he better than you all? Will you let him spit on Uruk?"

The words acted like a spark. Every chief raised his fist and shouted angrily, insult for insult.

"Bad form, Enmerkar!"

"You appeal to us!"

"We decide!"

They stepped forward, drawing their stone knives, and surrounded the prisoner in a defensive ring. Enmerkar's men hesitated. Sargon's blood leapt. The momentum had swung wildly in his favor. He turned to the mob, pushing his advantage.

"Tribes of Uruk! Who rules here? Enmerkar? Or justice?"

"JUSTICE! JUSTICE FOR WARAD!" the mob screamed.

"Then act!"

"LET IT BE DONE!" the crowd roared.

The chiefs, for their part, wanted only to appease the mob. Taking up the cry, they shook their knives and pushed Enmerkar's son down in the dirt, flat on his back. Their bodyguards joined them, and Enmerkar's warriors, unwilling to confront so many, melted away. Enmerkar was left alone outside the ring of chiefs, shouting: "My line . . . my heirs! NO!"

But it was inevitable now. Rogg and four other warriors grabbed the prisoner and held him fast. The young man wrestled desperately, but Rogg ripped off the lad's loincloth, exposing his private parts to the light of the fire, and raised a stone knife to the flashing light.

"Sargon!" the son shrieked, thrashing. "You were cut, too! Have you no pity?"

Sargon's stump tingled. He winced and looked away. The scene was too familiar.

But Nisaba said sharply: "Uruk must see its work, or not do it."

And Sargon felt the truth in that, so he nodded and lifted his face and watched as Rogg seized that of the prisoner's which had to be severed. The stone knife swept down. It was a swift, sure cut. The son gave a dazzling scream. Rogg tossed the severed matter onto the fire with a hiss. The young man curled over, holding the bleeding spot, panting in disbelief like a beached fish. Meanwhile, the entire tribe looked on, howling with approval.

"JUSTICE!" they screamed. "JUSTICE!"

"My son . . ." Enmerkar staggered toward the young man. Finding his way still blocked, he began to scream at Sargon, spit flying from his mouth. "I will break Uruk! I will scatter you like ash! I curse you! The god Enbilulu curses you!"

But everyone ignored him, and Rogg calmly finished his task.

"Take a hot stone from the fire," he ordered a medicine woman. "Char the cut and seal it. This is justice, not an execution." And as the woman knelt to obey, Rogg warned the prisoner: "Lie still and take the stone or you will bleed out and die." But the young man could not answer in more than agonized gargles. As the hot rock sizzled his flesh, shutting the wound forever, he fainted. Sargon turned away at last.

"What have I done?" he whispered to his friends.

"Justice," Aya said coldly. "Only justice."

Justice did not feel the way Sargon had expected. It felt sickening and hollow, like the slaughter of Ur-Baba in the gully. Was it really justice, then? Or perhaps he did not understand justice at all . . .

That night, Enmerkar's clan departed across the river to sleep on the opposite shore. Many threats flew back and forth over the water as the tribes separated. But it was not as bad as Sargon had feared, for Enmerkar's faction wanted no part of his shame, and not a single tribe joined him. Thus, nine tribes remained, cursing Enmerkar to be gone. And he left without fulfilling his threat to "break Uruk."

As his boats vanished into the darkness, Rogg doubled patrols in case of a sneak attack, and the rest of the clans went to sleep in their lean-tos. Then it was quiet and dark under the palms.

Exhausted, Sargon sat on a blanket by the fire pit. For a long time, he didn't know where he was. He just gripped his stump and stared dully into the glow of the pulsing red embers, hearing in his head the young man's screams over and over. He glanced down at his chopped wrist, unable to comprehend it. Is this what my two rules bid me do?

His friends sat in the mouths of their huts, watching him. The palm canopy rustled in the warm breeze. Night creatures scuttled by, foraging in the understory.

"The word 'justice,'" Sargon murmured. "It sounded beautiful to me once. But it is hard. Hard."

"What about the girl?" Aya demanded. "Her life will never be the same."

Sargon nodded. But he still felt sick.

He lifted his face. Across the river, the ruby fires of Enmerkar's new camp twinkled. Sixty workers, gone. A fifth of the camp's workforce. At sunrise, would the other tribes get discouraged and leave, too? Had one bit of justice been worth it?

Then Sargon felt a hand touch his shoulder, and looking up, he saw Nisaba beside him. He also heard footsteps approaching, crackling over the dead fronds. Many footsteps.

"Look," Nisaba whispered, and pointed.

From the shadows, many figures emerged. Fifty! A hundred! More! Sargon's hand fell to his knife hip. But then torches hissed up, lighting the somber faces in the bobbing glow, and he realized that over half of Uruk had come. Mostly women. But some men, too.

He glanced at Nisaba.

"Is it war?" he whispered.

Nisaba's hand was also on her hip-knife. "I don't know. Make no sudden move."

A marsh woman walked to the edge of their camp. Her shoulders were scarred. Her face, half-hidden in shadow, was inscrutable except for her eyes, which blazed like small torches. Seeing Sargon, she touched her bare stomach, the place of her *emittu*, and bowed in respect.

"I am Tau," she said. "Until today, I was of Enmerkar's clan. But when he crossed the river, I stayed."

Sargon sat up. "If you need to reach him, I can prepare a boat."

Tau shook her head. "I follow him no longer. I am of Uruk now."

Before he could reply, she pulled a knife from her waist-belt. Muttering a secret oath, she cut off a hank of her hair and tossed it into the fire. A sour burning smell went up. Then, without a word, Tau retreated.

Sargon looked at Nisaba in confusion. The bald-headed adviser quickly placed a finger to her lips.

"Let it happen, Sargon. This is for them, more than you."

A steady procession followed. Each woman did the same thing. She cut off a lock of her hair, threw it on the fire, said, "I am of Uruk," and melted away. They were not just from Enmerkar's clan, either, Sargon saw, but from all the clans. Soon the reek of their burning hair was overpowering. Yet still the women came. Men, too, including Togg, the wrongly accused. Like the other males, he cut off a piece of his beard, threw it on the coals, bowed to Sargon, said, "I am of Uruk," and vanished.

Finally, Warad approached. He brought his mate with him, and a small, hunched figure who refused to lift her face to the torch-light. After her parents completed the ritual, she swiftly slashed her hair and threw it on the fire, crying in a fierce girlish voice, "I am of Uruk!" before retreating with her parents. Sargon felt a chill. *Warad's wronged daughter.*

Above all, this had been for her.

Finally, it was over. Only his tribe remained. But now Nisaba went to the fire pit, saying, "I have no hair. But I am of Uruk, too." And extending her open palm, she cut the skin, and splattered blood onto the embers with a loud hiss.

"There was no need, sister," Sargon said.

"For me, there was."

Nisaba sat back on his blanket. "I was right about spying, Sargon. But you were right about this. Tonight, for the first time, Uruk is worth it."

The others came and sat close. For a time, they listened to the hooting of the tree owls, the ribbeting of river frogs. The clicking of rushes in the wind.

“I’m not sure what just happened,” Sargon said.

“I am,” Nisaba said.

They all looked at her, waiting for the answer.

Nisaba watched the fire. “Tomorrow you will see.”

37

The royal tent of Magog was packed. Generals, advisers, bodyguards, and top concubines knelt around the wooden throne several rows deep, heads bowed in reverence to the tattooed figure who sat upon it. At long last, Gog had returned!

Jakka knelt in the front row beside Hakka. Not for a million concubines would he have placed himself next to his hated younger brother. But tonight Jakka had no choice. Father wished it. Luckily for Jakka, the clouds of incense in the air were thick enough to veil his expression of disgust.

He leaned closer to his little brother. "Feeling good, are you?" he whispered. "Eager to make bad reports of me to Father? Go on, try it. See what happens."

Hakka didn't answer, just kept his eyes down submissively. It was the most infuriating answer of all. How dare he ignore me? Jakka could have strangled him. The blatant disrespect! But in public like this, nothing could be done. Moreover, it hinted at a *reason* for the arrogance. As if Hakka knew something Jakka didn't.

Nod walked up to the throne, bowed to Father, and began to make his report. Sure enough, he began to ruin the prince's reputation, one story at a time.

"It is a sad thing, Lord Gog." Nod shook his gray-bearded face. "I advised the prince not to go into the swamp. I warned him *you* never did. Alas, the prince is headstrong . . ."

Jakka listened in rapt horror. He hated Nod so much, he couldn't breathe. *Traitor! You promised.* But it was too late, the damage was done. Even the concubines were hearing the report. Jakka would be unable to show his face anywhere after this—even in the harem tent.

Nod finished, leaving the tent silent except for the fires that crackled in the clay pots, burning grass for incense. Slowly, Father's single eye swiveled from Nod to Jakka in the front row. Jakka's heart shriveled. *Don't demote me, Father, please, I'll do better!* But through the wafting clouds of incense, the eye gave no sign.

Finally, it swiveled back to Nod.

"The *baru* is at Uruk now?" Father asked quietly.

"Yes, Lord. The marshlings believe she will move the river and pull magic food from the desert." Chuckles rippled through the tent. "It sounds silly, I know. It's what our scouts heard."

Father's eye snapped dangerously around the tent, finding the laughter. It stopped.

"You mentioned something else, Nod. Some kind of power-struggle at Uruk."

"Yes, Lord. Our local spies report a civil war nearly erupted. But peace came. Thanks to a . . . code."

"A code!" Father sat up sharply.

"I'm not sure of the details, Lord. But yes, a code. Whatever that means."

Father stood. "This code. Is it the old Akkadian code? Of Sargon the Great?"

Nod looked embarrassed. "My Akkadian history is poor, Lord."

"Perhaps I need better advisers. How many camp at Uruk now?"

"Three hundred, Lord."

"THREE HUNDRED!"

"Yes, Lord."

"Then a rival power has come to Mesopotamia!"

Father grabbed his war club from its tripod and pointed its bulbous head, studded with stone spikes, at Nod's face. "What a favor. I go north to smash the Mitanni invasion, and when I return home, I find . . . what? An even larger threat on my southern flank?"

Nod licked his lips anxiously. "Uruk is hardly a rival, Lord. Magog still ranks first, by far. We have a thousand warriors, all men. Uruk has three hundred total. And it is so far south—"

"Think, Nod. That's your job, isn't it?" Father began to pace in front of his wooden chair. "If the *baru* springs magic food from the ground, the whole world will flock to her. She will recruit thousands from the Great Marsh alone. And if she can feed them, why . . ." Father stopped and stared at the tent entryway as if seeing a vision. "Uruk could outnumber us in a year."

"No one has ever fed so many—" Nod began to protest.

"SILENCE!" Father stepped forward threateningly. "She embarrassed you, Nod, yet even now you underestimate her."

Nod bowed. The snapping in the fire pots seemed to fill Jakka's ears.

"Her power will grow," Father said. "And once it equals mine, Mesopotamia will choose between two masters."

He fixed his eye on Jakka. "Tell me, son, which master would you pick? The one who insults his allies? Steals their women?" The eye flashed. "Or offers magic food, and the protection of a legendary code?"

"Father, I—"

Father waved a hand impatiently. "Yet it is just as I wished."

Everyone looked up in surprise. Father gave a half-smile. "I wanted her in the wild, to see what she could do. Now, thanks to my son, she has shown me. Here, at Uruk!"

He strode to the tent wall and pointed his club at the tapestry that hung there, a large elephant hide map of Mesopotamia speckled in blue, red, and green dots.

"She couldn't have obeyed me better had I bid her. Soon her plant-food will ripen, and once it does, Uruk will be our new home."

An excited murmur swept the tent. Father faced them. He seemed every bit the conquering warlord tonight. Copper bands glinted on his wrists. No fear showed on his scarred, tattooed face. Even his robe of lion fur had been ripped from the body of the dying Mitanni *lugal*, the fatal blow delivered by Father's club. This was what a true leader looked like, Jakka thought. One who could turn even his son's defeat into victory, like magic.

Bitterly, Jakka realized he didn't measure up.

I'm not what I thought I was, he brooded. Is it too late to change?

Father paced. "Months ago, none of you believed a nomad rat could feed us with magic. You doubted me."

"Never, Lord," the warriors cried. "Your word is truth!"

Father laughed. "Well, now no faith is necessary. Her magic will be proved when I steal it. We must move." He faced Nod. "How long before our gazelle herd runs out?"

"Half a year, Lord."

"Then we begin tomorrow. Slaughter the herd, smoke the meat, pack it. Sacrifice any slaves too weak to travel. In five days, we march south. Once we get the *baru* under our power again, Mesopotamia will be ours."

"GOG! HAIL, GOG!"

The tent shook with cries of admiration. This was the warlord of old! Always with a trick up his beard! Jakka could not help feeling awed. And did this mean he was forgiven?

But no, for now Father stretched forth his tattooed hand and beckoned *Hakka*, not Jakka, to the front of the tent.

"Young Hakka! Come, I need a general to assist me at the battle of Uruk. Receive my blessing."

Jakka's heart sank as his brother raced forward and knelt. Father placed his hand on the lad's head and spoke so the whole tent could hear. "I name you my heir, Hakka. Together we will crush this *baru* and show Mesopotamia what her 'code' is worth. And in the days to come, the world will see which master is worth serving—and which god. Baal! Ruler of the earth!"

"HAIL GOG!" the warlords roared. "HAIL BAAL! HAIL HAKKA!"

Jakka trembled. His future was lost. If he wanted to live, he had to challenge this *now*.

Clenching his teeth, he ran forward and threw himself prostrate on the dirt floor beside his brother.

"Father, please hear me."

A hostile, mocking silence filled the tent. Jakka felt their hatred. They despised him. Well, he despised them too. And when all this changed, he would punish them terribly. But for now, he had to beg.

"Father, I beseech you, let me redeem myself," he said. "Put me in the front line at Uruk where I can recognize the witch. She is no good to you dead. I will snatch her alive from the fight so you can use her. Please, give me this chance! For Magog's sake."

Murmurs of surprise swept the tent. No high-ranking man ever risked fighting in the front line. Only green troops fought there, expendables. Their purpose was to create chaos, smash up the enemy formation, so that the second line—the valuable veterans—could walk in and clean up the mess at low risk. Jakka would never have dreamed of fighting in front, especially after his awful time in the marsh. But now he saw no other way.

To his relief, Father's scarred face showed pleasure. He liked his sons to show courage.

"So be it, son. You fight in front."

"Thank you, Father."

Jakka scrambled back, shaking. His eyes flicked to Hakka. The brat had the upper hand for now, but he was inexperienced, as Jakka had once been. And who knew what tricks the *baru* might play in the battle of Uruk? Soon they'd all see what Jakka had been up against.

Careful, little brother, he thought. *Slip up once, and I'll never give you another chance.*

Hakka's eyes gleamed back as hard as stones. It was clear he felt just the same.

38

The sun rose hot and bright above Uruk. Palm trees waved in the breeze, and the river sparkled and flashed, reflecting the sun ferociously. The whole settlement of Uruk had gathered on the bank. All nine remaining clans—including Sargon's—were howling, cheering, and dancing in anticipation. Months of labor were about to pay off. The canyon was ready to fill.

"Ready!" Ki shouted across the trench, cupping her hands around her mouth.

"Ready!" the two rope teams shouted back.

"Here we go. May Enbilulu bless us."

"Ready, ready!" the tribes shouted. "Do it, *baru*!"

The channel was almost complete. It cut from the desert through the palm trees to the bank. Only a gate of palm logs divided it from the flowing water, now. Drums boomed, bone trumpets blared. Children ran back and forth along the channel lip. Sargon, Rogg, Ut, Aya, and Nisaba were all shouting encouragement. Everyone watched Ki. She stood by the gate, her fist lifted, her eyes on the gate teams. Once the gate panels swung open, the river would rush into the channel bed and flow out to the desert to fill Uruk Canyon—at least, so they hoped.

"Oh, I can't look." Aya covered her eyes. "Tell me when it happens."

Sargon studied the trench. It was so deep and wide, it looked as if it had always been there, a thing built by gods, not men. Yet men had done it. Nisaba's prediction had been correct. After the trial, the work pace had exploded. Especially among the women, who worked with an inhuman energy and motivated their men, showing fierce loyalty to a code that protected every one of them. A sense of unity no one had ever felt before had animated the dig. Fully committed, they'd not only maintained the pace they'd kept under Enmerkar—they'd tripled it.

Rogg gently removed Aya's hands from her face. "Come, sister," he commanded. "You must see this, if only to tell Shulgi about it someday." Hearing his name, Shulgi, lodged in his sling-pouch on Aya's shoulders, giggled and waved his hands. Rogg kissed him. "He deserves to know what his mother helped accomplish."

"As always, Rogg, you know best." Aya laughed. "Ki, hurry. I can't stand it!"

As if she'd heard, Ki cried: "Three . . . two . . . one . . . ," then chopped her fist down, giving the signal. "Pull!" Both teams hauled with all their might. The ropes stretched taut, dragging the two wooden panels apart with a great groaning. The green waters of the Euphrates rushed through.

"It's working!" yelled the Urukites.

They ran along the lip of the channel, chasing the water's progress. In the bed, the river galloped forward like a living thing, gathering momentum. Ki had designed the channel at a slope, inviting gravity to suck the river onward. Down the channel it rushed, gobbling up dry ground and spreading out in a frothy brown sheet, covering the bed as thinly as a deerskin blanket. But even when the bed flattened out, the water kept going, and that was everything. The enormous force of the main river behind it kept pushing it, and the water surged on into the desert, hit the channel bend in the distance where the old canyon began, took the curve, and flowed out of sight.

"Baru! Baru!" people cheered. "Gods be praised!"

Some fell to their knees and thanked the river god with loud cries. Others sprinted down the switchbacks and splashed in the muddy shallows, throwing up sparkling handfuls of water and rolling around with delirious joy. Sargon and his friends, however, ran to Ki and mobbed her with hugs. For a long time, they just danced and cheered, wiping tears of happiness from their eyes. But Ki was crying—really crying—and Sargon kissed her cheek.

"You did it, Ki."

He knew she'd hardly slept all month, wrenched with guilt for not helping her tribe, driven by that secret pain. This was her atonement.

Ki's eyes were red. "You saved me, Sargon. I'm here because of you. My life is yours."

Sargon wasn't sure what she meant, but his heart felt so good, it hurt. He hugged her, and she hugged back, while their friends leapt and sang.

"What about me?" Ut demanded. "My prophecy got us out of the marsh, remember?"

Everyone laughed.

"Oh, Ut," Aya teased. "You just need a mate to appreciate you, don't you?"

"I'm working on that," Ut said.

After that, things progressed at an astonishing rate. By the next morning, water had completely filled the old canyon, creating a new river that flowed far into the desert before curling back to rejoin the Euphrates. Seeing this, the tribes packed up camp and paddled down the new channel into the waste, moving far beyond any territory claimed by the neighbors. And there, at last, they established the permanent settlement of Uruk.

Within days, hundreds of reed huts went up in a grid along the beach. On each side of the grid, the tribes dug furrows in the earth and sowed them with grain. The seed came from many sources: the theft of Babylon, trade with the neighbors, and gathering far and wide. Thus Ki's "magic food" was begun. Every day the tribes tended the seed by lugging clay pots of life-giving water up from the new river and splashing it in silver flashes over the furrows. And before anyone could believe it, bright green shoots appeared, fighting their way skyward. The month of Nanna, god of the moon, changed to the month of Shamash, god of the sun. The shoots grew higher. Soon they rose to Sargon's waist, contrasting beautifully with the red desert.

"Is it how you imagined it?" he asked Ki one dawn as the group stood at the edge of the fields, admiring the glitter of dew on the emerald stalks.

Ki shook her head. "It's even more beautiful. I wish my family could see it."

"They can," Aya said. "I'm sure of it, Ki."

"I hope so," Ki said, and she shut her eyes as if to feel for their presences.

Meanwhile, camp life flourished. There were parties on the beach at dusk, and races and spear-throwing tournaments, and dances to the music of drums, wooden rattles, and singing. Storytellers from different tribes competed for audiences by roaring fires. And to everyone's delight, Uruk held its first mating ceremony when a young woman from Otter Clan became life-mate to a man from Turtle Clan. All Uruk celebrated with a feast that lasted into the night. Thus, the days flew by with a growing mood of hope, and Sargon was content.

Ki, however, would not coast on her success. She kept generating new ideas. Not least was one for a "Thinker Team," composed of Uruk's brightest minds. Pitching it to the council, she explained: "I'm not the only one with ideas. Many minds here could help us create. And the more creative Uruk is, the faster our progress will be. Four, five times faster. Who wishes this?"

The council approved her pitch immediately, for by this point, Ki's reputation was that of a living legend, and whatever she suggested was done. They awarded her a Thinker Team of ten people, and thenceforth, the ten took afternoons off from planting to think, conference, and test out new ideas. And soon they began to produce.

Their first idea was a "turtle shell"—invented by a Thinker from Turtle Clan, no less—and Uruk built hundreds of the shells, so that the round device could protect Uruk's warriors from blows. "I *hope* Magog comes at us," Rogg roared as he lifted the first turtle shell, a round wooden frame filled with reed matting and covered under a leather skin. He shook it at the council. "This'll break their teeth." And every day after work, he drilled the tribes under the blazing sun. He taught them to body slam each other with the shells, to knock each other off their feet, and leap back up again. To stab reed spears over the shells without exposing themselves. To maneuver in formation, charging in a long shell wall that guarded the warriors' flanks. The fighters learned to be flexible, too, to re-form into pods if the shell wall shattered. To maneuver independently, to sandwich foes. Daily, the movements grew more fluid and sure, and in all this Sargon felt the unity of Uruk growing. Neighboring scouts sometimes watched from a distance, small specks out in the desert that appeared, then vanished, going back to report to their chiefs. But there were no attacks, and Rogg credited the drills.

"We're flexing our muscles. Predators don't attack strength; they want weakness. They won't find that here."

But there was a better weapon, and this one Rogg hid from enemy scouts. He drilled it only in private, once his patrols had cleared the horizons. The weapon, of course, was Ki's deadly dart-flinger.

It was their great advantage, Rogg said. Their secret chance, if Magog ever came. Each day after shell-work, the tribes fired volley after volley into the desert, aiming at colored reed markers placed at different ranges in order to mimic hitting a charging army. Young and old shot, male and female. Everyone had their own device. Even Sargon bore one, for Ki designed him a special wooden cup fitted to a bow, so he could hold it and fire as well as any Urukite. Whenever the drill groups complained of weariness, Rogg would gleefully use Sargon as an example, shouting: "Come, friends. Our brother fires one-handed; can't you, with two?"

They were good days, Sargon thought. Hard ones, but fulfilling. There was companionship, and a sense of common purpose. Everyone felt something special was happening here and tried to live up to it.

"I keep expecting it to vanish, like a dream," he told Ki one afternoon as they took their daily walk out from camp. "Sometimes when I wake up, I'm afraid to open my eyes, lest I find myself in Akkad again, none of this real."

"It's real," Ki said. "If anything is real, this is."

The day always seemed lovely at this time, Sargon thought. The sun was setting in the west, casting a copper light over the desert, making the wheat stalks glint and shimmer. The air was dry and cool. Ki and Sargon, as was their habit, had gone far out, strolling nearly a league from camp so as to be free of the constant requests for guidance from the tribes. They spent the time talking . . . reflecting . . . joking. It felt necessary, Sargon thought. Each day was so full, it blurred and became unreal if they did not walk together like this and review it. Indeed, without the walks, he sensed his days would be half-lived.

Beside him, Ki's long black hair stirred in the warm breeze. Just looking at her made him happy. And how far away Akkad seemed. How incredible, that if not for his tribe's rejection, he might still be back there, living under the black feeling.

And what if I had mated that girl, Oona? he thought in quiet amazement. Stayed in Akkad? I might have a child with her now . . . and what a different life that would be.

He'd still be "Ta." Thief. Coward.

"What's wrong?" Ki asked.

Sargon stopped and scratched his beard, trying to find the words. "It was so close, Ki. So many times . . . *this* almost didn't happen."

"I know," Ki said quietly.

"In the desert, if I hadn't stolen food and been exiled from my group . . ." For now he had shared everything with her, even that awful moment. "Then, if the gazelle . . . if I'd stopped endurance running . . ."

Ki nodded.

"Then in the storm on the river . . . I almost heeded the vote. I almost didn't come for you."

He looked away. *One different decision.* One grain of cowardice at the wrong moment, and he'd never have known all this. It terrified him, how sad that alternate life was. And he shut his eyes and thanked El for guiding him here, somehow.

Taking his stump in her hands, Ki pressed his skin and looked up at him. Her whole heart was in her beautiful brown eyes, and his *emittu* rose within him, warm with joy.

"Sargon," she said earnestly. "Just wait. If we keep pushing, and don't let up . . . you won't believe how good this life can be."

Shortly before the wheat came ready to harvest, the council sent a delegation to the neighbors to establish a trade route.

Trade would be essential, the council believed. Uruk, being out in the desert, still had no reedbeds or palm trees of its own. The usual building materials were lacking, and until such things could be grown, Uruk would need to barter for them.

To Sargon's surprise, he was chosen to lead the delegation. But upon reflection, it made sense. Of the nine chiefs, he had the gentlest, friendliest manner. More importantly, he was a neutral outsider, with no history of local feuds like the marsh chiefs.

Thus, on the first day of the month of Anu, god of the sky, Sargon sailed downriver in a grass-bottomed boat. He took Rogg and Ut for protection, and Nisaba, of course, for counsel.

It turned out to be a wonderful trip. The sailing was restful, and in each village, the chieftains proved more than eager to set up trade. Wheat was rare on that part of the river, and every tribe wanted to lift its status by producing bread. In a few days, Sargon obtained pledges for a protected trade route, as well as permission to construct a dirt path linking the villages. Eager to report his success, he turned the wind-catcher back toward Uruk.

He had no idea how much was about to change.

It was just after sunrise, and they were a half-day's sail from home. Nisaba sat at the guidance plank, tacking upstream, while Rogg paddled in the prow and Ut and Sargon fished over the sides, using bone hooks attached to grass line. The sky was blue, the river brown. On shore, the palm tree forest made a slash of green against the red waste. The outlet of the new "Uruk River," where it emptied into the Euphrates, was coming into view. Far off in the desert, the smoke of Uruk's campfires could be seen. The Little Marsh was also visible, much-changed due to the drop in the water level, which had pulled the marsh significantly back from its old banks. Sargon shaded his eyes with his stump and observed the heaps of reeds lying dead in the exposed mud, shriveled and flattened as if a terrible brush fire had swept through and burned the land black for leagues.

"We didn't anticipate it drying out so badly," he said. "All those fish and frogs, dead. Birds, displaced."

"We made a choice," Ut said. "Us over animals. An easy choice, I'd think."

"Still," Sargon said uncertainly, "it is much power for men to wield."

Uruk, he felt, must not become like Jakka, a child wielding forces too big for it, damaging all around. Especially as the settlement grew more powerful and massive, there would be a great potential for harm, as well as good.

But Ut was thinking of other things.

"Listen, brother, I've something to ask you," he said tentatively.

"Yes?" Sargon turned, surprised. "What is it, brother?"

Ut cleared his throat. "It is a secret no one else knows so far . . . unless Nisaba's spies do?" He glanced sharply toward the stern. "Bah, of course she knows," he groaned. "Sargon, stop her. She's not allowed to use her resources on her own tribe, is she?"

Sargon laughed. "I'll talk to her about it."

Nisaba winked. "Don't worry, Ut. I haven't told anyone."

Sargon was worried now. "Come, Ut. Is everything all right?"

"Oh, it's nothing bad." Ut wiped his nose. "I . . . I've chosen someone. To be my mate."

Sargon gave a shout of joy and banged the boat's side with his stump.

"Wonderful, Ut! Who?"

Ut grinned bashfully. "Tau. The spy, remember? The ex-concubine of Enmerkar."

"Tau! How could I forget?" Sargon was so happy, he could hardly speak. He grabbed Ut and hugged him tight, laughing. "That's wonderful, brother! What news!"

Ut gulped. "I wouldn't be here without you, brother. The second chance you gave me . . ." He looked away, embarrassed. "That's why Tau and I hope you'll honor us at the ceremony with an official blessing. Would you?"

"Why, I'd be delighted to, brother. Delighted!"

Sargon leaned over the side and splashed a handful of brown water on his face to cool himself off. His heart was brimming with gratitude. This is Uruk, he thought happily. This, right here. People meeting, finding love, building families. Celebrating with friends. This was the *emittu* of a healthy tribe.

"What of you, brother?" Ut asked. "Who will your mate be?"

"Me?" Sargon didn't understand the question. "I . . . I have no one."

Ut laughed. "Not Ki?"

It felt like a terrible secret had been exposed. Sargon's cheeks burned. He didn't know what to say.

Ut chuckled. "It's obvious, brother. You two walk together every afternoon. You talk in camp as if no one else is around, and we're right there." He grinned at the others. "We'd have to be deaf and blind not to know."

Sargon looked around the boat. They were all gazing at him kindly. They must have known his feelings for some time. He became terribly embarrassed. Was it that obvious?

"Just deny it, and I'll stop bothering you," Ut teased. "Can you?"

Sargon looked away. Uruk was wonderful. But Ki made it *home*. Without her . . .

"I can't deny it," he said quietly.

"Hooray!" Ut shouted. "Thanks for telling us what we already know!"

In a group, the others laughed and crawled forward, hugged him and pounded him on the back. The boat rocked so much, they were lucky it didn't capsize.

"Finally!" they cried. "Took him long enough to admit it, eh?"

"Better today than too late," Ut said.

Still embarrassed, Sargon frowned. "Too late? What do you mean?"

"He doesn't know?" Ut looked at Nisaba sharply.

Nisaba rubbed her bald head. "Well . . . I didn't tell him."

"That's your job, spymaster," Ut cried. "What's wrong with you?"

"I was waiting for the right time," Nisaba protested. "He needed to focus on the trade meetings."

"What?" Sargon asked anxiously. "Come, tell me."

Nisaba sighed. "A few days ago, a young hunter visited our camp." She glanced at the others. "He asked Ki to be his mate."

Sargon froze. *His mate.* It felt like a knife had stabbed him.

"Who?" he whispered.

"A man named Ea. Otter Clan. A fine match, actually. He's on the Thinker Team. He respects Ki very much. He offered her a great number of otter pelts."

Sargon couldn't move. A hundred feelings rushed through him. Fear, grief, pain. Confusion. Somehow, he'd always seen Ki as a Great Person—the Thinker of Uruk, a gift from the gods. Not the mate of anyone. Yet . . . didn't Ki deserve to be happy, too? And who better than another strong mind, a Thinker, like her?

He began to breathe faster. The world swam. He gripped the gunwale to steady himself.

Nisaba interrupted quickly. "Don't worry, brother. Ki declined. She said, 'No.'"

"No," Sargon repeated stupidly. "No." Slowly, he found he could breathe again.

"But listen, brother, Ki needs to know her choices," Nisaba pressed. "It is no small thing for a woman to decline an offer from a fellow like Ea. He's a fine match. If you plan not to ask Ki yourself, she must know. She cannot waste her youth waiting for you."

Sargon's blood was pounding. His head felt empty.

"I . . . I don't know what to say."

"I think it's obvious!" Nisaba said.

"Easy, sister," Rogg said. "You needn't scold him. He's told us his heart." He crawled forward and put his arm around Sargon. "Let him breathe."

Nisaba shrugged. "Am I wrong? In love, a person must be as calculating as in politics."

"Perhaps," Rogg said. "But this case is special. It is Ki, Sargon."

His heavy hand patted Sargon's back.

"Brother, listen. You care for Ki, yes? More than any woman?"

Sargon nodded. No one else was even in his mind. The instant he'd met Ki, it had been her. In the storm and the river. In the desert and the swamp. Her.

"Then you know what you want. That is everything," Rogg said. "Listen, brother. I spent my life hunting and fighting, and it was good. But family is the best thing in life. I miss mine every day. If you have a chance to start one with a woman like Ki, by the gods, take it. Or you'll regret it all your years."

"Besides," Nisaba pressed, "if you don't, we'll be furious. You two are perfect for each other."

"Hear, hear!" Ut said. "Two strange ones, heads in the sky. Never seen two more suited."

"It would be a powerful alliance, as well," Nisaba said, a playful glint in her eye. "It would strengthen your position, Sargon. To be mated to the *baru?* To bond Uruk's Thinker to the creator of its code? Yes, very beneficial for us, going forward. Sargon, as your adviser, I recommend this course."

Sargon felt an upswell of gratitude for his friends. Everything they said felt true. So why hadn't he seen it himself? Perhaps he'd been so preoccupied with moving the river, growing food . . . No, that wasn't it, he realized. The truth was, he'd never dared to imagine Ki as his mate. His disappointments in Akkad were buried too deep. *Worthless cripple, no good for a woman* . . . It had never seemed possible *he* could be worthy of one like *her*.

Ut sensed his thoughts, and spoke.

"Brother, this isn't Akkad anymore. You're not the 'runt' who got passed over every year. You made all this happen. You and her, together." He waved a hand at the dead marsh and the channel, and at the smoke of Uruk's campfires in the distance. "You're a prize, brother. You speak at the council of chiefs. You beat Enmerkar. Beat Ishtar. Most women in Uruk would jump to be your mate."

A spark of hope entered Sargon.

"Really?"

"Really!" the whole boat laughed.

Sargon studied his stump. He still couldn't believe anyone would want him. But if they all said so . . .

"Should I offer her otter pelts, then?"

"By the gods, no." Ut faced the others. "Thank goodness he asked us first, eh?"

Nisaba bent forward. "I understand, Sargon. Most tribes have a system for mating. Elders decide it, or parents trade pelts. But here in Uruk, we are all free, so what do you do? I recommend this: do what slaves do. Like when I was a slave, before Ishtar. We had no guardians anymore, so we made our own customs. We just spent time alone with a person, as you and Ki already do. Now let her know the rest. It is that simple. Life is too short and full of suffering to delay such a thing." She nodded. "As for Ki, now that you've made up your mind to pursue her, believe me, she will sense the change. After all, she is the *baru.*" Nisaba smiled. "She'll know. And she will let you know how she feels."

"What if she feels different?" Sargon rubbed his stump nervously. "We're a tribe. I don't want to make things uncomfortable for us. It could hurt Uruk. It could—"

Rogg laughed. "Is this the man who killed Ur-Baba? 'Sargon, Highly Praised One?' Who cannot tell someone he cares for her?"

Sargon wrinkled his nose. "I see your point."

He felt overwhelmed. But they were right. Ki should know his feelings, whatever she felt in return.

And was it really possible? The two of them? Might such a wonderful future be his?

Oh, El, he prayed silently to his god. *More than anything in my life, I beseech you, let this be.*

They were still talking about this when they neared the channel outlet. There they adjusted the sail, meaning to tack up the Uruk River to the settlement. But Rogg stopped them, pointing at the bank.

"Is that us?"

Onshore, a campfire smoked between two hide tents. A wind-catcher boat was pulled up on the beach, sail rolled. Sargon was puzzled. Uruk was still the only tribe down here with wind-catchers. So this had to be an Urukite mission. But he didn't know of it. He scanned the shore. Where was everyone? He saw no movement. Just the rustling of the green palm canopy, and the waving of the water reeds.

"It's a Thinker Team mission," Nisaba said. "I remember now."

"How do you figure?" Rogg asked.

"Ki informed me before we left. She sent two Thinkers to explore the Little Marsh, to check water levels and so on. I don't know, Thinker things."

Rogg chuckled. "Indeed."

Sargon watched the empty bank. Part of him was afraid one of the Thinkers would be Ki. How could he face her now? Yet part of him was hopeful, too.

"Anyone see the Thinkers?" he asked.

Ut chuckled. "Maybe they're still in the tent, sleeping. Mind-work makes 'em lazy."

"I'd like a hot breakfast." Rogg lifted a big fish he'd caught that morning. "A fire would be nice. Any objections to going in?"

Ut laughed. "Is that a question?"

They glided in and nosed the boat ashore. But as the prow scraped the mud, Sargon stiffened, for a scream burst from the shade deeper under the trees.

Everyone reached for their weapons.

"Was that human?" Ut whispered.

No answer was needed, for the scream came again. Human, sure enough.

Peering into the darkness between the trunks, Sargon saw six tall figures moving around. They were muscular, with long hair flowing down their backs. And the backs were hideously tattooed. *Magog.*

Sargon's jaw clenched. Luckily, the tattooed backs were turned. The warriors seemed too preoccupied to have noticed the boat.

Torture, Sargon realized. They're torturing our Thinker Team! What if Ki is there?

Rogg faced Nisaba. "Quick. Sail upriver and hide offshore. I'll go in."

"What? Alone? No, you can't waste yourself," Nisaba said.

"I won't be alone. Sargon and Ut will join me."

Ut paled. Sargon began to sweat.

"Shouldn't we go tell the others?" Ut whispered. "They need to know this."

"That's our Thinker Team," Rogg said. "If they confess about the dart-thrower, it ruins us. We must stop this from reaching Gog."

He turned to Nisaba. "If something happens to us, don't wait. Warn Uruk."

Nisaba nodded. "I understand."

Rogg reached into the boat and handed Sargon his dart-thrower. It was the special one Ki had designed for him, fitted with a cup attached to the bow so his stump could hold it.

"Remember, brothers, you're trained now," Rogg said. "Take courage. They won't know what's coming."

They climbed out of the boat with their weapons as Nisaba pulled back into the water and began to paddle downstream, out of sight. Meanwhile, Sargon and Ut crept after Rogg into the palms. Sargon was shaking. He and Ut weren't warriors like Rogg. And this was a real fight, against the best warriors in the world.

Then another scream shot from the trees, and Sargon's rage kicked in, overriding his fear. He hated Magog for this. *Help your people.*

Rogg crept catlike into the shadows, scanning for stray Magog warriors on their flanks. But as they drew closer, they saw only the six, ahead. Magog hadn't even posted a lookout.

Overconfident as usual, Sargon thought. Sloppy.

At the edge of the clearing, they crouched behind a bush and took in the scene. It was hideous. One Thinker lay dead, his head bashed in, sprawled on his face where they'd clubbed him to the dirt. The other Thinker was lashed to a tree, sitting upright. Five Magog warriors stood by, leaning on the shafts of their spears and mocking him. The sixth held a stone blade to the Thinker's chest, tapping it playfully with the sharp point.

"No more withholding, Uruk worm. I want the *baru's* secrets. She got a new weapon? Eh?"

"I told you!" the Thinker cried. "It's just the wind-catcher—AHHH! AHHHHH!"

The knife went in again, and nothing but screaming remained, underscored by laughter from the warriors. Sargon's heart twisted.

"It's just a scouting patrol," Rogg whispered. "We'll take them in two volleys. Ut, you target the two on the left. The center two are mine. Sargon, shoot the right two."

The men nodded and nocked their feathered darts into their bows.

"No need for a shot to the head or anything fancy," Rogg whispered. "Just aim for the body. Any hit is good."

They silently drew back their darts, tensing the gristle strings. And to Sargon's surprise, his hand wasn't shaking anymore. Thanks to his practice in the desert, the feel of the bow calmed him, as if he'd been born to this.

"Aim," Rogg whispered. "Three, two, one . . . fire!"

The strings *twanged.* Three Magog warriors flopped down, screaming. The others turned, eyes big with surprise. Before they could find their attackers in the foliage, however, the Urukite bows twanged again, and the final three fell, clutching darts in their stomachs. Every shot had been a hit.

"RAAAAAHHHHH!"

Rogg tossed his bow aside and stood up holding his war club.

"Come, brothers. Time to ask *them* a question or two!"

With a lion's roar, he smashed through the bush, uttering his battle cry. Ut and Sargon followed, yelling, shaking their spears.

The battle for Uruk had begun.

39

That night at the edge of Uruk, Ki stood alone, studying the red fires of Magog's camp on the black horizon.

The smells of flowering thornbushes and desert sagebrush floated to her on the hot breeze. So did faint screams. Magog's camp was far away, but Gog had sent a group much closer, just half a league off, to build brushwood pyres to scare the Urukites. The great fires blinked as warriors passed in front of them, driving slaves at spearpoint toward the pyres. Ki cursed softly. Even from here she could see a tiny figure suddenly break free of his ropes and attempt to flee—only to be stabbed by two warriors, then heaved onto the nearest fire, so that his screams mingled with the rest of the awful night-music. Ki shook her head, sickened. Once again, Gog used fear to his advantage. With each sacrifice, his troops would grow more confident of the war god's favor. And the Urukites would grow more fearful, luring them into mistakes.

For the first time, Ki felt glad that her people were dead. If they were still alive, Gog would be torturing them hideously now to break her spirit. In the Underworld, at least they were safe.

Unable to take it anymore, Ki covered her ears with her hands and turned and walked wearily back to the council fire. But even there, Gog's fear tactics seemed to be working. As she arrived, she found the chiefs in a circle around the blaze, arguing and shouting and banging their staves, casting blame just as they had under Enmerkar. No one wanted to become a human sacrifice. Nor join in hand-to-hand combat with the most feared fighters in the world.

Uruk's newly elected *lugal,* the chief of Otter Clan, provided little help.

"A thousand Magog warriors," he yelled, pointing at the darkness. "Meanwhile, what've we got? Just *two hundred and fifty,* since Enmerkar left. That's odds of . . . of . . ."

"Five to one," chipped in the Turtle Clan chief, who was better at numbers.

"Right. And we're half women, with old people thrown in."

"So, really, ten to one," the Turtle Clan chief said helpfully.

"Right!" the *lugal* shrieked. "Why, that's the whole thing right there."

Until now, he'd done a fine job as *lugal,* Ki reflected, mostly agreeing with the council's moods. But tonight, his lack of a spine was being exposed.

"Do you see this?" he screamed, waving at the fires in the distance. "We must flee. Now!"

Rogg was there, his big arms folded.

"Must?" he said calmly. "What we *must* do is review our options."

"Options? What options? You failed us, Elamite. Your job was to forewarn us."

"Right," another chief shouted. "Rogg promised us a warning. He said if Magog approached, we'd see smoke-signaling from the river tribes first. Well?"

Rogg clenched his jaw, losing his temper. He was not built for politics, Ki knew. Luckily, he'd asked Nisaba how to deal with these types, and heeding her advice now, he bowed his head and counted to five before answering.

"Gog didn't do what we expected," he said slowly. "He skipped the river and came from the desert. Marched deep into the waste, got even with us, then cut in. It was clever. He probably realized we'd anticipate him if he came in boats, so he took a route we couldn't fully watch."

"Clever, yes. He was too clever for you."

Rogg frowned. "Remember, *lugal,* a month ago, I asked this council for a desert patrol. *You* vetoed it. This is not to cast blame on you," he added quickly, "but to prove that Gog is not a god. If we proceed sensibly—"

"I've heard enough. If Magog raids us tonight, we're dead," the *lugal* shouted. "It's over." He scanned the darkness as if expecting tattooed warriors to burst from it at any moment.

"We have time," Rogg said patiently. "We know from the scouts we captured today that Gog dislikes night fighting. He intends to attack tomorrow, to capture the maximum number of slaves. If we use this time to prepare—"

"No." The *lugal* faced the river. "We must abandon this place. Get in our boats and go to the Great Marsh tonight. I am your leader; this is my decision. On the water, marshmen are safe. A foreigner, an Elamite, cannot understand. The swamp has saved marshmen before."

The meeting was about to break up. Ki saw Nisaba looking at her intently—*Do something*—so she nodded and entered the circle of orange light. Rogg looked relieved.

"Just in time, sister," he said in her ear. "I was about to start breaking noses."

Ki patted his arm. "I don't blame you. Stay close, we might still need it."

"Gladly."

Seeing her, the chiefs quieted. They still held a grudging respect for the *baru*.

I hope I merit it, Ki thought.

Taking her place in front of the fire, she rubbed her forehead, searching for the right tone.

"I share your concern, brothers. We must look at this honestly. Gog is strong. But we must not forget our own strengths, either. If we fight, we *will* hurt him. We have the weapons for it. The training. The critical question is, will it be enough?"

"Don't equivocate, *baru*," the *lugal* said. "What is in your mind? Fight? Or flee?"

The group fell silent, watching her. Ki gulped.

Be honest. Don't lie. You know the costs of losing.

She shut her eyes. Behind her lids, she saw the horrors of her past. Father's brain, clubbed out. Asha's temple, spurting blood. Inanna's idol, shattered. What if that happened to her friends? Could Ki bear it?

For a long moment she pondered that question. Finally, she opened her eyes.

"I say we fight."

The council burst into an uproar. Rogg shouted them down, and Ki continued.

"Yes, we could escape tonight to hide in the Great Marsh. But for how long? I tell you, the world has changed. Your old ways will not save you anymore. Once Gog's advisers study our fields and replicate them, growing unlimited food, Gog will have the resources to build a bigger army than anyone can imagine. Nothing will stop him. He will conquer all Mesopotamia, even the Great Marsh. With unlimited bread, he'll bribe other marsh tribes—who hate you, by the way—to hunt you down in the swamp and kill you, one by one."

"Why would he go to such trouble?" the *lugal* asked.

Nisaba stepped in. "To make an example of Uruk. To show Mesopotamia that Magog is the only way. What we've done here is challenge his model of the world. He must crush our model utterly, to make his point."

The council listened in bitter silence.

"We should never have come here," one said. "Adad was right."

"No." Ki's voice rose. "If we fight, we have a real chance. It will cost us; we *will* lose people. But we stand to win everything. A real home. And an end to Magog's terror, for good."

Sargon joined her, his face set.

"None of us believe in suicide, brothers. If it was hopeless, I'd agree to flee. But if Ki says there's a chance, there is. And I'd rather die fighting for it than sulk in the marsh for the rest of my life, a man without dreams, wondering *what if*."

Ki could have hugged him. That was exactly how she felt, too.

"What is your opinion, general?" Sargon turned to Rogg.

"Fight," the giant said simply. "It will be close. But we can win."

"The experts have spoken," Sargon said.

Still no one answered.

"Very well," Sargon said. "No one should force this decision on you. Everyone will risk his life. Therefore, everyone must enter this willingly, or not at all."

"What are you suggesting?" the *lugal* asked suspiciously.

"Confer with your people. Tell them the situation honestly. Let anyone who wishes to leave do so. But if enough wish to stay to protect our home, then we owe them that chance, too. This is their work at stake, as much as ours."

The chiefs nodded, pleased. Sargon had spoken wisely. They turned to go. But now Nisaba interrupted with a warning. "Wait, brothers." And she pointed.

Turning, Ki nearly fell over in surprise. In the darkness outside the ring of firelight, all of Uruk stood listening. All two hundred and fifty! They must have crept up during the meeting and watched silently, overhearing it all.

One small figure pushed her way to the front. As she stepped into the light, Ki's heart tightened. It was Warad's daughter, the victim from the first trial. Her face was as hard as stone, her eyes bright. Lifting her fist, she spoke directly to Sargon.

"Sargon, Defender of the Code. We heard you, and we are here. Ask us, Sargon. *Ask*."

Sargon bowed in respect. "What do you wish, sister?"

The girl's eyes flamed. Her voice filled with emotion.

"There is only one Uruk. In all Mesopotamia, nowhere else do we have dignity. If we lose Uruk, we lose all." Sounds of agreement rippled through the crowd, and the girl touched her stomach, the place of her *emittu*, her true self. "For Uruk, I will give all," she said. "Every drop of blood—FOR URUK."

"FOR URUK!" the tribes shouted. "FOR URUK!"

The shouts grew louder and louder. Fists thrust skyward. Heads nodded. It grew so deafening, it entered Ki's blood like fire, and she, too, lifted her fist in salute to the girl.

"FOR URUK! FOR URUK!" she heard herself shouting.

Even the chiefs were nodding in agreement.

So, Ki thought, lowering her fist. It was decided. Tomorrow, their dream would live or die.

40

The next morning, Magog's forces marched out from camp. They stopped a quarter league from Uruk. There in the waste, they spread out and formed two lines. The rear line contained the high-ranking warriors, where it was safe. The front held the low rankers, who would absorb the first shocks of battle. Jakka stood with these unlucky ones.

His blood ran so hot, he hardly noticed the sun blasting his face. He knew he might die today, or be crippled for the rest of his life. But if he failed to capture the witch, Hakka would become heir and kill Jakka anyway. That would be the most bitter death of all.

So I must get her. I must, he thought, gripping his wood spear. Or die trying.

Uruk's army stood in the distance in a single line, the brown Uruk River sparkling behind it. At this distance, it was impossible to find the witch among the blur of bearded faces and fluttering reed skirts. Still, Jakka peered at the line anxiously, trying to sense her presence. What if she wasn't there? What if she had died, somehow? What if . . . ?

"First battle?"

Jakka glanced right, startled. His big neighbor was eyeing him. A hulking beast with fat lips and the strange accent of a Hittite.

"You look scared," the big man said. "What tribe were you captured from? Mitanni?"

Jakka refused to make eye contact. Stupid slave. "What do you care?" he asked.

The fellow sighed. "If it is your first battle, you'll probably fall. And if you fall, my left flank will be exposed. And maybe I'll get hurt." He shoved his tattooed face menacingly into Jakka's. "Don't fall."

Jakka scowled and said nothing. The man didn't recognize him, of course. Jakka was wearing heavy war paint. Besides, it was unthinkable that a prince would stand in the front line. Part of him wanted to threaten the fellow, reveal who he was. Then again, in a melee . . . it might not be safe. The man could easily stab Jakka in the ribs when no one was looking.

And he just might, Jakka thought sourly. Since his disgrace, he'd realized how many in the army hated him. Not only for losing the witch, but for losing so many lives in the swamp. Even now, down the line, warriors were mocking him.

"Foolish nomad rat," one said. "Why didn't she flee in the night? She thinks she can win?"

A second warrior laughed. "She believes she's facing Jakka again, that's why. She knows if Jakka lost all those warriors in the swamp, he'll easily lose another thousand here."

"Of course, *he* came out of the swamp all right," snarled the first. "High ones always do."

"Hakka's much better," said the second. "He is like Gog. Quiet, clever. Spends his days on the training grounds, not in the harem tent. We'll be all right."

"I hope to Baal you're right."

Glancing down the line, Jakka memorized the two speakers' faces. They'd pay later. By Baal, they would. Still, it shook him. He'd never imagined people thought of him this way. He even found himself rooting for the witch. *Good hunting, baru. Slaughter these fools today. Show them what I had to deal with.* As for him, he would not underestimate her again.

Sure enough, when he studied the battlefield more closely, he saw two odd features in the Urukite line. His arm hairs prickled.

First, in the center of the army was a small hill of earth. It had steep sides and a flat top. Thirty figures stood on it, as if to see better over the battlefield. Jakka didn't like it. What was the point? Once Magog arrived, they'd easily climb the hill and knock the thirty Urukites off.

The second feature was more understandable. In the earth along the Urukite front, a shallow trench had been dug. Clearly, the witch intended to force Magog to cross the trench to get to her. Yet this was strange, too. The trench might cause Magog some discomfort as they charged across it, going down, then up. But not enough to stop them. Uruk had two hundred and fifty. Magog, one thousand. Jakka licked his lips. Even magic couldn't defeat that difference. What was she up to?

"Make ready," an officer shouted.

The warriors began to limber up, stretching and hopping in place. A pouch of seeds was passed around. Jakka grabbed a handful and chomped anxiously. Combat was exhausting, and the extra burst of energy might make the difference between life and death when it counted. Swallowing, his mouth grew dry, and looking around, he saw that everyone was drinking from water bags, draining them, tossing them aside.

He faced his neighbor. "Ey, gimme some water. I forgot mine."

The Hittite laughed. "Everyone else brought theirs. Why should I suffer for you, eh?"

Jakka's temper flared.

"I'm Prince Jakka, that's why," he snarled. "Gimme it. Or I'll cut your tongue out."

"You're Jakka? Hoho! That's a good one. Well, I agree you must be as stupid as him, if you forgot your bag." The Hittite wiped his eyes in mirth. "But I suppose it's bad for me if you flop from thirst. Go on."

He handed the bag over, and Jakka grabbed it and drank deeply. He was suddenly so afraid, he didn't even feel angry anymore. Not being recognized was awful. Nobody cared how you felt.

Handing it back, he turned and peered through the second line. Magog's rear guard stood in a circle around Father, finalizing the battle strategy. Hakka was there too, basking in Father's every word. Jakka felt like a ghost, watching the scene. No one was even thinking about him.

Then a priest stepped forth, waving a kicking rabbit above his head, and all attention returned to the front.

"Great Baal, Lord of War! Who will win today?" the priest shouted.

Raising a stone knife, he ran the tip down the rabbit's belly, spilling its blue and red intestines on the earth. The army watched in tense silence as the priest studied the messy entrails. "Baal be praised! Magog will be victorious!" the priest shrieked.

A cheer rose from the men, and Jakka rolled his eyes. "Children," he muttered.

"What's wrong with you?" the Hittite asked. "Don't like good news?"

Jakka scoffed. "If he predicted anything else, he'd be skinned alive."

The Hittite seemed to think this was blasphemy and started to lecture Jakka on the finer points of religion, but suddenly a roar burst from the ranks, interrupting him. Gog was marching forward to address the men.

"HAIL! HAIL!" the line roared.

Jakka watched attentively. Father looked more inspiring than any priest. The warlord's scarred face, his broad tattooed shoulders, his cold single eye—every aspect spoke *death*.

For a moment, the eye fixed on Jakka, and his heart flickered with hope. *Father.* But then it looked away as if Jakka didn't exist, and Jakka's heart plunged. To be scorned by common lowlifes like his neighbor was one thing. But by Father?

No, Father doesn't mean it, Jakka thought. He is just busy.

"Brothers." Gog's eye seemed to glow as he spoke to his troops. "Baal has prepared you a great feast. Two hundred weak ones. What say you?"

"HAIL, BAAL," the army roared. "HAIL, GOG!"

"The right of the strong is your birthright!" Gog roared. "That of strong over weak! Baal offers it to you! But you must take it! Will you?"

The army began to jump and scream, shaking their weapons. "HAIL! HAIL!" Automatically, Jakka did the same, yelling so hard, his throat hurt. It felt good to work himself up, scream the fear away. "KILL! TAKE! RAPE!" the thousand roared.

Before the frenzy could diminish, Gog chopped his club at the enemy. "MARCH!"

With a great crunching of gravel, the line began to move.

A moan rose from the Urukite army as Magog started across the waste. It was a terrifying sight. A wall of tattooed flesh advanced, raising a cloud of dust like a demonic fire. A prickling swath of bone weaponry glinted wickedly along its front, coming *here*. Sargon stared. It was one thing to plan for death. Quite another to see it marching toward you, step-by-step.

El, help us, he prayed. *If we have earned your favor, we beg it now. And if some of us must die . . . protect my friends.* He gulped. *And if it must be me . . . help me bear it well.*

"Make ready!" Ki shouted.

In unison, all the Urukites began hugging and kissing, giving final blessings to each other. Sargon did the same. First, he embraced Ut and Aya, perhaps for the last time. Second, he whispered a prayer for Nisaba up on the hilltop, then for Rogg on a secret mission in the desert.

Finally, he turned to Ki.

She looked exhausted. Her hair was askew. Deep hollows darkened her eyes. She had stayed up all night planning the battle, draining her of vitality. But to him, she was still utterly beautiful. With all his heart, he wanted to tell her how he felt. What if he never got another chance? At the same time, he knew he mustn't distract her from the battle, either.

"Ki," he began uncertainly. "I . . ."

She grabbed him and hugged hard. And in that hug, he suddenly knew she felt as he did.

"Ki," he said. "I want you to be my mate."

She pulled back, and for a moment, he feared she was pulling away. But no, her eyes were bright with tears, and she nodded, too overcome with emotion to speak. His heart filled with joy. It felt the most natural thing in the world, then, to pull her in and kiss her. And she kissed him back, wrapping her arms around him, holding him as tightly as she had during the river storm.

Ut and Aya cheered and pounded their backs.

"Finally!" Ut laughed. "Took you long enough."

"Oh, they're so wonderful," Aya cried, wiping her eyes.

Sargon wished he could stay in that moment forever, holding Ki and feeling her heart beat against his. But then Ki grew deadly serious, and she pulled away.

"Sargon, listen. Today, we can't lose."

"I know," he said, puzzled.

"No. I mean, if something happens to me, keep fighting, understand? Gog *must* not win. It would be too terrible to imagine. Do you promise?"

"Ki, I—"

"Promise, Sargon. Choose Uruk over me today. Promise."

Unable to speak, Sargon nodded dumbly. Before he could collect himself, she kissed him again, fiercely, then marched off to her post in front of the army.

His heart ached as he looked after her. Why did this wonderful moment—the best in his life!—have to be so rushed? Rage filled him. Magog! *Thieves!* They couldn't make their own happiness, so they stole everyone else's.

Down the line, Ki raised her fist and began to pace, shouting at her troops.

"Dart-throwers, up. Remember your training."

Hearkening to her cry, the army reassembled and lifted their dart-throwers. A great shout answered her. "Uruk! Uruk!"

Everything was set. Those too weak to fight had paddled across the river to hide. The infirm and the babies were gone, including Shulgi. Only warriors remained.

As the cheers grew louder, Sargon's pulse boomed in his throat. Magog would soon be here. Then his friends, everyone he loved, would start to die.

Jakka's heart thundered as his sandals crackled over the dry desert ground. Ahead, the Urukite position was coming rapidly into focus. He scanned it as well as he could, searching for the witch. He still saw no sign of her. Only a blur of sand-colored skin, black hair shining in the brilliant dawn, red specks of mouths open and shouting. *Baal, where is she?* He had to find her soon or the lines would clash, and in the chaos who knew what might happen?

His Hittite neighbor nudged him. "What's your worry, brother? They'll break and run. Always do."

"I'm calm," Jakka snapped.

The man laughed. "You're about to soil yourself, is how calm you look."

Jakka wanted to strike him. But in truth, he was rather afraid of the big fellow.

"The witch," he tried to explain. "Don't you see? If *Gog* thinks she's powerful—"

"She's witched *you,* sounds like," the man chortled. "You should see yourself."

"Wait, look." Jakka pointed with his spear. "What are they doing?"

Ahead, the Urukites were all bending in unison, grabbing something off the ground . . . a kind of tiny stick. A faint voice shouted a command, and suddenly a flight of the tiny weapons went up into the white globe of sun, vanishing into its glare like a flock of birds. Jakka gawked. What was the witch doing? The armies were well out of throwing range. No human could throw a dart that far. *You're better than this, witch,* he thought furiously.

Why had Uruk just wasted a precious volley? It made Jakka look more stupid for losing her.

Laughter exploded from the warriors.

"Dumb nomad rat. Too easy."

"Marshlings. I tell you, they can fight in a swamp, but not on land. I pity 'em."

"Not me," the Hittite said. "I enjoy an easy slaughter." He bent toward Jakka, smirking. "You were saying? Mighty witch, eh?"

"I . . . she always has a reason," Jakka protested. "Believe me, I . . ."

Then he trailed off, for a spatter of cries shot down the line. "The sky! The sky!" Jakka looked up and gasped. What in Baal's name? The darts were diving out of the sun, right at him. Impossible! Nobody could throw that far. Yet it was happening.

A clattering erupted on the stones. Also, a sickening *chunk-chunk* of wood piercing flesh. Men crashed to the soil, screaming. Others doubled over, grabbing darts protruding from their stomachs and thighs. The front line came to a halt. Jakka was stunned. Everywhere, feathered darts protruded from muscles, and blood streamed down tattooed skin.

"Gods! Gods!" the big Hittite was roaring in shock. "How . . . ?"

"I told you," Jakka shrieked. "It's the *baru*."

"The witch, it's all true, then?" someone asked.

"I'm not doing this," another said. "I won't fight magic."

He turned to run, but suddenly the veterans' line was there. A club descended on the fellow's head. He flopped to the dust, twitching, slain by his own army.

Jakka stared at him stupidly. They just . . . so quickly . . . all for that?

"How could they . . . ?" he croaked.

"Welcome to Magog, first-timer," the Hittite snarled. "Now shut up and keep walking. Don't you know anything? Keep covering my flank."

So Jakka kept on, even as the line commander ran out front, waving his club.

"She's just a nomad. A stupid filthy nomad. Advance! Advance!"

With the pressure of the veteran line behind them, the first line staggered on resentfully, hating the second line with all their hearts. Jakka had no choice but to follow. Now they will sėe, he thought bitterly. By the end of this day, the name of Jakka will be restored.

He hoped he was alive to see it.

As the first volley fell, Sargon bent and grabbed another dart from the pile at his feet.

"Nock," Ki shouted.

Sargon obeyed, his love for her growing with each moment. She stood in front of the army like a character from the legends, demonstrating the proper stance, feet perpendicular to the enemy, torso swiveled at the waist, face toward Magog. Following her lead, the army copied her stance and fitted their darts to their bows. Sargon did, too, using the special wooden cup Ki had designed for him.

"Draw," she shouted.

Stretching the bowstrings, the Urukites pulled their feathered darts back to their cheeks.

"Aim."

Every dart tip pointed at the sky.

"FIRE!"

The gristle strings *twanged*. The darts lofted easily up into the sun-drenched blue. Up, up they went, as if a god's breath was whooshing them higher. Rogg's countless drill sessions had taught the squads to aim not where Magog was, but rather where they would be as their march carried them forward. And it was working. The first volley had hit Magog's ranks with devastating force. Now bodies lay everywhere in the desert, half-obscured among the red clouds of dust, flopping in agony, pulling darts out of bellies, legs.

"Pick up," Ki shouted.

Even as the second volley floated higher, the Urukites bent for their third darts.

"I got a Magog warrior. Me!" Aya said breathlessly, fitting her dart in. "I saw him fall."

"Nock," Ki shouted. "Draw."

Two hundred and fifty bows drew as the second volley fell. Sargon heard more screams, saw more holes open in the Magog line. He couldn't believe the damage. It was working just as Ki had predicted.

"Aim!" Ki yelled.

All obeyed. Confidence rippled through the line. But even so, Sargon knew Magog was approaching fast. Soon it would mean hand-to-hand combat, and that phase would favor Magog.

"FIRE!"

The third volley flew. Sargon released, then lowered his bow and looked nervously into the desert toward Magog's camp. Somewhere out there, Rogg was hiding, waiting to begin the second part of the attack. Sargon whispered a prayer to El for him. Everything might depend on the big Elamite.

In a shallow wash behind Magog's camp, Rogg lay on his chest, eyeing the black tents he'd dreamed of for so long.

He clenched his big fists. It had been torture to sit here all night listening to the poor slaves scream their lives out on the wood pyres. Everything in him had wanted to rush to their aid and bludgeon the brutes inflicting it. Now at last he could act. The two armies were engaged. Rogg's skin was black with fake Magog tattoos. A bag of special weaponry lay at hand. Best of all, Magog's sentries were out of position, backs turned, watching the distant battle. Only a short sprint separated Rogg from the camp.

Taking a breath, Rogg shut his eyes and felt for the spirits of his dead family. How many months he'd waited for this moment. How many nights he'd lain awake, his guts twisting with an anguish his lips could never speak. *My dear mate. My younglings.* He could almost feel their small hands in his, hear their sparkling laughs, see their bright happy faces in the tent in Elam, picking apart roast grouse, laughing, dozing, playing games, crawling over his feet. He smelled his mate's damp hair as she lay beside him in the tent after a bath in the nearby stream. He felt her warm face pressed to his hairy chest, both of them in harmony, not needing to say a word as they listened to the noises of their children on the blankets. It was the family music, something he'd never hear again.

My dear ones. This is for you.

Opening his eyes, he turned and tapped his lone companion on the shoulder. The fellow gave a crooked grin. He was a strong hunter with a square jaw and a hardness in his eyes that told Rogg he'd seen battle, real battle, more than once. Good. He'd need it now.

"Brother, did you really volunteer for this?" Rogg joked. "You're as mad as I am."

"Thanks, General. Greatness and madness go hand in hand, they say."

Rogg liked this fellow. "Last chance to turn back, brother."

"To stop me now, you'd have to kill me."

"Good man."

They uttered a quick prayer to their separate gods, then sprang out of the wash and sprinted across the empty patch of earth. The Magog sentries didn't see a thing. Rogg felt a dark pleasure.

Overconfident again, Magog. Bad fundamentals. It costs you every time.

Darting between the tents, he saw that this was the barracks quadrant. Its residents were off in battle, leaving it empty, vulnerable to attack. Ki's analysis had been correct. Her time here as a prisoner had paid off.

Choosing a tent at random, he ripped aside the entry flap and ducked in. It was quiet and dark inside, stinking of sweat and urine. A few rumpled sleeping mats and personal trinkets lay about. Rogg's hunting instincts surged.

"They roast slaves. Now we roast them," he said. "Watch the lane, brother."

"Gladly." His companion rubbed his nose at the stench. "Fire will do this place good." He peeked out through the door flaps, keeping watch, while Rogg set down the bag.

Opening the bag, Rogg lifted out a ball of reeds painted in sticky bitumen. It was a fireball waiting to happen. Setting it against the hide tent wall, Rogg built a nest around it of anything flammable he could find. Garments, rags, blankets. Finally, the great black egg was ready. Lifting two flint chips, he struck them together over the ball, scattering sparks onto the bitumen. It ignited instantly, shooting red light up the tent panel and filling Rogg's nostrils with the sour smell of burning hide.

"Pretty," his companion said.

"About to get prettier."

In five other tents they repeated the action. Finally, they stepped into the lane and looked up at the rising smoke.

The puffs looked innocent enough, Rogg thought. For now, they appeared like simple discharge from breakfast fires. But soon the smoke would thicken, and orange light would flash skyward, engulfing the whole quadrant. By the time the sentries noticed, it would be too late to quench it. On the battlefield, the army would look back and see its camp aflame. Then Gog would be forced to make a choice. Ignoring it would risk damaging his army's morale. But sending a party back to address it . . . well, that could turn the whole battle.

Rogg's mission was a success.

Now he wanted more. The council had ordered him to flee after this stage of the mission, but he had no intention of doing that.

"You're free to go, brother," he told his companion. "You earned it."

The man didn't like this. "What's your plan?"

Rogg looked around. Hundreds of slaves were lodged in the adjacent quadrant. If he could inspire a revolt, it might make an even bigger difference than the fire.

His companion laughed when Rogg told him. "Sounds fun, brother. I want in."

"We probably won't survive," Rogg said. "I've got a family to avenge. But you—"

"I've a debt, too," the fellow interrupted. "I owe Sargon my life."

"How?"

"It's me, Togg. From the trial. Remember?"

Memory sparked. Togg! The man falsely accused at Uruk's first trial.

Togg's voice hardened. "Sargon saved me, brother. For him, for Uruk—I'm with you."

Rogg was moved. He punched Togg lightly in the chest. "Well spoken, brother. For Uruk."

They ran on. Rogg's senses grew sharper as they neared the slave quadrant. Here it was far more dangerous. Magog warriors would be in this area, guarding the slaves.

Sure enough, as they neared the end of the lane, voices stopped them. Rogg motioned for Togg to wait in the path. Then he strode forward and peeked around a tent—and found himself face-to-face with a young Magog warrior.

Cold fear prickled over his body. The youth was not alone. Three more fellows sat around a cookfire, gnawing racks of meat. Beyond, slaves huddled underneath a canopy, thirty or so. Just who Rogg wanted to recruit! They didn't look like fighters, though. Their feet were bound with grass rope, and their faces were subdued, skeletal. The guards, in contrast, ate merrily, laughing and spitting into the ash-filled pit. All except the young fellow, who kept looking at Rogg, his face blank.

Rogg looked back, confused. Why didn't the lad shout the alarm? For a moment, neither man moved. Then, suddenly, Rogg remembered. He was covered in fake tattoos! He looked like a Magog warrior.

Thinking fast, he pointed at the sky above camp where the smoke was beginning to thicken. "Look, brothers, fire," he said. "Stop slacking and help, will you?"

The men burst into shouts of surprise.

"Who started it?" one asked. "Slaves?"

"I bet it was those new Mitanni recruits," another said. "Never seen men more careless."

"What's your name and squad, soldier?" a third barked at Rogg. "We won't be held accountable for that damage."

"Just shut up and come," Rogg said. "It's getting out of control."

He ran back up the path, ignoring their cries for him to stay. Togg was waiting. He handed Rogg his dart-thrower, and they knelt and aimed darts back down the lane. A moment later, all four Magog warriors burst around the corner into an ugly surprise. *Twang. Twang.* Two fell, darts in their chests. The others turned, yelling the alarm. *Twang. Twang.* They also fell, darts in their backs. Pulling out their stone knives, the two Urukites raced forward and finished the task.

"Fine shooting," Rogg said, wiping his stone knife clean in the dirt.

"Hard to miss at that range," Togg said. "Get us a real challenge next time, eh?"

"Will do." Grabbing one corpse by the feet, Rogg began to drag it backward. "Now let's show off your work."

Pulling the body around the corner, he dropped it beside the fire and faced the slaves. Thirty miserable faces stared at the body from under the tarp. Rogg's stomach turned. This was ugliness. The slaves' eyes were hollow and staring, shattered by suffering. One woman made a guttural noise of puzzlement, her tongue cut out. Another man flinched away, as if expecting to be struck. They were terrified of him, of course. He was still wearing his Magog disguise.

Spitting on his palm, he smeared his face clean. "See? I'm one of you." He held up his palm, revealing the smeared dye. "I'm an Elamite. A friend."

No one moved. This would be harder than he'd thought.

"Listen," he said. "There's a battle out there. A big one. All Gog's army is engaged. Help me burn these tents and tip the balance. Take back a piece of what they took from you, eh?" He looked from face to face. "Come, brothers and sisters, the camp is almost empty. Let's free it and break Gog's spine forever!"

Silence. The slaves wouldn't even look at him. Their eyes flicked away, watching the approaching lanes for more Magog warriors, expecting more punishment, more pain. Bile filled Rogg's mouth. How many catastrophes had these poor people endured? Were they too ruined to help? *No*. He didn't believe that.

"Friends," he urged, "you've suffered. You're not ready, I know it. But the gods are giving you a chance *today*. One chance." He kicked the dead body. "Look at him. We *can* win. But you must remember who you are."

No answer. Rogg clenched his teeth, searching for the right words—never his strong point. *Family, help me. Gods, help.* His mind churned. Nearby, angry shouts were rising. Fresh footsteps thudded his way. He glanced at Togg, who had gone pale, another dart nocked in his bow. Magog was coming.

On the battlefield, more darts zipped down. Jakka couldn't understand what was happening. Men were shrieking in pain, staggering, falling, dying. His Hittite neighbor was down, too. Jakka knew that anytime, a random dart might hit him. He was terrified. Yet he also felt a dark satisfaction. No one could mock him anymore for losing the witch. She'd organized her attack brilliantly, positioning her line in the east to take advantage of the rising sun, which blinded Magog to the falling darts and prevented dodging. A friendly breeze also increased the darts' range, expanding the kill zone. How many warriors had she hit so far? A hundred? Two hundred? All before Magog could land a single blow. If he captured the *baru* now, Father would surely forgive him.

Jakka checked the enemy line. This time he saw her. She stood in the center of Uruk's formation, slightly ahead of everyone, shouting orders at her troops. He might grab her! But he was out of position. He needed to be in the center.

"Double your pace, front line," the commander shouted. "Almost there. Let's hit them hard!"

The first line broke into a jog, leaving the veterans behind. Jakka took his chance. The veterans were too far back to club him now, so he slowed a little, giving himself room. Then he sprinted diagonally across the battlefield, running behind the first line toward an open spot closer to the witch's position. Darts sliced through the first line and past his ear as he sped behind the shield of running bodies. Then he was there, slowing to fill his new slot, the witch straight ahead. He nodded to the men on either side of him, then focused on the Urukites, his blood racing. *Did you see that, Hakka? Are you impressed? Afraid?*

"Spears up," the line commander roared.

Jakka's breaths grew ragged. They were just forty paces from the enemy line. Thirty . . .

He lifted his spear, arm shaking.

"Take aim," the commander screamed. "MAKE THEM PAY!"

Twenty paces!

"THROW!"

The first line gave a roar and launched their spears. Finally, after so many unanswered injuries, they could strike back! Jakka willed the dark storm of wood into his enemies' flesh. He'd seen the spear-volley before. It always hit with devastating force, obliterating resistance. But now something else happened—something so unexpected, Jakka nearly stopped running.

As the spears flew, each Urukite stooped and grabbed a new thing off the ground. A strange round thing. A sort of *shell.* As the Magog spears arrived, the shells lifted, covering the Urukites' bodies in an unbroken wall, and—*Crack. Crack. Crack.*—the shells flicked the spears harmlessly away. Jakka's gut twisted. The *baru!* How much magic did she have?

Then the trench appeared. In the panic, everyone had forgotten it.

Magog's front line skidded to a halt and looked down. The trench wasn't much of a defense: just half-a-man deep, and four man-lengths across. Easy. The only trick was, along the bottom, a barrier of reed stakes prickled like teeth, impeding the crossing.

"A few sticks is nothing," the line commander roared. "We have them now! Cross, cross!"

The first line was ragged, but it obeyed. The men scrambled down into the trench and began picking their way over the sharp stakes. The darts continued to spit into their ranks. But as the men made it over and ran up the far slope, they roared with excitement. They had arrived! Hand-to-hand combat, Magog's specialty, was here at last. Now the tide would turn.

Jakka, however, was still wriggling between two stakes when he heard the witch shout, "Now!" And looking up, he saw the shell wall suddenly charge down into the trench. He was shocked. No one had expected the weaklings to actually *charge*.

He managed to free himself just as the prickling wall arrived. A shell swung toward his face, giving him no time to lift his weapon and defend himself. *BAM!* The shell hit his nose with the force of a hammer. He fell back into the dirt, narrowly missing a spike. For a moment he lay stunned, blood running down his mustache into his teeth. His head was buzzing. His teeth ached. His eyes wobbled. His club was lost somewhere, leaving him defenseless.

I hate the first line, he thought. By the gods, I hate it.

Yet there was no time to reflect. The shells were upon him. Spears darted out and retreated, then darted out again in a killing frenzy. Feet mashed the earth. Blood sprayed the air. Terrible sounds filled Jakka's head, sounds of fleshy grappling and wet bloody stabbing, *cracks* of stone on bone, and howls of strong men begging for mercy. Some warriors managed to rise and fling themselves against the formation, but their clubs clattered uselessly off the surfaces of the shells, while again and again Uruk's spear tips darted out to stab, drawing life-juice. This was bad, Jakka realized. It was a slaughter.

A spear came at him. He squirmed aside, and the spear missed narrowly, striking the ground and spraying dirt over him. Above the shell, a pair of hard eyes, red with battle fury, fixed on Jakka's gut. The spear drew back for a second strike. Jakka, still on the ground, realized with ice-cold clarity that he would be hit. But then a roar exploded across the battlefield, sending chills down his neck, and above him, Father appeared, swinging his club like an emissary of Baal.

"To me! To me!" the warlord roared. "Break them!"

BLAM! Father's mighty war club slammed the shell above Jakka, knocking the attacker back. *BLAM!* Another attacker went flying up out of the trench, sailing as easily as if he was a child.

Jakka's hopes surged. The line of veterans had arrived!

"Up, boy!" Father roared. "Find her!"

Without waiting, the warlord charged onto the flat earth at the base of the hill. He swung his spiked club in a blur. No Urukite could stand against him. His club smashed shells left and right, sending bodies soaring. In that moment, Jakka loved his father. It was plain why so many hundreds followed him.

But the surge was not to last.

Somewhere, an Urukite shouted: "Withdraw! Protect the hill!"

In unison, the shattered Urukite line reformed into pods and retreated up out of the trench, back to the hill's base. Jakka was astonished at their self-command under pressure. They moved in good order, shells up, spears out, leaving no flank exposed. The *baru* must have drilled them well, for in no time they reformed neatly into a perfectly intact shell line around the hill base. Fatigue hit Jakka like a stone. Magog would never break that wall.

But maybe they wouldn't have to. The *baru* was there!

She knelt at the edge of the trench, just a hand's reach away. She was lifting an injured companion up onto her back. Her face was mud-streaked, hardly recognizable. But Jakka had seen her so often in his dreams, he'd have known her anywhere.

Fire swept back into his blood. Jumping from the trench, he grabbed the *baru's* ankle and yanked. She was so light. He got her off balance and dragged her down into the trench. She tried to wriggle free, but she was so small, it was easy to punch her in the temple with his fist. She went limp. She was his!

"Back!" Father shouted, covering Jakka's retreat. "With me! With me!"

Swinging his club, he created a space for Jakka to lift the senseless witch over the barrier of spikes and then stagger with her up the other side. There on the trench lip, Jakka threw her on the flat ground, and fell back, panting, as Father bent over her.

"Is it her?"

"It is, Father."

The warlord studied her intently for a moment, his scarred face dripping sweat. Then he grunted and nodded and looked around for his retinue. They ran up promptly, eyes tight with fear.

"Cowards!" Father shouted. "Where was my support? I broke them, they were falling back."

In reply, Nod, Hakka, and several high-ranking generals pointed at the veterans' line. Indeed, many had stopped at the edge of the trench, choosing to throw spears across it rather than advance. Their weapons hit the Urukite shell wall and clattered off. Things had stalled. And stalling meant failure for, from the hilltop, Uruk's thirty dart-throwers kept firing darts into Magog's ranks, picking men off. Meanwhile, down in the trench, the first line lay slaughtered, their bodies draped across spikes, their guts and blood everywhere. Magog's sub-commanders kept shouting, "Forward! Forward!" But the veterans on the trench lip just hovered there, hesitating. They didn't consider themselves expendable enough to risk it.

"They fear to go in, Lord," Nod said. "We've lost a third of our men."

"We still have six hundred," Father said. "Uruk only has two hundred and fifty, remember? We just need to break their shell wall. Once we do, Uruk is finished."

"How do we break it?"

"I will."

Father seized Nod's shoulder. "You distract them with a feint on their flank, draw their fire. Once their focus is on you, I will attack their other flank. I'll smash a wedge through the wall, climb the hill, and sweep the dart-throwers off like grasshoppers. Then I'll leap down from above and break the line's formation from behind. The instant I do, you lead an all-out charge from the front, Nod. We will massacre them from two sides."

"Outstanding, Lord."

"This is a battle for the world, Nod. The whole world! The stuff of legends!"

Father did not look shaken, Jakka thought in awe. Rather, he looked more alive than ever. His enthusiasm was infectious, and the generals all began roaring and beating their chests.

"Yes, Lord! Yes!"

"Hakka, you stay close to me." Father grabbed his son and shook him. "Time to build your name."

Jakka lost his breath. Why wasn't Father paying attention to him? He'd captured the witch. Why wasn't *he* invited to stay close?

Panicking, he blurted across the dirt: "Father!"

The group looked at him with contempt. Jakka withered.

"Father, I . . . I want to help, too."

"I've no time to save you again, boy." Father's voice dripped with scorn. "Stay here. Guard the girl. Surely you can do that."

He marched off, taking his retinue with him. Jakka looked after him, stunned. What was happening? He'd done it! Captured her! She lay like a dead thing under his hands, blood oozing from her eyebrow where his knuckles had cut her skin. The great *baru* of their time. But it didn't matter. *Guard the girl.* As if Jakka was good for nothing else.

Jakka began to shake. Nothing had changed. Father still favored Hakka.

At the base of the hill, Sargon lay prostrate, aching. Gog's club had thrown him hard. His turtle shell was shattered. His head was buzzing. Somehow, he rose weakly to his feet and looked for Ki.

He saw her across the trench, unmoving. Jakka knelt over her like a dog guarding a kill. Sargon's heart ripped out of his chest. *NO.* Magog's entire army surrounded her, shaking their spears like a wall of teeth. *Ki.* He had to get her back. But how?

His mind scrambled, frustrated at every turn. If he ran to her alone, it was certain death. If he ordered a full charge, the Urukites would cede the advantage of their defensive position and lose the battle. What, then?

Promise me, Sargon. Whatever happens, choose Uruk over me. Gog must not win.

Ki's words echoed in his head like a prophecy. Sargon shut his eyes. *I'm sorry, Ki. I can't lose you. I have to try.* Maybe he could lead a small charge, ten people strong, to grab her from Jakka and retreat. Could Uruk risk that?

But wait.

Something new was developing across the trench. On the flank, Magog's forces were massing. Troops rushed to Nod, shouting, stamping their feet, making a great noise. In response, Urukite troops were rushing to bolster that side. And atop the hump, Nisaba was focusing her archer fire there, slaying many tattooed men. But something confused Sargon. If that was the main assault, why wasn't Gog there?

He scanned Magog's line. On the opposite flank, a group of forty or so warriors stood around Gog, listening intently as he yelled and made another speech. What was more, Jakka himself was looking at his father instead of at Nod's flank, almost as if . . . as if Nod was a distraction!

In a flash, Sargon understood. Gog was the real push. The warlord would form a wedge, drive through Uruk's flank, mount the hill, then hit the confused Urukite line from above and behind, while Nod hit them from the front. If it worked, it could shatter Uruk.

But if it failed . . .

Sargon felt a jolt of excitement. We could win! I could let him through. Trap Gog up there. Kill him. End the battle.

But to do so, he'd have to abandon Ki. There wasn't time for both. A terrible choice faced him. Ki? Or Uruk?

Oh, Ki! What do I do?

◆

Jakka watched the final maneuver in a state of anguish. The battle was about to be decided, yet he had not redeemed himself. He needed one more chance.

How? Where?

Magog's false attack began. "Charge!" Nod screamed on the left flank. On cue, his men began to scream and hurl spears over the trench. Some even made short rushing feints into it, drawing bursts of Urukite darts. But on the right flank, Father's troops were gathering, getting ready for the real push.

But what was this? Trouble! Across the trench from Father stood the crippled Akkadian Jakka had seen in Babylon. The cripple stood under the hill whispering to a clustered group of Urukites. He was pointing at Father with his stump-arm. And suddenly Jakka saw the whole thing. The runt had anticipated Father's charge. He was setting a trap! Father, who had never met the cripple, didn't realize the runt was a leader and a threat. Only Jakka caught it.

I'll warn him, Jakka thought eagerly. Father will reward me, and—

He stopped. *Would* Father reward him? Father might not care at all. Jakka had brought him the witch, yet Father still favored Hakka.

A curious idea entered Jakka's head. What if both Father and Hakka died in the trap? Who would inherit Magog? *Jakka*. That's who.

Jakka's fingers tightened into a fist. Father's scornful words came back to him. *Guard the girl.* As if Jakka was good for nothing more.

Well, Father. If that's all I'm good for, that's all I'll do.

Jakka sat and watched.

Sargon gripped his spear and braced himself. "Here they come. Make ready."

Ut punched his arm. "Good fighting with you, brother."

Sargon nodded. "Let's finish this."

Across the trench, a roar burst out. "CHARGE!"

So it began. Magog ran into the trench. Everyone braced for impact as the wedge of tattooed bodies flowed over the spikes and up toward the shell wall. But as Gog arrived, swinging his club, Sargon screamed, "Part!" And Rogg's training paid off again. In unison, the shells opened, allowing Gog through and up onto the hill slope, ahead of his warriors. "Close!" Sargon yelled. The parted shells swung back together like jaws and bit hard into the throat of the enemy, blocking most of the others. Spears and shells struck Magog's wedge from both sides. Their momentum was mangled. The plan was working. Only two warriors followed Gog up the hill.

"Hold them! Push them back!" Sargon roared. "Ut, with me!"

The slope was steep, but climbable. Sargon scrambled up it on all fours after Gog. Then he was on the hilltop in the high fresh air, smelling the desert breeze.

Three tattooed figures stood before him. Gog's tattooed figure stood in the center, swinging his club at Nisaba's thirty dart-throwers. "TO ME! TO ME!" he roared, driving them back. Nisaba and her archers gave ground strategically, keeping the men at bay with their spears. But the hill's drop-off was behind them, and they couldn't back up much farther. Moreover, the fight was so close, they couldn't get off clean shots with their bows. Sargon had to act fast.

He ran forward, spear leveled. Rogg's voice echoed in his head, memorized from days of training. "Strike low and to the right of the spine, at the kidney area. It causes excruciating pain." Yet Gog looked too terrifying to hit, even from the rear. His great back rippled with muscle as he swung his club, tattoos of hideous images swirling across it like living demons. Sargon would have hesitated, if the love of Ki had not filled him. But it did, and he rammed his spear deep into Gog's kidney, just as Rogg had drilled.

"FOR KI!" he cried.

The spear hit true, puncturing the soft area and plunging deep. The warlord let out a scream that almost broke Sargon's ears. But instead of falling, Gog whirled around and ripped the spear out of himself, glaring at the bloody tip with his one eye. Then he cast the weapon aside as if it hadn't slowed him at all, and came at Sargon, who was empty-handed now, only his stump raised in defense. Gog lifted his club.

"DIE, CRIPPLE!"

The club swung down, straight at Sargon's head. Sargon shut his eyes. It was over.

But somehow, the club did not land. Instead, a shadow passed across Sargon's face, and a great *crunch* sounded in his ears. A body fell against him, knocking him onto his back. When Sargon opened his eyes, he found Ut lying across him, protecting them both under his turtle shell. Gog's great club smashed down again and again. *CRACK! CRACK!* With each blow, Ut gave a cry of pain, and the shock waves ripped through both their bodies, driving their bones into the earth.

Then the blows stopped. They were alive! How?

Sargon looked past Ut. Nisaba! She and her team of thirty dart-throwers were now pressing toward Gog, jabbing at him, drawing his focus.

Sargon grasped Ut's body. "Brother," he croaked. "You saved me."

Ut was too bruised, too stunned to move. "Get him, Sargon," he whispered.

So Sargon tried again.

Exhausted, bones buzzing from the blows, numb, hardly thinking, he crawled out from under Ut and grabbed a spear lying in the dirt. Gog's back was to him again. Two fresh darts protruded from the warlord's torso, but they seemed not to affect him. The loss of his two warriors, slain beside him, made no difference either. Nisaba's dart team was falling back before his club. Once more, Sargon took his chance. He plunged his spear tip into the already open, red-gushing wound at the kidney. And this time Gog went down.

The great warlord fell to his knees with a choking gasp, dropped his club, and reached around with both hands to press the spot, as if to keep the lifeblood from pouring out. But Sargon did not stop. He struck again and again. For Ki! For his companions! For Uruk!

Gog crashed onto his face.

"Sargon! You got him!" Nisaba cried.

It wasn't over. Even as Gog thrashed on the ground, Sargon realized what he had to do. Crawling forward, he yanked a stone knife from his loincloth belt and straddled the shuddering body. He pushed the long black hair aside with his stump and began to hack at the thick neck with the knife. One after another, the small bones in Gog's muscular neck were severed. Finally, the head was free. The round bearded object rolled away, eyeball staring, grotesque, terrible. Sargon scrambled after it. He grabbed the blood-soaked head, and stood, hugging it to his chest. Everyone on the hilltop stared.

"Someone give me a spear."

Nisaba nodded with understanding. "Do it, Sargon."

She gave him a spear, and he stabbed the tip into the neck hole, then hoisted the trophy high, waving it back and forth over the battlefield. He lifted his voice for all to hear.

"GOG IS DEAD! GOG IS DEAD!"

Across the trench, Jakka stared at the hill, awestruck. Father's charge had been totally repelled. The unit had retreated, leaving many dead in the trench—including Hakka, who lay impaled on the yellow stakes, blood bubbling from his lips, his arms flopping feebly.

Meanwhile, above the hill, rising like a bloody black sun . . . was Father's bearded face.

Jakka couldn't believe it. As the head waved back and forth—soaked in mud and red gore, its single eye devoid of life—Jakka felt gutted. He had wished this. And yet now . . . now . . .

What have I done?

"Gog is dead! Gog is dead!" the cripple shouted, waving the head like a flag.

A hush gripped the battlefield. Fighting stopped. The groans of the injured filled the void. Suddenly cries of shock and despair exploded from the Magog warriors. The Urukites, in contrast, gave a roar of euphoria that burst over the trench, echoing the cripple's cry.

"GOG IS DEAD! GOG IS DEAD!"

All Magog shrank back from the trench. Their faces were horrified. They looked as if they'd just witnessed the death of a god. Warriors began to moan, covering their faces. For the first time, the word *retreat* entered Jakka's mind.

Yet his ambition still lived, and now it whispered: *This is your time. Seize it.* And in a burst of fantasy, Jakka imagined leading a final charge up the hill. Retrieving the head. Winning fame forever.

Gathering his courage, he rose above the fallen witch. Burying the hollow ache he felt at losing Father, he cupped his mouth and yelled hoarsely: "Avenge him, Magog! He was my father, but he was yours, too. Fight, brothers! The man who slays the cripple wins any favor he asks."

For a moment, many Magog warriors looked between him and the hill as if considering a fresh charge. But before they could rally, another surprise came. Back in the desert, a ram's horn blew. Louder and louder it sounded, drawing every ear. The camp!

Jakka turned. There in the desert was a sight even more horrifying than Gog's head.

Smoke filled the sky, billowing up from the black Magog tents. Yellow flames danced in the pathways. Far worse, a horde of slaves streamed toward the battlefield, waving Magog's own weapons at them, hollering savagely from tongueless mouths. They looked like a horde of beasts released from the Underworld. Leading the charge was the giant Elamite, his long hair flapping, a stone battle-ax whirling above his head.

Jakka paled. How could this be? Magog's full army had never been defeated. Never even challenged. But this was one surprise too many. Dread filled the tattooed faces, groans burst from their lips. One man croaked: "It is ended." Then, as if his words had broken a spell, the horde fled.

“Wait,” Jakka shrieked. “They’re just slaves! Marshlings! Nomad rats! We are Magog! I have the *baru*!”

No one listened. The battlefield was emptying, leaving Jakka alone beside the trench. Turning, he found more darts flying at him from the hilltop. Fresh terror filled him. He had no intention of ending up like Father or Hakka. With a curse, he stooped, grabbed the witch, threw her over his shoulder, and ran after his fellows, the girl’s face flopping limply against his spine.

“Come back!” he screamed at his men’s retreating backs. “We can still do this!”

No one listened. More darts hummed by like bees.

Jakka gritted his teeth and *ran*.

41

Numb, Sargon lowered the spear and let Gog's head slip off the spike. It rolled away over the hilltop, leaking blood. Someone grabbed it and threw it into the air, and it landed amidst the mob below, where they began to kick it around like a melon, screaming, "Sargon! Sargon! Gog-slayer!" Others banged spears on their shells, shouting: "Uruk! Uruk!"

Sargon suddenly grew so faint, he collapsed on all fours on the hilltop, shaking. He felt flattened with weariness, as if a mountain had fallen on him and crushed him. Ut crawled toward him, embraced him. Nisaba knelt and did the same. Holding them tightly—all of them weeping with relief—he looked off at the tattooed backs of the Magog warriors retreating in the distance. They were moving so fast up the riverbank, they had already shrunk to specks. The battlefield was empty, leaving many wounded and dead. But something was missing . . . he struggled to remember . . .

Ki.

He glanced swiftly at the place beside the trench where he'd seen her before. She was not there. Heart sinking, he looked at the fleeing horde again. And there he saw her, bouncing on Jakka's shoulder, nearly out of sight.

"Ki," he gasped, reaching for her in the distance.

"Sargon, are you all right?" Ut cried. "You killed him. It's over, why're you crying? Are you hurt?"

He leapt to his feet. "Ki."

Nisaba and Ut both turned gray.

"Dead?" Nisaba stood and clutched both his shoulders.

"Jakka." He pointed at the warriors, hardly able to speak. "He . . . he took her."

"Alive?" Nisaba demanded.

Sargon nodded, a scream rising in his heart. He struggled with it, sensing dimly that he must keep sturdy for the troops below.

Nisaba shook him, hard. "She's alive, Sargon. We must praise the gods for it. And find Rogg."

"Rogg . . . yes," Sargon croaked, grasping at hope. The Elamite would know what to do.

They staggered down the hill, heading for the desert. It was not easy. Hands reached out to touch him. People chanted: "Gog-slayer! Sargon for *lugal!*" Then Aya appeared, and Sargon felt a burst of relief through his despair. He hugged her tightly.

"You're alive," she wept. "And look, Shulgi's home is saved." She shook him. "We did it. Uruk will live. All Mesopotamia will know it. And in Akkad, they will hear of 'Sargon,' but never know it is 'Ta.'" She laughed at the sky. "Poor, ignorant Akkad."

Sargon pulled back. Aya's face was shining with joy and triumph. Ah, if only he could feel the same! He would not tell her of Ki, yet. That could come later . . . once Rogg made a plan.

"Remember what Rogg said," he urged. "The faster we treat people, the more we save. Quickly, Aya."

"Of course. We'll rally the healer teams," Aya said. "We'll get them working nonstop. Ut, follow me."

They rushed off, crying back: "You did it, Sargon. Uruk will live!"

Wiping tears from his eyes, Sargon pressed on toward the trench. Rogg. He could fix this.

But Sargon had to reach him first. People kept running up to cheer him, blocking the way. And in the trench, the sight of so many Urukite dead and wounded made Sargon hesitate. People were kneeling, weeping beside corpses twisted in awkward positions among the stakes. Some were so streaked with gore and mud that he hardly recognized them. Everyone begged for water. Magog survivors, too, were desperately trying to crawl away. Urukites ran after them, stabbing them with spears.

"Horrible." Sargon grabbed Nisaba's shoulder. "What are we doing?"

Down in the trench, an Urukite woman screamed and stabbed a Magog man in the back. The man writhed and cried out in despair as she stabbed him again and again . . . Sargon felt revulsion. This was murder. Awful as they were, under the tattoos they were not just Magog warriors, but captured slaves twisted by Gog until they no longer knew themselves. Tortured Hittites, Canaanites, Assyrians, even Akkadians. Sargon felt a soft clear urging. El does not wish this, he thought. Baal does. Baal, the evil god at Babylon who'd whispered: *Power*. Sargon knew he must always reject that voice.

"Stop them, Nisaba."

Nisaba shrugged. "Better they die quick than a slow lingering pain."

"We can tend them."

"Tend the enemy?" Nisaba was astounded. "Why?"

Rule one. Do what you admire.

"Uruk should be merciful," he said, already moving on in his mind. "Do it, Nisaba."

Nisaba looked at him strangely. "Very well, Gog-slayer. I'll try." And she ran off to whisper a few words to the nearby chiefs.

Sargon pressed on. He had to get to Rogg as fast as possible and begin the chase for Ki. Again he was delayed, however. A hand reached out and grabbed his stump, halting him. A face glistening with tears confronted him. "Gog-slayer, my son is dying. Give him your blessing." He could not deny her. She knelt over a boy no older than fourteen. He lay cut open, disemboweled, ropes of squishy blue guts hanging out of him like worms. The mother was trying to put the worms back in, but it was hopeless. The boy's face paled more each moment. "My son, my son," she whispered. "Don't go yet. The Gog-slayer is here. He'll get the *baru*. She'll fix you."

Kneeling, Sargon grabbed the slick hand, hot with blood, and leaned close. The boy's sacrifice felt beyond words. He could not leave without honoring him, somehow.

"We did it, little brother."

The boy was quivering, head to foot. Froth flecked his lips. It was a wonder he was not screaming in agony, as others were, nearby. Perhaps he was numb, his life so nearly out.

"Is it true?" the boy asked. "You killed Gog?"

"We all did. Together."

"Uruk is safe for my mother?"

Sargon squeezed his hand tighter. "It is."

"Then I'm happy," the boy said. "I can face the next life with a strong *emittu* and a clear heart, like Rogg says."

Then his face twisted, and something slipped out of his eyes. He was gone.

"My son!" the mother cried.

Sargon hugged her. But he knew nothing could touch her pain. So he gave his best effort, then rose and moved on into the desert, wiping his face. War is horrible, even for the victors, he thought. May whoever brings it to this world be cursed.

Ahead was Magog's camp, engulfed in flames. He hurried toward it, passing many tattooed bodies lying in the dirt, stuck with darts. Some were still alive and tried to crawl away, but Sargon ignored them, and soon he arrived at the camp perimeter, where slaves were dragging supplies out of the burn to salvage. Nisaba caught up to him.

"Did you find Rogg?" she asked.

A bellow of joy answered her. From the curtain of black smoke, Rogg marched forth, cheekbones smudged with ash. Seizing Sargon, he crushed him in a hug.

"Brother, I heard them calling you 'Gog-slayer.' Is it true?"

Sargon nodded, and the giant kissed his forehead, tears in his eyes.

"My family is avenged. Ah, brother, what this means—I cannot tell you. But what's this?" He pulled back, his eyes suddenly worried. "Quick, I see it in your face. Who did we lose? Don't spare me."

"Ki."

Rogg staggered back, clutching his chest. "No."

"She's alive," Sargon added quickly. "Jakka has her."

Rogg smashed him in another hug. "Then Ki is alive, brother. Alive! And I tell you, she is rejoicing in her heart that Uruk is born. It is as she wished."

"Can we get her back?"

"Let me think."

Rogg turned and studied the fleeing horde. On the bank, Magog was now just a cloud of dust.

For what seemed like an eternity, Rogg studied the cloud, scratching his black beard. Then he dropped his hand. "Alas, it's not so simple."

"No?" Blackness filled Sargon's eyes.

"A chase could turn victory into defeat." Rogg pointed at the horde. "There are six hundred warriors out there. And cornered men fight twice as hard. We're in no shape for that. What's more, we must prepare tonight's defenses." He looked toward the main river. "Neighbors love to strike when a tribe is weak, such as after a battle."

Each word crushed Sargon's chest, but he knew Rogg spoke the truth. "So she is lost?"

"Never. Our odds are good. Magog is broken. They have no camp, no food, they are in hostile territory. Their tattooed skin makes them targets for all the world, unable to hide. All Mesopotamia hates them." Rogg clapped him on the back. "With Gog dead, many will rally to us, eager for revenge. In the coming days, we'll gather a force and hunt them down. I swear it, brother."

"And Ki?"

It was Nisaba's turn to comfort him. "Don't underestimate her, Sargon. She knows Jakka needs a Thinker. He'll try to use her to get his power back, and she'll string him along like she did before."

Sargon nodded weakly, too faint to speak.

Rogg put his heavy bloodstained arm over Sargon's shoulder. "In the meantime, come and meet our new family." He guided him toward the smoking camp. "Brothers and sisters! Meet the Gog-slayer."

A horde of skeletal bodies poured out and surrounded them. The ex-slaves were tongueless, burned, pierced with sharp bones through their noses, ears, and lips. Brands scarred their chests to mark who they belonged to. They smelled awful, too, Sargon thought, and an instinctual revulsion filled him. Still, the ash-streaked faces were raw with yearning—even tears of hope. It struck him profoundly. With a great murmuring, they all came forward to touch him. Several even knelt and bowed. Sargon felt moved to tears himself.

He quickly pulled the nearest kneeling slave to his feet. "No, brother, no. Everyone here is family. No masters."

The slave looked at Rogg, confused. Rogg patted him manfully.

"Worry not, brother. The Gog-slayer is not rejecting your service. He only means you are free, welcome to live in Uruk as long as you like, as brothers. You won this victory, too. Uruk is yours as much as ours. And soon we shall feast on bread." He gestured at the wheat growing on the riverbank. "BREAD! For Uruk!"

A great roaring rose. "AAAAAAH! AAAAAH!" Not words, for their tongues were cut out, but an open-throated howl so filled with emotion that even Rogg seemed shaken.

"Gog couldn't break them," he said quietly. "He certainly tried."

He raised his voice again. "Now, brothers and sisters. Before we rest, let us work. Grab all the supplies you can before the camp burns. Then join us at Uruk for the celebration feast."

The ex-slaves gave another shout, then returned to looting. Great heaps of weapons were piled up for Uruk's future defense.

Unburned tents were torn down and rolled up for safekeeping. There were many riches, too. Sargon saw hyena pelts, tools, clay pots, jewelry, lapis lazuli, and other precious stones, as well as rolled-up maps of faraway lands. Everything Magog had stolen from Mesopotamia over the years was now Uruk's.

"Best of all," Nisaba told Sargon, "we have several hundred recruits here. Do you realize what that means? We've tripled our numbers. Uruk, not Magog or Babylon, is now the mightiest tribe in the world."

But Sargon was still struggling. He wiped blood from his beard and faced Rogg again.

"There's a thing I can't understand," he said quietly. "Just now, I watched a boy die in the trench." He hesitated. "If brave ones like him cannot enjoy what we've won . . . what does it mean?"

"I don't know, brother. But I know this," Rogg said. "We must live good lives, even great ones, to honor him."

"Then we will," Sargon said fiercely. "We will begin right now."

And rubbing his face, he turned and strode back toward Uruk, his friends close behind.

42

That night, Ki lay in a small village on the Euphrates in the dirt. She was bound hand and foot, unable to move. Hot flames snapped by her face. The yellow moon shone down pitilessly, illuminating the pathways between the reed huts. The paths were dotted with the corpses of the slain inhabitants. All around her, Magog warriors chomped meat and gnawed bones. They were eating the village children, the tenderest flesh, an emergency measure to replace the meat rations lost at Uruk. Their voices were tense with fear, and Ki kept silent. The slightest twitch might cause the warriors to lose their tempers and start eating her, too.

Nearby, a warrior spat a finger-bone into the fire. It landed with a wet hiss. His eyes glittered on her. "They'll come for us now, I expect. They'll be wanting their witch back."

"I say we club her and be done with it," another growled. "We've had a lot of trouble for this *baru*."

The first looked skeptical. "What if the giant comes? You see that big ax he swung? We're better off keeping her alive to barter with, if things get tight."

"I'd rather we split up. They can't track us all."

"The world hates us, fool," the first snapped. "We'll be picked off one by one."

The second lifted his face slowly and looked back with dead eyes. "Careful, brother. You speak proper to me. I don't like to be called 'fool.'"

The first met his eyes coldly. "I'll speak how I like. *Fool.*"

Roars burst up. A stone knife flashed. The two men rolled in the dirt. The first warrior gurgled and died.

Nod ran over, his face mottled with rage. "What's this? One more dead?"

The group sat sullenly, refusing eye contact.

"It's the third death tonight! You do Uruk's work for them!"

The men said nothing. They'd lost faith in their leaders. Their emotions were in charge. It might mean death for Ki, but she was glad. They'd be easier to hunt and kill like this, and Rogg would do it well.

She shut her eyes and thought of Sargon. He'd won. That was all that mattered. Of course, she ached to be with him and her friends. But another part of her felt this was inevitable. Uruk was safe. Gog was dead. Her debt had been paid. Now she could join her tribe in the Underworld.

Mother, Father, Asha, Esarhaddon, she prayed silently. *I hope you're proud of me. I'll see you soon.*

Around midnight, she woke to a strange sound in the darkness. Someone was gargling softly. Ki rolled over and saw the dim shape of her guard rolling on his back, clutching his throat. Drowning in his own blood!

Horrified, she opened her mouth to cry out. A hand slapped over her lips, silencing her. Strong arms hoisted her up and dragged her down the bank, away from the fire embers. She twisted her head. In the corner of her eye, she saw grass boats floating in the shallows, carrying men. The moon glinted on their tattooed arms and muscles. Magog warriors, escaping!

"Not a sound, now," Jakka whispered in her ear. "Or I'll slit you like I slit him."

He waded into the warm water, dragging Ki toward the nearest boat. Slowly, Ki understood. Jakka was abandoning his comrades, leaving them to fend for themselves. The others in camp wouldn't like this. If she screamed, the others would wake and fight. In the chaos, maybe she could slip away.

With a sudden jerk, she sank her teeth into Jakka's hand. She thrashed her head back and forth, hard, like a dog pulling at raw meat. But Jakka must have been expecting this. Enduring the pain, he didn't let go, and instead punched her in the head. For the second time that day, the world exploded with lights, and she blacked out.

When she woke, something felt broken inside. Groaning, she sat up and clutched her throbbing forehead. The world rocked under her. But it wasn't her head. She was on a river, far from shore. Moonlight glinted on palm trees on a distant bank. She was sitting in the prow of a reed boat, her feet bound so tightly, they felt blue. Jakka sat behind her, his warriors paddling steadily, grunting as they strained in time. Their escape had worked.

"Nice try, witch." Jakka chuckled. "You wanted a fight, didn't you? Make us kill each other? You've always got a scheme. I know your ways, though. There'll be no more tricks from you."

"This is a mistake," Ki said coldly. "You're vulnerable here on your own. You should turn back."

Jakka laughed cruelly.

"You're worried, nomad. You should be. All those things you fear, I'll do."

His words pierced her, but Ki mastered herself and sat upright, straining at her grass bindings. Her mind cleared. She would probably die, but until then, she'd play Jakka all she could. Sargon would expect no less.

"You won't hurt me," she said.

"Oh?" Jakka sneered.

"No. If you do, I won't give you what you want."

"And what do I want?" Jakka said angrily. But his voice wavered, and she knew she'd struck home.

"You want a weapon," she said. "Something good enough to give you power again."

Tension filled the darkness as the warriors leaned in, listening. This was Ki's chance.

"You lost everything because of me," she said loudly, so all could hear. "My darts. My trench. My turtle shells. But I can help you, too. Keep me safe, and I'll build you a weapon better than anything Uruk has. Your men here aren't much. But with my newest weapon, these few will overpower hundreds."

"You lie," Jakka said.

Ki twisted and looked at him.

"The world has changed, Jakka. In Gog's time, numbers meant everything. Now weapons do. Whoever has the best weapon will draw men in herds. If that's you, you'll recruit whoever you wish. Magog will live again. I can make it so."

"You filthy rat." Jakka grabbed her hair and shook her head. "I'll drown you right now."

"Prince," a voice barked. "We should hear this."

Jakka flinched. But he released her, then breathed out slowly.

"Go on, rat," he said softly. "Just out of curiosity, what is this weapon?"

"It's too hard to explain. I'll show you."

"I could torture it out of you."

"You could try. But I'd leave things out. Make the weapon imperfect. Finally, I'd kill myself as soon as I got the chance, leaving you stuck like this forever. A sad, frightened fugitive. No better than a marshling stuck in the swamp."

She turned away to show him she didn't care. "Make your choice."

There was a long silence. The men slowly dipped their paddles, thinking it over.

Reluctantly, Jakka asked, "How fast can you make this weapon?"

"Fetch me a few materials, and it is done," Ki said.

A deep voice boomed from the back. “Let her try.”

“I was going to.” Jakka sulked. “Don’t forget who’s in charge, eh? I’m still the son of Gog.”

The men didn’t answer. They just paddled in silence. Jakka pouted and said no more. And as the quiet stretched on, fresh hope sparked in Ki’s chest. If she stayed alive, who knew what might happen? Sargon had kissed her. He would come for her. Rogg, too.

Your troubles are our troubles.

This time, she wasn’t alone.

EPILOGUE

At the month's end, the harvest came ready, and Uruk's members made short work of bringing it in. They beat the husks with sticks to release the wheat berries. Then they ground the berries into flour, and using rows of new mud kilns built by the Thinker Team, they baked the flour into bread and threw a great feast to honor the slain.

Magog fared less well.

Shortly after the battle, an army led by Rogg attacked. They rained darts on Magog from above, drove them into the desert, then surrounded them and destroyed them utterly. But Ki was nowhere to be found. A great search commenced, and Sargon, newly elected *lugal* of Uruk, offered rewards for her whereabouts. Many claimed to have found her, but all proved false, and the search went on.

In the meantime, Uruk prospered.

In the marshes and deserts, hills and caves across Mesopotamia, the name of "Sargon, Gog-slayer," became legend. So did "Ki, Thinker" and "Nisaba, Bald One." Nor was "Rogg, Giant of Elam," forgotten. But greater still was the fame of the Code of Uruk itself. Hearing of it, many grew restless with their chiefs and plotted rebellions to install their own codes. Others made plans to run away. Settlers flocked to Uruk's shore. The camp expanded and expanded again, growing in power. Merchant boats thronged in the shallows.

A wooden quay had to be built to handle all the trade. Young palm trees were planted along the new pathways, giving shade to strollers on the bank. And within the settlement, whitewashed dwellings of mud brick arose—another invention of the Thinker Team—the lintels painted in bands of red, green, blue, and yellow, like a flock of birds. Uruk was becoming beautiful.

Still, Ki was not found. Her friends sought her ever farther, probing into Elam and Akkad, inquiring even into Assyria and the Zagros Mountains. Some in Uruk started to complain. They said Sargon was wasting Uruk's resources, favoring a personal romance. Others said life was good at home, and the Gog-slayer deserved to rest. "Let him enjoy life again," they said. "Take a mate, start a family." Too much loneliness could affect their *lugal's* decision-making. Besides, there were greedy chiefs on the high council, men eager to undermine the code to enhance their status. The *lugal's* attention was needed at home.

But Sargon kept searching.

Time passed. New chiefs joined the council. New factions formed. More tribes along the Euphrates copied Uruk's wheat and weapons methods, and built up power bases of their own. In the north, Babylon took more vassal villages, levying tribute like Magog once had. In the south, wild desert tribes began using dart-throwers to raid local trade routes, capturing goods and slaves. Still, Sargon hunted for Ki. Her troubles were Uruk's troubles, he said. Until Uruk found her, it would not be satisfied.

The End

AUTHOR'S NOTE

Much of ancient Mesopotamian history remains enshrouded in mysteries. The story of Uruk takes place around 12,000 BCE, several thousand years before any histories are written. Where gaps exist in our current research, I have invented numerous details of ordinary life and experience. I have also condensed and sped up the rate of technological progress, and fitted together myths from various religions to create a unified belief system for the characters. Like any work of fiction based on history, this book takes these liberties in order to present a clear and compelling narrative.

ACKNOWLEDGMENTS

I am deeply grateful to the following people:

First, my agent, Russell Galen. He took a chance on me at a critical moment.

Second, my editor, Toni Kirkpatrick, and the whole team at Diversion Books. Special thanks to Alan Dingman for his cover design.

I have been blessed with writing teachers who are beyond excellent. At Johns Hopkins, Stephen Dixon took me under his wing. At UC Irvine, Michelle Latiolais treated me like family. Ron Carlson helped me publish my first story. But I wouldn't have made it that far without my mentor, editor, and friend from before high school, Tom Noe. Tom, my writing debt to you cannot be repaid.

I also offer my sincere thanks to Ann Collette, who pushed me to keep improving through multiple drafts. Thanks to John DeMasi for hiring me, so I could teach at a great school while I finished this manuscript. And thanks to John Anderson, who supported my children's books and kept me writing.

I will always owe much to my fellow writers from the UCI workshop. Kim Parker, you revived our JHU writing group at exactly the right time. Fox, Toni, Josh, Dave, Brooke, Liz: thank you for reading this in its roughest form. For commenting on my early drafts—Dan M., Annie Z., Johnny Z., Mary Elaine, Anne K.—thank you.

Of course, I owe the most to my parents.

James Zwerneman
April 13, 2025
Naples, Florida